THE STRANGER WITH A STRANGE SPELL

The stranger did not notice them at all, and Shoogar began to fidget with impatience. Just as Shoogar was about to interrupt him, the stranger straightened up and touched his device. It responded by hurling red fire across the canyon—directly at the cairn of Musk-Watz!

Lant turned to Shoogar: "This could be serious."

The wizard shook his head. "Lant, you are a fool. *This is already serious . . .*"

> The planet wasn't big enough for both of them—at least not on the ground. So Shoogar was determined to learn how to fly . . . no matter what the cost!

THE
FLYING SORCERERS

David Gerrold
and
Larry Niven

A Del Rey Book

BALLANTINE BOOKS • NEW YORK

Dedicated to the men of NASA;
We understand their problems

A Del Rey Book
Published by Ballantine Books

Copyright © 1971 by David Gerrold and Larry Niven

A shorter version of this novel was first published as a serial titled "The Misspelled Magishun," in *If* Magazine, copyright © 1970 by Universal Publishing & Distributing Corporation.

ISBN 0-345-30494-2

Manufactured in the United States of America

First Edition: August 1971
Fourth Printing: June 1982

Cover art by Boris Vallejo

I was awakened by Pilg the Crier pounding excitedly on the wall of my nest and crying, "Lant! Lant! It's happened! Come quickly!"

I stuck my head out. "What's happened?"

"The disaster! The disaster!" Pilg was jumping up and down in excitement. "I told you it would happen."

I pulled my head in and dressed. Pilg's joy was a frightening thing. I felt my fur rising, fluffing out in fear as I wondered . . .

Pilg the Crier had been predicting disaster for weeks—as was his habit. He predicted his disasters twice a year, at the times of the equinox. The fact that we were leaving the influence of one sun and entering that of the other would make the local spells completely unstable. As we approached conjunction—the time when the blue sun would cross the face of the red—Pilg had increased the intensity of his warnings. This was disaster weather: something dire would certainly happen.

Usually it did, of course. Afterward—and after we of the village had somehow picked up the pieces—Pilg would shake his heavy head and moan, "Wait until next year. Wait. It'll be even worse."

Sometimes we joked about it, predicting the end of the world if Pilg's "next year" ever arrived . . .

I lowered the ladder and joined Pilg on the ground. "What's the trouble?"

"Oh, I warned you, Lant. I warned you. Now maybe you'll believe me. I warned you though—you can't say I didn't warn you. The omens were there, written across the sky. What more proof did you need?"

He meant the moons. They were starting to pile up on one side of the sky. Shoogar the Magician had predicted that we

1

were due for a time of total darkness soon—perhaps even tonight—and Pilg had seized on this as just one more omen of disaster.

As we hurried through the village I tried to get Pilg to tell me what had happened. Had the river changed its course? Had someone's nest fallen from its tree? Had the flocks all died mysteriously? But Pilg was so excited at having finally been proven correct that he himself was not sure what exactly had happened.

One of the hill shepherds, it seemed, had come running into town, panic-stricken and shouting something about a new magician. By the time I got this information out of Pilg, we were already at the village clearing where the frightened shepherd was leaning against one of the great housetrees, gasping out his story to a nervous group of men. They pressed in close to him, badgering him with questions. Even the women had paused in their work, and hanging back at a respectful distance, listened fearfully to the shepherd's words.

"A new magician," he gasped. "A red one! I saw him!" Someone handed him a skin; he sucked the Quaff from it noisily, then panted, "Near the cairn of the wind-god. He was throwing red fire across the mountains."

"Red fire. Red fire." The villagemen murmured excitedly among themselves. "If he throws red fire, he must be a red magician." Almost immediately, I heard the word "duel". The women must have heard it too, for they gasped and shrank back from the milling group of men.

I pushed my way through to the center of the crowd. "Ah, Lant," said one of the men. "Have you heard? There's going to be a duel."

"Is there?" I demanded. "Have you seen the runes of the duel inscribed across Shoogar's nest?"

"No, but——"

"Then how do you know there's going to be a duel?"

"A red magician——" gasped the shepherd. "A red magician——"

"Nonsense. No red magician could have the powers you describe. Why don't you wait until you know something definite before you start spreading silly rumors that frighten women and children?"

"You know Shoogar as well as we! As soon as he discovers there is a new magician in the district, he'll——"

"You mean Shoogar doesn't know yet?"

The man looked blank.

I raised my voice. "Has anyone thought to tell Shoogar?"

Silence. No one had. My duty was clear. I must prevent Shoogar from doing something rash. I hurried through the trees toward the magician's nest.

Shoogar's nest was well suited for a wizard, a squat misshapen gourd hung from a forbidding black ogre of a tree well beyond the limits of the village. (The Guild of Advisors was afraid to let him move closer; he was always experimenting with new spells.)

I found Shoogar already packing his travel kit. His agitated manner told me he was worried. Then I caught a glimpse of what he was packing and *I* was worried. The last time he had used that ornate bone-carved *tarinele* was when he had hurled the curse of the itching red boils at Hamel the Failure.

I saw what he was packing in on top of the *tarinele* and I flinched. "I believe that's against the Guild rules," I said.

For a moment I thought he'd hurl a spell at me. I cringed and instinctively made a spell-cutting gesture, (forgetting for the moment that Shoogar himself had made the protective amulets I wore; he couldn't possibly break through his own protections; at least not for a few more days—they would expire with the coming of the blue dawns).

"You!" he snapped. "What do you know of magic? You who call yourself my friend! You didn't even have the courtesy to inform me of this intruding sorcerer!"

"I didn't even know of him myself, until just a few moments ago. Perhaps he only arrived today."

"Arrived today? And immediately began throwing red fire about? Without first informing himself of the local gods, tidal patterns, previous local spells and their side effects? Ridiculous! Lant, you are a fool. You are an idiot of the first circle where magic is concerned. Why do you bother me?"

"Because you are an idiot where diplomacy is concerned!" I snapped back, my fur bristling. (I am one of the few people in the village who can bristle at Shoogar and survive to tell about it.) "If I let you go charging up the mountain every time you felt you had been wronged, you'd be fighting duels as often as the blue sun rises."

Shoogar looked at me, and I could tell from his expression that my remarks had sunk home. "Smooth your fur, Lant. I did not mean that you were a complete fool. I just meant that you are not a magician."

"I'm glad you are aware of my skill as a diplomat," I said, and allowed myself to relax. "Our abilities must complement each other, Shoogar. If we are to succeed in our endeavors, we must maintain a healthy respect for each other's powers. Only thus can we protect our village."

"You and your damned speeches," he scowled. "Someday I'm going to make your tongue swell up to the size of a sour melon—just for the sake of some peace and quiet."

I ignored that remark. Considering the circumstances, Shoogar had a right to be testy. He closed up his travel kit, tugging angrily at the straps.

"Are you ready?" I asked, "I'll send a message up to Orbur, telling him to ready two bicycles."

"Presumptuous of you," Shoogar muttered, but I knew that he was secretly grateful for the thought. Wilville and Orbur, my eldest two sons, carved the best bicycles in the district.

We found the new magician near the cairn of Musk-Watz, the wind-god. Across a steep canyon from the cairn, there is a wide grass-covered mesa with a gentle slope to the south. The new magician had appropriated this mesa and scattered it with his devices and oddments. As we pulled our bicycles to a shuddering halt, he was in the process of casting a spell with an unfamiliar artifact. Shoogar and I paused at a respectful distance and watched.

The stranger was slightly taller than me, considerably taller than Shoogar. His skin was lighter than ours, and hairless but for a single patch of black fur, oddly positioned on the top half of his skull. He also wore a strange set of appurtenances balanced across his nose. It appeared that they were lenses of quartz mounted in a bone frame through which the stranger could see.

The set of his features was odd and disquieting, and his bones seemed strangely proportioned. Certainly no normal being would have a paunch that large. The sight of him made me feel queasy, and I surmised that some of his ancestors had not been human.

Magicians traditionally wear outlandish clothing to identify themselves as magicians. But even Shoogar was unprepared for the cut of this stranger's costume. It was a single garment which covered most of the stranger's body. The shape of the cloth had been woven to match his own precisely; and an oddly bulging shape it was. There was a hood, thrown back. There were high-flared cuffs on the pantaloons to allow for his calf-high boots, and over his heart was a golden badge. Around his middle he wore a wide belt, to which were attached three or four small spell devices.

He had also set up a number of larger devices. Most of them had the blue-white glimmer of polished metal. (There is little metal in our village—it rusts quickly—but I am a man of the world and have traveled much. I am familiar with the sight of metal, having seen it in the highlands; but nothing so finely worked as this.)

These devices stood each on three legs so that they were always level, even where the ground was not. As we watched, the stranger peered into one of them, peered across the canyon at the sacred cairn of Musk-Watz, the god of the winds, and then into his device again. Muttering constantly to himself, he moved across the clearing and adjusted something else. Evidently this was a long and complicated spell, though just what its purpose was neither Shoogar nor I could fathom.

Occasionally he would refer to a large egg-shaped nest, black and regular of shape, sitting on its wide end off to one side of the pasture. As there were no trees in the area large enough to hang it from, he had set it on the ground. (An unwise course, to be sure, but the shell of that nest looked like nothing I had ever seen—perhaps it was able to resist marauding predators.) I wondered how he had built it overnight. His power must be formidable.

The stranger did not notice us at all, and Shoogar was fidgeting with impatience. Just as Shoogar was about to interrupt him, the stranger straightened and touched his device. The device responded by hurling red fire across the canyon—directly at the cairn of Musk-Watz!

I thought Shoogar would suffer a death-rage right then and there. The weather gods are hard enough to control at best, and Shoogar had spent three long lunar configurations trying to appease Musk-Watz in an effort to forestall another season of hurricanes. Now, the stranger had disrupted one of his most careful spells.

Redder than ruby, eye-searing, bright and narrow, straight as the horizon of the ocean (which I have also seen), that crimson fire speared out across the canyon, lashing Shoogar's carefully constructed outcrop. I feared it would never end: the fire seemed to go on and on.

And the sound of it was dreadful. There was a painful high-pitched humming which seemed to seize my very soul, a piercing unearthly whine. Under this we could hear the steady crackling and spattering of the cairn.

Acrid smoke billowed upward from it, and I shuddered, thinking how the dissipating dust would affect the atmosphere. Who knew what effects it would have on Shoogar's weather-making spells? I made a mental note to have the wives reinforce the flooring of our nest.

Suddenly, just as abruptly as it had begun, the red fire went out. Once more the silence and the calm descended over the mesa. Once more the blue twilight colored the land. But across my eyes was a brilliant blue-white afterimage. And the cairn of the wind-god still crackled angrily.

Amazingly enough, the cairn still stood. It smouldered and sputtered, and there was an ugly scar where the red fire had touched it, but it was intact. When Shoogar builds, he builds well.

The stranger was already readjusting his devices, muttering continuously to himself. (I wondered if that were part of the spell.) Like a mother *vole* checking her cubs, he moved from device to device, peering into one, resetting another, reciting strange sounds over a third.

I cast a glance at Shoogar; I could see a careful tightening at the corners of his mouth. Indeed, even his beard seemed clenched. I feared that a duel would start before the stranger could offer Shoogar a gift. Something had to be done to prevent Shoogar from a rash and possibly regrettable action.

I stepped forward boldly. "Ahem," I began. "Ahem. I dislike to interrupt you while you are so obviously busy, but that bluff is sacred to Musk-Watz. It took many cycles to construct the pattern of spells which . . ."

The magician looked up and seemed to notice us for the first time. He became strangely agitated. Taking a quick step toward us, he made a straight-armed gesture, palms open to us, and spoke quick tense words in a language I had never heard. Instantly, I threw myself flat on the ground, arms over my head.

Nothing happened.

When I looked up, Shoogar was still beside the other bicycle with his arms outstretched in a spell-breaking pattern. Either the stranger's spell had miscarried, or Shoogar had blocked it. The stranger threw no more spells. Instead, he backed toward his oddly shaped nest, never taking his eyes from us. He continued his strange words, but now they were slow and low pitched, like the tone one uses to calm an uneasy animal. He disappeared into his nest and all was quiet and blue.

Except for the crackle of cooling rock which still reached across the canyon to remind us that Musk-Watz had been defiled.

I turned to Shoogar, "This could be serious."

"Lant, you are a fool. This is already serious."

"Can you handle this new magician?"

Shoogar grunted noncommittally, and I was afraid. Shoogar was good; if he were not sure of his skill here, the whole village might be in danger.

I started to voice my fears, but the stranger abruptly reappeared carrying another of his metal and bone carved devices. This one was smaller than the rest and had slender rods sticking out on all sides. I did not like its looks. It reminded me of some of the more unpleasant devices that I had seen during the dark years.

The magician watched us all the time he was setting it up on its three slender legs. As he turned it to face us I tensed.

It began to make a humming noise, like the sound of a water harp when a string bow is drawn across its glass tubes. The humming rose in pitch until it began to sound disturbingly like that of the device of the red fire. I began gauging the distance between myself and a nearby boulder.

The stranger spoke impatiently to us in his unknown tongue.

"You are discourteous," rumbled Shoogar. "This business can wait, surely?"

The spell device said, "Surely?"

I landed behind the boulder. Shoogar stood his ground. "Surely," he repeated firmly. "You violate custom. In this, my district, you must gift me with one new spell, one I have never seen. Were I in your district——"

The spell device spoke again. Its intonation was terrifying and inhuman. "New spell gift—never known—surely."

I realized that the stranger had spoken first. His device was attempting to speak for him, but in our words. Shoogar saw it too, and was reassured. The device was only a speakerspell, and a poor one at that, despite its powerful shape.

Shoogar and the speakerspell and the stranger stood on that wind-swept mesa and talked with each other. Or rather, they talked at each other. It was infant's talk, most of it. The thing had no words of its own. It could only use Shoogar's; sometimes correctly, more often not.

Shoogar's temper was not improving. He had come to demand gift or duel from an intruding warlock only to find himself teaching a simpleminded construct to talk. The stranger seemed to be enjoying himself, unfortunately at Shoogar's expense.

The red sun was long gone, the blue was near the horizon, and all the world was red-black shadow. The blue sun settled behind a clump of deep violet clouds. Suddenly it was gone, like a taper blown out by the wind. The moons emerged against the night, now in the configuration of the striped lizard.

During certain configurations Shoogar's power is higher

than during others. I wondered if he were master or servant to the striped lizard. He was just drawing his robes imperiously about his squat and stubby form. Master, apparently, from his manner.

Abruptly, the stranger repeated his palms-out gesture, turned, and went back to his nest. He did not go inside. Instead, he briefly touched the rim of the doorway, and there was light! Garish light, it spurted from the flank of the nest, bright as double daylight.

And such a strange light. The ground and the plants seemed to take the wrong colors and there was something not right with their shadows, an odd blackness of shade.

The new magician's motive was obvious, even to me—and even more so to Shoogar. He leapt back out of the light with his arms raised for defense. But it was no use. The light followed him, swept over him and dazzled him, effectively cancelling out the strength of the lunar light. The stranger had effectively negated the power of the striped lizard. Shoogar stood trembling, a tiny figure pinned in that dazzling odd-colored glow.

Then, for no apparent reason, the stranger caused the light to vanish.

"I think that the light disturbs you," said the speakerspell, talking for the magician. "But, no matter. We can talk as well in the dark."

I breathed more easily, but did not completely relax. This stranger had shown how easily he could cancel the effect of any lunar configuration. Any powers Shoogar might have hoped to draw from the sky would have to be foregone.

I watched the striped lizard slink dejectedly into the west. The moons rode their line across the sky, milk-white crescents with thick red fringes. On successive nights the red borderlines would narrow as the suns set closer and closer together. Then there would be no colored borders. Later, blue borders would show after second sunset . . . and Shoogar could make no use of any of this . . .

Shoogar and the new magician were still talking. By now the speakerspell had learned enough words so that the two could intelligently discuss the matters of magicians.

"The ethics of the situation are obvious," Shoogar was

saying. "You are practicing magic in my district. For this you must pay. More precisely, you owe me a secret."

"A secret . . .?" echoed the speakerspell device.

Still cold and cramped, I was suddenly no longer sleepy. I cocked an ear to hear better.

"Some bit of magic that I do not already know," Shoogar amplified. "What, for instance, is the secret of your light like double daylight?"

". . . potential difference . . . hot metal within an inert . . . doubt you would understand . . . heat is caused by a flow of . . . tiny packets of lightning . . ."

"Your words do not make sense. I take no meaning from them. You must tell me a secret that I can understand and use. I see that your magic is powerful. Perhaps you know of a way to predict the tides?"

"No, of course I can't tell you how to predict the tides. You've got eleven moons and two primary suns tugging your oceans in all directions. Tugging at each other too. It would take years to compute a tidal pattern . . ."

"Surely you must know things that I do not," said Shoogar. "Just as I know secrets that you are unaware of."

"Of course. But I'm trying to think what would help you the most. It's a wonder you've gotten as far as you have. Bicycles even . . ."

"Those are good bicycles!" I protested. "I ought to know. Two of my sons built them."

"But bicycles!" He moved closer eagerly. I tensed, but he only wanted to examine them. "Hardwood frames, leather-thonged pulleys instead of chains, sewn fur pelts for tires! They're marvelous! Absolutely marvelous. Primitive and hand-made, with big flat wheels and no spokes, but it doesn't matter: they're still bicycles. And when all the odds were against your developing any form of . . . at all!"

"What are you talking about?" Shoogar demanded. I was silent, seething at the insult to Wilville and Orbur's bicycles. Primitive indeed!

". . . starts with the perception of order," said the magician. "But your world has no order to it at all. You're in an opaque dust cloud, so you cannot see any of the fixed lights-in-the-sky. Your sky is a random set of moons picked up from the worldlet belt . . . three-body configuration makes capture easy . . . tides that go every which way under the influence of all those moons . . . moons that cross and recross at random, changing their . . . because of mutual . . ." The speakerspell was missing half of the stranger's words, making the rest gibberish. "And then the high level of . . . from the blue sun would give you a new species every week or so. No order in your observable . . . probably use strict cut-and-try methods of building. No put-it-together line techniques because you wouldn't normally expect a put-it-together belt to produce the same item twice in a row . . . but it's a human instinct to try to control nature. You must tell me——"

Shoogar interrupted the babbling stranger. "First, you must tell me. Tell me some new thing that you may satisfy the Guild law. What is the secret of your red flame?"

"Oh, I couldn't give you a secret like that!"

Shoogar began to fume again, but he only said, "And why couldn't you?"

". . . For one thing, you couldn't understand it. You wouldn't be able to work it."

Shoogar drew himself up to his full height and stared up at the stranger. "Are you telling me that I am not even a magician of the second circle? Any magician worth his bones is able to make fire and throw it!" And with that Shoogar produced a ball of fire from his sleeve and casually hurled it across the clearing.

I could see that the stranger was startled. He had not expected that. The ball of fire lay sputtering on the ground, then died away leaving only the burnt core. The stranger took two steps toward it, as if to examine it, then turned back to Shoogar, "Very impressive," he said, "but still . . ."

Shoogar said, "You see, I can throw fire also. And I can control the color of the flame. What I want to know is how to throw it in a straight line, like you do."

"It is a wholly different principle . . . coherent light . . . tight beam . . . small clumps of energy . . . vibration of . . ." As if to demonstrate, he touched his spell device again, and once more the red fire lashed out. Eye-searing flame played across Musk-Watz's cairn. Another smoking hole. I winced.

The stranger said, "It boils the rock and tells me what it is made of by telling me what color the smoke is."

I tried to conceal my reaction. Any idiot could have told

him the smoke was bluish-gray, let alone what rocks are made of. I could tell him myself.

He was still talking, "Absorption of light . . . but I couldn't teach you how to use it; you might use it as a weapon."

"*Might* use it as a weapon?" Shoogar exclaimed. "What other use is there for a spell to throw red fire?"

"I just explained that," the stranger said impatiently. "I could explain again, but for what purpose? It's much too complex for you to understand."

(That was a needless insult. Shoogar may be only a magician of the second circle, but that does not mean that he is inferior. In actuality, there are few secrets he is not privy to. Besides, gaining the first circle is a matter of politics as well as skill, and Shoogar has never been known as a diplomat.)

I could see that Shoogar was fuming.

It was high time that the oil of diplomacy be applied to the rough edges of these two magicians. I knew it was my duty to prevent friction between them, especially now that the barrier of language had been removed. "Shoogar," I said, "let me speak. I am the diplomat." Without waiting for his assent, I approached the speakerspell, albeit somewhat nervously.

"Allow me to introduce myself. My name is *Lant-la-lee-lay-lie-ah-no*. Perhaps it may strike you as a bit presumptuous that I claim seven syllables, but I am a person of no mean importance in our village." I felt it necessary to establish my rank from the very beginning, and my right to speak for the village.

The stranger looked at me and said, "I am pleased to meet you. My name is . . ." The speakerspell hesitated, but I counted the syllables of the name. Three. I smiled to myself. Obviously, we were dealing with a very low status individual . . . and I realized something disquieting as well. Where did this magician come from, that individuals of such low status controlled such mighty magic? I preferred not to think about that. Perhaps he hadn't given his full name. After all, I hadn't given him the secret side of mine.

The speakerspell abruptly translated the stranger's three syllable name, *"As a color, shade of purple gray."*

"Very odd," said Shoogar, speaking low. "I have never known a magician to be named for a color."

"Perhaps that's not his name, but an indication of which god he serves."

"Nonsense," Shoogar whispered back. "Then he would be either Something-the-red or Something-the-blue. But he isn't either."

"Perhaps he's both—that's why he's purple."

"Don't talk foolishness, Lant. It's impossible to serve two masters. Besides, he isn't all purple. He's Purple the Gray. And I've never heard of a gray magician."

I turned back to the stranger, "Is that your full name? How many syllables are in the secret side of it?" He couldn't be offended; I was not asking for the name itself.

He said, "I have given you my full name. As-A-Shade-Of-Purple-Gray."

"You have no other? No secret name?"

"I am not sure I understand. That is my full name."

Shoogar and I exchanged a glance. The stranger was either incredibly foolish, or exceedingly cunning. Either he had betrayed his full name to us, thus delivering himself into Shoogar's power; or he was playing the fool in order to keep Shoogar from discovering his real name. Perhaps the name he had given was some kind of spell trap. It certainly wasn't a clue to his identity.

As-A-Shade-Of-Purple-Gray was speaking again. "Where did you come from?"

"From the village," I started to point down the mountain, but covered the gesture quickly. No sense in telling this stranger where the village was located.

"But, I saw no village from the air . . ."

"From the air . . .?" Shoogar asked.

"Yes, when I flew over the area."

At this Shoogar's ears perked up. "Flew? You have a flying spell? How do you do it? I have not yet been able to get anything larger than a melon to fly—and I have been trapping the bubbles of noxious odor as they rise from the swamps." Indeed, Shoogar had been trying to perfect a flying spell for as long as he had been a magician. He had even contrived to get two of my sons to aid him, Wilville and Orbur. Often they would neglect their bicycle carving to work on some strange new device for him. So great was their enthusiasm for

Shoogar's project that—much to my annoyance—they had been accepting no payment at all for their labors.

The new magician smiled at Shoogar's description of his flying spell. "Primitive," he said, "but it could work. My own vehicle uses somewhat more complex and efficient principles." He pointed at his huge black nest. No, he must have meant one of the devices in it, or near it. Who could conceive of a flying nest? A nest is a home, a fixed place, a locality of refuge, a place of returning. Philosophically a nest cannot so much as *move*, let alone fly. What is philosophically impossible is impossible to magic. This law constrains even the gods.

"Well, show me how it works. Teach me *your* flying spell!" Shoogar begged excitedly.

The stranger shook his head. "I could not show that one to you either. It is beyond your understanding. . . ."

This was too much for Shoogar. All evening long, this new magician had continued to insult him. Now, he refused even to gift him with a secret. Shoogar began jumping up and down in exasperation. He pulled his *tarinele* from his travel kit, and had actually begun to pack the blow chambers with cursing powder before I could calm him.

"Patience, Shoogar! Please!" I begged him. "Let us return to the village. Call for a meeting of the Guild of Advisors first! Don't challenge him to a duel until we have a chance to talk this thing out."

Shoogar muttered something under his breath. He muttered a whole bunch of somethings. "I ought to use this *tarinele* on you. You know how I hate to waste a good curse." But he emptied the blow chambers, wrapped it up again in its protective skins and returned it to his pack.

He stood and faced the new magician. "We return to our village to confer. We will visit you again before the time of the blue dawns."

But the stranger did not seem to hear this. "I will accompany you," he said. "I would like to see your village."

Shoogar can be clever when he puts his mind to it. "Certainly you may accompany us," he said. "It would be inhospitable for us not to welcome you. But you cannot leave yourself so far from your nest. Tonight the moons are down and the red curses roam the land." (I wished Shoogar hadn't brought that up. I remembered how far we were from home.)

Shoogar spread his hands helplessly. "If we had empty nests in the village, you would be welcome to use one——but as it is, with the time of total darkness approaching, I would not recommend straying too far from one's own nest."

"That's all right," said the stranger, "I'll just bring it with me."

"Huh?" said Shoogar. "How? We certainly are not going to help you. That is, neither of us has the strength to——"

As-A-Shade-Of-Purple-Gray seemed to laugh. I was becoming most tired of his laugh. "Don't worry about that," he said. "You just lead the way and I'll follow."

Shoogar and I exchanged a glance. Obviously this dumpy-legged stranger would be unable to keep up with our bicycles —especially if he was going to try to bring his nest. We waited respectfully, however, while the magician collapsed his artifacts and devices. I was amazed to see how easily they folded up and how compactly they stored, and made a mental note to get closer to one of them if I could. I was curious to see how the bone was carved and how the metal was worked. Perhaps I could learn something from the construction of such devices. They were carved too precisely, too delicately for me to see much in the dim light.

I glanced involuntarily at the sky. We were fast approaching the time of total darkness. Only six of the moons were left in the sky. No wonder the light was fading. I certainly did not intend to tarry for this stranger.

Within a remarkably short time, the stranger had packed up all of his devices and stowed them within his nest. There was something about his manner that made me feel vaguely uneasy; a sureness of self that implied he knew what he was doing. "All right," he said. "I'm ready," and he disappeared into his nest, shutting the door behind him. That was when my feeling of unease gave way to one of pure terror. Purple-Gray's whole nest began to hum, like the speakerspell and the red-fire devices within it, but louder. Suddenly it rose into the air and hung there at twice the height of a man. It began to glow with a color we had never seen before. The plants and the trees shone like garish hallucinations. *Green* is a dark color—not a dreadful bright fluorescence.

I thought Shoogar would fall off his bicycle from astonishment. I was having trouble with my own hands and feet.

Even when you are not trembling all over, a bicycle is hard enough to control.

The ride back to the village was a nightmare. Shoogar was so unnerved, he forgot to chant any of his protective *canteles,* and we both kept looking back over our shoulders at that huge looming egg which came floating silently, dreadfully after us, throwing off light in all directions, like some terrifying manifestation of Elcin, the thunder god.

It didn't help matters that every time I looked up, another moon had set, plunging us ever closer to the time of total darkness. One of us was moaning, but I wasn't sure whether it was Shoogar or me.

The bicycles clattered roughly down the mountain path, and I was so concerned about getting safely back to my nest that I did not even think to urge Shoogar to be careful with my other machine. The way he kept looking back over his shoulder I was sure he would hit something and split a wheel. Fortunately, he did not; I did not know if I would even have stopped to help him. Not with that bright black egg chasing us, always keeping perfectly and terrifyingly upright.

Somehow we made it down to the grasslands. Several of the women saw us coming—they were out in the fields gathering the night fungi—but when they saw that huge glowing nest looming along behind us, they turned and ran for the safety of the village. Shoogar and I did not even think to park our bicycles on the hill, but rode them right down into the settlement. (Well, the women would have to clean the mud from the wheels later.)

We reached the village none too soon. The last of the moons was just settling in the west. We paused, out of breath, in the center clearing. The great black nest floated ominously above us, lighting up the whole village with its odd-colored aura. The great trees and the gourd-shaped nests hanging from their mighty branches took on strange and terrifying colors.

From out of the air the magician's voice boomed louder than any natural voice, ". . . no wonder I didn't see it from the air . . . houses are structured spheres, suspended from the limbs of tremendous trees . . . must be at least. . . . Wait until . . . hears about this! Where should I park?" he asked suddenly.

"Anywhere . . .," I gasped weakly, "Put it anywhere," and made an appropriate arm-sweeping gesture. I looked around myself to see if we had any trees strong enough to hang such a nest from. There were none big enough that were not already occupied; but if this magician could make his nest fly, then he could surely hang it even from a sapling.

But even this the stranger did not do. He landed it on the ground.

And not just on any ground. He swept through the village toward the river, and brought it to land on the crest of the slope overlooking the frog-grading ponds. The ponds were dry now, drained for their ritual purification and reseeding spells, but I was appalled at such callous disregard for the property of the village. I winced as the magician's nest sank into the ooze with a loud squishy *phloosh*.

I did not sleep well at all. By the time the smoky rim of the red sun began to appear over the horizon, I was already up and about. I felt better after my cleansing and purification, but still haggard and drawn. The events of the night before had taken their toll.

A glance out the door of the nest was enough to confirm that the stranger was still in our midst. Pilg the Crier was already moving through the trees moaning of this new development. Disaster was all the more certain now that the strange magician had moved his nest into the village. Even from here I could see a curious crowd gathering around it—though keeping a respectful distance.

Ang, the frogmonger, was wringing his hands and moaning over his frog-grading ponds. He would have to repurify them again after the stranger left, and if that were not soon, he might miss the spawning season altogether.

Shoogar and I went out to watch him, that first day. As soon as he saw us he straightened from his examination of a local herb and disappeared into his nest. He returned almost immediately with an object in his outstretched hand. "A gift," he said. "A gift for Shoogar, the magician."

Shoogar was caught by surprise. He had not expected the stranger to produce the required gift. Now he had fulfilled his obligation as a magician, and had the legal right to remain in the district. By the same convention, Shoogar was bound to respect the rights of the new magician as well as his spells. Guild rules are quite specific.

Shoogar, as resident magician, had the seniority. The stranger could do nothing to interfere with Shoogar's practice or previous spells; but aside from that, he was free to do as he chose.

Shoogar examined his gift. It was small and light, easily held in one hand. One end had a glass lens mounted in it. The stranger demonstrated how it worked. When one pressed forward on the thing's sliding nerve, the glass lens made light.

It was a trivial thing. I could sense that Shoogar was disappointed, and insulted that the stranger had not given him something more spectacular. Shoogar had other ways to make cold light. But there was little he could say. It is extremely bad form to test a gift spell in the presence of the giver.

The only advantage to the gift was that its light was of a shape we had not seen before. By twisting a knob on one side the shape could be varied from a bright narrow beam— like the stranger's red-fire device, but nowhere near as damaging—to a broad glare, wide enough to illuminate half a countryside.

Using the sliding nerve, the brightness of the device could be adjusted too. It could be muted down to a dim glow, no brighter than a lightmoss, or it could be pushed up until it was too bright to look at. Purple-Gray advised Shoogar not to use the spell too much in this latter form, or its *something* would drain away too fast. The speakerspell didn't translate the word.

Shoogar turned it over and over in his hands. He had had his heart set on the flying spell or the red fire device. Yet manners compelled him to accept this gift graciously. I could see he wanted to ask for something else, but couldn't figure out how to do so without the risk of offending the other magician.

Purple-Gray was saying, "I cannot understand why your world has life at all. Your evolution patterns don't seem right; yet who would have settled here? *We* certainly wouldn't. For one thing, the dust clouds hide you from space. For another, you don't really get yellow, dwarf, sunlight." Much of it was like that: coherent sentences trailing off into strings of unrelated words. "Though I suppose the red and blue suns do combine to give the same effect . . . the plants all look black because there's so little green light, but the *something* in plants doesn't use the green anyway, so that's all right. It's these double shadows that would drive anyone insane."

Shoogar waited through this stream of gibberish with commendable patience. Purple-Gray's words about different colors seemed to hint at something very important, and Shoogar wanted to know what it was. "You speak of 'this world,'" he said. "May one assume that you know of other worlds?" I wondered if Shoogar was baiting the stranger.

"Oh, yes. My world——" He looked up, considered, then pointed into the empty sky. "My world is in that general direction. . . . I think. Beyond the dust clouds."

"Dust clouds?" Shoogar peered up into the sky. I looked also. So did the crowd of onlookers. "Dust clouds?" The sky was an empty blue. What was he talking about?

Shoogar looked at the other magician, "Do you mock me? I see nothing. No dust clouds. No other worlds. There is nothing in the sky."

"Oh, but there is," said Purple-Gray. "It's just too small for you to see."

Shoogar raised an eyebrow—threw me a look—turned back to the other magician. I could sense some of the onlookers trying to restrain their mirth. Some of the lesser women were already giggling and had to be herded away. "Too small?" repeated Shoogar. "Too small . . .?" His patience was growing thin. Shoogar has no temperament for children, fools or madmen.

"Oh, no—you misunderstand," said Purple-Gray quickly. "It's too small to see because it's so far away."

"Oh . . ." said Shoogar slowly. Purple-Gray still had not explained the dust clouds——or the lack of them.

"Yes. In fact, it's so far away that if you tried to get there on say, a bicycle, it would take you many generations. You

would grow old and die before you had covered a significant
fraction of the journey."

"I see . . .," said Shoogar. "Then how did *you* get *here?*
By pedaling faster?"

Purple-Gray laughed, "Oh, no, no. Even that wouldn't
help. I . . ." The speakerspell hesitated, then said, ". . . went
around . . ."

Shoogar shook his head in confusion. Several more of
the women had to be led away. It was not good for them to
see a grown man making a fool of himself, nor was it advisa-
ble that they witness Shoogar discomfited. Several of the men
began muttering among themselves. Shoogar gestured for
silence—he still had not given up. "Went around . . .?" he
asked. "Went around *what?* The dust clouds?"

"Oh, no. I went through the dust clouds. I . . . went
around the distance."

Shoogar repeated this sentence slowly, to see if there was
something in it he had missed. There wasn't. He looked at
Purple and shook his head. "Uh uh," he said. That was all,
just, "Uh uh."

Then he turned and walked away, up the slope, shaking
his head and turning the small light-making device over and
over in his hands.

Purple-Gray spent the next several days collecting small
plants, pieces of larger plants, handfuls of mud and water
and dirt. There were plenty of sprats and adults to watch
him, but he took little notice of them.

A floating three-legged clicking device followed him about
with its legs folded, unnoticed and untended until he needed
it. Each time he took a sample of something he would mount
this device on its legs and point it at the site. It seemed a
harmless enough testing device, but Shoogar would grit his
teeth every time it came floating by.

Shoogar went into seclusion then, determined to discover

the secret of the stranger's light-making device. When I visited him for the purpose of checking his progress, he glared angrily at me, and muttered, "Curse that single-shadowed demon!"

"Perhaps it would help if you tried to find out which god the spell draws its power from."

Shoogar gave me another look, more scathing than the first. "Do I tell you how to carve bone? Why do you tell me magic? Don't you think I know my own business? I have *already* tested this device for the presence of every god in the known pantheon and it responds to none."

"Perhaps," I suggested, "perhaps it is based on a different principle. Purple appears not to call on any gods at all. Could it be that . . ."

"Then how does he work his devices?" Shoogar demanded. "By superstition?"

"I don't know——but perhaps he draws his power from some different source. Or perhaps . . ."

"Lant, you are a fool! Why do you continue to prattle on about things you do not know? If you are going to try to talk to a magician about magic, you should at least try to talk intelligently."

"But that's why I'm asking——"

"Superstition, Lant, is harmless prattle that gets repeated so often that people start to believe it—and then it is no longer harmless. The belief of the people gives it power. Magic, on the other hand, involves a carefully constructed equation of symbols intended to control specialized forces or objects. Magic works whether one believes in it or not."

"I understand that," I said. "And I do not think that Purple operates by superstition."

"Nor do I," said Shoogar. "His powers are too great."

"But it does not appear that he operates by magic either."

"Are you suggesting that the stranger's devices are independent of the gods?" Shoogar's look and tone made it clear that he felt he was talking to an imbecile.

I stiffened my tone. "Such a thing is not impossible. Wilville once confessed to me that he has often test-ridden new bicycles without bothering to bless them first. One grows careless and forgets. But nothing evil has ever happened to him."

"Wilville and Orbur are under my protection—remember? In payment for helping to construct a flying spell."

"Yes, I remember. I had preferred they take something tangible."

Shoogar ignored me. "I am protecting both your sons as a matter of course, so Wilville's occasional ride on an unblessed bicycle proves nothing. Besides, if everything else has been properly prepared, the bicycle blessing is superfluous."

"I still say that such a thing as a device independent of the gods might be possible."

Shoogar gave me a look. "You seem very sure of yourself."

"As a boy, I once used an unblessed fishing rod. I made it myself."

"So?"

"So I caught a fish."

Shoogar snorted. "It still proves nothing, Lant. If you had blessed that rod and washed your hook as you should have, you might have caught ten times as many fish. All that you proved otherwise was that you had constructed a usable fishing rod. What you needed for that experiment was a valid control—an identical fishing pole that had been blessed and washed. Then you would have seen which one could catch the most fish."

"You talk as if you have done such an experiment."

"Not with fish, no. But with traps."

My surprise must have shown, for he said, "As an apprentice, every new magician must prove to his own satisfaction, at least once, that there is truly great power in magic. One cannot be a magician if there is a seed of doubt in his mind. By allowing the apprentice to satisfy his curiosity, we generate faith in him. It is a simple experiment—one that anyone can construct for himself—a test that can be repeated as often as you choose. Each time the results are the same and can be verified."

"And what happens?"

"The traps with the blessed bait will catch twice as many rabbits."

"So? Maybe it was only because the bait is more attractive to the rabbits."

"Of course," said Shoogar. "That's exactly what it is supposed to do. The whole purpose of the spell is to make the bait more attractive. These traps are simple devices, Lant. A simple device may not always need magic, but when it is used the results are easily demonstrable. Now, how many parts were there to your fishing pole?"

"Three. Stick, line and hook."

"Right. There is little that can go wrong with it, but still the string can break, or the bait can slip off, or the hook may not catch. And this is only a simple device—a thing that does not have to be very precise. Think, Lant! What of the construction that has many moving parts? It has to have all of them in absolute working order before any of them will work. What of, say, the bicycle?"

I started to answer, but he cut me off. "Don't interrupt. The bicycle has many moving parts, the wheels, the pulleys, the steering bar, the pedals, the axles. All of these things must be precision carved and in delicate adjustment with each other, or the device simply will not work. Now, theoretically, a perfect machine is possible . . . but in practice—well, when you get a machine that has to be that precise simply to function, that is when the effect of the magic becomes most important. If only one part fails—one part—then the whole machine is useless. The simple device does not need magic, so its effect is enhanced by the simplest of spells; but a complex device needs a more complex spell–just to keep it working at all. There is just too much that can go wrong. Tell me, Lant, how many parts are there to a bicycle?"

I shrugged. "I have never counted. A good many, I would guess."

Shoogar nodded. "And how many parts does the stranger's flying nest have?"

I shook my head. "I don't know."

"More than a bicycle?"

"Undoubtedly," I said.

"Very perceptive of you, Lant. I feel sure that there must be at least a thousand different parts in that flying nest. From my own flying experiments, I can tell you that a flying spell is a very complex device indeed. Purple-Gray's nest must have many moving parts, all of them working together in precision. The smallest error and—*Poff!* Nothing happens. It's quite obvious to me that the more parts a machine has, the more opportunities it has to go wrong. Now, are you going

to stand there and try to tell me that the stranger keeps all
of those various parts working in absolute precision without
the aid of any magic at all . . .?"

I shook my head. Shoogar made a very convincing case.
Certainly, he had already given the whole matter much more
thought than I had imagined. But, of course, that was his
job as magician. It was reassuring to know that he was doing
it so well.

I beamed proudly at him, "The same thing must apply
to all of his other devices, right?"

Shoogar nodded, "You are beginning to see the obvious,
Lant."

"They must need so much magic that they must be reeking
of spells, right?"

Shoogar nodded again.

"Then, you have already figured out the secret of the light
device, Shoogar!" I exclaimed. "It is so complex that it is
obvious, right?"

"Wrong. It is so simple that it is a mystery."

"Huh——"

"The most I've been able to do is to take the device apart
—but look at what that leaves me!" He waved his hand at a
workbench. On it were only four pieces, the elements of the
stranger's light. These consisted of a hollow shell, a crystal
lens, a flat plate and an interior canister, roughly the same
shape as the outer shell. Shoogar turned this flat bulging object
over and over in his hands, but he could not find an opening.
It was hard and solid and we both puzzled over what it might
contain. It resisted all of our attempts to open it, and
Shoogar would not use force for fear of destroying the devices
within.

"And you have been able to make no changes at all in
its condition?" I prompted.

"Not exactly. I have made one change. . . ."

"And what is that?"

"The light. It has failed completely and will no longer
glow."

"Oh."

Shoogar glumly fitted the pieces together again as I watched.
He activated the sliding nerve. Nothing happened. He twisted
the turning knob back and forth. Still nothing. "I thought

not," he muttered. "I had hoped the spell might restore itself if given a chance to rest—but apparently I was mistaken."

"Why don't you take it back to Purple?" I suggested.

Shoogar whirled on me, "What?!! Do you think I am not capable enough on my own to solve this problem?"

"No, Shoogar!" I protested. "I am sure you are capable. I just thought that——uh, well, perhaps Purple has done something to cancel the original spell that you can't know about. Perhaps he has insulted some god."

Shoogar considered this. "You could be right . . . you're sure you're not doubting my ability as a magician?" He peered at me.

Hastily, I reassured him, "Shoogar, I have no doubts about the level of your knowledge."

This seemed to placate him, "Good. Then we can pay a visit to Purple and find out why the device doesn't work."

We found Purple out in the west pasture, doing something with a set of his devices. I looked for, but did not see the red-fire throwing device. Apparently, he had not brought it with him. The devices he was using here in the meadow all seemed to be rather harmless.

Purple was puttering contentedly, murmuring and humming busily to himself when Shoogar interrupted and handed him the device. Purple took it, fiddled with it several times, then opened it and examined the cylinder within. He noted that its surface had gone red. "Well, of course it won't work. The battery is dead."

Shoogar went pale. "The battery? Why did you not tell me there was a living creature within this device? I did not even know what to feed it."

"No, no," said Purple with a laugh. "You don't understand."

"I understand all too well," said Shoogar. "You entrusted a living creature into my care without even telling me. Small wonder that it died—imprisoned in that tiny box without food or water! You have caused the death of a living being to be on my head, and now I must offer up prayers for its soul!"

Purple managed to check his laughter, "Listen to me, Shoogar. Listen. A battery is not a living creature. It is a device, a thing that stores power."

"Oh," said Shoogar. "A latent spell." He smoothed his fur and said in a calmer tone, "Well, which god must I placate in order to restore its power to it?"

Again Purple laughed, "You still do not understand. Here, give it to me, and I will do it for you." He reached for the device, but Shoogar did not give it to him.

"Why will you not tell me how to restore it?" demanded Shoogar. "What good will the device be to me, if I must continually come to you when its power is exhausted—what kind of a magician would that make me look like? And furthermore, what happens after you leave—how will I restore it then? If I at least knew which gods—"

"No gods," said Purple. "No gods at all. Your gods are not able to restore this device's power. Here, give it to me, Shoogar. I will do it."

Shoogar jerked his hand back as if stung. "The gods not able to restore the device's power? Only *you?*"

"Relax, Shoogar," Purple said. "The device works without the gods; it doesn't need them."

Shoogar said slowly, carefully, "Do you mock me? No device works without the gods."

"This one does. So do the rest of my devices."

Shoogar gently stiffened his tone. "Purple, you are not making sense. It sounds as if you are denying the power of the gods. Such talk will cause Elcin to rain lightning down upon your head. I urge you to——"

"That would be true," Purple interrupted, "if there *were* an Elcin. Or any other god. You have over a thousand gods here—and I still have not numbered them all. Oh, these primitive superstitions, borne out of the ignorant need to explain the inexplicable! I'm sorry, Shoogar; I can't explain it to you—you're as much its victim as its master." Abruptly, he was silent.

"Is that all?" Shoogar asked.

"Yes, I'm afraid so," the other replied.

Shoogar looked thoughtfully at the device he still held in his hands. "Purple," he began slowly and evenly; his voice showed great control. "Were it not for your devices, I would think you either a fool or a blaspheming red magician. But the abilities of your devices are such that you can be neither foolish nor false. Therefore, you must be something else." He paused, then said, "I want to know what that something is. In your conversations you continually refer to things that do not make sense, but they *hint* at meaning. I am sure that you know things that I do not. Your devices prove that. I wish to learn these secrets." He paused again; it was very hard for him to say what he said next, "Will you teach me?"

Shoogar's words startled me. I had never heard him so humble. His passion for the secrets of the stranger must have been all-consuming for him to debase himself like that.

Purple looked at Shoogar for a long moment, "Yes . . ." he said, almost to himself. "Yes . . . It is the only way— teach the local shamans, let them introduce the knowledge. . . . All right; look, Shoogar, you must first understand that the gods are not gods at all, but manifestations of your belief."

Shoogar nodded, "That theory is not unfamiliar to me."

"Good," said Purple. "Perhaps you are not as primitive as I thought."

"This theory," continued Shoogar, "is one of the key theories upon which all of magic is based—that the gods will take the forms necessary to their functions, and those functions are determined by—"

"No, no." Purple cut him off. "Listen. Your people do not understand how the moons make the tides, so you create N'veen, the god of tides and patron of mapmakers. You do not understand how the winds are created by great masses of hot air, so you create Musk-Watz, the god of winds. You do not understand the relationship between cause and effect, so you create Leeb, the god of magic."

Shoogar frowned, but he nodded. He was trying very hard to follow this.

"I can understand how it happened, Shoogar," said Purple condescendingly. "It's no wonder you have so many gods— single god worship starts with a single sun. Here you have two suns and eleven moons. Your system is hidden away in a dust cloud . . ." He saw that Shoogar was frowning and said quickly, "No, forget that last. It would only confuse you."

Shoogar nodded.

"Now, listen to this carefully. There is something more than these gods of yours, Shoogar, but you and your people have forgotten that you have created the gods yourselves, and you have come to believe that it is the other way around— that the gods have created you."

Shoogar flinched at this, but he said nothing.

"Now, I will try to teach you what I can. I will be glad to. The sooner you and your people are ready to lay aside your primitive superstitions and accept the one true . . ." And here, the speakerspell hesitated again, ". . . *magic,* then the sooner will you inherit . . . the lights in the sky!"

"Huh?" said Shoogar. "What lights in the sky? Do you mean those faint nonsubstantial things that appear at random and rarely in the same place twice?"

Purple nodded, "You are not able to see them as I am— but someday, Shoogar, someday, your people will build their own flying spells and———"

"Yes, that's it!" said Shoogar eagerly. "Show me the flying spell. What gods———"

"No gods, Shoogar. That's what I have been trying to explain to you. The flying spell is not derived from the gods, but from men; men like myself."

Shoogar started to open his mouth to protest, but he Swallowed mightily and croaked out instead, "Derived from men . . .?"

Purple nodded.

"Then it must be a simpler spell than I imagined———you will teach it to me?"

"I can't," Purple protested.

"Can't? You just said you would."

"No, no—I meant that I would teach you my . . ." the speakerspell seemed to be having some trouble with the word, ". . . *magic;* but I can't teach you my flying spell."

Shoogar shook his head, as if to clear it, "Your flying spell is not magic then?"

"No, it isn't. It's . . ." Again, the device hesitated, ". . . it's *magic.*"

I could see that Shoogar's temper was shortening. "Are you or are you not going to teach me how to fly?"

"Yes—but it is your people who will fly——"

"Then what good is it to me?"

"I mean, your children and your grandchildren."

"I have no children," Shoogar fumed.

"I did not mean it that way," Purple said, "I meant . . . your children and your grandchildren. That is, the spell is so complex that it will take many years to learn and build."

"Then let us begin," prompted Shoogar impatiently.

"But we can't—" Purple protested. "Not until you learn the basics of . . . *magic*."

"I already know the basics of magic!" Shoogar screamed. "Teach me the flying spell!"

"I can't!" Purple screamed back. "It's too difficult for you!"

"Then why did you say you would if you wouldn't?" A red-faced Shoogar cried.

"I didn't say I wouldn't!" bellowed Purple. "I said, I couldn't!"

And that's when Shoogar got mad. "May you have many ugly daughters," he began. "May the parasites from ten thousand mud creatures infest your cod-piece!" His voice rose to a fearful pitch. "May dry rot take your nesting tree! May you never receive a gift that pleases you! May the God of Thunder strike you in the kneecap!"

They were only epithets, nothing more, but coming from Shoogar they were enough to pale even me, an innocent bystander. I wondered if my hair would fall out from witnessing such a display of anger.

Purple was unmoved—and I must credit him for his courage in the face of such fury. "I have already told you, Shoogar, that I am not concerned with your magic. I am above such things."

Shoogar took another breath. "If you do not cease and desist I will be forced to use *this!*" And Shoogar produced from the folds of his robe a doll. I knew from its odd proportions and colors that the doll had been carved to represent Purple.

Purple did not even quail, as any normal man would have done. I knew then that he must be mad. "Use it," he said. "Go ahead and use it. But don't interrupt me in my work. Your world-life-system-balance has developed in a fascinating direction. The animals have developed some of the most unusual fluids-secreted-for-the-control-of-bodily functions that I have ever seen." Purple bent back to his devices, did something to one of them, a stabbing gesture with a single forefinger, and a whole section of the west pasture erupted.

Shoogar covered his eyes in despair. Purple had just violated one of the finest pastures of the village—one of the favorite pastures of Rotn'bair, the god of sheep. Who knew what the mutton would taste like this winter?

Then, to add injury to insult, Purple began gathering up fragments of the meadow and putting them into little containers. He was taking the droppings!

Was it possible for one man to violate so many of the basic laws of magic and still survive? The laws of magic are strict. Any fool can see them in operation every day —even I am familiar with them—they operate the entire world, and their workings are simple and obvious.

But Purple, this man of the flying nest was blind even to the simplest of spells!

I was not surprised when Shoogar, grimly intent, set the doll down on the grass and set it afire. Neither was I surprised when the doll had burnt itself into a pinch of white ash without Purple even bothering to notice.

Purple ignored it—and us; he showed not the slightest effect. Flaming sting things! What powers this magician must have! Shoogar stared at him aghast. How dare he not be affected! Purple's very casualness was the ultimate insult. When we left him he had one of his clicking boxes open and was fumbling inside. He never even noticed us leaving.

Shoogar was peering into the sky, a frown on his face. Both suns were still high; broad red disc and blue-white point. The blue sun was poised on the edge of the red, ready to begin the long crawl across its face.

"Elcin's wrath!" he muttered. "I cannot use the suns—

all is unstable. That leaves me only the moons—and the moons are well into the mudskunk." He hurled a fireball across the clearing. "An eight-mooned mudskunk at that!" He put his hands on his hips and shouted into the sky, "Why me, Ouells! Why me? What have I done to offend you that you curse me with such unusable configurations? Have I not sworn my life to your service?"

But there was no answer. I don't think Shoogar expected one. He turned back to his spell devices. "All right, then. If it is a mudskunk you have given me, then it is a mudskunk I shall use. Here, Lant, hold this," and he thrust a large pack at me.

He continued to rummage through his equipment, all the while muttering under his breath. A fearful collection of cursing devices began to grow around him.

"What is all this for?" I indicated the pile.

He appeared not to hear me, continued checking off items in his head, then began loading them into the pack.

"What is all this for?" I repeated.

Shoogar looked at me, "Lant, you are a fool. *This*," he said and hefted his kit meaningfully, "is to show the stranger that one does not trifle with the gods of the full belly."

"I'm afraid to ask. What is it?" I asked.

"It's the spell of the. . . . No, you'll just have to wait and see it in action, with the others." He strode purposefully toward the frog-grading ponds. I hurried after him; it was amazing how fast Shoogar's squat little legs could carry him.

There was already an uneasy crowd of villagers standing on the rise above the flying nest. None dared approach it. When Shoogar appeared, an excited murmur ran through the crowd—the word of Purple's insult had spread quickly; the villagers were tense with expectation.

Shoogar ignored them. He pushed through the milling throng and strode angrily to Purple's nest, ignoring the mud that splashed up and over his ankles and stained the hem of his robe.

He strode around that nest three times without pause, looking at it from all sides. I was unsure whether he had already started spelling, or whether he was just sizing up the situation. For a long moment he stood looking at the landward side of that nest, like an artist contemplating a blank skin.

Then, abruptly, he made up his mind. He stepped quickly forward and with a piece of chalk he inscribed the sign of the horned box on the side of Purple's nest.

An interested murmur of speculation rose from the crowd, "The horned box . . . the horned box . . ." This spell would be under the domain of Rotn'bair, the sheep god. Members of the crowd discussed it busily amongst themselves. Rotn'bair is neither very powerful nor very irritable. Most of the Rotn'-bairic spells deal with fertility and food gathering. Few things will anger the sheep god; but if Rotn'bair could be angered, Shoogar would know how. The crowd buzzed with an excited curiosity, each speculating on just what form the final spell would take.

Shoogar finished the sketch. Absent-mindedly wiping the chalk from his hands, he strode down to the mudbanks of the river. He paced back and forth along its edge, casting about for something. Abruptly he spotted what he was looking for, something just below the surface of the water. He grabbed quickly for it, his hands dipping into the river with no splash at all. When he straightened, the sleeves of his robe were dripping, but there was a brownish-looking slug in his grasp, and after a moment I caught the repellent odor of mudskunk.

The scent reached the rest of the crowd at the same time, and a murmur of approval went up from them. The antipathy between Rotn'bair, the sheep god, and Nils'n, the god of the mud creatures, was known even to laymen. Evidently Shoogar was constructing a spell that would play on the mutual antipathy of the two gods.

My guess was right—I pride myself on a fairly good understanding of the basic principles of magic—Shoogar slit the belly of the mudskunk and deftly extracted its anger gland. He placed this into a bone bowl. I recognized the bowl, having carved and cleansed it for him myself. It was made from the skull of a newborn lamb and had been sanctified to Rotn'bair. Now he was defiling it with the most odious portion of the mud creature. No doubt, he now had Rotn'bair's attention.

He laid this to one side and returned to the mudskunk which lay writhing in a swampy pool. He picked it up and

deftly sliced off its head without even offering up a prayer
for its soul. Thus he defiled its death. Now, he had Nils'n's
attention.

Using the bladder of the slug as a mixing bag, he began
to construct a potion of powdered ramsbone, extract of
hunger, odour of sheepsblood, and several other elements
that I could not identify; but I suspected that all of them
were designed to arouse the wrath of Nils'n, although in what
manner was not yet clear.

Shoogar surveyed the nest of the mad magician on its
riverward side. Then he began to paint his soupy potion in
broad lines across its black flank in a pattern of eleven
stripes by eleven. Having finished, he sketched in the sign
of the deformed changeling, the favored son of the sheep
god. This half of the spell would anger Nils'n. Shoogar had
defiled a mud creature in order to celebrate the greatness of
Rotn'bair. To complete the other half of the spell, Shoogar
would now desecrate his earlier celebration of Rotn'bair, the
horned box sketched on the other side of the nest.

He returned to the bone bowl, the one containing the anger
gland of the mudskunk, and using the leg bone of a ram,
he crushed the gland into a sick-smelling paste. This he
mixed with ramsblood, defiled water and a greenish powder
from his travel kit. I recognized that powder—it was an
extract of fear, usually used where potent action is desired.
It is derived from animals of the cloven hoof. Six sheep must
have been sacrificed just to provide the small amount Shoogar
was now mixing into his spell.

Stepping to the landward side of the nest, and chanting
a song of praise for Nils'n, Shoogar began painting a familiar
symbol across the chalk sketch of the horned box. It was the
sign of Nils'n, a diagonal slash with an empty circle on
either side.

The crowd gasped appreciatively. Such originality in spellcasting was a delight to behold. No wonder he was called
Shoogar the Tall. Rotn'bair would not allow such a desecration of his sheep to exist for long. And Nils'n, the god of mud
creatures, would not long be complacent while mud-skunks
were being sacrificed to Rotn'bair.

The antipathy of the two gods is demonstrated every time
the sheep are led to the river. Sheep are careless and clumsy.

As they mill about on the banks, they trample scores of frogs, snakes, salamanders, lizards, chameleons, and other amphibians that live in the mud. At the same time many of the more dangerous mud creatures, the poisonous ones, the fanged ones, the ones with venom lash back at the sheep, cutting their legs, ruining their wool, infecting them with parasites, giving them festering sores, leaving them bleeding from angry cuts and slashes. The two gods hate each other, and in their various incarnations, as sheep and mud creatures, they work to destroy each other at every opportunity.

Now Shoogar had inscribed insults to both upon the same nest. He had defiled creatures of each in order to celebrate the greatness of the other. If Purple did not make immediate amends, he would have to suffer the wrath of both simultaneously.

Purple had said he did not believe in the gods. He denied their existence. He denied their powers. And he had stated that he was above Shoogar's magic.

I hoped he would return in time to see the spell take effect.

I followed Shoogar down to the river, and helped him with his ritual purification. He had to cleanse himself of the odours of offense against the gods, lest he be caught up in his own curse. Sometimes the gods are nearsighted. We bathed him with six different oils before we even let him step into the river. (No sense in offending Filfo-mar, the river god.)

Even before we finished with the cleansing we could hear the curse beginning. We could hear the cheers of the crowd; and beneath that was a dull sort of booming. Shoogar wrapped his robe around himself and hurried back up the hill, me trailing excitedly in his wake.

We reached the crest of the hill in time to see an angry ram butting his head insistently against the side of Purple's nest. More rams were arriving, and they too began to attack the looming black globe. The focus of their anger was the desecrated homage to Rotn'bair, and it seemed as if the very substance of the Nils'n symbol was enough to anger them. The smell of the mudskunk was potent enough to raise anyone's hackles.

Red-eyed and breathing heavily, the rams jostled and shoved and butted even at each other in their frenzy to attack that odious desecration on the side of Purple's nest. Each time they struck it, that same dreadful booming echoed up and down the hill, and each time a great cheer went up from the crowd. I expected at any moment to see one of the rams go crashing through the walls of that fearful nest, but no— those walls were stronger than I had thought. Perhaps even as strong as metal.

The only effect I could see was that each time a ram struck it, it seemed to lift slightly out of the mud for a moment before sinking wetly back. Bleating in frenzy, the rams raged at that offensive spot——they were the living incarnation of Rotn'bair's anger. Again and again, they hurled themselves at that dull black surface.

Old Khart, the lead ram, had shattered both of his horns (sacred items in themselves—I mourned the loss), and several of the other rams were also injured. Their eyes were red with fury, their nostrils flared wide; their breath came in hot puffs of steam and the sounds of bleating and snorting filled the air with a madness born of wrath. The steam rose from their sides; their hoofs slashed wetly through the ground, churning the grass and mud into a meaningless soup.

Some of the rams were having trouble with their footing already, and indeed, as we watched, one of the older ones slipped and slid through the mud. He crashed against two others and brought them both down with him; all three were caught under the frenzied slashing hooves of the others.

Their angry snorts were punctuated by grunts of pain, and by the dull thud and hollow boom that rolled up and down the slope each time they struck the side of Purple's nest. But the creatures had strength beyond all natural endurance, and continued to clamber over one another, butting at that offending spell.

And each time they did so, each time they struck it, the nest rose up out of the ground and threatened to slide down the slope and into the river; but each time it would pause and

then sag wetly back into its hollowed out cradle of mud.
Several times it trapped slow-footed beasts under the curve
of its wall. I felt a great surge of emotion within myself——
any moment now Purple's great egg-shaped nest would be
toppled onto its side.

Then, abruptly, three of the rams hit the nest at the same
time, and it seemed to leap into the air. One more struck it
at just the right instant, and as it rose out of its hollow it
just seemed to keep on moving. Suddenly it was sliding
downslope with a great wet slosh. Angry rams scrambled
after it, butting at it all the way down, churning the mud
with their hoofs and leaving a long angry scar through Ang's
carefully terraced frog-grading pools. I shouted in triumph
with the rest.

The great black globe struck the river with a resounding
smack and splash; a loud cheer of delight went up from
the villagers. Only I was silent, for the terrible nest had not
deviated even a thumbnail's width from its perfectly upright
position. Had Shoogar noticed too? His puzzled frown was
a match for mine.

But the nest was in the river! The rams slid and skidded
down the slope, destroying what was left of the frog pools
in the process. Almost joyfully they leapt into the water,
still butting at Purple's nest.

Others milled around the banks, churning the mud. Mud-
skunks and salamanders ran panic-stricken under their hoofs
and a new shade of red added itself to the stains on the
heaving flanks of the crazed rams. Crushed mud-skunk
mingled with the blood of the sheep, and the terrible smell
reached us on the crest of the hill along with the hysterical
splashing and bleating.

Now the black nest was within Nils'n's reach. So far only
Rotn'bair had had a chance to avenge the insult. Now the
banks boiled with life as salamanders, lizards, crabs, venom-
bearing snakes and other river creatures came swarming up
out of the mud and darkness. They scrambled across the
churning surface and attacked anything that moved, even
each other, but more often the rams.

The rams continued to charge the nest, oblivious to the
mud creatures caught in their wool, hanging from their sides,
biting and slashing at their legs. Their once proud flanks, now

torn and slashed, were stained with angry strokes of red
and great washes of muddy brown river water. It was an
awe-inspiring sight, sheep and mud creatures together attacking that ominous unmoving sphere.

The villagers stood on the flanks of the hill and cheered
the frenzied activity below. One or two of the braver shepherds tried to work their way down the slope, but the snapping
claws of the mud crabs drove them quickly back up to the
crest.

The rams were slowing down now, but still they continued
to mill about Purple's nest——still they continued to push
at it, occasionally clambering over the body of a fallen
comrade. The water was pink. Angry mud-skunks swarmed
along both banks of the river. It was a heartening sight. The
crowd continued to cheer wildly, and began to chant a chorus
of praise to Shoogar. Pilg the Crier was leading them.

Down below, their anger spent, some of the rams were
already climbing back up the hill, slipping and skidding
in their own blood and falling back down the mud-slicked
surface. Two or three slipped beneath the water and failed
to surface.

The mud creatures too were beginning to calm——and
the shepherds once more dared to work their way carefully
down the slopes to tend their wounded flock.

"A beautiful spell, Shoogar!" I congratulated him, "Beautiful! And so powerful!"

Indeed, as the churning foam of the river continued to
subside, revealing the full extent of the devastation, several
of the villagers even began to mutter that perhaps the spell
had been a bit too powerful. One of the members of the
Guild of Advisors remarked, "Look at all this destruction!
This spell should be banned."

"Banned?" I confronted the man, "And leave us defenseless
before our enemies?"

"Well," he amended, "perhaps we should only keep Shoogar
from using it on friends. He could still use it on strangers."

I nodded. I would accept that.

At least eleven of our sheep lay dead in the churned
mud of the slope, mud creatures feeding indiscriminately on
their stilled or still heaving flanks. Four of the rams were
trampled into the landscape; others lay with their heads at

oddly twisted angles, their necks broken from butting against
Purple's nest. Three more bodies lay below the water with
their mouths open.

What remained of the flock would show countless mudskunk bites upon their legs and flanks. Many of those bites
would undoubtedly become festering sores and probably more
of the rams would die later.

The vermin of the mud would be vicious for days to
come. It would not be safe to bathe for a while, and probably
the sheep would not dare to return to the river for a long
time; they would have to be led to the mountain streams to
drink.

The frog-grading ponds had been completely obliterated
and would have to be completely resculptured elsewhere. Ang
stood moaning and wringing his hands as he surveyed his
mud-churned slope.

And finally, the wreck of the mad magician's nest now
blocked the river. Dammed water spilled over the south bank
in a torrent. Already it was carving a new course for itself.

And none of it mattered. These were all small prices to
pay for the damage done to the stranger. Considering the
magnitude of the task, it was one of Shoogar's less expensive
efforts and we were proud of him.

Then why was the scene so utterly silent?

I looked to my left and saw Purple standing on the crest
of the hill.

He stood there with his devices floating behind. Every
eye was on him. His hands were on his hips as he looked
thoughtfully down at his nest. How long had he been standing
there?

"Fascinating," he said. And he started briskly down the
slope. His devices followed.

The nest sat like a great egg in the middle of the river.
Water backed up behind it, flowed in great torrents past its

bulging flank, splashed angrily up and over the trampled shore. Angry mud creatures clambered over its dull black surface, scratching determinedly at the spell designs. Gobbets of mud and bloody fur streaked its sides, but still the spells of Shoogar were visible, almost etched into its surface. It stood perfectly, almost arrogantly upright.

That made me uneasy. My eyes searched for the dents in the stranger's ruined nest, the dents surely put there by the horns of the rams. I couldn't find them.

Purple strode straight down the slope and into the water. Not a droplet of mud stuck to those peculiar boots of his ——in contrast to Shoogar's legs and mine, which were mud to the hip. A pair of mud-skunks attacked the magician as he entered the water. Purple ignored them; and they couldn't seem to get a grip on his boots.

He stood under the bulge of the nest, and we waited for his scream of fury.

Carefully, with a small edged tool, he began scraping off bits of Shoogar's curse signs and putting them into small transparent containers. His mindless speakerspell continued to translate his ramblings. "Fascinating . . . the power of these fluids-secreted-for-the-control-of-bodily-functions is like nothing I've ever seen before . . . I wonder if these effects could be produced artificially?"

Twice he sniffed at what he had scraped off, and twice muttered a word the speakerspell did not translate. When he finished, he dipped his hands in the river to wash them, incidentally offending Filfo-mar, the usually gentle river god.

Purple turned to the egg-shaped door of his nest; it was flush with the curved wall, but outlined in orange to make it visible. He punched at a square pattern of bumps on the nest. The door slid open and Purple disappeared inside.

We waited. Would he continue to occupy his nest, living in the middle of our defiled river?

The flying nest hummed and rose twenty feet into the air. I screamed with the rest, a wordless scream of rage. The nest turned in an instant from black to silver; and it must have become terribly slippery, for every particle of mud and blood and potion from Shoogar's spell slid down the sides, formed a glob at the bottom of the nest and dropped in a lump into the river.

The nest turned black. It moved horizontally across the land and dropped gently to the ground——just a few yards west of where it had stood an hour ago. Only now it rested at the edge of a region of churned mud where the rams and mud creatures had fought to destroy it.

I could see Shoogar sag where he stood. And I feared for my village, and for Shoogar's sanity and my own. If Shoogar could not defend us from the mad magician, then we were all doomed.

There was an angry rumble from the villagers as Purple emerged from his nest. Purple frowned and said, "I wish I knew what's gotten you people so angry."

Somebody threw a spear at him.

I couldn't blame the lad. No sound, no pattern of mere words could properly have answered the magician. But the young man, enraged beyond sanity, had hurled his bone spear at the stranger's back——without a blessing!

It struck Purple hard in the back and bounced off to the side without penetrating. Purple toppled, not like a man, but like a statue. I had the irrational conviction that for a single instant Purple had become as hard as stone.

But the instant was over. Immediately he was climbing to his feet. The spear, of course, had done no harm at all. One cannot attack a magician with an unblessed spear. The boy would have to be brought before the Guild of Advisors.

If the village survived that long.

The suns rose together, the blue sun silhouetted off-center within the other's great fuzzy-edged and crimson disk.

I woke at noon. The evacuation was already well under way. My wives and spratlings had already done a good deal of the packing, though the fear of disturbing my sleep had slowed them somewhat. With my supervision, however, and the necessary discipline, the packing progressed quickly. Even so, we were very nearly the last family to leave the village.

The lower rim of the red sun was already near the mountains when I dropped behind the procession of my wives to tarry at Shoogar's nest.

Shoogar looked tired, but curiously determined. His eyes were alive and dancing, and his fingers moved with a life of their own, weaving spell knots into a leather strap. I knew better than to speak to him while he was in the midst of a duel.

For though no formal declaration had yet been made by Purple, this was a duel. Perhaps Purple thought that so long as no duel was declared, Shoogar would sit peacefully by and allow him to continue with his duel-mongering actions.

But I knew Shoogar better than that. The fierce glow burning in his eyes confirmed what I—and all of the rest of the villagers—already knew: that Shoogar would not rest until there was one less magician in the village.

I hurried on after my wives. Burdened as we were, we would be traveling well into the night. I had even removed the hobbles from my women so that they could travel faster; it would not do to underestimate the seriousness of the situation.

By the time the moons were overhead, we had reached our destination. Most of the families of the village were settled on the steppes to the north, a series of long sloping rises that overlooked the river and the cluster of housetrees that marked our village.

The encampment was a sprawling place of lean-tos and tents, smoky campfires and shrill women, milling groups of men and boys. Already scavengers were rooting busily underfoot; even before we had selected a campsite, many of my own spratlings had melted away into the bustle.

Although it was well into the night, few slept. The eerie glow of the moons gave us a twilight neither red nor blue, but ghostly gray—a strange half-real quality for the waiting time before the next step of the duel. An almost festive air pervaded the settlement.

From somewhere in the bachelor's section came the brawling chant of a game of rolling bones, and an occasional cry of triumph as one of the players scored a particularly difficult pass. It does not take much to please the lower classes.

An unpleasant surprise awaited us in the morning.

Hinc and I were standing at the edge of the encampment, looking down the slope toward the village, discussing the forthcoming duel, when we heard a dull distant slam, like a single cough from Elcin's throat.

We looked down to see a tremendous plume of black smoke wafting through the village treetops.

"Look," said Hinc. "Shoogar has started already."

"No," I shook my head. "I think he is only warming up. That looked like a preparation spell more than anything else. Something to get the attention of the gods."

"Pretty fierce attention-getter," noted Hinc.

I nodded, "It's going to be a pretty fierce duel. I wonder if we should move again? Farther back."

"If we are not out of range already, Lant, we haven't time to get out of range," said Hinc. "Even at a dead run. And even if you are right, you could never persuade the others. They are too tired."

He was right, of course, but before I could speak, we were interrupted by a crowd of frightened women running hysterically through the encampment as fast as their hobbled legs would carry them. They were screaming Purple's name.

I caught up with and cuffed my number three wife to attention. "What is the matter with you?" I demanded.

"It's the mad magician!" she cried. "He's trying to talk to the women!"

"The mad magician—here?"

She nodded fearfully, "He brought his nest to the spring where we wash—and he's trying to talk to us! He wants to know why we moved!"

Had the man no self-respect at all? Talking to women? Even from the mad magician I found this hard to believe. I strode purposefully through the crowd, now milling nervously

42

about, women comforting other hysterical women, men interrogating their wives, sprats crying for attention.

As I moved toward the spring, some of the men caught up with, and followed along behind me. They were muttering nervously. Pilg was moaning loudly, "We cannot escape. The duel follows us. Alas! Alas!"

It was as the women had said. Purple had brought his nest to a spot just above the encampment, near the spring the women had chosen for washing. The great black egg-shape was closed, and the magician was nowhere to be seen.

The others waited only long enough to see that the women had spoken the truth. Then they turned and fled quickly back to the settlement.

Hinc and I exchanged a wordless glance. Why had Purple followed us? Was he fleeing from his duel? I had never heard of such a thing before. What did he want of the villagers?

I circled the nest warily. It looked much as it had on the fearful night that I first saw it. I crept closer. There, lightly pressed into the dust, were the imprints of Purple's strangely shaped boots. But where was Purple now?

Suddenly, that booming hollow voice. "Lant! Just the person I was hoping to see."

This was too much for Hinc. He turned and disappeared down the slope after the others. I ached to join him, but I had to find out what the magician was up to.

The door to the nest slid open and Purple stepped out, his strange paunchy shape oddly disquieting—he had a fearful grin on his bare face and advanced toward me as if I were an old friend; his speakerspell drifted along behind.

"Lant," he said, moving closer, "perhaps you can tell me ——why have you people moved your village? The other spot was so much nicer."

I looked at him curiously. Could it be that he did not know of the duel? Was it possible for anyone to be that naive? Well, so much the better——his liability was Shoogar's asset. I certainly would not tell him. Why should a layman be concerned with the affairs of magicians? I didn't want to get involved. Instead, I just nodded, "Yes, the other spot *was* nicer."

"Then why do you not stay there?"

"We hope to return soon," I said. "After the time of the

conjunction." I pointed to the sky where the suns were setting together, Ouells's blue-white point near the bottom of Virn's crimson disk.

"Oh, yes," Purple nodded, "very impressive." Turning, he gazed admiringly at the ground behind him, "And it makes the shadows very pretty too."

"Very pretty——!" I stopped in mid-sentence. Dark and blue they were, each with a bloody edge—constant reminder that the time of terror was upon us. Was the man fearless ——or foolish? I shut up.

"Very pretty," Purple repeated. "Quite striking. Well, I will remain here with you and your people. If I can be of any assistance . . .?"

Something within me shriveled and died. "You—you're going to stay here?"

"Yes, I think so. I'll go back to the village when you people do; this will give me a chance to 'test' the mountain area for a day or so."

"Oh," I said.

He seemed to lose interest in me then, turned and went back to his nest. I waited to see how he caused the door to slide open. I had been puzzling about it since I had first seen him do the trick. There was a pattern of bumps in the surface of the nestwall. He tapped at these in a quick precise pattern.

I presumed that the pattern must have been the spell to open the door, but it was too quick for me to memorize. He stepped inside; the door slid shut and he was gone.

Dejectedly, I trudged back to the encampment—or what was left of the encampment.

Already the villagers were fleeing from their makeshift homes. Men were hastily packing travel kits, women were calling for spratlings. Children and dogs ran excitedly through the crowd, kicking up dust, chickens and scavengers.

Panic-stricken families were already moving across the steppes, upslope, downslope, sideways, anywhere, just as long as it was away from Purple; the magician who brought disaster with him.

My own wives were standing about nervously, waiting for me. Numbers one and two were trying to comfort number three, who was most upset. "He kept trying to talk to me! He kept trying to talk to me!"

"It wasn't your fault," I told her. "You will not be beaten for his trespass. You did right to run." My words had an immediate calming effect on the distraught woman, more so than all the stroking and soothing of the other two wives, once more proving that only a man can know how to handle the unusual situation.

"Pick up your packs," I told them. "We must be on our way."

"On our way?" questioned one. "But we just got here."

"We must move again," I said, "before this area is blasted. The mad magician's animal manners have blinded you to the true danger. Shoogar will follow Purple up here. Now, pick up your packs or I will beat all three of you."

They did as I bade them—but with no small amount of grumbling. Even though I thought to remove their hobbles so as to speed the journey, they grumbled—and for once they had cause. For a day and a half we had fled the site of the coming duel. Purple had easily, thoughtlessly nullified that effort with only a few moments of flight.

Within an hour the encampment was deserted. As we moved down the hill, I thought I saw Purple moving like a lost soul through the empty lean-to shelters.

We were the only family to return to the village. Where the others had fled I did not know. Probably south, away from the whole region. They had likely lost all interest in watching the duel, even from a distance. Now they wanted only to save their skins.

In the fading daylight, we approached the village warily. The blue sun winked out behind the edge of the world, leaving only the semicircular bulge of the red. The mists rising off the distant swamps took fire from the glow. It was as if the whole western edge of the world were aflame. I could almost smell the burning of it, a smell of disaster on the evening wind.

I left my wives at the nest, the nest to which I had thought we would never return, and headed toward Shoogar's. I carried a pack with me—a meal for him—perhaps his last. As I made my way through the village I could see the many effects of his spellcasting. Here and there, some of our proudest housetrees lay on their sides, as if they had been blasted out of the ground with great force. Others seemed to have withered and died where they stood.

Here and there a nest lay on the ground, shattered walls laying it open to the elements. Everywhere were great patches of dying vegetation. The scavenger animals were gone. There were no sounds of nightbirds. Except for my wives, myself, and of course, Shoogar, the village was empty. And dead.

Even if Shoogar won the duel, none would ever be able to return to this village. Nor would they want to. Its stability had been permanently destroyed.

All was silent and brooding.

The dead grass crunched under my feet as I approached Shoogar's nest. I knocked cautiously on the wall.

When he appeared I gasped in horror. Shoogar had gone gray and haggard; new circles had appeared under his eyes and his skin was discolored in angry red patches as if he had been caught too close to one of his own spells.

But what had startled me most was that Shoogar had shaved off all of his fur! He was totally naked and hairless— a frightening caricature of the mad magician!

He greeted me with a wan smile, grateful for my company. I began to lay out the ritual supper for him. It is traditional that on the night before a duel the men of the village serve a meal of faith to their patron warlock. But the others had fled, so that duty had fallen on me alone.

I stood silently by and waited, serving him at each gesture or grunt. It was not much of a meal, but it was the best I could prepare under such circumstances. Shoogar seemed not to mind. He ate slowly, savoring every bite. He looked tired and his hands trembled as he moved. But he ate heartily.

By the time he laid aside his bone food-stabber, the red sun had long disappeared from the west. The moons had not yet appeared. He moved slowly, but whether from satiation or exhaustion, it was impossible to tell.

"Where are the others?" he asked.

"They've fled." I explained what happened. Shoogar listened carefully, occasionally picking at some previously overlooked morsel in the bowls before him.

"I did not expect the stranger to move," he muttered. "It is a bad thing—but clever. Now I must alter my spell to account for this new factor. You say he tried to talk to the women?" He bit into a fruit.

I nodded, "My number three wife."

"Ptah!" Shoogar spat out the seeds in disgust, "The man must have no taste. Hmp. If one is going to lower oneself to talk to women, one could at least choose the women of a worthy rival."

"You have no women," I pointed out.

"It is still an insult to me," brooded Shoogar.

"Perhaps he doesn't know any better. Remember, he said that the ways of his homeland are very different from ours."

"Ignorance could be the excuse for his bad manners," Shoogar grumbled, "but only madness could explain the man's trespasses against common sense."

"It is said that a madman possesses the strength of ten . . ."

Shoogar gave me a look, "I know what is said. Most of the time *I* said it first."

We sat there in silence. After a while I asked, "What do you think will happen on the morrow?"

"There will be a duel. One will win, one will lose."

"But who . . .?" I prompted.

"If it were possible to tell which magician would win a duel, there would be no need for duels."

Again we sat in silence. This was the first time Shoogar had referred to the duel with any indication of doubt. Always before he had expressed confidence in his own abilities and skepticism for the powers of Purple. Clearly the duel had taken its toll even before the first spell had been cast.

"Lant," he said abruptly, "I will need your help."

I looked up startled. "Me? But I know nothing of magic. You have told me that I am a fool countless times. Is it wise to risk such an important undertaking in the hands of a . . .?"

"Shut up, Lant," he said softly. I shut. "All you have to do is help me transport my spellcasting equipment up the mountain to Purple's nest. We will need two bicycles or some pack animals. I cannot carry it all myself."

I breathed easier at that. "Oh, well, in that case——"

We were on our way within the hour.

It was close to dawn when we reached the site of the encampment. The deserted lean-tos and shelters stood bleak and empty in the night, like some fearful city of the dead. I found myself trembling.

We rode through it wordlessly, finally parking our bicycles on the slope just below the spring. We could hear it babbling carelessly in the dark.

Taking care to keep as quiet as possible, we edged forward, up the hill. I held my breath till we topped the rise, then let it out in a whoosh. Yes, the nest was still there.

I believe I would have cried bitter tears had it been gone. I am sure it would have killed Shoogar. The frustration of having an enemy flee from him in such a manner would have been too much.

We crept back to the deserted encampment, there to wait the coming of dawn. I ached for a chance to sleep, but Shoogar gave me a potion to keep me awake. To keep him company, he said. He began laying out his equipment, organizing and sorting. "If I can only take him by surprise," he muttered. He paused to oil a metal knife. "And if only there were some way to draw him away from his nest . . ."

"That's not needed," I blurted. "He will probably leave it by himself. He is testing again. He said this when I spoke to him. He wants to test the mountain."

"H'm," said Shoogar. "This is a bit of good fortune. I hope that he tests the mountain the same way that he tested the village; for when he tested the village he was gone from his nest almost the entire day."

"What if he doesn't? What if he returns before the curse is finished?"

"Let us hope he does not."

"Can't you do something?"

Shoogar paused, thought for a moment, then rummaged in his kit. He produced a small leather pouch of dust and another of herbs. "Here, go and spread this dust around the outside of his nest. It is very fine dust; it will float in the air for hours. If he breathes any of it, it will produce a very strong yearning in him. He will not return until that yearning is satisfied."

"But, what about me?"

"That's what the herbs are for. When you finish with the dust, you will take half of those herbs and chew them well. When they turn bitter in your mouth, swallow them, but not until they turn bitter. Bring the rest of the herbs back to me, so I may chew them. They will make us both immune to the power of the dust."

I nodded, then crept up the hill and did as I was instructed. When I brought the two leather pouches back to Shoogar he was just laying out the last of his equipment. One swollen pouch he handled most carefully. "Powdered magician's hair," he explained. I did not blame him for handling it carefully. He had sacrificed much to produce it; his squat and shaven body trembled with the cold.

Abruptly, a troubled look crossed his face, "I am sure that Purple's power is in some way connected with his nest. I must get into it somehow. That is the only part of my curse that I am in doubt about. I must get into that nest . . ."

My heart leapt. "But, I can help you there——" I fairly shouted, then remembered to lower my voice. "Today—I mean, yesterday (for dawn was fast approaching)—I was able to get close enough to Purple to observe how he worked his doorspell."

Shoogar nearly leapt at me, "Lant, you are a fool!" Then he thought to lower his voice. "Why did you not tell me this earlier?" he hissed.

"You did not ask me."

"Well, I am asking you now—how does it work?"

I explained what I had seen, the pattern of bumps on the nestwall, how Purple had tapped at them in a certain way and how the door had slid open immediately after. Shoogar listened carefully. "Obviously, the order in which he touches the bumps is the way the spell is controlled. Think, Lant! Which bumps did he touch?"

"That I did not see . . ." I admitted.

Shoogar cursed, "Then why bother to tell me how to open the door if you do not know? Lant, you are a fool."

"I am sorry—but it happened so quickly. If I could only remember——If I could only see it again——"

"Perhaps . . ." said Shoogar. "Perhaps . . . Lant, have you ever been placed under the spell of the open mind?"

I shook my head.

"It is a spell of great power. It can be used to make you remember things that you think you have forgotten."

"Uh, is it dangerous?"

"No more so than any other spell."

"Well," I said, picking up my bicycle, "good luck with your duel, Shoogar. I will see you when it is——"

"Lant," he said evenly, "if you take one more step down-slope, I will work your name into the curse along with Purple's."

I laid the bicycle down again. It had been worth a try.

My feelings must have shown, for Shoogar said, "Don't be so fearful. I will do my best to protect you. Suddenly you have become a very important part of this duel. The knowledge locked up in your mind may make the difference between success and failure."

"But, Shoogar, I am a fool. You have told me that too many times for it to be otherwise. I admit it. I am a fool. You could not be wrong in your judgment of my character. What good could I be to you?"

"Lant," said Shoogar, "you are not a fool. Believe me. Sometimes in my quickness of temper I have made rash statements. But I have only the greatest respect for your judgment, Lant. You are not a fool."

"Oh, but I am," I insisted.

"You are not!" Shoogar said. "Besides, it does not take any great mental prowess to remember something as simple as you have described. Even an idiot such as you could do it!"

"Oh, but I will be only in your way, Shoogar. Please let me return to my family——"

"And have the other men of the village think you a coward?"

"It would be a small burden to bear——"

"Never!" snapped Shoogar. "No friend of mine shall wear the brand of coward. You will stay here with me, Lant. And you should be grateful that I care so much for you as a friend."

He turned again to the equipment laid out upon the ground.

I sighed in resignation and sat down to wait. Dawn was already seeping into the east.

Shoogar turned back to me, "Your part in this will be easy, Lant. There is no reason to fear."

"But, the danger——"

He dismissed it with a gesture, "There will be no danger if you follow my instructions exactly as I give them to you."

"I will follow your instructions."

"Good. There can be no room for error. Even the tiniest mistake could cost us both our lives."

"But you just said there would be no danger——"

"Of course not. Not if you follow instructions. Most of the hard work has already been done. Don't forget, I had to construct the equations: I had to prepare the ingredients, and I had to stabilize the symbology necessary to make the various incantations and potions work. All you have to do is help me place them in the proper place at the proper time."

"I thought all I had to do was help you open the nest——"

"Of course. But if you are going to be there anyway, you might as well help me with the rest."

"Oh," I said.

"And whatever you do, you must not try to speak to me. This is very important. When the suns rise, we shall begin— and once we begin, I must not be distracted at all. Except as is necessary to the curse I will not speak. Do you understand?"

I nodded.

"Good. Now, listen. There is one more thing. A very important thing. It has nothing to do with the curse, Lant, but for your own protection you must be exceedingly careful not to lesnerize."

"Lesnerize?" I asked. "What is lesnerize . . . ?"

But he pointed instead to the east. Day had seeped

red/flashed-blue over the hills. Shoogar fell to his knees an
began chanting to the suns.

The curse had begun.

The first step was a ritual cleansing, a purification s
that we would not contaminate the curse with some long
forgotten residual spell.

Then came the sanctification, the prayer for forgivenes
to the suns, Ouells and Virn, and to the moons, all eleven o
them—now in the configuration of Eccar the Man, he wh
had served the gods so well that he had been elevated to god
hood himself.

Other prayers were offered to the river god, the wind god
the gods of violence and magic, of engineering, of birds an
duels, of wars, of past and present and future, of skies an
seas and tides. And, of course, to Elcin, the thunder god. W
offered sacrifice to all of them, and sought their blessing
in the endeavors to come. We prayed that they would blam
the stranger and not us for the affronts about to be done to
them.

Then we cleansed ourselves again.

We gathered up the spellcasting equipment and crept u
the slope to where the mad magician's nest waited. Behind an
below us the mist which had covered all the lowlands at daw
thinned as the two suns rose higher. The ponderous red su
had turned the mists pink while the pinpoint blue burne
them away. We could see for miles.

We topped the rise slowly. Slightly below us, on the othe
side, was the black egg of Purple's nest, waiting grim an
brooding in the silent morning. It was closed, but was it de
serted?

I wanted to ask Shoogar what the next step was, but hi
last instruction made me fear even to breathe without being
told. Shoogar must have sensed my indecision, for he said
"Now we wait . . ."

The suns rose higher in the sky. The last of the mists disappeared from the land. And the egg sat silent on the steppes. The only sound was the gurgling of the spring.

Abruptly, the door of the nest slid open and Purple emerged. He stretched slowly and took a deep breath, then let it out with a sigh. I wondered if the yearning dust was still floating in the air. If it were, then Purple had just filled his lungs with it. He showed no reaction though as he closed the door of his nest behind him. If the dust was working, then it was very subtle.

We held our breaths as he began climbing up the slope of the hills. Shortly he disappeared over the top of one, and we were alone with the nest. Shoogar scrambled eagerly for it, I followed in his wake, not quite so eager.

Shoogar surveyed the nest carefully. He strode around it three times, finally coming to a stop in front of the orange and oval outline that was the door.

This first important step was the crucial one. Shoogar had to gain entrance into Purple's nest. If he could not, then all of the rest of his careful preparations would be for naught. He would be unable to complete the rest of the spell.

So much depended on the spell of the open mind——

He positioned me in the exact spot I had been standing when I observed how Purple had opened his nest. Then he brought out a device of glass and held it before my eyes, commanding me to look into it.

I wondered if the strain of the past three days had been too much for my friend. I saw no answers within the device of glass. But I did as he said, and looked into it. He began chanting at me softly, slowly, in that high croaking voice of his. I tried to concentrate on his words, but the crystal thing kept flickering light into my eyes.

Nor could I focus my sight upon the thing. It seemed to fade in and out of existence even as Shoogar held it. I tried to follow where it went when it disappeared, but it was revolving too fast. The sound of his chanting wove in and out with the flashes of light, and all of it together seemed to be whirling and twirling, churning and turning and——the world was——

Abruptly, I was wide awake.

Nothing had happened.

The spell of the open mind had failed. I remembered noth-

ing. I opened my mouth to speak, but Shoogar stopped me.
"You did fine, Lant. Just fine."

I wondered what he was talking about, but he was once
more fussing with his equipment. His manner was confident,
almost cheerful. He found what he was looking for, a piece
of chalk, and proceeded to draw a rune about the square pattern of bumps beside the door. Only once did he speak to me,
"You told me almost all of what I need to know, Lant. Almost
all. The rest I can fathom for myself."

I shrugged and sat down to watch. Obviously he knew what
he was doing.

He sat cross-legged before the door and began chanting,
working himself into a trance. He sat motionless on that
patch of ground before the door, the only sounds his thin
reedy voice and the gushing of the spring.

The suns crept up the sky, Ouells glowing like a blue-
white diamond at Virn's fading edge. So much to do, so little
time! How long would Purple be gone? Could we complete the
spell in time?

Shoogar sat silent and unmoving. His eyes were glazed.
Occasionally he would give a little grunt; but he said nothing.
I began to perspire.

Could Purple throw red fire *at a man*?

At last, when I had begun to fear that Shoogar would
never speak again, he rose, stepped to that pattern of bumps,
and touched four of them in a particular pattern.

Nothing happened.

Shoogar repeated the touch.

Still nothing happened.

Shoogar shrugged and returned to his place, Again he
went into his trance. This time, after an even greater wait,
he approached that door even more cautiously. Once more
he tapped out a pattern on the nestwall bumps; the same four,
but a different order.

Nothing happened again.

Shoogar sighed and returned to his squatting position. I
began to fear that we might spend the whole day just gaining
entry to Purple's nest and have no time left for the cursing.
Indeed, I had almost given up all hope of ever completing
the task before us when Shoogar rose again. He approached

the nest slowly, looked at the bumps for a long time, then touched four of them in a carefully precise manner.

And the door to the nest slid open.

Shoogar allowed himself a smile, but only a small one. It was a smile of anticipation: there was still much to do.

Quickly, we gathered up the equipment and moved into Purple's nest.

The walls themselves glowed with Purple's odd-colored light —bright and yellow, it made my eyes see colors that were not there. Slowly, as my vision sorted itself out, I began to see that this nest was furnished like no other nest I had ever seen. All around were tiny glowing eyes, raised knobs and more bumps like those in the pattern outside the door.

In the center was a zigzagged piece of padded furniture, a fit couch for a demon. Set into the nestwall just ahead of this were a series of flat plates like windows, but infinitely more transparent—like hardened air! Indeed, the whole nest showed workmanship finer than I had ever seen.

Shoogar peered carefully at the flat plates like windows. Some showed images of the areas around the nest. Others held odd patterns in colored light, carefully drawn lines and curves —obviously the demon's runes. Shoogar indicated one of these. "Do you still think he does not use magic?" he asked me; then, remembering his own injunction against unnecessary chatter, silenced himself.

Apparently it was not a very strong injunction, for Shoogar had been muttering back and forth all morning. Perhaps he had only warned me against speaking because he feared I would distract him. Well, he need not have worried; I had too much respect for Shoogar's abilities to question him in the middle of a spell. I opened my mouth to tell him so, but he cut me off.

Next to the padded thing was a plant, a vegetable well suited for the interior of this nest. It too was of a type I had never seen before. It was the shape of a white rose, but its color—could such a color be *green*? The leaves glowed like an hallucination. Green is a dull color, almost black; but here it seemed to glow as bright as any shade of red or blue. I touched the plant, expecting it to be as delicate as any I was familiar with; but here too, I received a shock: the leaves were as stiff and hard as an uncured hide. What a strange

world Purple must come from! I thought— then realized that
I was giving the mad magician too much credence. This must
be a plant that would ordinarily be familiar to me. Purple
had only cursed it.

I turned my attention away, began looking for a door
leading to the area above. But there was none. Apparently
the nest included only this one compartment. The rest of
its huge interior must be all spell devices. Shoogar had been
right all along.

But how small the nest was, if this was all there was to
it! Barely room for two to stand!

Shoogar had spread his travel kit and his equipment on
the floor and was methodically organizing the materials he
would use first. It was as if he cursed flying nests every
day. He paused, put a finger into the stubble on his chin
and scratched. He began to examine a piece of parchment
which he took from his robe, a checklist, "Yes . . ." he decided after a brief pause. He pulled out the metal knife that
I had seen before. "We will begin with the defiling of the
metal."

He spat on the knife, then began to carve runes into the
surface of the floor. Or tried to. The knife would not pene-
trate. Frowning, Shoogar pressed harder. The tip of the knife
broke. Then the blade snapped in half.

Shoogar returned the pieces of the knife to his travel kit
without comment and looked at his checklist again. This time
he pulled out a pouch of reddish powder, the dust of rust.
He emptied a bit of it into his hands and blew. A smoky red
cloud filled the room. I coughed and he threw me an angry
glance.

A whirring sound started somewhere. Then a wind blew
through the nest, plucking at my hair and clothing. I looked
around in fear—could Purple have trapped the wind god?
Even as I looked for traces of such a thing, the reddish dust
in the air thinned. Shortly the wind stopped, and the dust
was gone with it. There was not even a fine red layer on any
of the polished surfaces. Odd.

Still Shoogar was undismayed. He consulted his list again.

Abruptly, he produced a ball of fire from under his robe.
Then another and another, throwing them as fast as they

came, at the walls, the ceiling, the floor. Where they struck they stuck, sending up acrid sparks and oily smoke.

There was a hissing sound—and jets of water spat from apertures in the ceiling. They aimed themselves straight at the fireballs, drenched them to ash in seconds. And then, as Shooger produced a last fireball from under his robe, they all turned on Shoogar.

When the water went off, Shoogar turned his hand over, and allowed the drenched fireball to drop stickily to the floor. Dripping, he held up his sodden checklist and consulted it again. Water dripped from it onto the floor, then drained away into places we knew not.

I felt my hopes draining away with the water. Shoogar had begun three separate attempts—and all of them had failed. The stranger's magic was much too strong. We were doomed even before we had begun.

"Ah, yes—" said Shoogar. "It goes well."

I doubted my ears. I dared a question, "it goes *what*—?"

"Obviously, Lant, you have not been paying attention. This nest is equipped with very efficient protective spells. I had to find out what they were, so that I could nullify them. Now, let us curse."

Shoogar began by inscribing runes on all the surfaces of the nest, floors, walls, ceiling, the back of the oddly shaped couch, the panels of knobs, everything. He called upon Fineline, the god of engineers and architects, to blast this nest with a spell of deformity to make it crack and shatter.

Onto each of the sacred signs, inscribed with chalk instead of knife, he dripped evil-smelling potions. As they combined, they began to smoke and sputter. "Waters of fire, burn and boil," Shoogar urged them. We watched as the fluid ate holes into the runes and the surface below.

Beautiful. Blasphemy is the heart of a good curse.

Next he began to fill the ship with dust. Apparently he wanted to overload the spell of the protective wind, for he blew great clouds of the red dust of rust. The whirring started up immediately, but Shoogar kept blowing.

"Well, don't just stand there, you goat—help me!"

I grabbed handfuls of the red powder and blew—somehow we were able to keep great swirling clouds of rust swirling and churning throughout the compartment. The dust of rust is a symbol of time, sacred to several gods at once: Brad of the past, Kronk of the future, and Po who causes the decay of all things.

When we had run out of the dust of rust, Shoogar continued with a fine white powder. It looked like the grindings of bone. "Aim for those wind pockets," said Shoogar, pointing at a square, screened-over opening.

Eyes streaming, coughing vigorously, I did so. Once Shoogar hurled a fireball at the screen, where it stuck. Water jetted briefly, splashing through the screen. Some of the grindings gathered around the water droplets.

Presently the whirring became uneven, threatened to stop. "Cover your nose and mouth, Lant. I do not want you to breathe any of this." He pulled out a fat leather pouch. I put a cloth across the lower half of my face and watched as he produced a thick double handful of powdered magician's hair.

With a care borne of great sacrifice he aimed cautiously and blew a great sneeze of it toward the wind pockets. Within a moment, it was gone.

The whirring sound labored, the wind seemed to be dying. And suddenly, both stopped.

"Good, Lant! Now get the pots." Shoogar was beaming with triumph. I pulled my kit from its place by the wall and produced a collection of six pottery containers, each with a close-fitting lid.

"Good," said Shoogar again. He began placing them carefully around the interior of Purple's nest. Into each he put a sputtering ball of fire, then closed the lid on it.

There were tiny holes in the lid of each pot, to allow the fire-god to breathe, but too tiny to allow entrance of the water. The liquid jets arced out, but unable to reach the flames directly, they continued playing over the pots and over everything else.

Shoogar watched to see where the water was draining, began pouring defiled water and other viscous syrups into the drain holes. Once he paused to add a generous handful of the white dust bone-grindings. As it swirled down into the drain, the mixture began to thicken ominously.

Shortly, it seemed as if the drains were not working as efficiently. Pools were gathering on the floor. The odious smell of defiled water was strong in the hot, steamy smoky air. I thought I would retch. But no matter, the defiled water would certainly anger Filfo-mar, the river god.

By now, Filfo-mar and N'veen, the god of the tides, would be engaged in their ancient tug of war. Only this time they would be tugging not at the waters of the world, but at opposite sides of the black nest. The more water that poured into the cabin, the stronger grew their powers—and the more vicious their battle.

By the time the water jets stopped hissing, we were several inches deep in water and Shoogar and I were both dripping wet. But not chilly. The nest was steaming hot and growing hotter. Shoogar shucked off his robe and I followed suit.

My eyes were watering, and I was still coughing up the dust from my lungs. When I pointed this out to Shoogar he only said, "Stop complaining. Nobody ever said a curse was easy. There's more to come yet."

Indeed, we had only begun.

Now Shoogar turned his attention to the various panels and plates that lined the interior. There were a great many knobs and bumps. Many of these came in sets of eight, each labeled with a different symbol. One we recognized: a triangle, the symbol of Eccar the Man.

Could it be that some of Purple's spells were based on the symbol of Eccar? If that were so, could Shoogar use that fact as a wedge, his lever with which to unbalance the rest of the spells of Purple's nest?

Shoogar pursed his lips thoughtfully, scratched at his stubbly chin. "Push the bumps, Lant. Wherever you see the symbol of the triangle, push the bumps—we will activate all of Purple's Eccar spells and dissipate their power."

We moved through that compartment, looking high and low for the knobs and bumps. The knobs could all be twisted so that the triangle would appear at the top, and the bumps could all be depressed. There were blank knobs also; with a little experimentation Shoogar found that these could be turned in such a way that tiny slivers of metal behind layers of glass would move and point to triangles etched there.

Strange things happened, but Shoogar cautioned me to ignore them. Once, one of the flat mirror-like plates glowed with an unearthly light and images appeared on it—images of the village, images of people we knew, Hinc and Ang and Pilg. I stared in fascinated horror—and then abruptly, Shoogar nullified the spell by painting over it with a thick gray potion that obscured the plate entirely.

"I told you not to look," he reproved me.

We continued. Eventually we had turned every device in that nest to the symbol of the triangle, the symbol of three. We began the next phase of the curse.

The fire pots had begun to cool, so Shoogar replenished them. Already the metal where they sat was too hot to touch, and portions of other devices had begun to crack.

Now Shoogar began painting his thick gray paint over everything. First he nullified the image windows. Then he painted all the dials over, and all of the bumps too. Only the gods would know what symbols had been activated. In almost no time the interior of that nest was entirely gray. Klarther, the god of the skies and seas, would be furious. Fol, the god of distortion, would be chortling. Thus had Shoogar brought them to battle with each other, with the black nest between.

Shoogar began to sketch new runes into the painted surfaces, oblivious of their relation to the runes beneath. Where the upper and under surfaces conflicted, the gods would engage in random battle. Always when he could, Shoogar worked the name of Elcin, the thunder god, into the runes.

Into a crevice between two of the surfaces of knobs and bumps Shoogar pushed the narrow point of a sword-wand and called on Pull'nissin, the god of duels. Calling on Hitch, the god of birds, he broke eggs into three apertures. They sizzled angrily where they slid down; for Shoogar was using the egg-shape image of the nest against itself. He continued chanting, calling on Musk-Watz and Blok, the god of violence; and at one point he even cast a rune defiling Tis'turzhin, the god of love, for love turned to hate can be the mightiest force of all.

Shoogar consulted his checklist again, and produced a container of dormant sting things, and another of fungusoids and leeches. He brought forth things with barbs and things with claws, and began scattering them about. Torpid though they were, some tried to attack us; but we were careful to place them where they were not immediately dangerous. And we had had the forethought to wear our thickest boots and gloves; the fanged creatures could not cut through.

As he called on Sp'nee, ruler of slime, Shoogar spread great viscous gobs of goo into cracks and crannies between the boards of knobs and bumps. The air was already unbreathable with heat and wet, but the boards were far hotter. In some places Shoogar's gray ointment had blackened and cracked, and the surface beneath glowed red with such heat and stench that one could not bear to approach too near. Eggs sizzled and smoked in places we could not see.

And always Shoogar continued to call upon Elcin. The God of Thunder. The God of Fear.

"Elcin, oh, Elcin! Come down, Oh Great and Tiny God of Lightning and Loud Noises! Come down from your mountain, oh Elcin! Come down from your mountain and strike down this infidel who dares to profane the sacred name of your magic!"

Shoogar stood atop the demon couch and stretched his arms toward the sky. Triumph was spread across his face as he chanted the final *canteles* of the spell. The nest was hung with webs of pain and painted with runes of despair.

The swimming heated compartment crawled with fuzz balls and stingers, crabs and krakens and leeches. Somewhere something was burning, and oily smoke seeped up the walls. I choked on the rotting air and blinked the tears from my eyes.

It was a masterpiece.

I followed Shoogar out of the nest. The dry grass crunched underfoot as I dropped to the ground. We had spent a lifetime in that Shoogar-generated hell.

I was amazed to find that it was still day. The double sunlight washed the world with a reassuring familiarity. Trees and plants and grass looked black to me; and I wondered if my eyes had seen too long by the light of Purple's nest.

My head swam in the cool clean air. Waves of dizziness swept over me. Even so, it was I who had to help Shoogar to walk. I had only observed the curse. Shoogar had executed it, and it had taken its toll of his strength. We moved unevenly down the slope. Our shadows wavered before us, tinged with red and blue edges. As the curse had ended, so had the conjunction. Once more the suns were separate.

It seemed a miracle that Purple had not interrupted us, but it was still only mid-afternoon. We had finished with time to spare.

We collapsed behind a clump of bushes. The unfouled air was like strong Quaff, and I was drunk on it. We lay there under the familiar black leaves, taking deep heaving breaths.

After a while I rolled over on my side, looked at Shoogar, and asked, "When does it begin?"

He didn't answer, and for a moment I thought he had fallen asleep. It would not have surprised me. The exertions of the past days had left him pale and haggard. His eyes were red when he opened them, and rimmed with deep circles. He sighed slowly, "I don't know, Lant, I don't know. . . Perhaps I forgot something."

I sat up and looked uneasily at the black nest. It waited there in a hollow between two hills, its door invitingly open. Its door——!!

"Shoogar!" I cried. "The door! We left it open!"

He sat up suddenly, stared horrified across the hill.

"Can we close it?" I asked.

"It must need another spell for that," said Shoogar. "And we don't have it."

"Couldn't you——"

"Couldn't I what?" he demanded. "Make up a door-closing spell? Not for that nest, I couldn't. I'd have to know what activates the door-opening spell first."

"But, I saw you open the door——"

"Lant," he said wearily, "you are a fool. I know how to use the spell—but I do not know *why* it works as it does. You saw what trouble I had with the light device. No, Lant—— unless you know something else about the way that door works —and I know you don't, for I peered into your mind—it's going to stay open."

"But the curse——"

He cut me off with a gesture, "I don't know—It must be waiting. It needs something to activate it, probably the closing of the door. Without that . . ." He shrugged, let the sentence trail off into silence.

The suns crept westward, the blue now visibly ahead of the red. I peered uneasily across the hill. How long would that curse wait before it went bad? Only the gods could help us if this, the greatest of Shoogar's spells, were to go foul— and if it did go foul, there would be no gods left who *could* help us. They would all be against us.

Slowly the shadows lengthened; the chill of the dying day crept across the world while Shoogar and I stood helplessly by. The black nest waited, grim and forbidding, yellow light poured from its door.

The world waited. We waited. The nest waited.

The curse waited. . .

And then, abruptly, a sound. Footsteps crunching up the side of the hill. We dropped down behind the bush.

Seconds later, Purple came into view, striding up over the rise——I wondered if he had satisfied his yearning——then down the slope toward his waiting nest. He could not see the open door from the direction he approached.

He rounded the curve of the nestwall and stopped. Then he stepped hurriedly forward and peered within. For the first time we saw Purple react to Shoogar's magic. He screamed like a hunting banshee-bat.

No doubt a translation would have been most instructive, but the speakerspell was silent. Purple clambered into the door; the jamb caught him across the forehead, knocking the glass appurtenances from his nose. (How had Shoogar managed that?)

We heard his voice from inside the nest; great anguished cries, hardly recognizable. Occasionally, words would come from the speakerspell, booming across the hollow, "My god in . . . ! How the . . . did they get in? Stung me! Get off my foot, you . . . son of . . . Why isn't the pest killer working?!!"

"The sting things are giving him trouble," I whispered.

"God-damned sting things . . . !" Purple's booming voice corrected me.

"But the sting things are not the spell, Lant," Shoogar

hissed. "They would sting whether they were part of the curse or not."

Shoogar was right. The curse had not yet been activated. Anguished, I tore at my fur. What were the gods waiting for? Would they wait so long that Purple would have time to nullify the elements of the spell and turn it back on Shoogar?

More words came hurtling across the slope. *"Eggs! . . . Eggs?"*

"At least you have ruined his composure," I whispered to Shoogar. "That's a beginning."

"Not enough. . . . The gods should be tripping over each other in their eagerness to destroy him. . . . It must be the door! It must be! Lant, I fear. . . ."

He trailed off ominously. I felt ice melting along my spine.

"Savages!" boomed Purple's voice. "Primitive savages! This damned gray paint——Where the hell is the . . . ? Incest, lovemaking, illegitimate, compound incest, excrement, excrement, excrement, oral-genital contact, rectum, castration, diseases passed by lovemaking, primitive anal lovechildren! I'll kill the lovemaking offspring of dogs! I'll burn this lovemaking world down to the bedrock!"

Purple may have been incoherent, but he certainly sounded sincere. I readied myself to run. I could see him moving about within the nest; he was stabbing furiously at the various bumps and depressions that we had painted over. Savagely Purple twisted the knobs, one after another, trying to nullify Shoogar's spells.

"And as for that fur-covered animal, Shoogar——"

The heavy curved door slid shut and cut off Purple's last raging howl.

A gentle breeze tugged at the leaves, the bushes and the cuffs of our robes. The shadows had lengthened until they stretched eastward into darkness.

The blue sun twinkled and vanished, leaving only the

bloated disk of the red. Below us the hills lay like the folds of a crumpled red cloth. All was deathly silent.

Slowly Shoogar and I crept out of our hiding place. The black nest sat quietly in its depression. The door, closed now, was only an orange oval outlined on its smooth featureless surface.

We edged forward, curiously, cautiously.

"Has it begun yet?" I whispered.

"Shut up, you fool! Every god in the pantheon must be listening!"

We moved closer. The black egg waited there, motionless. Shoogar put his ear to its surface and listened.

Abruptly, the egg rose noiselessly into the air, throwing Shoogar back. I threw myself flat on the ground, began praying for forgiveness. "Oh, gods of the world, I cast myself upon your mercy. I plead to you. Please, do not let me——"

"Shut up, Lant! Do you want to foul the spell?!!"

I lifted my head cautiously. Shoogar was standing there, hands on hips and staring up into the red twilight. The black nest hung unmoving and patient a few feet above his head.

I climbed wearily to my feet. As a curse this spell was turning out to be a dull bore. "What is it doing?" I asked. Shoogar didn't answer.

Abruptly the nest turned from black to silver and began sinking back toward the ground as gently as it had risen. The red dusk glinted across its surface, the color of blood.

We stepped back as it touched the ground; it continued sinking downward without so much as slowing. Now, at last, there was sound, a churning crunching grumble of rock being forced aside. The nest moved downward, inexorably. The rocks screeched with the sound of its passage.

In moments it was gone.

The crackle of rock sank to a distant mutter, then died away entirely. Dazed, I walked to the rubbled edge of the hole. Darkness swallowed the bottom of it although an occasional distant rumble of movement could be felt.

Shoogar came up beside me.

"Brilliant," I said, and I never meant anything more. "It's gone, Shoogar. Completely, totally gone. The world has swallowed it up as though it never existed. And——" I gasped breathlessly, *"and there were no side effects at all."*

Shoogar harrumphed modestly. He bent to pick up the glass appurtenances which had fallen from Purple's nose. He pocketed them absent-mindedly. "It was nothing," he said.

"But, Shoogar! No side effects! I wouldn't have believed you could do it! I wouldn't have believed anyone could do it. Why didn't you tell us you were planning this? We wouldn't have had to leave the village."

"Best to be safe," Shoogar mumbled. He must have been dazed by his triumph. "You see, I wasn't sure . . . What with the tidal equations acting to pull the nest *down* instead of . . . and with Eccar the Man tending to—well, it was highly unusual; experimental, you might say. I——"

The whole mountain shook under us.

I landed jarringly on my belly looking downslope. Two hundred feet below, the black nest erupted out of the hillside, shrieking in agony.

It plunged up and southward, screaming with an unholy sound——we had hurt it terribly. The egg wailed its pain— a rising and falling note—piercingly loud even as it moved away from the mountain.

Some weird side effect had pulverized the very substance of the hill beneath us, turning it to sliding dirt and pebbles. The entire slope was sliding, shifting, carrying us majestically downward. We were powerless to move; we rode the rumbling avalanche, a massive churning movement of dust and sand. The black nest was a speck of shrieking red brightness fast disappearing into the southern horizon.

The sliding mountain came gradually to a stop. Whether from caprice or Shoogar's magic, it had not buried us. We had been fortunate enough to be standing at the top of the affected area, and had ridden it down unhurt. Now I found myself on my belly, deep in soft sloping dirt. Shoogar was several yards below me.

I climbed to my knees. The black nest was no more than a dot above the horizon: rising and dwindling, rising and dwindling. It was going almost straight up when my eyes lost it.

I scrambled down the slope to Shoogar, each step creating tiny echoes of the bigger slide. "Is it over?" I asked, helping him to his feet.

Shoogar brushed ineffectually at his robe, "I think not." He peered into the south, "There are too many gods who have not yet spoken."

We were ankle-deep in the newly pulverized dirt, and would have to walk softly lest the slope be jarred loose again. We began to work our way down cautiously. "How long must we wait for the curse to complete its workings?" I asked.

Shoogar shrugged, "I cannot guess. We called heavily on too many gods. Lant, I suggest you return to the village now. Your wives and children will be waiting."

"I would stay here with you until the curse is complete."

Shoogar frowned thoughtfully, "Lant, the black nest will probably return to attack the one who injured it. I dare not return to the village until that danger is past, and I would not want you here with me when that happens." He put his hand on my shoulder, "Thank you, Lant. I appreciate all you have done. Now go."

I nodded. I did not want to leave him. But I knew that this had to be. Shoogar was not just saying good-night; he was saying good-bye. Until he knew for sure that the black nest had been destroyed, he could not return.

Dejectedly, I turned and trudged down the slope. I did not want him to see the tears welling up in my eyes.

The village was as I had left it. Silent, deserted, and bearing the scars of Shoogar's preparations.

I had been fortunate to find one of my bicycles halfway down the hill. Now I parked it beneath my own nest. Miraculously, both bicycle and housetree had remained undamaged.

My number one wife was curled up on the floor sleeping when I hoisted myself into the nest. She awoke at the swaying of the structure and rubbed the sleep from her eyes.

"Where are the others?" I asked.

She shook her head, "They fled when Purple came to the village this morning."

"Purple came to the village?" I was aghast.

She nodded.

I seized her by the shoulders, "You must tell me what he did! Did he curse Shoogar's nest? Did he——"

"No, it was nothing like that. He just walked around for a while."

"The fire device? Did he use the fire device?"

"No. He wanted something else."

"What was it, woman?"

"I cannot say if I understood right, my husband. He did not have his speakerspell with him. We had to use gestures."

"Well, what did he want?"

"He wanted to do the family-making thing, I think."

"And you let him . . . ?"

She lowered her eyes, "I thought it would help Shoogar's part of the duel if the mad magician were distracted for a while . . ."

"But, how could you? He is not a guest of ours! I should beat you!"

"I am sorry, my husband. I thought it would help." She cringed before my upraised hand, "And you did not beat your third wife when Purple talked to her."

She was right. I lowered my hand. It would not be fair to beat one and not the other.

"He is built most strangely, my husband. He is almost completely without hair, except for——"

"I do not want to hear about it," I said. "Is that all that you did?"

She nodded.

"And then he left the village?"

Again she nodded.

"He did not touch anything? Take anything?"

She shook her head.

I breathed a sigh of relief, "Thank the gods for small favors. The situation *could* have been very bad. Fortunately you say nothing was damaged." Gratefully, I lowered myself to the floor, I had not realized how weary I was. "You may serve me a meal," I said.

She did so, wordlessly. If she had to exercise her jaw, there were always my dinner leavings. I had taken two bites, when abruptly from overhead came a weird kind of shrieking whistle.

It was a sound of disaster, of emergency and panic. I dropped out of the nest and ran for the clearing. Through the treetops I could see——

The flying nest! It had returned to the village. It was no longer silver. Now it was yellow with heat. It hurtled across the sky, then circled and returned for another shrieking pass.

Shoogar's words flashed across my mind, ". . . the black nest will probably return to attack the one who injured it . . ." Could the nest have confused me with Shoogar? I stood there in the central clearing, too panicked to move.

It stopped jarringly a few yards above the treetops, as if it had hit a soft wall. Its door was missing, ripped away. The opening showed black against the orange glow of what could only be heated metal.

The nest turned, questing. I imagined eyes in the blackness behind the doorway. I waited for them to find me.

The nest turned faster.

Suddenly, it was spinning, terribly fast. All details blurred and vanished; the surface seemed a liquid red-orange. I heard the drone of it rising and I covered my ears. A wind swept through the trees.

As it spun, the nest was carrying the air with it. Great gusts spun through the village with a rising shriek, different from the agony-cry of the nest, but terrifying all the same. It was a great whirlpool of wind with the nest at the center. I clung to the trunk of one of the nearby housetrees.

Was Musk-Watz attacking the stranger's egg? Or was the latter attacking the village? The wind roared through the trees, through the leaves and branches and nests; it tried to pluck me from where I clung tightly to one of the root limbs. I wrapped my arms and legs about the branch and buried my face in the trunk. Leaves, bark, bits of wood sprayed me. It went on and on and on. . . .

After a while, I became aware that the sound was lessening. I raised my head. The wind was dying. . . .

Not a tree in the village carried a leaf. Every nest had been knocked to the ground. Many had been shattered against the trunks of their host trees. Others lay yards from where they should have fallen.

Purple's great black egg, still spinning, had moved south-ward toward the river. It was above the new course of the rushing waters when it began to drop. Filfo-mar, angry and implacable, was pulling the black nest down to destruction.

I had to see. I followed the nest, unmindful of the possible danger. I had to know if Purple's nest was truly being de-stroyed.

The nest was spinning ferociously, as if it were trying to escape the power of the river god. When it touched the water a great cloud of steam burst into the air. At the same time, the river and its muddy banks all rose up in one huge wave of earth and water. It blackened the sky, covered the moons— I tried to run—it splashed across the world in one vast wave. A scream forced itself out of my throat as the rushing water swept me back through the village. Filth and mud flooded my mouth, my nostrils.

Abruptly I was struck a jarring blow from behind, found myself caught between two limbs of a tree. Water rained down in fat drops and mud in stinging gobs.

The water began to recede then, flowing back toward the river in a great mud-streaking wave. Churning debris left in its wake.

Shoogar had miscalculated. The nest had not returned to attack him. Even now I could see that there was nothing left of the village: just a few blackened trees, naked against the night.

I lowered myself from the branch. My back twinged warn-ingly and I wondered if I had cracked a rib. Painfully I limped toward the river. If I were destined to die, I would first know the fate of my enemy.

Black mud squelched beneath my feet as I plodded. The bare trees dripped muddy goo. It was as if the whole world were uninhabitable, drowned in a rain of earth and water. It was tricky going; often the viscous mess beneath my feet hid shards of debris. —

Under the shadowless light of seven of the moons, I began to cross the old course of the river. The mud and the smooth wet rocks all worked to slow me. Probably they saved my life. I had forgotten that one god had not yet spoken.

I cursed as I balanced on the slippery surfaces. The nest lay ahead. In its spinning it had churned a great dish-shaped cavity for itself. As I topped the lip of that cavity I saw the nest, black again and lying in shallow silvery water. Its spin had stopped, and—finally, finally—*it was no longer upright.*

It rested on its side with water pouring into the hollow around it, flooding into the doorway. Garish light reflected in that opening and across the surface of the water.

No doubt, that final awry tilt of the egg was the work of Fineline, the god of engineers. Perhaps in his last moments, Purple had finally believed in the power of Shoogar's magic. I worked my way closer, eyes open for one glimpse of the mad magician's body. Nothing could be left alive within that nest.

I was not one quarter of the way down when the interior of the nest began to sparkle and flash. This was not the steady yellow which had lit the compartment earlier. This was a sick sputtering sparkle, the color of lightning. I paused, unsure. I could hear crackling sounds and the hiss of water turning to steam. I began to inch my way back up the mud slope. The nest was still dangerously alive.

The blue flashing grew brighter behind me—and then a thick puff of black smoke erupted from the gaping door. I reached the mud lip of the churned-out hollow none too soon and dropped behind it. Cautiously, I raised my head.

The nest seemed to pause, as if wondering what to do next.

It decided.

It leapt upward, up and out of the pond. It rose in a steep arc, glowing white, paused at the apex, and fell back. It landed right in the middle of the village. Instantly it bounced, leaving a clutch of burning trees behind it. A hot wind fanned my face. It bounced again.

The nest had forgotten how to fly. Now it moved by bouncing, and it glowed with a terrible heat. Each time it struck it would give off one enormous spark, and the land would burn. But only momentarily: the village was too much a swamp to support a fire.

And still the nest was bouncing. As it left the village, other patches of flame were spreading. They led in a straight line, west toward the mountains where Shoogar waited.

The nest bounced uphill, like a ball in reverse. I could see it, a glowing white speck moving erratically up the mountain-side. It ultimately disappeared behind a ridge.

The wind followed it, crackling with the presence of the one god who had not yet spoken; then it too faded into the west. A semblance of calm crept over the landscape, leaving only the sound of water dripping from the trees and branches.

I stood up and looked off across the black mud to where a pillar of greasy smoke still rose from the center of the village. Brushing at the mud which permeated my clothing, I wondered if my first wife had survived. I would regret it very much if she had not. She was a good woman, obedient and almost as strong as a pack animal.

It occurred to me then which god had not yet spoken.

I sat down.

There was a slow and deathly silence now. Only the crackle of the mud, the hiss of water trickling into pits of melted rock disturbed the night. The wind died to nothing. The last of the moons was dropping toward the west. Darkness would soon be creeping across the land. It would not be safe to be about.

Could Shoogar have been mistaken in this one aspect? After all, *He* was an unpredictable god, known to have fits of pique—and also known to have failed when most expected to perform. Perhaps the experimental nature of Shoogar's spell had not been enough to arouse him . . .

Behind me the east began to hint at deep blue instead of black. I stood, cursing the stiff cold weight of my clothes . . . Then an eye-searing flash of white filled the world . . .

My eyes clenched in pain. But in the after-image, burned into my skull, I saw a great ball of fire, like one of Shoogar's but magnified to the size of a mountain. Then my eyes could open, and I saw a great rising mass of flaming cloud, a toadstool of red-lit fury——fiery smoke standing up behind the mountains, reaching, ever-reaching into the sky——

I was slammed backward, slapped rolling across the mud as if struck by a giant's hammer made of air. And the sound —oh, the sound—my ears seemed to cry with the pain of a sound so loud.

If I had thought the sound of Musk-Watz earlier sweeping through the village had been loud, he was only a whisper compared to this. It was as if Ouells himself had come down, and clapped his mighty hands together in a sudden howling wind. But the sound continued—mutated into a continuous rumbling thunder that rolled up and down the hills. It grumbled and rumbled, rumbled and grumbled across the world. It echoed and re-echoed in a never-ending wave. I was sure I could hear it long after it actually had died away. That great bass roar went on and on and on. Small rocks began to fall from the sky.

Elcin had spoken.

I found my wife huddled in the crotch of two branches, beneath an uprooted tree.

"Are you all right?" I asked, helping her to her feet.

She nodded.

"Good. Then find some bandage and tape up my ribs. I am in pain."

"Yes, my husband." She began dutifully to tug at her skirt.

I recognized that; it was one of her favorites. I put out my hand, "No, do not tear that. Find something else. That is all that you have left in the world. Keep it intact."

She looked up at me, grateful tears flooding her eyes, "Yes, my husband . . ." She paused, and I knew she wanted to say something else, but feared.

"Go on . . ." I urged.

She fell to her knees, unmindful of the mud, and clasped fiercely at my hands, "Oh, my husband, I feared so for your safety. My heart is filled with such gladness at the sight of you, I cannot bear it. I could not bear the thought of life without you." She kissed my hands, buried her face against my waist. I stroked the fur on the top of her head, mud-smeared though it was. It did not matter; we were both soaked through.

"It's all right . . ." I murmured gently.

"Oh, tell me it is, tell me. Tell me that the danger is over, that all is right with the world again."

"Stand up, woman," I said. She did. "I have lost everything. My nest is gone and my tree has been uprooted. I know not where any of my children are, nor where my other wives have fled to. I have nothing. Only the clothes I am wearing. But I am still not a poor man . . ."

"Not . . . ?" She looked at me, brown eyes wide with wonder.

"No, I am not. I still have one woman, a good woman." I looked into her eyes, wide and glowing with love. "A woman with a strong back and a willingness to work. And it is enough. I can rebuild. Now go and find that bandage. My ribs ache with the pain of standing."

"Oh yes, my husband. Yes." She began moving cautiously across the mud-covered landscape. I lowered myself carefully to the ground. To rest, to sleep . . .

B̲efore leaving the village we searched through the mud to see if anything of value remained intact. We found little. I had hoped to find my bicycle, but that had been smashed under a falling tree. I ached to see that finely carved machine crushed to sodden pulp. Truly, I had been right when I had said that we had nothing but the clothes on our backs.

We stood in the ruins of the village and surveyed the disaster.

"What will we do, my husband?"

"We will move on," I said to her. "There is nothing left for us here." I turned and looked at the distant blue prairie. "There," I pointed, "we will go south. Probably most of the others have had the same thought."

She nodded in acquiescence and shouldered her miniscule pack. Painfully we started the long trek.

The suns were high in the sky when we saw a single tiny figure on a bicycle hurrying to catch up to us from the west.

There was something familiar about that——no, it couldn't be.

But it was! "Shoogar!" I cried, "You are alive!"

He shot me a look and climbed off the bicycle, "Of course, I'm alive, Lant. What did you think?" He paused, looked at the dried mud caked on our clothes, "What happened to you?"

"We were in the village. We saw the end of Purple's nest. But it headed toward the mountains to die. We thought that——"

"Nonsense, Lant. *I won the duel.* Only the loser gets killed. I saw the black nest return. It attacked the village instead of coming up into the mountains after me. If it was going to destroy the village anyway, there was no longer any reason for me to stay up in the hills. So I dug out the other bicycle."

"The nest must have just missed you."

Shoogar nodded, "I saw it coming. When it finished with the village, only then did it go for the mountains. Only I was no longer there."

"Shoogar, that's brilliant!"

He shrugged modestly, brushed a speck of dirt from the sleeve of his robe. "It was nothing. I had it planned that way."

There was nothing more to say. We watched as he mounted the bicycle again, his dignity and reputation were tall and triumphant. Once more he began pedaling into the south. It made me proud to know him.

* * * * *

Blue twilight had faded and flashed into red dawn before we found a place to stop. We were on a rocky outcrop overlooking a series of rolling hills, a black wooded slope, and beyond that we could make out the vague distant shapes of a village of brooding housetrees.

Behind us, what had been a desert was fast becoming a sea.

It was not necessary to give the order to halt. Instinctively we knew we had done enough traveling for one day. Exhausted, the women sank to the ground, discarding their heavy packs and burdens where they fell. Children sank immediately into fitful slumber, and men stooped to massage their tired legs.

We were a sorry, shabby crew. The healthiest of us was in none too good a shape. Many had lost most of their body fur, and the rest had lost their grooming. (The knots and tangles in my own fur would be there until they grew out; they were too far gone for repair.) Open and running sores were not uncommon, and too many of our ailments did not respond to Shoogar's ministrations.

My number two wife, one of the balding women, began to lay a meager meal before me. Under any other circumstances I might have cursed the poor quality of the food and beaten her for there being so little of it—but under our present conditions I knew that this was a hardwon feast. She had probably spent many extra hours searching for these pitiful greens and nuts. Still, it wasn't what I was used to and I forced myself to eat it only with the greatest distaste.

As I sat there, silently chewing the tough vegetable fibers, a figure approached. I recognized the now nearly hairless Pilg; once our village crier, now a homeless vagabond, as we all were. He was thin and wan and his ribs made an ugly pattern under his skin.

"Ah, Lant," he cried effusively, "I hope I am not interrupting anything."

He was and he knew it. I pretended not to hear him at first, and I concentrated on a particularly tough root instead.

He threw himself down in front of me. I closed my eyes. "Lant," he said, "it appears that we are nearing our journey's end. Doesn't that gladden your soul?"

I opened one eye. Pilg was eagerly eyeing my dinner bowl. "No," I said, "it doesn't."

Pilg was uncrushed. "Lant, you should look on the joyous side of life."

"Is there one?" I choked down the root and bit off another, smaller chunk.

"Of course. You should count your blessings. You still have four of your children and two wives and all your hair—

and your first wife is with child. That is far more than I can claim."

That was true. Pilg had lost his only wife and all but one of his children—and that one a girl—no credit there. Yet what I had lost was greater than what I had saved. I could not help feeling bitter.

We have lost our whole village," I said. I spat out a bitter shred at Pilg's feet. He eyed it uncertainly, but pride won out over hunger. He would not eat it unless it was offered to him.

I would not do so. I had fed him three times in the past three hands of days and I had no intention of taking Pilg any closer into my family than that.

"But in no time at all, we will have won a whole new village," Pilg exulted. "Surely, Shoogar's reputation as a magician must have preceded us here. Surely, they will honor him and us alike."

"And surely they will just as soon wish us elsewhere, Pilg. Look behind us. Look at where we have come from. Boggy marsh! And beyond that, water! The oceans are rising almost as fast as we can travel. The darkless season is upon us, Pilg. Hard times for any village. Surely they will have harvested their crops by now, and stored up only enough food to last them through the wading season. They will have none to spare for us. No—they won't be very happy to have us join them."

My mention of food had caused Pilg to salivate; the spittle ran down his chin—but social protocol held him back. He glanced again at the discarded bit of root near his foot. "But, Lant—look at the lay of the land here. This village that we are approaching is on a slope overlooking a great plain. They will have at least another twenty or thirty days before the water menaces them."

"Granted," I swallowed the mass I had been chewing.

"Perhaps we will be able to exchange some of our skills for some of their food."

"And what skill will you trade them for?" I grunted. "Rumormongering?"

Pilg looked hurt. Immediately I felt sorry, it had been a cruel and unkind thing to say. Pilg had indeed suffered more than I, and it was unfair for me to add my mockery to his already heavy burden. "That was cruel, Lant," he said, "if you want me to go, I will."

"No," I said, and immediately wondered why, for I did want him to go. "Don't go until you have at least had something to eat."

Curse it! He'd done it to me again! I had sworn I was not going to invite him to partake—but he had annoyed me until I had insulted him, and then to assuage the insult, I had to prove to him that he had not annoyed me. I wondered if I was going to have to start eating my meals in secret just to avoid Pilg.

But he was right about that one point. Perhaps we would be able to trade some of our skills for some of their food. Probably my own trade of bonemongering was not as skillfully practiced this far south as it was in the land we had journeyed from.

But so much of it depended upon the magician of this village. Would Shoogar be willing to swear an oath of truce for the duration of the wading season? Would the new magician even want Shoogar around, considering the strength of his reputation? Would you feel safe if a magician of such power wanted to move into *your* neighborhood? If this new magician could not match Shoogar's knowledge and skills, would Shoogar deign to treat him as an equal? Was there a magician anywhere who could match the powers Shoogar had already so dramatically demonstrated?

Shoogar might, just might, consider dueling this village's magician for the right to rule the magic of this area. If he lost (an unlikely chance), we would have to keep moving—only this time without our magician. More likely, if he won, we would incur much ill will in this area, for is it not said that a new magician must take nine generations to be accepted by a tribe?

I feared for the inevitable meeting with these villagers and their Guild of Advisors. Hopefully, we would have time to rest before that meeting, but probably not. As soon as they became aware of our presence here on the slopes of their mountain, they would send an emissary.

There wasn't much left of our Guild—we would be a sorry group of representatives: myself, of course; Hinc the Weaver, Pilg the Crier, Damd the Tree Binder, and one or two others. Ran'll the Quaff-Maker had drowned in one of his vats, Tavit the Shepherd had been lost with much of his flock, and none of the remaining shepherds was yet old enough to replace him in the Guild. Some of the others had not survived our long trek south.

But the two Guilds would meet and hopefully we would work out some kind of agreement whereby we could camp on this land until the waters should withdraw. Then we would either seek a new area to plant our village, or petition for the right to remain.

But again, so much depended on the magicians.

Later, as red sunset/blue dawn approached, our tired group of Advisors trudged across the slope to the lower village and the obligatory meeting with them. We had spent most of the red day bathing in the cold stream that ran through the pasture, and allowing the women to massage us and rub precious oils and fats into our skins. The oils and fats had been saved specifically for such an occasion as this. Had we not had this eventual confrontation continually in mind, we would have eaten them long ago.

We had exchanged our traveling skins for other garments. We would not be presenting ourselves as poorly as we really were, for we had stripped nearly every member of the tribe naked in order to assemble enough fine clothing for our Advisors to wear to this all-important council.

Shoogar stayed behind, to meditate; the time was not yet right for the other village to cast its eyes on his magnificence.

As we walked, Damd the Tree Binder remarked on the fine quality of woods in this area. There were thin strong shoots of bambooze, the fibrous tubular plant that could be used for building, or that could be eaten as food or fermented for Quaff. There were tall slender birts, stippled in gray and brown; there were sparkling aspen, white spirit pine and sturdy red vampire oaks. There was rich, dark

shrubbery, and wild houseplants, stunted and twisted for lack
of a magician's blessing and a proper Binding. There were
streams aplenty, and as we walked we trudged through a
thick carpet of crackling discarded leaves.

Yes, this was a rich wood. One which had been finely
cared for, but had not yet realized its full potential. Before
we were halfway through this thick arm of forest, it was
obvious that this was as fine an area in which to live as anyone could hope for. Froo, the eldest shepherd, exclaimed
over the grazing grounds; Jark, who had some moderate
skill at quaffmaking, expressed delight over the quality of
the bambooze. Hinc the Weaver munched thoughtfully on
a fiber plant as he walked. If they allowed us to stay, we
would be lucky indeed.

I speculated that there must be more work here than any
one village could hope to do. If they had had a good harvest
this year, they might be in an expansive mood. It was our
hope that we could trade our labors for some of their food, or
for the right to use some of this land.

Their village was on the crest of a hill, lowest of the
range below the wooded slopes. It was larger than our own
had been, but not impressively so. Most important, many of
their housetrees appeared unused, and those that were had
considerable distance between them. Where our village had
had a solid-packed floor of dirt from the extensive comings
and goings of commerce, this village had a gentle carpet of
blackgrass, cut through only here and there by dirt paths.

Clearly they did not trade on the scale we were used to.

As we approached, we could see their Advisors gathering
in a clearing near the edge of the village. We raised our
hands and gave them the finger gesture of fertility. They returned it.

A tall man covered with sparse curly fur, brownish red,
stepped forward. "I am Gortik, Speaker of this village. These
are my Advisors." And he introduced them. There were more
than thirty—traders, weavers, fishmongers, Quaffmakers and
craftsmen were amply represented. To my ill-concealed delight, they did not introduce a bonemonger. Could it be that
this village lacked one of my skill? If so, I was sure to find
much work. Or—a dampening thought—could it be that

they did not consider a bonemonger important enough to belong to the Guild of Advisors?

I thrust that thought away. A bonemonger was as good as anybody.

Gortik finished pointing out the last of his Advisors, then turned to us. "Who Speaks for you?"

That *was* a poser. We had not yet designated any of our number as Speaker. We had buried Thran, our old Speaker, only two hands of days previously. His memory was still too warm for us. There was much shuffling and whispering amongst ourselves. Finally Pilg pushed *me* forward, saying, "You, Lant. You Speak for us. You have been an Advisor as long as anyone."

"I can't," I whispered back. "I have never been a Speaker. I do not even have a Speaking Token. We buried it with Thran."

"We'll make a new one. Shoogar will consecrate it. But we need a Speaker *now.*"

One or two others nodded assent.

"But there's the chance they might kill me if they find me too audacious a Speaker," I hissed.

The rest nodded eagerly.

Hinc said, "You'll cope with it, Lant."

Pilg added, "It would be an honor to die for our village. I envy you."

And with that he pushed me out of the huddle and announced, "Lant here is our Speaker. He is too modest to admit it."

I swallowed hard, but a man must recognize and accept his duties. "I speak for us," I quavered. I had the feeling that at any moment, ancient Thran would step forward to question my impudence. Or that somehow Gortik would recognize me as an impostor and fail to grant me the respect due my uneasy office.

But he merely nodded his acceptance and said, "And why do you journey?"

"We are pilgrims," I said. "Migrants seeking a new home."

"You have not chosen wisely," he said. "This is not the best of places to live."

"You live here," I countered.

"Ah, but we don't enjoy it. I envy you—your ability to travel—I wish you luck in your journey—"

"It seems to me that you are eager to see us go, friend Gortik."

"Not so, friend Lant—it is just that I am not eager to have you stay! This is a poor land. You would not want to be caught here during Wading Season."

"Wading Season?"

"During interpassage, the days are hot, Speaker Lant; the seas get high. Most of the year, this section of land connects to the mainland——"

"This section—of land—connects—to the mainland?"

"That's right. You go by the Neck. It's convenient because nobody lives on the Neck. They might be caught there the wrong time of year, so it's free passage for everybody—"

"—except during Wading Season," I finished for him.

"Right." He smiled obliquely. "We're an island during the season—so it is important that you hurry. You do not wish to be caught here."

"How big an island?"

"Not big. Four villages and some land between them. And the Heights of Idiocy. That's where you people are camped now." He added, "Nobody lives on the Heights. Mostly because nothing grows. We stay there during Wading Season, but only because the ocean covers everything else. Otherwise, it's free land."

"An island—" I repeated. A thought was starting to take form. "Yes, you are right. We must hurry to move on." I gestured to my council. "Come, we cannot waste any more time on talking. Gortik has given us fine advice and we must hasten to take advantage of it." I gave him the finger gesture of fertility, wrapped my robe about me, and swept from the glade. My advisors followed behind.

We tramped back up through the woods, Hinc and the others hastening as fast as they could. "Hurry, Lant, hurry," they called. I dawdled along behind them, occasionally pausing to admire the view or a particularly fine stand of trees.

"Lant!" insisted Pilg, "Hurry!"

"Hold on, Pilg," I said. "What's your rush—?"

His eyes were wide. "You heard them! This is an island

during the season—" The others paused in their flight, began to gather round. "Yes, Lant, hurry."

"Why?" I said.

"Because, if we don't, we'll be trapped here."

"So?" I said. "What happens if we get trapped?"

"We're stuck here—we can't move on," said Hinc.

"And then they can't refuse us sanctuary, can they?"

The council considered it.

I said. "Of course, we must hurry to get away from here—Gortik said so. But if we do not hurry fast enough, then we have no choice in the matter. Then we have to stay."

"Hm," said Damd. He was beginning to get the point.

"Hmmmmm," said Jark. He had already gotten it.

"Look around you," I said to the rest. "The woods here are *terrible*, aren't they? Remember how we noticed it on the way down—?" They nodded thoughtfully. They remembered what they had noticed. "This would be a miserable region to settle, wouldn't it."

They looked about them. "Yes, this would be a miserable place," said Damd. "I would have to weave housetree nests twice as big as before—that's much too much work for me to do. And what would a man do with a nest that big?"

"You're right," said Jark. "Look at the bambooze, so strong and sturdy. Think of the Quaff I could make from it—no, it is not right for a man to have such fine, sweet Quaff!"

Hinc was kneeling, examining a fiber-plant. "Hmm," he said. "It would not be good for a man to wear such fine clothes, it would spoil him for the harshnesses of life."

"And we should not get used to eating regularly, should we?" added Pilg. "We might get fat and lazy."

We all sighed in unison.

"Yes, this would be a terrible place to settle," I said, stretching out beneath a comfortable tree. "Come, we must hurry to consider how we will move on."

Hinc settled himself beneath another tree, "Good thinking, Lant," he said. "But we should not do anything rash—let us take some time to discuss the quickest way to travel."

"Ahhh," sighed Pilg. "But, we do wish to be gone from here, before we are sealed off by the sea." He had found himself some soft meadow grasses.

"You are right," said Jark, from his soft bed of fern. "We must not tarry too long."

"No," added Damd. "I think nightfall should be sufficient."

"And of course," I added, "no one would expect us to travel by night—"

"And besides," said Pilg, "by then the women will have put up the tents."

"It would be good to get a full night's worth of sleep before traveling on," added another.

I sighed, "A full night of sleep? That sounds tiring; I think I shall begin to rest up for it now."

"Tomorrow we will have to get an early start though," said Jark.

"Yes. I think noontime, or shortly thereafter, should be soon enough."

"Oh, but there are so many other things to do first," said Hinc. "For instance, there is breakfast, and then lunch."

"Ahh," sighed Pilg. "Yes, the women will not have time to take the tents down before lunch."

"And even then, they may not have time," I said sleepily. "For they will have to gather food for the journey before we can leave."

"That might take all day."

"Or even two . . . or three."

Another round of sighing. And yawning. Someone mumbled sleepily, "I hope there won't be any problem introducing Shoogar to the new magician . . ."

"I don't think there will be. We should be able to work something out. Why don't you ask Pilg what he thinks?"

"He's asleep."

"Then ask Hinc."

"He's asleep too."

"And Jark?"

"The same."

"And Damd?"

"Also asleep."

"—Then what are you keeping me awake for!" I grumbled. "It's hard work being a Speaker and making decisions all day!"

Sure enough, a terrible thing happened.

Try as we could to hurry, the seas rose up and sealed off the island. It took eleven days.

It would have taken us only a few hours to cross by way of the Neck, an ever-narrowing strip of land, but somehow, we just couldn't get the women organized. The confusion in the camp was terrible. It took six days just to get the tents down, and then it was so late we had to put them back up again so we could get to sleep. After all, the red sun was high in the sky and it was night.

Gortik and his advisors came up to see us on the second day. They stood about and fretted, urging us constantly to hurry faster.

"But we are already hurrying as fast as we can. As you see, our women are so stupid, they cannot keep two orders in their heads at the same time."

"It is a wonder you made it this far," murmured Gortik.

"Yes, isn't it?" I chimed brightly, and scurried off.

Thereafter, Gortik came up every day to fret and moan and worry over the delay of our departure. Finally, though, we were on our way. Gortik and his advisors were only too happy to act as our guides.

It took us five days to cross the island.

We arrived at the Neck just in time to see the seas crash over its peak. Gortik sighed, a sound of despair. I sighed too.

He looked at me, "Lant, if I didn't know better, I'd say your people wanted to stay here." He shook his head. "But that's impossible; no people could be as stupid and confused as yours."

I had to agree with him.

He said, "Well, let us turn back. Apparently, you are going to be with us throughout the season."

I nodded. Reluctantly, I gave the order. "Turn back, turn

back! It is too late to cross the neck. We must go back to our
old camp!"

We were settled in again on the Heights of Idiocy well
before nightfall.

It was time to introduce our magicians.

I was extraordinarily pleased with myself.

Lant the Speaker! Speaker of one of the finest villages in
the world! Speaker for Shoogar the magnificent! I beamed
proudly.

Shoogar was an impressive figure in a purple and red robe,
one that changed colors as the suns changed their positions in
the sky. On a string around his neck he wore the quartz lenses
of the mad magician, a trophy of the kill and a token of proof
that he was who he claimed to be.

In a high singsong chant he told them of his skill, how he
had defeated his most dangerous enemy, Purple, the mad
magician who had claimed to come from the other side of the
sky. There was a stir among the listeners at that. Evidently,
Shoogar's fame had preceded us. He told of how he had
flattened the mountain, Critic's Tooth, how he had called
down the thunder and laid waste to the land for miles around.
As proof, he held high Purple's quartz lenses. He embroidered
the story hardly at all—the truth was impressive enough.

When he finished, I detailed how we had had to flee our
former village because of the side effects of Shoogar's spell;
how we had been travelling south for nearly a quarter of a
cycle. Our journey had begun at the blue conjunction, and
stretched across hundreds of miles and the floor of the
empty ocean. The suns had moved farther and farther apart
in the sky as we traveled, Red Virn and Blue Ouells stretching
the days longer and longer between them until the darks
shrank away to nothing.

I told how, at great danger and loss of life, we had crossed
the great desert mudflats. As the darkless time approached

the seas had returned to this land, and the latter part of our
journey had been a pell-mell flight from the ever-encroaching
waters. Many were the times we awakened to find the ocean
lapping at our tents.

I did not mention that that was how we had lost Thran,
drowned in his tent one night. It would not do for them to
know that I was so new to Speaking for my village.

Now Virn and Ouells were living at opposite ends of the
sky, and the darkless time was upon us. As the oceans crept
to their height, I related how we had arrived here at the base
of the southern mountains, seeking refuge and a place to
build a new village.

Gortik smiled, "Your stories are most impressive, especially
that of your magician. If his magic is merely half as good
as his story telling, then he is a challenge to the Gods themselves."

"Is your magician as good?" I said calmly.

"Better," said Gortik, "his spells don't produce side effects
that destroy villages."

"Our magician's spells," I countered, "are so strong that
even after the side effects are minimized they lay waste the
countryside."

"How fortunate for you that he minimizes his side effects."
Gortik's smile mocked us. It was obvious he did not believe
in Shoogar's power. I hoped it would not be necessary to
demonstrate it to him.

"Our magician," Gortik continued, "came to us quite suddenly. He killed the old one with a single blow that wakened
the whole countryside, but damaged nothing—except, of
course, the old magician."

The shrubbery rustled behind Gortik as if someone were
hurriedly being moved into place. Gortik stepped aside then,
saying, "Behold! Our magician is *Purple, the Unkillable!*"

I thought my heart would stop.

Shoogar stood trembling and speechless, unable to move.
The man who had stepped forward was indeed Purple, the
living breathing man whom Shoogar had killed—*had thought
he had killed*—in fiery combat at the last conjunction.

Around Shoogar the others of our village shrank away as if
to escape Purple's inevitable lightning strike.

I wanted to shrink within myself. I wanted to run. I wanted

to die. Well, at least the latter wish would be granted—and soon.

Purple looked us over carefully. He wore his suit of sky blue——all of one piece, it fitted his bulk like a second skin. Several objects hung from the wide belt around his formidable waist. The hood was thrown back. His glance was squinty and unsure; his eyes were watery and wavered back and forth from one to the other of us. At last his searching gaze came to rest on—oh, Elcin, no!—on me.

He strode forward eagerly, grasping my shoulders and peering close into my face, "Lant! Is that you?" His words were oddly pronounced, but they came from his own mouth. With his speakerspell destroyed he had had to learn to talk like a man.

He released me before I could faint and looked around, "And Shoogar? Is Shoogar here?"

He caught sight of the shorter magician then; Shoogar was stiff and trembling. This was it—I braced myself. Let it at least be painless.

"Shoogar," he said, stepping past me, hands outstretched. "Shoogar, there is something I've been wanting to ask you."

Shoogar uttered a single, inhuman shriek and leapt at his throat.

The two of them tumbled to the ground, the big magician and the small. Shoogar was making unholy grunting noises, Purple was choking for air.

It took nine of us to pry them apart. The youngest and strongest members of our council bore Shoogar kicking and screaming out of the clearing. His cries carried back to us through the woods until they were cut off by the sound of a splash. The river.

In a moment, a chastened, dripping Shoogar returned to us, flanked on one side by Jark the Shepherd and on the other by Wilville, my eldest son. He stood there glowering.

Meanwhile, Purple was brushing himself off. He was surrounded by solicitous and concerned advisors. They patted at his bulk like anxious women. Gortik was nonplussed. He looked at me and said, "It appears that our two magicians already know each other."

I looked from him to Purple. My head reeled. I felt I was drowning. My mouth opened and closed like a fish tossed upon the bank to die. How could this disaster have found us out?

"You were dead," I said to the magician, "how did—how could—which God—" but there I got stuck for the question itself was insane. Purple believed in no Gods, he had said so many times. I could not look at him, at his paunchy frame, his alien flesh, his pale hairless skin and his patches of unnaturally straight black fur. He was ugly in my eyes, and menacing to my soul and sanity.

Gortik was smiling, pleased at our discomfiture. I gestured at Purple and managed to croak, "How?"

"He was a gift from the gods," Gortik said. "For many years we lived with a magician who was not as well appreciated as he might have been." He frowned darkly. "Dorthi was a fine magician and strong, but there were those who were unhappy with his spellcasting."

"Dorthi? We trained together," Shoogar murmured.

I nodded. Gortik's was a familiar story. Sometimes magicians endure long after their powers and their respect have vanished. Villages suffer because of it.

"It happened at the last conjunction," Gortik continued. "A miracle. There was a great storm that night, a great wind and a fireball of Elcin that swept across the sky and turned and made another pass. Then suddenly there came a crash from the edge of the village. When we came forth from our houses we discovered that a strange magician had fallen on old Dorthi's house and smashed him flat. A strange magician indeed."

"He fell from the sky?"

Gortik nodded. The other Advisors interrupted each other in their eagerness to explain, "From the sky he came!" "Yet he suffered no hurt!" "Like a great falling star——" "None

89

suffered hurt, not even Dorthi——" "He must have been killed instantly." "There was much singing and dancing then——"

"Quiet!" Gortik roared.

There was quiet; Gortik said, "We gave Purple Dorthi's scarlet sandals and his robe and made him magician immediately. What else could we do? But he was little help to us, for he could not even talk. We had to burn Dorthi without incantations."

"We trained together," Shoogar repeated. "Poor Dorthi."

"But how could a man fall from the sky and not be killed?"

"Purple is no ordinary man," Gortik said, as if that were explanation enough.

"He's a demon," said Shoogar, and that *was* explanation enough.

"It was my impact suit," Purple said. He took a step forward and thumped himself hard in the belly with his fist. His belly was big and soft, so the blow should have made him wince. It did not. I thought for a moment that Purple had become as rigid as stone.

"My impact suit," he repeated. "Normally it flows like cloth, but under a sharp blow it becomes a single rigid unit. Lant, you remember that a boy threw a spear at me in your village."

"I remember. You were not hurt."

"The suit is skin tight. With the hood up it covers all of me but my eyes and mouth, and of course it holds my shape. It saved my life.

"I did not realize," said Purple, "that my flying egg was moving. You had painted thick gray goo over all the knobs and dials, so that I could see none of the settings on my——" he hesitated, then used the word, "——spellmakers." The loss of his speakerspell must have taught him to think his words out more carefully.

To his own villagers, Purple explained, "Somehow they had gained entrance to my flying egg—which I have told you about—and done terrible things to it." To us, he continued, "I was furious, Lant. I would have killed the pack of you."

I shuddered. He still might. In fact, what was he waiting for?

"Later," he continued, "I realized that you had acted from ignorance. Perhaps you thought that the egg was alive and dangerous. Perhaps that was the reason for Shoogar's earlier attacks on me. I wanted to know why, *why* you had dirtied and broken implements in my flying home——

"Unfortunately, I did not realize how badly you had damaged it. There is a spell in any flying device that compensates for sudden, sharp motion. It also compensates for the lack of a world underfoot. Well, I did not know that I was in the air. The windows had been painted gray, the screens likewise, the dials had all been tampered with.

"When I opened the door to go looking for you, the wind of my passage picked me up and sucked me out. When I realized I was falling, I pulled my hood up and curled in a ball. My impact suit saved me by holding my shape—much as water in a vase does not change shape when you set it down hard."

"I wish the vase had broken," muttered Shoogar.

"The fall knocked me out," continued Purple, "but I broke no bones. But I saw very little of the landscape coming down. I still don't know just where *here* is——my flying egg does not respond to my signals. It has not answered me for months. I fear it may be beyond my scope."

"True enough," I answered. "Shoogar's spells entirely destroyed it. It was over the mountain called Critic's Tooth when Elcin's hammer struck it."

"Elcin?"

"The small, but mighty, god of thunder."

"Ah, yes. I know him. You say he struck my egg?"

"He struck it with a great flash, and a sound loud enough to shake the world and shatter the sky. I could neither hear nor see for many moments afterward."

Purple made an odd strangled sound. "Tell me, Lant, does the ground glow blue at night now?"

"In the old village, yes. And all the trees and grass have died. Villagers and animals as well. Look, Pilg and Ang have lost their fur, and Pilg is covered with sores."

Purple looked, he stepped closer; Pilg, brave man that he was, did not shrink from Purple's feverish examination. Both

their faces were pale. "It's true," Purple murmured, "I am
marooned." He used a word from his own demon's tongue.
"Those are *radiation* sores.

"Radiation sores," he repeated. "You blew up the pile."
He was trailing off into gibberish in his excitement. He looked
blindly around. "You hairy half-humans have smashed my
flying machine. I'll be lost here forever! Curse you, curse you
all——"

We all shrank back, even Purple's own villagers. He was
being too free with his curses. But Gortik and several of his
Advisors stepped forward to comfort Purple. "There, there,"
they murmured, patting his shoulders with visible reluctance.

"Let me alone!" Purple cried, jerking loose from the hands
that held him. He collided with Pilg who still stood forward
baring his naked and festering chest. Purple hesitated.

"Can you cure me?" asked Pilg with a quaver.

Purple looked at Pilg's disease-ridden body as if for the
first time, he looked into his eyes, then he stepped forward
and took Pilg by the shoulders. "Oh, my friend, my friend,
my poor dear friend." He released the shaken Pilg and turned
to the rest of us. "My friends, all of you——"

Again we shrank back. There was not a man in two villages
who wanted to be the friend of a raving, hairless madman.

"My friends, I need you more than ever now. I have lost a
major source of my power. My flying egg has been destroyed.
All the wonderful things I said I would do for you when I
recovered it, I can never do now."

At that Shoogar straightened a bit. "And I did it," he
reminded us. There was a hint of pride in his voice. He was
the only one smiling.

"And you did it," Purple echoed, in such a way that two
Advisors stepped up to take his arms.

Gortik glanced at me, at Purple, at Shoogar. He must have
been thinking furiously. He had thought his magician better
than ours; but now Purple had admitted to being hurt, and
hurt badly, by Shoogar's dueling spells. Obviously both magicians were powers to be reckoned with.

How they must hate each other! It boded not well for either
village.

Gortik, the Speaker, drew me aside. "I think we had best
break up this meeting."

"Before our magicians do it for us," I agreed.

"You take yours back to your encampment, we will return ours to his nest. You and I will meet later, privately, to discuss this situation. If either of our villages is to survive, there is much that we will have to work out."

I nodded immediately. How much longer would Shoogar restrain himself? We had to get away from Purple's own dueling ground as fast as we could. I waved my hands frantically at my Advisors. "Let's go, let's go." All I wanted was to put as much distance between Shoogar and Purple as possible.

We hurried back up the slope. One thought was uppermost: we were trapped on an island with two mad magicians— Elcin's Wrath—what had we done to deserve such a fate? Could we have possibly angered the Gods that much?

It did not take long for the word to spread. The wave of dismay was a visible thing as it washed across the encampment. Women began wailing, strong men trembled, children bawled in confusion. Dogs barked.

Many began tugging at their tent ropes, pulling them down. Exhausted as they were, they were ready to move on, so great was their fear of Purple.

Incredible!—that these few pitiful families had once been a strong and fruitful village. Yet so we had been before the coming of Purple. We had seen that village reduced to rubble, seen our friends and neighbors dead, and our property obliterated because of the feud between Shoogar and the mad magician.

And the duel was not yet over.

Purple still lived. He had followed us, and he would destroy us.

No. He had flown here in a single night. For a quarter of a cycle, he had been waiting for our arrival!

Shoogar was unapproachable. That Purple still lived, was indication of his failure. He had cast his finest spell, and the

other held not even a grudge. Angrily, Shoogar shook off his
two escorts and stamped off across the already sea-dampened
field. The crowd parted before him like goats from a pool of
defiled water. Anxious mothers herded their children safely
out of sight.

All over the camp tents were falling now as the word
spread. The people were ready to flee; they did not know
where they would go, but they were willing to die trying, so
great was their fear of Purple.

Here and there, sobbing women were loading their packs.
Children tugged at their skirts. Many of the men I passed
were putting extra sets of hobbles on their wives—there is no
telling what a hysterical woman will do.

Several members of the Guild of Advisors were standing
and arguing. They broke apart when they saw me. "Ah, Lant,
we were just discussing whether to go east or south—or
perhaps west, into the hills——"

"What foolishness are you babbling, Pilg?"

"The journey, the journey—we cannot possibly stay here?"

"We cannot possibly go anywhere else—unless you have
learned how to walk on water——"

"This is not the only spot on the island, Lant," said Hinc.
"You heard Gortik. There are others."

"You heard him too," I snapped back. "This is a small
island. Four villages and the Heights of Idiocy."

Hinc shrugged, "If we must flee to the Heights, then so be
it. We can be a renegade tribe, moving by night——"

"That way we'll have every village on the island after our
necks."

"We have no choice. Shoogar is going to start a duel!"

"Has Shoogar said so?"

"Hah! We don't need to talk to Shoogar to know he's
planning a duel—he's sworn to kill Purple, remember?"

"Now, listen," I said, "you are making foolish conclusions.
This is what we are going to do. First, there is not going to
be a duel. Second, I am going to go back to the lower village
and dicker privately with Gortik. I am going to try to stick
to our original plan of trading our services for their food and
land. It is the only way."

"Hah!" snorted Hinc. "Do you think you can stop Shoogar
from planning a duel?"

"I am the Speaker now," I said. "That gives me the authority—"

"Just a minute, Lant—" Hinc said. "When we let you be Speaker, it was only to talk to the villagers down below. We had no intention of letting you—only a bonemonger—assume any of the other rights and privileges of Speaker."

There was a murmur of agreement from the others.

"You are right, of course, Hinc. And I did not want to be Speaker in the first place. But you insisted—*you* were one of the loudest——and now that you have taken me as your Speaker in dealings with other men, you must also accept the fact that I represent you in your dealings with the Gods."

"Huh?"

"Well, think about it. Obviously, we are being tested by them. This set of tribulations that has been thrust upon us is nothing more than a test of our faith and our worship. The Gods wish to see if we will continue to believe in them despite our troubles and pray to them for relief, or if instead we will forsake them in our despair."

"What does that have to do with whether or not you should be allowed to give orders?" demanded Hinc's half-brother, Lesser Hinc. They shared the same father, of course, but were of different mothers.

I fixed him with my best angry stare. "Certainly it should be obvious, even to a frog brain like you! If you deny the traditions and the ancient ways, you are denying the Gods themselves. Our whole way of life is based upon the whims of the Gods we serve. Only a magician can control the Gods, and only the village speaker can control the village magician. Shoogar engraves his secret name into the Speaking Token, so that only the owner of that token has power over him."

"But you don't have a token," Lesser Hinc said.

"Right!" snapped Greater Hinc. "We owe you nothing! Come, let's go." They started to turn away. "We can choose another Speaker. Shoogar can just as easily make a token for him."

"Wait!" I cried. I had to think fast. "You have forgotten one thing."

There was something about my tone. They stopped. "You have forgotten about Gortik, the Speaker of the new village. He does not know how new I am to the art of Speaking—as far as he is concerned, I am as experienced as he. But if you introduce another man to him as your Speaker, he will know just how inexperienced that man is—and he will wonder why you have elected a new Speaker at such a crucial time for the village. All of the villages on this island would be able to take advantage of us, knowing that they were dealing with an unskilled Speaker."

They muttered among themselves. They moved a bit away and discussed the subject heatedly. "Better no Speaker than——" "But there is this new village——" "We don't need another inept Speaker——" "But we are already committed to——"

"And there is one more thing," I called. They paused, looked over at me. "There is Shoogar. How do you think he will react when you tell him that his best friend is no longer Speaker? Is there one among you who thinks he can control an angry magician?"

There wasn't. They looked at each other warily. At last, Hinc nodded his assent, and the others nodded with him. "All right, Lant—you win. Next time we will be more careful who we push forward."

"It certainly won't be anyone with such a fast tongue," muttered Lesser Hinc.

"Let's just hope he can use it against Gortik," said Snarg.

"Don't worry," said Greater Hinc. "If he can't, we can always strangle him with it."

"I am more concerned that he use it on Shoogar," babbled Pilg. "And quickly. He is probably planning a duel right this minute."

"Nonsense," I said, "he can't be planning a duel! It's the darkless season. There are no moons."

"Oh, you know your seasons well enough, Lant—but I don't think you know Shoogar."

"I am a bonemonger," I said with dignity. "I have to have a good layman's grasp of magic to make bone implements. Believe me, Shoogar cannot possibly be planning a duel."

Shoogar was alone with his shelter and his bicycle. I found him staring up into the sky and muttering to himself. "Goat kidneys, frog follicles, ant feathers—why did this have to come during the darkless season?"

"Shoogar," I said. "What is the matter?"

"The sky, you idiot—the *sky!*"

"I am not an idiot. I am the Speaker now."

"Being a Speaker does not preclude you from being an idiot," he snapped. His eyes were watery-red from peering so long into the sun. "If only it weren't for that god-cursed sky!"

"What is the matter with the sky?"

"I can't see the moons." He stood and gestured, "Elcin's Wrath! How can I know what the configurations are if I can't see the moons? Red day, blue day, red day, and no darkness ever. I've stared and stared——"

A dreadful certainty was stealing over me. "Shoogar, what are you doing?"

"*I'm trying to plan a duel*—Gods protect us, Lant! How can I even hope to defend myself if I can't see what the configurations are?"

"It is unfortunate," I agreed. Virn knows how I managed to keep my voice steady. "But perhaps it is also auspicious."

"Auspicious?" He whirled on me. "Auspicious? How can it be auspicious? How can I plan a duel when all the auspices are hidden?"

"Maybe," I said carefully. "Maybe, it's a sign that you shouldn't duel."

"Shouldn't duel?—Are you mad? Lant the Speaker——" he mocked, "he only knows how to speak in circles."

"I am not speaking in circles," I said firmly. "I mean that for once you won't be able to depend on your magic for an easy solution. Perhaps, for a change, you will have to think out the wisest course of action instead of just rashly casting a spell with dangerous side effects. Remember, whatever you

97

do, we won't be able to flee the side effects of it until the waters recede."

"Are you questioning my magic?" He peered at me, narrow-eyed.

"Me? Never! I am your staunchest supporter—but you have to admit, Shoogar, you do sometimes use your magic in situations where a little diplomacy might be better. You are too hasty to cast spells before you know how they will work out—"

"How else will I find out how they work??" he snapped.

I ignored the interruption. "You must admit, Shoogar, that my skill with words is better than yours."

"Yes," he said. "You use more of them than I do. You should be better."

"Be that as it may—if you don't know how the moons are positioned, then you are unable to cast any kind of moon-dependent spell. Instead, you must depend on me, as Speaker, to avoid situations where your magic will be needed."

"It's too late, Lant. We're already in a situation where my magic is necessary. I have to protect us from Purple. Obviously, he's going to try to kill me—and you—and the rest of the villagers! If only to retrieve *these*!" He held aloft the trophy that he had picked up when he vanquished the black egg: Purple's quartz lenses, their black bone frame glistening in the blue light.

"Nonsense," I snapped back at him, surprising even myself with my audacity. I was already beginning to feel like a Speaker. "Obviously, you don't remember Purple as well as I do. I don't recall that he ever once used violence, or ever once tried to cast a spell against you. In fact, all of the spell-casting done at the old village was done by you. Purple has yet to retaliate for any of your attacks."

"All the more reason to beware. We're in his village now—when he does retaliate, it will be a moon-destroyer, Lant."

"Again, nonsense. Purple is a talker, not a doer."

"My magic is necessary to protect us, Lant——"

"Granted, that you should protect us, but that does not mean that you must attack Purple right off—"

"The only good defense is a strong offense—"

"And you will have the moons falling out of the sky on top of us! Why don't you wait to see what he is planning? You forget that you have power over him, Shoogar—you have his lenses. He'll want them back. He'll do anything to get them back, perhaps even swear an oath of truce."

"Truce?" exploded Shoogar. "Truce?!! Lant, you have the mind of a flea! There can be no truce with magicians. I ought to know!"

"And you have the temper of a goat!" I snapped back. "If it weren't for me, you would have killed yourself long ago attempting to hurl fire balls at Elcin!"

This stopped Shoogar for a moment. He looked at me speechlessly. "Lant," he said quietly. "You surprise me. I had no idea you were so violent."

"It's been a long hard journey, Shoogar—I'm tired. Most of all, I'm tired of suffering because of poor judgment on the part of a magician. Now use your brain for once——or if you haven't one, let me use mine for you."

"What is it you are suggesting . . .?" he sighed.

"Wait—that's all. Wait. Swear an oath of truce, if necessary. It is too soon to duel with Purple, much too soon. If you attempt to duel with him on his home ground you are doomed to lose. Wait until you are on equal terms at least."

Shoogar didn't say anything. He examined his fingernails thoughtfully, and scratched at his thin fur.

"Well . . .?" I asked.

He didn't answer. He continued to scratch.

"There is one other thing you should consider, Shoogar. Purple always claimed that his spells did not depend on the gods or on the configurations of the moons. You've always thought that he was lying. But if he is not, then the endless sunlight does not hamper him."

He didn't answer—but at least he stopped scratching.

"Well? Will you wait? Or will you at least agree not to do anything until you talk it over with me?"

He looked up. "I'll talk it over with you before I do anything."

"Fine."

When I left he was still cursing the sky—but at least he was packing away his spellcasting equipment.

That settled, I went back to Hinc and the others and reported that we had nothing to fear from an immediate duel. Shoogar would not move without consulting me first. I told them we would stay here.

There was again some grumbling, but we were committed to this course of action—if not by my authority as Speaker, then certainly by the authority of the all-encompassing sea. Clearly, they had not expected me to fare so well with Shoogar, but since I had, they were left with no choice but to honor my claim to the office. It was as if the Gods themselves were backing me up.

As they wandered back to their tents I called my two sons, Wilville and Orbur, to me. Wilville, noticing my smile, asked, "Why are you so eager to stay here? This area teems with trouble. That Purple is still alive bodes not well for us."

"Oh, I think that situation can be handled. The advantages of staying here far outweigh the disadvantages."

"Advantages?" asked Orbur incredulously. He was the darker of the two.

"Certainly—you're a bicycle builder—you must have noticed the quality and variety of woods around here. Fine bambooze shoots, spirit-pine, sparkling aspen, birts, vampire-oaks——also fibertrees, nevergreens and cranials. One can build fine bicycles with the materials at hand here. In fact, one could probably build anything with the materials here. Did you not notice there are no bicycles or bicycle builders at all in the lower village? You will have the market all to yourselves."

Wilville nodded eagerly. "Our father is right, Orbur. There is much work here."

"You are thinking right, Wilville—there is. You can start by contacting the neighboring villages for me. I want you to locate the nearest sources of dry bone, wet bone, petrified bone and so on. It seems they don't have a good bonemonger here either . . ."

N ow I headed down toward the lower village and my meeting with Gortik.

This time it would be just the two of us, without our squabbling councils to hinder us. We had finished with the formalities of the greetings, and now we could get down to the real business of negotiating.

Of course, we had no choice in the matter. I and my fellow villagers were here for the duration of the wading season. Gortik and I had to come to some sort of agreement on how our two villages could survive till the onset of the next conjunction.

To tell the truth, I was uneasy. This would be the first time I would have to Speak for my whole village and make decisions for them. It was one thing to browbeat one's own people for their own good—quite another to attempt it with a perfect stranger.

I carried with me a token of luck in lieu of the new Speaking Token which Shoogar had not yet begun to build. (One of the most important ingredients he still had not located— a stone the weight of a small child. Indeed, we had not even selected the small child yet, whose weight was to be the standard of the token.)

I felt unsure of myself without a proper Speaking Token ——and worried that I might not do a proper job. "A token, a token," I mumbled, "my village for a token." But I tottered down the slope, determined to do the best Speaking I could without it.

There was a shout from behind me. I paused. My first wife came running down the hillside, her skirt flapping, her breasts bouncing, her hobbles giving her a peculiar short-gaited run. "Lant, oh brave Lant, wait!"

I waited.

She hurried up to me, "My brave Speaker, you have forgotten your amulet of shrewd mongering."

"But I don't need it, woman," I admonished her. "I am going to Speak. I have a token of skillful language as well as one of luck. What do I need with a monger's token?"

She looked crestfallen. "I am sorry, my brave one. You are right. It is just that I wanted to do something to help you—I wanted to give you something to aid your Speaking and all I could think of was your monger's amulet. I thought perhaps it might help——a little bit anyway."

"How could it?" I scoffed. "I am not going there as a monger, but as a Speaker."

"You are right, my wise master." She began kissing and stroking my feet. "I do not know what it is that Speakers do—but I thought it was something like mongering, so I——I'm sorry. I take up your time. I will go and flog myself."

She looked so unhappy and woebegone: her hair had fallen out in patches and lost its once-proud sleekness, her shape was heavy with child; I felt a surge of pity for her. "Here, woman, wait. Give me the amulet. It could not hurt to carry it. It will not help, of course, but I will take it because you thought it important."

Trivial words, of course, easy enough for me to say—but they cheered her immensely. She smiled gratefully and threw herself at my feet in gratitude.

"Here now, here now—that's enough kissing. You want the other wife to think I am favoring you with an inordinate amount of affection?" I bade her rise, took the amulet and sent her back to the encampment.

I continued downward to the lower village.

The wide river swept through it on its surging course to the sea. Great black housetrees lined both sides of its banks. There were many frog-tending ponds and dams, and there were terraced riceblossom pools along the river banks. Off to one side, well away from the village proper was a tree so misshapen that had it been human, it surely would have been stillborn. Clearly, that was the nest of Purple the Magician.

But that was not my destination. Not yet. First I would speak to Gortik.

As I entered the village proper, a curious ragtag of villagers and children began to follow me. Some of the children tried to taunt me, but were hushed by their elders. All followed curiously as I strode between the shady trunks. The black-grass crunched under my feet.

I could not help but admire the size of the trees and the skillfull weaving of the nests hanging from them. They spoke of prosperity. It takes extensive care to make a tree grow as big as it must to support a house. That this village had so many spoke well of the wealth of its inhabitants.

The Speaker's glade was a shady area lined with gentle birts and yellow aspen. Here no women, no children and no villagers outside the first circle were allowed.

I held a rank which allowed me to enter, but in the interests of politics I gave Gortik the courtesy of officially granting me the right. He stepped forward, bade me enter—but not before he had first chased away a by now sizable crowd of onlookers. The arrival of my village must have been the most exciting thing to happen here for some time.

Gortik and I sat in the glade and exchanged formalities. We chewed raba-root and talked about the Gods and the weather. We each traded two syllables of our respective names, more an indication of a growing—and necessary— mutual trust than a sign of respect.

We traded our histories as well. I did not go into much detail in the telling of mine—merely that I had been chosen Speaker by acclamation of my fellow villagers because of my bravery and courage.

Gortik was impressed. He told me how he had become Speaker for his tribe—how he had fought for the honor many times, and how each time he had been defeated—but only narrowly, mind you—how his village had had a succession of terrible Speakers one after the other, how one had been killed for his audacity, how a second had been disgraced and a third laughed out of power. At last these gentle villagers had realized that Gortik had been right all along, and they hailed him as their new Speaker.

It was an impressive story, all right. I didn't believe him any more than he believed me; but I was thoroughly im-pressed with Gortik's skill as Speaker.

"It is no secret," Gortik said then, "that your tribe needs a place to settle permanently."

I nodded. "You are right, it is no secret. One can get tired of traveling."

"I find that hard to believe. Why, the excitement, the adventure!"

"Yes," I admitted, "we love to sit and talk about them. We were a brave people to have faced the dangers of such a migration. It was the dangers behind us that helped to make us brave." Then, changing the subject, "This is a rich area you have here."

"Oh, no," Gortik protested. "We are really quite poor. Quite poor. We go hungry throughout much of the ungrowing season."

"Then you have not been exploiting the land properly," I countered. "Our tribe could grow enough on this land to feed both villages."

"Ah, you exaggerate again. We have trouble feeding ourselves. There is not space enough for a good crop, let alone room to plant a decent number of housetrees."

"Your village belies that—there are more than enough housetrees in your village. Many are empty. And there are other housetrees high on the slope, unused as well. There is room for us there, above the aspenwood."

"That is our migration ground. We will need it later when the waters rise."

"It is still a roomy area—there are a great many housetrees there."

"Hardly enough," he shook his head. "Hardly enough— and in poor repair. Poor repair."

"Nonsense. My villagers could put those trees in shape within a hand of days and have decent nests hanging from every one within a second hand."

"I find that hard to believe."

"We could show you. As I said, we have many skills that your village obviously must not have, or you would be living better than you do now."

"We live as well as we can."

"Do you have a decent bonemonger among you?"

"Bonemongering is a northern trade. We do not—*honor* it here."

"More's the pity—you are missing out on much that would

make your life easier. We have other trades as well, which you lack."

"And suppose we did let you demonstrate your vastly superior talents and abilities—what would you expect in return?"

"The right to settle—say, on that piece of land above the woods."

Gortik shook his head slowly. "That is not living land. That land is unusable for men."

"It is unusable for you, you mean. We are not cropmongers as you people are. We do not need to live near the rivers, nor do we need to migrate every year to avoid the swelling waters. We are mountain folk and make our living off the sheep, the goats, the high pastures. We do not go hungry during the time of ungrowing, the season of sweat."

"Humph, Lant, I doubt much of what you say—your clothes are rude, badly woven to say the least. And animal skins do not indicate the quality of spells you claim to have. One who is civilized no longer needs to wear animal skins."

"That's true for your village," I said, "because you are weavers. We are not. We are craftsmen—have you any bicycle makers?"

"Bicycles——?"

"Ah ha, you do not. It is a vehicle with wheels which enables its rider to travel great distances in one day."

"And I suppose you use scavenger pigs and dogs to pull it in the manner of the western barbarians?"

"Ah, you show your ignorance, Gortik. The bicycle requires no animals at all—it moves by magic alone."

"By magic alone?" He was incredulous.

"Of course," I said, not without some small tone of superiority. If these people did not know even of bicycles, they must be stupid indeed. "One sits astride it and chants and pedals——the harder one chants, the faster he goes. You must chant hard, of course, to get up a hill; but that stores so much magic in the machine that one need hardly chant at all on the way down."

"I would like to see one of these fabulous devices."

"Shoogar has one now—he has had it since his duel with Purple. It used to be mine, but I would not dare ask Shoogar for its return—it would be an insult. It is no matter. My sons can build others."

"Could they build one for me?"

"Quite probably."

"I would be the only one in my village with such a device, wouldn't I?"

"You are the Speaker here," I said. "If you felt that the magic of a bicycle was too dangerous for the rest of your people, your word would be law."

His eyes narrowed shrewdly, "Do you think I could get away with it?"

I nodded reluctantly. It was obvious what Gortik wanted. Being the only owner of a bicycle would enhance his *mana* greatly. I did not want to do such a thing, nor did I want to limit the market for my sons' devices—but if it was the only thing which I could offer him in return for the right to stay, then I had no choice. He still had the right to demand we move on when the wading season ended. I sighed and nodded again.

He beamed. "Then it is settled, Lant. You and your village will give me a bicycle, in return for which I will allow you to demonstrate your supposedly very great housemaking skills by clearing and cleaning our migration ground for us."

"Ah, Gortik, my friend," I answered, "you are correct in your manner, but you have misstated the terms of the agreement. We are lending you a bicycle for your use. In return you are granting us your migration area for our use. As a sign of our goodwill we will offer to teach your people what skills they will need to survive the season of ungrowing."

"Ah, Lant, my devoted friend, my lifelong companion, you are the one who misstates the agreement. You have forgotten the bounty of ten sheep which you have offered me for a great feast in my honor."

"Ah, Gortik, my faithful brother, my generous colleague, I have not forgotten them—indeed, I have not thought of them at all. Such a feast is an honor intended only for those Gods who have wrought mighty miracles."

"Lant, you are the playmate of my spratling years. Have I not earned such an honor?"

"Ah, Gortik, we are more than playmates—we are suck-lings at the same breast. I would deny you nothing. You need only ask and it is yours. I offer you, out of the boundless affection of my own heart, six sheep so that your people may start a flock of their own."

"Ah, but Lant, my illustrious advisor—my people are not shepherds. The animals would die."

"Gortik, Gortik, your wisdom is unsurpassed. Of course we cannot give the sheep to the untrained shepherd. You will grant us three young men to watch them. We will keep your sheep with ours and teach your men how to be shepherds. Shoogar will teach them the necessary spells."

"I have not the men to spare."

"Boys, then. Boys love sheep. Our shepherds will teach any three of your boys how to properly care for sheep and keep them from grazing too long in one spot."

"Sheep have much magic in their bones, do they not? Is that where your magician gets so much of his power? From sheep?"

"I do not know the source of Shoogar's power," I said. "But you are right that sheep are powerful."

"Then what guarantee do we have that you will not use that power against us?"

"Your village is not without its strength. What guarantee do we have that you will not use *your* power against *us*?"

"You have your magician," he said.

"And you have yours," I countered.

"Yes, there is that," he said.

There was silence for a moment.

"We must decide what they are going to do—before they decide for themselves," I said. "A feud between them would not augur well for either of our clans."

"Yes," he nodded. "It would tear the two villages apart."

"And much of the surrounding countryside too," I added. He looked startled.

"I have already spoken to Shoogar," I said quickly, "and I know that he is not planning to attack Purple—that is, not without sufficient provocation. I have convinced Shoogar that it is important enough for us to settle here for him to swear a truce with Purple. In return, of course, he—and all of us— would like some guarantees from Purple."

"Well," said Gortik, "I cannot speak for Purple. No one speaks for Purple but Purple. To tell the truth, I do not like the idea of having two hostile magicians in the same village—but just as much, I do not like the idea of having even one magician in this village—one particular magician, that is. There is little love between myself and Purple. Dorthi and I were good friends. Dorthi's strength supported me as Speaker; but since Purple has replaced him, he has done nothing."

"H'm," I said thoughtfully, "is it not said that a land with two magicians will soon have only one."

He nodded. "There is only so much magic in an area—enough for one magician, not for two. It is inevitable that one of them will die."

"I know. Shoogar has thought long on that."

"So have I. If we have our magicians swear a truce, it will be a very artificial situation. It cannot last long."

I nodded. He was right, of course. "But perhaps it will at least buy us time until the oceans again recede."

"Ah, but then what? You want a permanent village site. I want a permanent magician."

"Purple is planning to leave you?"

"He has been talking that way ever since he first fell into our midst. At the moment he is forced by circumstance to stay—like you—but if that were not the case, there are many in this village who would be happy to speed him on his way."

"Are you suggesting that you would like to see Purple removed?" I asked.

"Of course I wouldn't suggest such a thing," he replied. "A Speaker must never question his magician. But—if a duel were to occur between our two warlocks, I would not be disappointed if Purple lost."

"But you have said that you do not wish a duel."

"Oh, yes—I did, didn't I. To be quite honest, Lant, I would prefer to see him leave of his own free will—quietly, if possible—but by force, if necessary."

"I see," I said. And I did. Purple was not aiding Gortik as a magician should. Gortik wanted him gone. Even no magician at all might be better than a bad one. I could understand it. "Let me suggest this to you, Gortik: if there is some way that we can remove Purple from your village, we will do that for you."

"And replace him with Shoogar?"

"Uh—" I asked cautiously, "Is that what you want?" I did not want to lose Shoogar to another village.

"Definitely *not*!" he said.

"Fine. Then we will keep Shoogar."

"One thing, Lant," said Gortik. "Yes, I would like to be rid of Purple, but not if it means devastating this land. I do not wish to be a migrant like you."

"H'm," I said. "That makes the problem a little more difficult. We will have to take things one at a time. First, we will secure an oath of truce from both our magicians. This will give Shoogar time to acquaint himself with the local spells."

"That will be a simple task," said Gortik. "Most of the spell-charts were destroyed with Dorthi when he was killed. There are few local spells left, and Purple has not renewed any of them."

"Shoogar can do that," I said expansively. "He knows all one hundred and eleven spells of village tending."

"Good. We can make good use of them. Perhaps you have noticed that we have many empty housetrees? Many of our most religious people have fled since Purple's arrival—they fear to live in a village with an inept magician."

"I know exactly how they feel," I said.

"Of course, of course; a good Speaker always empathizes with the people."

"You must be one of the finest then," I said.

"And you as well, Lant. You are a veritable fountainhead of faith."

"Ah, Gortik, I am but a shadow compared to the brightness that is you."

"Ah, would you compare one sun to the other?"

"No, of course not—there can be no comparison. One is bright, but small; the other is huge, but dim—and yet, both light up the world equally well."

"Both are necessary, and both are beautiful," said Gortik.

"Like ourselves," I added.

"Of course, of course. It is well that we agree on so many things, Lant. It will not be difficult at all to make an agreement which is fair to both of us and our villages."

"How could it be difficult when each of us is thinking more of the other than of himself?"

"Ah, Lant, you have such a way with words, such a beautiful way. Now about those sheep—six is not enough—"

"Ah, Gortik, it is more than enough if all you are planning to send is three boys—"

And so it went.

We stayed and chewed *raba*-root till well into the blue afternoon. There was much to discuss, and much root to be chewed.

And when we finished what we had, we staggered off in search of more. We were thoroughly under its influence by now. It was good root. Jark could make a fine Quaff from it.

"Purple!" said Gortik. "Purple has some *raba*-root. He chews it whenever he gets depressed—which is often these days."

"Ah, good. Let's pay him a visit. And while we are there, we can inform him of our agreement."

"Again you are thinking, Lant. I am continually amazed by your prowess."

We found Purple tending his small patch of herbs and plants. *Raba*-root was not the only fermentable spice he had. He had several others that I recognized, and many more that I did not. Jark would be overjoyed at the news.

"Purple, ahoy," we hailed him. He looked up, squinting in our direction in the blue light.

"It sounds like my old friend, Lant," he said.

I shuddered—*friend?* I gritted my teeth and said, "Yes, it's Lant. Gortik and I have come to speak with you." I tried to sound as stern and formal as I could.

"Uh——" Purple hesitated. He seemed to be uneasy at something. "How are you, Lant. How is your family, your wife?"

What a strange question to ask. Why would anyone want to know about the condition of a wife? But then, Purple always had been a strange one. "My wives are fine," I said.

"My number one wife is expecting a child soon. Shoogar says it will be a daughter, but as she has already presented me with two sons, I cannot fault her."

Purple looked startled, "Expecting a child?" He counted hurriedly on his fingers, "It's been almost nine—" He looked at me, "When is it due?"

"In another three hands of hands of days."

He counted again, "Three times five times five—seventy five. That would be blue days, of course; now let's see, convert that into standard—that would be four and a half months from now." He exhaled loudly and looked relieved. "Whew! For a moment there I thought it could have been—"

"Could have been what?"

"Uh, never mind. I'm just glad that there's no such thing as a thirteen-and-a-half-month gestation period."

He was talking gibberish again—a pregnancy lasts no longer than two hundred and fifteen blue days. What a month was, I had no idea, although he used the term as I might discuss a hand of days. Perhaps it was his way of measuring clusters of days. Purple had once mentioned that his days— "standard days" he had called them—were only half as long as ours.

Our days, of course, are measured by the passage of the blue sun, regardless of where the red is. Gortik had told me how Purple had once been confused—he could not believe it was midnight because the red sun was still high in the sky. How odd—why should the periods of light and dark have to correspond with the concepts of night and day? Only during conjunctions did such a thing occur.

In any case, I could not understand his concern with the child. I said, "Why should you care, Purple?"

"Uh—uh—"

"Is it because you did the family-making thing with my wife on the day of the last conjunction?"

Purple went pale. "I—I—forgive me, Lant. I—"

"Forgive you? How can I forgive you?"

He took a startled step backward and held up a hand as if to ward me off.

I said, "Shoogar had scattered a dust of yearning around your nest. You could not help yourself."

"You mean, you think I did it because of a spell?"

"Of course, it was a spell. It was part of the duel."

He looked relieved again. The color flowed back into his face. "Then I have been worrying needlessly—and I do not need to worry about the child either."

"Why should you? Shoogar knows when the child was conceived and when she will be born."

Purple nodded, "Yes, Shoogar is probably quite good at those things."

"He is," I confirmed. "The child is your daughter, all right."

He went pale again. This time I thought he would faint altogether. The blood had been flowing into and out of his head at such a rate that he was having trouble standing.

I continued, "When we first realized that the child was yours, I almost killed my wife—"

"Oh, no, Lant—not just because I—"

I looked at him oddly. "I told you, Purple, you could not help yourself. And she is only a woman. A woman doesn't know how to refuse a kindness. No, we would have killed her because she was carrying a demon child, but Shoogar forbade it. The child must be carried to term and born as any other. At that time we will determine if the child is a good demon or a bad demon. Shoogar thinks she will be a bearer of much magic—and if so, he thinks he can control her."

"Humph," snorted Gortik, "it sounds like Shoogar wants to emulate the legend of the poor fisher and the demon tailor. The demon demanded three wishes—"

I shrugged. "It is of little concern to me. If the child is a demon, then Shoogar will have to pay me for the right to destroy or control her. If she is not, then at least I gain another bride price. Why else would one allow a woman to breed indiscriminately? Another son is always a pride and a strength. A daughter is at least a price of a drink. One offers one's wife to guests as a matter of course. Now that our two villages are going to live peacefully together, the child's birth will be of no importance at all. It will be as if I had offered you the guest privilege to insure good relations between our two groups. That she is a magician's daughter will add somewhat to her value when I sell her on her seventh yearday, but a daughter is only a daughter and not worth the air wasted discussing her."

"Uh, yes," said Purple. He was obviously disturbed about

something. "Just one question. Are all your women's pregnancies so long?"

"What do you mean 'so long'? Two hundred and fifteen days is the proper length of a pregnancy."

"Two hundred and fifteen—" Purple began counting again. "Thirteen and a half months," he said. "Oh." He began mumbling to himself. "Well, I guess such a thing is not impractical—probably the extra four and a half months are needed because conditions here are so unstable. It gives the developing infant an extra length of time to grow and be more ready for a hostile world. Yes, yes, I can see why such a thing—"

Gortik and I exchanged a glance. I said, "I see he still talks gibberish to himself."

"Not as much as he used to," Gortik replied. "He hardly uses the demon tongue any more."

"Ah, that's good. How can a man be civilized if he does not speak a civilized language?"

To Purple, I said, "Actually, we have come here to talk about something much more important."

"Yes," put in Gortik. "Have you any ripe *raba*-root?" I could see that this other Speaker was one who did not waste words—he got right down to the subject at hand.

Purple scratched his hairless chin, which was gray with many tiny black dots. How odd. He said, "I think I might be able to spare some." He rummaged through his herb patch, then decided against it and disappeared up into his nest instead.

He returned almost immediately with a basket of tubers. "Here, these have already been cured. Take what you need."

Gortik slung the whole basket under one arm. "Thank you, Purple. This will do nicely."

Purple looked a bit askance, but said nothing. I found myself wondering what kind of a magician this was who was treated little better than a common cropmonger. Did Gortik have some strange kind of power over Purple? No, such a thing was not possible—or was it instead that Gortik knew that Purple would not use his vast powers against him. But why?

The thought crossed my mind—perhaps the only reason Purple was allowed to endure here was because he was unkillable. Otherwise they would be rid of him in a minute if they could. No wonder Gortik was so eager to accept my offer to remove their magician for them. Purple was worse than inept—he was a dangerous fool.

And they were stuck with him just as we had been a quarter of a cycle ago.

No wonder Gortik treated him so shabbily—he was hoping to drive Purple away with his rudeness.

H'm, he would not try that with Shoogar, I thought. Shoogar would curse him hairless without even blinking.

Gortik handed me a *raba*-root and I chewed it slowly, savoring its rich bitterness. Ah, that was nice. Its pungent smell filled the glade and saturated the air. I and my clothes would reek of it for days.

We started to wander back toward the village when abruptly I remembered something. I caught Gortik's arm and turned back. "Oh, Purple," I called.

He looked up, "Yes? What is it, Lant?"

"I almost forgot to tell you. I and my tribe will be settling in this area—but we cannot do it if you and Shoogar intend to duel."

Purple looked puzzled, "I have no intention of dueling with Shoogar."

"You don't?"

"Of course not. Dueling never accomplished anything."

I looked at Gortik, "You see why we thought him mad?"

Gortik returned the look, "You think you are pointing out something we have not already noticed?"

To Purple, I said, "I am overjoyed to hear that. Shoogar will also be glad."

Purple nodded thoughtfully. He said, "Lant, it seemed to me that I saw my seeing pieces hanging from a string around Shoogar's neck when he came to the conference."

"A trophy of the duel," I explained. "Although under the circumstances—"

"I will exchange an oath of peace for those devices, Lant. I need them to see."

"Um," I said. "I don't know. Shoogar regards that trophy quite highly. He would not be eager to give it up—"

"No seeing pieces, Lant, no oath of peace."

"—but since you put it that way, I'm sure he will be delighted."

"Not half so much as I," said Purple.

Well! It had been easier than I had thought. I was overjoyed. Expansively, I offered Purple a piece of *raba*-root to seal the deal. "It is a more than reasonable request."

His mouth full, Purple nodded his agreement.

"I don't think so," said Gortik. "You really should ask for more."

I frowned at him.

"There is really nothing more that I need," said Purple. "except perhaps—"

"Perhaps what?"

"No, it is nothing. There is no way you could help me."

"But if we at least knew, perhaps we could offer some suggestions——"

He looked at us as if we were children. "Don't speak foolishness," he said. "There is no way either of you could help me get home."

"Huh—!!" Gortik and I exchanged a glance. Why, he was asking for the very thing that both of us wanted. We practically tripped over each other in our eagerness to answer. "But we will do anything to help you, Purple, anything! We only wish the same as you—that you can return to your home as soon as possible."

He sighed, "That is very generous of you, but I am afraid there is no way. My flying egg is destroyed. I have no way to lift into the sky." He sighed again and fingered a device on his belt. "I have the means to call down the mother-egg, but the call signal will not work this far south."

"The mother-egg—?" I found myself choking on a piece of root.

"The egg that Shoogar—sank, that was only a small vehicle for exploring the contours of a world. I left the larger vehicle in the sky."

Nervously, I looked upward.

Purple laughed, "No, you need not fear, Lant. It will not fall—not unless I call it down. But I am too far south to do that. If there were some way I could return to the north—"

"You mean you would leave us?" Gortik was astounded.

Purple misinterpreted it. "Oh, my friend Gortik, I know

how it must hurt you, but please try to realize—I yearn to return to my home in the sky, to converse, confer and otherwise hobnob with my brother wizards."

Gortik danced a little jig of grief.

Purple continued, "But, alas, there is no way. I cannot travel north overland because the sea already covers everything. And I dare not attempt it by boat. I am told that it will be all whirlpools and dangerous uncharted reefs. There is no path by land, and there is no path by sea. I am marooned, marooned." Purple sighed and sat down.

I sighed with him. "If only there were a path through the air—but nothing goes through the air but birds and eggs." He sighed again and nodded. "If you had been willing to teach Shoogar your flying spell," I pointed out, "perhaps today you might not be in this predicament."

"Flying spell?" he said. A strange look came over his face.

Gortik looked at him curiously, looked at me, looked at Purple again. "What are the two of you talking about?" The magician was muttering curiously to himself.

"No, no—the whole idea is preposterous. It would never work. Yes, it would——" He trailed off into the demon's tongue. He shook his head impatiently as if trying to thrust that thought away. But it wouldn't go—that peculiar look kept returning to his eyes, and he argued frantically with himself in words not known to men.

Suddenly he leapt to his feet. "Yes, it must be tried," he shouted. "It must be! It must be! It is the only way!"

He leapt at me. I jumped back, but he grabbed my robe. "Tell me, Lant—does Shoogar still want to fly?"

"Is the sky red and blue?" I asked in reply. "*Of course*, Shoogar still wants to fly."

He was delighted. "Oh, yes, yes—what a wonderful idea." He began capering around his housetree. "Go—go tell him, tell him—go, go! I'm going home—I'm going to fly!"

"Tell him?" I echoed. "Tell him what?"

"Tell him I'm going to build a flying machine—no, *we're* going to build a flying machine—and I'm going to fly north for the *winter!*" And he laughed hysterically.

Gortik and I exchanged another look. We shook our heads sadly. I did not know who to feel sorrier for—Purple for being deranged, or Gortik for being his Speaker.

When we left, Purple was still dancing about his housetree and singing at the top of his lungs.

When he heard the news, Shoogar was neither pleased nor angered, merely curious. "So, now he *wants* to build a flying machine. Before, he would not tell me how to do such a thing—that was why I fought him—now he wants to." He shook his head. "I don't like it, Lant. I don't like it."

"But Shoogar, don't you see what it means? You win after all—you fought him because he wouldn't show you how to fly—you didn't kill him, but you put him into a position where he has to show you how, or he can't go home."

Shoogar remained unexcited. "So what? Why should I help him build a flying machine? He will leave in it and I will still have no flying spell."

"But he won't be taking it with him—" I said. "—only to the north country."

"He lives in the north country? I thought he lived on the other side of the sky."

"No—he has to go to the north country to get to the other side of the sky."

"Lant, you're talking in circles again. The north country is not the other side of the sky—it's not even anywhere near it. I ought to know; Dorthi and I trained there."

"The north country is not his destination," I explained. "But he has to go there to call down his mother-egg."

"Mother-egg? You mean he has another one?"

"Apparently so—at least that's what he says."

"Pfah!" said Shoogar. He didn't believe it.

"He showed me a spell device—it's attached to his belt. It's a calling thing, but he can't use it here because his mother-egg isn't in this sky, it's in the northern sky. So he has to go to the north country to use it. For that he needs a flying machine."

"H'm," said Shoogar. "And what happens to the machine afterward?"

"After what?"

"After he leaves in it."

I shrugged. "I don't know. I guess he will leave it in the north country—after all, once he calls down his mother-egg, he won't need it any more."

"H'm," said Shoogar again.

"You could probably have it for the taking," I suggested.

"Pfah! You're not thinking, Lant. If I wanted it, I would have to go north to get it. Or go there with Purple in order to bring it back. No, I don't like the idea."

"But if he builds a flying machine, obviously he will need help. You and Wilville and Orbur can help him—and if you can build one flying machine for him, you should certainly be able to build another for yourself."

"H'm," said Shoogar for a third time. His eyes lit up as he considered the possibilities. In fact, his whole face took on that same peculiar expression that I had seen on Purple's when he had been thinking of flying machines.

"Then it is decided?" I asked.

He fingered the lenses on the string around his neck. "To cooperate with him on the flying machine means first securing an oath of peace, doesn't it?"

I nodded.

"And that means giving up my trophy, doesn't it?"

I nodded again.

"Um," he said. He continued to finger the lenses.

"But a flying machine, Shoogar—" I suggested softly. "Think of it! A flying machine!"

"Umm," he said. He was thinking of it.

"And there will be no other magician in this region either, after Purple leaves," I whispered. "Certainly not one who could compare with you. You will be without equal—you can be the magician of both the upper and lower villages."

"Ummm," said Shoogar.

"And think about this," I added slowly. "You will be able to accomplish all of this without a duel!"

"No, Lant—then I cannot do it."

"Huh?!!"

"Not without a duel—if I am truly to earn my position

here, then I must demonstrate that I am a better magician than Purple. I must best him in a duel."

"Erk," I said. I had talked myself out of a peaceful solution. "Uh, well, uh—"

He shook his head firmly. "I'm sorry, Lant, but you know how things are—a duel between two magicians in the same region is not only necessary, but proper."

"Uh, but, Shoogar—" I said quickly, "you have already bested him in a duel."

"No, I haven't. I've only inconvenienced him by destroying his black egg. The duel is still to be fought."

"But you said you wouldn't duel him right away—"

"No, I didn't. I only said I wouldn't duel him without talking it over with you first. I'm talking it over with you now."

I felt like I was drowning. "But the flying machine—"

"The duel," he insisted.

"But—but—" I stammered helplessly, but it was hopeless. When Shoogar made up his mind, he was a solid lump of stubbornness. "All right, Shoogar, I know when I am defeated. If you must, you must. I will go and warn the villagers."

"You do that, Lant—but tell them not to be too alarmed."

"Why?" I asked bitterly. "Are you planning to minimize the side effects again?"

"No," he said. "But there is no reason that the duel must be held *today*. We might build a flying machine first."

My heart leapt. "Then you'll do it! You'll cooperate with Purple?"

"Of course not. I am merely going to let him show me how to build a flying machine—if he can," Shoogar said.

I relaxed.

"After he finishes," he added, "*then* I'll kill him."

The blue sun was at one side of the sky; the red sun was at the other. The world was bathed in red and blue light;

shadows stretched in two directions. We waited in the meadow
below the heights. All was still.

This would be the first meeting of the two magicians—
would they be able to live up to their truce?

Purple, fat and paunchy, was already waddling up the
slope, escorted by Gortik and his advisors. He was a bright
figure in his suit of strange cloth. He paused and squinted up
the hill.

I looked too. Shoogar was stumping imperiously toward
us, magnificent in his shortness.

Shoogar caught sight of Purple then, and stopped. The
two of them surveyed each other, one up the hill, one down.
For a moment, all was still and silent. I held my breath and
prayed.

And then Shoogar took a step forward, another. Purple did
likewise. I exhaled loudly in relief; the two magicians carefully closed the remaining distance. They ended up facing
each other, one standing to either side of me; Gortik was
standing opposite my position, also between the two
magicians. As Speakers for our villages, we had thought it
best to place ourselves so. If the magicians should attack
each other, we would be there to stop them (I hoped). If
we couldn't stop them. . . . Well, I would be in no position
to worry about it.

Shoogar and Purple eyed each other warily, Shoogar looking Purple up and down, Purple only looking down.

"The oath—" I prompted.

"Him first," they both said, pointing in unison.

"Both together!" Gortik and I cried.

Reluctantly, Shoogar and Purple reached out and took
each other's right hand; then they joined left hands too. Now
neither could reach his spellcasting equipment without first
letting go, which would allow the other to reach for his. They
glared at each other across their linked arms.

I looked at Gortik and nodded. He nodded back. Simultaneously, we each turned to our respective wizard and
snipped off a lock of his hair, two fingernail clippings, and
took a droplet of blood and a nasal dropping.

While the two magicians watched, we mixed these ingredients together in a bowl between them, then separated

the result into two equal portions which we put into spell bags, one for Shoogar, one for Purple.

"Here. Now neither will be able to cast a spell on the other without also affecting himself. Any harm that befalls one will befall the other, so it will be for the benefit of both to watch out for each other's welfare."

They continued to scowl.

"Repeat after me," I said, "in unison, so that your oaths will be taken as one: I (state your full name, including the secret syllables) do solemnly swear . . ."

"Do solemnly swear . . . "

"To love, honor and cherish . . . "

"To love, honor and cherish . . . "

"My brother magician as myself."

"My brother magician as myself."

I turned to Shoogar. "Do you, Shoogar, agree to uphold the terms of this oath?" His eyes were fierce.

After a moment, I repeated, "Do you, Shoogar, agree to uphold the terms of this oath?"

He muttered something.

"Louder." I kicked him.

"I do!" he snapped.

Gortik leaned forward then and slid a leather-and-hair ring around the third finger of Shoogar's left hand.

I turned to Purple. "Do you, Purple, agree to uphold the terms of this oath?"

He grumbled, "I do."

"Fine." I slipped a ring around his finger. "As long as either of you is on this island, that ring will remind you of your duty as a magician, and your duty to your brother magician. See that you use it well. Now, by the authority vested in me as Speaker for the upper village, and by the authority which each of you has seen fit to grant me by your presence here, and also by the authority which Gortik has given me in allowing me to perform this ceremony, I now pronounce the two of you magicians united in trust!"

Simultaneously, they let go of each others' hands and leapt apart, glaring angrily. I closed my eyes and waited. There were no explosions, no hissing fireballs.

I opened my eyes.

They were still standing there, looking at each other.

"An auspicious sign," murmured Gortik. "They haven't tried to kill each other."

"Mm," I said.

Purple drew himself up and took a step forward, hand outstretched. "My seeing pieces?" he asked.

Shoogar slowly lifted them from around his neck. Reluctantly, he handed them over.

Purple took them reverently, carefully. Hands trembling, he wiped them with a soft cloth and placed them across his face. He squinted around at us, "Lant, Shoogar, Gortik—it's good to see you. I mean, really *see* you!" He stepped impulsively forward and clasped Shoogar's right hand. "Shoogar, thank you, thank you, for taking such care of my seeing pieces!" He was smiling—He actually meant it!

Shoogar was caught by surprise. He muttered, "You're welcome," without even realizing he had. "Now we can build a flying machine?"

"Yes," laughed Purple, "now we can build a flying machine!"

Gortik and I looked at each other. It was a start. If only they didn't kill each other trying.

I was beginning to understand what old Thran had meant when he used to say, "A man is not fit to be Speaker until he has first led a flock of goats through a forest of crazyfern."

In fact, I was beginning to suspect that the goatherding task might be easier.

For instance, it appeared that *I* had to organize the flying machine construction. I appointed Wilville and Orbur as officials aides and instructed them never to leave Purple and Shoogar alone together—not for any reason whatever.

The boys nodded soberly. They understood all too well, but they were willing to accept the task—they were as eager to build the flying machine as Purple and Shoogar were.

Now if only the other men of the village would be as willing to accept my leadership.

I smiled bitterly at the thought. If only the seas were Quaff, we could all get drunk—I might as well wish for a moon to fall out of the sky and carry away all my problems. The way things were going, if the seas were to turn to Quaff, I would find only a bladder with a hole in it.

Hinc and the others had wanted to stay, then they wanted to migrate, then they wanted to stay—then they found out that staying meant they would have to clear the upper slopes, bind new housetrees, build extra nests and make the area livable—and they wanted to move on again. They wanted to do everything but work.

To tell the truth though, the woods here *were* wild—they were a savage tangle of red crabvines and scraggly blackbushes. Broken branches hung everywhere, and stingbee nests were a common sight. Graygauzes hung from almost every branch, and once we found a hollow of nesting vampire kites.

Everywhere else the woods seemed delightfully tame and well cared for—but here, where we were supposed to settle, here it was as if all the wildness had been stored for the rest of the forest.

Or perhaps we had not noticed these things until we began to work.

We all nursed stings and bites. The women were never less than exhausted.

We men ate badly—sometimes worse than on the trail— and lived in chaos. That the work was tiring was no secret. For once even the women were allowed to grumble. The children helped or hindered as suited their whims, and in general had a fine time.

Shoogar appeared each morning at the rising of the blue sun and blessed the day with a hasty chant: *"blessèd art Thou, Ouells, father and mother of all the gods, who hast commanded our women to work for us."* Then he disappeared back into his nest to sleep until noon.

Meanwhile the shepherds had located several excellent pastures on which to graze the sheep. And they were delighted —at first—with the workforce sent up from the lower village. One of the lads was identical twins—so that though he was counted only as one, he did the work of two. In effect we had four novice shepherds to pick the burrs out of the wool and comb the sheep.

That, of course, freed several of the more experienced novices to work alongside the rest of us in the sloping wood. They appreciated that not at all.

Life in the sloping wood gradually became more pleasant than wandering across the deserts—that is, once we had housetrees and nests enough for our own needs. Hinc began to talk of weaving again, and began testing various fiberplants and trees. Jark was daily to be seen testing some new and exotic kind of root or herb as a flavoring for Quaff. Ang, faced by an absence of frogs, changed his vocation and set up fishing rods along the stream. And I——

Now that I had settled the affairs of two villages and their magicians, I was ready to return to bonemongering.

Trone the Coppersmith was a dealer in metals and a member of the Guild of Advisors of the Lower Village. He was a broad scowling man who spoke in monosyllables. The hair of his head and torso was brown and coarse. He seemed to regard my wares with disfavor.

I was at a loss to understand his hostility. At the beginning of our trek I had taken only the most valuable pieces of petrified bone from the ruins of the village. Later, on the trek, I had increased my store from a desert trove, an ancient runforit skeleton, dry and hard as stone. Trone should have been impressed, but he wasn't.

"What's the matter?" I asked him. "Do you fear the competition?"

"Hah!" he snapped. "Bone is no competition for metal. It is not strong enough. A copper hammer will not break, a bone hammer will."

"There are other uses for bone. I can carve out ceremonial bowls and ritual ornaments."

"True," the coppersmith admitted, "but why don't you

discuss this matter with Bellis the Potter—he might have something to say about that."

Bellis the Potter. What was a potter?

I learned that by watching him at work. He took clay from the bottom of the river and worked it into the shapes of bowls. When it dried, it was as hard as any bone though far more brittle. Bellis had worked this into a high art, baking the clay ornaments in the hot sunlight until they would not go soft in the water, and could be used to carry water, soup, stews. He had even learned ways to paint and decorate the bowls and harden them by fire.

It was possible to make other things as well out of clay. Bellis was considered one of the best workers of his craft in the region. Indeed, he could do things with his clay that I could not do with my bone.

"But," I suggested, "you cannot use these devices for rituals and festives. Surely the Gods would be offended by the use of a bowl or ornament without a soul. Only bone has a soul."

Bellis was a squat man, short and bent, almost deformed. He looked up at me through wizened eyes. "My father used clay bowls to consecrate the births of all of his children, and my family has used clay bowls for as long as there has been either family or clay to make bowls out of. If there were Gods who would be offended by such use, we would have heard from them by now."

Which might account for his twisted shape, I thought. But since I had no wish to quarrel with him, I said only, "But clay has no soul."

"All the more reason to use it. You can cast a spell without having to allow for or nullify the powers and attitudes latent in your utensils." Like a bonemonger in my own region, Bellis the Potter understood some rudimentary magic, at least enough to discuss his needs with a magician. "Your trade is outmoded, Lant the Speaker. You will soon find that there is little market for bone here."

"Oh, I will always have a trade," I said. "Shoogar will not easily abandon the old ways—at least, he will always have a need for my craft."

"Oh?" said Bellis. "You see that pile of bowls and pots over there? You see this one that I am making now? All of these are for Shoogar. I can make clay bowls faster and easier than you can carve them out of bone, and Shoogar can use them right away. There are no latent influences to neutralize."

I felt betrayed. Bellis was right, of course. To a magician at least, the advantages of clay over bone were enormous. And to the average person as well—one need not say a prayer of sorrow if one broke a clay bowl, one need only throw away the pieces—and that was that.

I knew it instinctively—there was no market for bone here. Probably there never would be, for the best bone is petrified bone and bone would not, could not, petrify here—the climate was too wet. I should have realized it earlier.

I could understand now why Hinc and the others had wanted to move on. Hinc was a weaver—but there were better weavers here. Jark was a Quaff-maker—but there was such an abundance of fermentable plants here, everybody made their own Quaff or chewed *raba*-root. And I was a bonemonger—but nobody used bone at all.

Even though we *wanted* to move on, we could not do so until the seas receded—and that time was a long way off. And I doubted that anyone would want to migrate then—already many had announced themselves satisfied with their new homes.

During the dry seasons, Gortik had told me, when the seas were down, this island was actually a peninsula off the main southern continent. We could see the larger mass of it across the swollen channel, some twenty-odd miles away. But for all the good it could do us, it might have been beyond the world's edge.

There was just our double village and four others on the island. All were near the shoreline. Every second hand of days, a trading caravan came round bringing the news and goods of the other towns and taking away the news and goods of ours. I soon found out that they had no use for a bonemonger either.

No wonder I had seen no bonemonger here—they had all starved to death. When the local villagers wanted to indi-cate futility, they said, "You might as well go carve bone."

It was a fine time to find that out, I thought bitterly.

Well, so I had no trade I must concentrate instead on Speaking for my village. I wondered if I dared tithe my people to pay me for the labor of Speaking for them. I had heard of

villages where the Speaker collected a toll from each fully
grown man. But I sensed that my tribe would object strongly.
My control was still too weak for me to risk such a test of
power.

Then Wilville and Orbur would have to support me, that
was all there was to it. But no, Wilville and Orbur were working for Shoogar and Purple in the lower village. Shoogar and
Purple were accepting responsibility for the two of them.

Hm. If they were taking care of my sons, they could easily
accept the care of the rest of my family, including me.

After all, it was the two villages that supported the magicians. If they were to support me too, they would in effect
be paying my tithe without ever knowing it.

Yes, it would work. I could tell Gortik that I had decided
not to ply my trade until after the affair with Purple and
Shoogar was settled. My skill as a diplomat would be required
to help them work together in order to speed Purple's ultimate
departure.

Yes, Gortik would accept that.

I went to tell them what I had decided.

I found Purple and Shoogar wrangling over a writingskin
with complicated markings all over it. Wilville was sitting on
a stone crying in frustration. Orbur was patting him on the
back.

The source of the trouble was a perplexing one. Purple was
trying to convince Shoogar that the lines on the skin were a
flying machine. Shoogar didn't understand and neither did I.

"Listen, lizardhead," he was saying, "animal skins don't fly.
They need animals in them even to move."

"The skin doesn't fly!" Purple screamed. "It's only something to put the flying machine lines on!"

"Oh? Then the lines fly?"

"No—these lines don't, but they are a flying machine.

That is, they are a—" He paused, having trouble choosing
the right word, "—simulacrum."

"Nonsense," said Shoogar, "if this were a simulacrum, it
would be a flying machine in itself. How can it be a simulacrum and not be a flying machine?"

"It's a nonworking simulacrum—" insisted Purple.

"Don't be silly—the two terms are contradictory. It's like
saying it is a nonworking spell."

Purple muttered something in his demon tongue. "It's like
a doll, Shoogar, it's—"

"That's what I mean!" Shoogar cut him off. "A doll is the
person and the person is the doll. What more do you need
to know?"

"The doll isn't the person. The doll is a doll!" snapped
Purple.

"And you are a frognose," Shoogar snapped back.

"Hah! You would be honored if a sheep emptied his bladder
upon you!"

"And you would be honored to be that bladder!"

As one, they both rolled up their sleeves, preparatory to
hurling curses.

Without thinking, I stepped between them. Had I thought
about it, I'm sure I would have been moving in the opposite
direction. "Now stop this, you two—do you want to devastate
another village?"

"If it will remove this fungus eater from my eyesight, it
will be worth it."

"A toad like you should be honored to live in my droppings."

"And where will you go?" I answered. "You'd both do
better to wait until the waters recede before you destroy the
island."

They hesitated. Before they could work up their fury
again, I added, "Besides, you both swore oaths of fealty and
truce. There will be no feuds and no duels. I will mediate all
disagreements—now what is the problem?"

Both spoke at once—like children, they were: "This clot-
sucking dung beetle doesn't know how to do the simplest
of—"

"Stop it! Now stop it!" I turned to Orbur, "Do you understand the conflict?"

He nodded, "They're both fatheads."

Both magicians turned on him, spells at the ready, but Orbur didn't blanch. He said, "Wilville and I understand what it is that Purple wants. If he'll shut up long enough for us to do the work, we can begin building the framework for it. But not if we have to keep stopping to explain it to Shoogar, and not if we have to keep stopping to look at Purple's drawings."

"But these are blue-drawings," insisted Purple. "You need them in order to build the flying machine."

"Fine," said Wilville. "Draw them when we finish. Then you'll have the machine as a model to draw them from."

"But—but that's not the way you're supposed to do it," Purple wailed. "These are *blue*-drawings."

I looked at the animal skin. The lines were black on a brown background. Even with his seeing pieces, Purple's eyesight was none too good. "I don't see that the color of them is that important," I said.

"But it is—you're supposed to have blue-drawings before you build the machine."

"It's part of the spell, then?" I asked. Shoogar looked up.

"Yes, I guess you could say that."

"Well, then why didn't you say so?" Shoogar said.

"I—I don't know."

I looked at them both. "Then it is only a misunderstanding, isn't it?"

"I guess so," said Purple, still looking confused. Shoogar nodded.

"Fine. Then this is what we will do. Wilville and Orbur will start building the framework of the machine and Purple will do the blue-drawings. Shoogar will—well, he'll do something, I'm sure. And I will stay here and help you organize."

They all looked at me. "You? Organize?"

"You will need somebody to help round up labor for you, and materials."

They saw the wisdom of the point and nodded.

"Besides," I added, "someone like me will always be needed to mediate your differences. Now, Wilville, you and Orbur can start building the framework or whatever it is over there and—"

"No, Father. We were thinking of building it up on Idiot's Crag."

"Appropriately named. Why there? You would have to carry all your materials up."

"But it is a high place, a good place to launch a flying machine. And the sea will not rise that high. We can continue to build through Wading Season, if need be."

"H'm. A good suggestion. Then you and Orbur can start building the framework up on Idiot's Crag and Purple will stay here and draw his blue-drawings. And Shoogar will uh— Shoogar will cast a rune of good luck."

Shoogar didn't look any too pleased with his duties, neither did Purple. They both started to object, but I wouldn't hear any of it. I insisted that Wilville and Orbur get to work assembling their tools up on Idiot's Crag.

"Now then," I said to Purple, "if I am to organize this project, I will need to know what I am organizing. What other materials will we need?"

Purple said, "What we are building is a giant boat, one which will be at least five manlengths long, maybe six. We'll attach—"

"Wait, wait. A boat? I thought you intended to fly."

"Yes, that was what I thought too. I would have used a basket, but if I have to come down on water at all, I would rather be in a boat than in a basket."

"That makes sense," I said. Even Shoogar nodded. "Now how will your boat fly?"

"We will make huge bags in which we will trap air that is lighter than air. We will attach them to the boat—they will lift it and the boat will float through the sky."

Shoogar looked up at this. "Air which is lighter than air? Is that like the bubbles of noxious odor that rise from the swamps?"

"You have tried to use swamp gas to make a flying machine?"

Shoogar nodded eagerly.

"That's more intelligent than anything I would have expected of you, Shoogar. You are more advanced than I thought—that is just what we are going to do. In principle, that is—we will not be getting our gas from a swamp."

"Gas?" asked Shoogar. "You use a word—"

"Yes, gas," said Purple, waving his hands excitedly. "Air is many gases mixed together. The gas we will use will come from water. Now, do you see this?" Purple pointed to a circle on his animal skin. "This is a big bag. We will fill——"

"That is not a big bag!" Shoogar screamed suddenly. "That is a blue-drawing!"

At that, I took Purple aside and explained to him that he'd better not try to use his blue-drawings to explain anything to Shoogar. Shoogar did not like blue-drawing spells because he did not understand them.

Purple shrugged and turned back to Shoogar, "Uh, forget the blue-drawings, Shoogar. You are right, this is not a big bag, this is a blue-drawing. But we will use big bags to lift the boat. We will fill them with my lighter-than-air gas." He turned to me. "We will need several things. We will need a boat shell. These people here do not know how to build boats as big as you did up north, and Wilville and Orbur know much about working with wood. They can teach the local boatsmith a thing or two. We will also need cloth, fine cloth, out of which we will tailor the bags. Fortunately, the weaving here is among the finest in the region. Thirdly, we will need gas to fill the bags. I can supply that."

"Then all is settled," I said. "We can easily build the flying machine."

"Wrong," said Purple; "unfortunately, Wilville and Orbur have so far been unable to find the proper materials for a boat frame."

"Huh? I thought you just said——"

"They know only how to build boats out of heavy wood," said Purple, "and this boat must be light as well as strong. It must be made out of the lightest wood possible. Secondly, the quality of the cloth here is still unusable for the gasbags. It is too coarse. We are going to have to teach these people how to weave finer material."

"And what about the gas?" asked Shoogar. "Is there some reason why we can't get that either?"

Purple shook his head, "No, it should be an easy matter to separate the water. I can use my battery, or Trone the Coppersmith can build me a spark-wheel."

"Separate the water? Battery? Spark-wheel?"

"Water is two gases. We will separate them and use one in the gasbags."

Shoogar shook his head at this, but if it worked, it worked.

Apparently Purple knew what he was talking about. The rest
of us would have to wait and see. I delegated Shoogar the
task of obtaining samples of cloth from the various weavers
in the region. He protested at first, but I took him aside and
impressed upon him the importance of having the right kind
of spell materials. He protested until I pointed out that he
could take advantage of the fact by acquainting himself with
the local spells in the process. He nodded agreeably and left.

Wilville and Orbur had already begun to mark out the
outlines of the boat with stakes and twine. It looked like a
large flat-bottomed barge.

"No, no!" screamed Purple, when they explained to him.
"It should be narrower, and it should have a keel, like so!"

"Put away the blue-drawings," I insisted. "We don't need
them."

After he calmed down, we began again—this time at the
beginning. Wilville and Orbur moved the stakes in to form a
narrower outline. They shook their heads. "What will keep it
from capsizing?" they asked.

"Outriggers, we will have outriggers," Purple explained
that the boat should have narrow pontoons, held out like
so from the sides.

"Then what will keep the thing level when it is suspended
in the air?"

"A keel, of course—a heavier beam of wood at the bottom
of the hull."

"But if it is heavier, won't it weigh down the boat too
much?"

He considered that. "You may be right. If it does, we may
have to add another gasbag."

To tell the truth, I didn't understand much of the discussion. It began to get too technical for me—but once
Wilville and Orbur started to understand what Purple meant
they began discussing the project in excited terms. The three

of them argued happily back and forth, Wilville and Orbur nodding and gesticulating with every new idea.

Indeed, at one point they began scratching diagrams in the dirt in order to help them understand. When they did this, Purple tried to bring out his blue-drawings again, but they rejected them as having little or no relevance at all to the project. It was the dirt-drawings which were necessary to the construction of the device.

Obviously my sons understood what needed to be built and how to do it. The why of it sometimes eluded them, but Purple was willing to explain. Several times the boys suggested alternative and better ways—especially when the discussion turned to how they would rig the gasbags to the boat frame.

"Why not sew up just one very big bag as large as all the others?" Orbur asked.

Purple held up the hem of his robe of office in two hands and gave it a yank. It did not rip, but the weave parted easily. It looked like a piece of strainer cloth. "If all I have is one bag and this happens," said Purple, "then I am marooned at sea, or even high in the air! But if I have many bags and this happens, I can only lose one at a time."

Orbur nodded excitedly. "Yes, yes, I see. I see." They turned back to the problem of rigging the boat with a variable number of gasbags.

When Shoogar returned from his task two days later, he bore with him a double armful of samples of different kinds of cloth. "I have visited every weaver on the island," he puffed. "All are eager to supply our needs. This is their finest cloth."

That evening we met with them—it was a council of all the weavers of both the Upper and Lower Villages, and representative weavers from the four other townships of the peninsula/island. The five of us sat with them and discussed the possibilities of using each type of cloth.

The only jarring note was Hinc—he demanded to know why I was officiating—a mere bonemonger.

I replied that I was here as Speaker, and also as organizer of the project.

That failing, he challenged my sons, "And why are they here? I thought this was to be a council of weavers and magicians."

"It is—but they are helping to build the flying machine. They have as much right to participate in these discussions as you. Perhaps more."

Chastened, he sat down.

Purple had two simple tests for each type of cloth. First, he would give each one a yank to see how easily the weave would spread. More than half of the samples failed this test. Purple said to the weavers who had submitted them that if they could not do better than that, then there was no point in their staying. Several left, just as glad that they wouldn't be working with the mad magician.

The second test was just as easy. He formed a sack out of each piece of cloth and poured water into it. He then counted slowly while the water leaked out. Clearly he was searching for the cloth that was tightest and would hold water longest. "If the cloth will hold water," he explained, "it can be made to hold air. But if none of these cloths work, we will have to find one that will. Even if we must weave it ourselves."

We went through the finest goods in the region, while Purple shook his head sadly and told them that each was too coarse. None would hold water for more than a minute.

Naturally the weavers bristled. Several more left in a huff. Had they not been facing the two greatest magicians in the world, undoubtedly they would have challenged us all to a battle for the right of survivorship at the following blue dawn.

"Humph," said white-furred old Lesta; "why do you want to carry water in a clothbag anyway? Why don't you use a pot like a normal person?"

"The spell calls for a bag, you butter-wart!" snapped Shoogar. Lesta hissed back, but said nothing else.

Purple ignored this interchange. He lay down the last piece

of cloth sadly and said, "It is as I feared—these are all too coarse for our purposes. Can't you do better?"

"Those are our best—and if they are the best we can do, then you will not find anyone anywhere who can match them, let alone surpass them."

Purple opened what he called his "impact suit" and peeled it away from his arms and torso. He took off the shirt underneath—revealing (Gods protect us!) his pale, nearly hairless chest. I had known about this already from my number one wife, but the men of the other villages gasped in disbelief. The sight of Purple's fat paunch was almost too much.

Purple ignored it. Instead he handed them the shirt—he pushed it at the man who had spoken. "Here is finer cloth," he said.

The man took it, he turned it over curiously and examined both sides. He rubbed it between his fingers.

"That should prove to you that finer weaves are possible," Purple said.

Other weavers were reaching for it now. Quickly, the shirt was passed around the circle. It was sniffed at and tasted, touched and murmured over. The weavers were incredulous at its quality.

At last it reached old Lesta. He held it up to the light and peered. He gave it a yank and peered at it again. He rubbed it between his fingers. He sniffed at it, made a face, and tasted it. He made another face. At last, he folded it into a sack and stepped to the center of the clearing. One of the other weavers, perceiving what he was intending, hefted a clay pot of water and poured it into the sack. It held.

Lesta counted slowly, but only a little water seeped out ——and at such a rate that it would take all day to empty the sack. "Humph," he said and let the water splash to the ground. It glinted wetly in the red light. "You are right," he said. "This is a fine piece of cloth—why don't you use this?"

"Because I haven't got enough of it," said Purple, retrieving his shirt. He began wringing the water out of it. "I want you to match this."

"Why should I even bother to try?" grumbled Lesta. "If you want cloth that fine, go where you got that piece."

"I'm trying to!" Purple exploded. "I want to go home. I am marooned in a strange land, and I want to go home."

I pitied him. I couldn't help it. We too were marooned in an alien land. Even though it was Purple's fault, I still pitied him.

Purple turned away from the circle of weavers and began shrugging back into his still-damp shirt. Clearly, he was embarrassed at his outburst.

I waited until he had covered his alien pink flesh. Then I turned to Lesta. "You cannot weave cloth like that, can you?"

Lesta muttered something under his breath.

"What was that?"

"No," he said. "No, I cannot. Nobody can. It is demon-cloth."

"But if you could learn to weave cloth like that," I suggested, "that would make you the greatest weaver in the land, wouldn't it?"

"I am already the greatest weaver in the land!" he screamed.

"Oh," I said, "but what would happen to you if *another* learned how to make cloth like this——?"

He stopped breathing.

"and if you could not . . .?"

He didn't answer. He glared at me, at Purple, at me again. Abruptly he regained himself. "Nonsense," he said. "It can't be done."

"Purple has a shirt that shows it can be done. If necessary he will teach other weavers how to duplicate it."

Lesta bristled. He started to turn away, then turned back. He opened his mouth to speak, then closed it. He started to gesture to Purple, then pulled back his hand. He glared. "It can't be done," he repeated. "But if it could be, then I could do it! If anyone can do it, it's going to be me!"

At that Purple turned back to us, still fastening his impact suit. "All right, Lesta," he said. "I accept your statement——"

Lesta looked pleased.

"and I am going to help you prove it."

Lesta stopped looking so pleased. He swallowed hard. Suddenly he no longer had any choice in the matter; the alternative was to lose face—and his position as head weaver.

We went to examine the looms.

Purple's claim that he could teach a finer quality of weaving was accepted, but his insistence that he be allowed to examine the looms met with some resistance.

"But how can I teach you anything unless I can see the looms you are working with?"

Lesta shrugged, "You will have to teach us here."

"But I can't," said Purple. "I have to see the looms."

"And I can't allow that."

"Then there will be no new cloth. I will have to seek a weaver who will show me his looms."

At that the old weaver relented and led us toward his secret clearing. Only weavers were allowed to enter it. That Lesta was willing to break a generations-old tradition showed how important he considered Purple's cloth.

As we approached we could hear the sounds of great creaking machinery, shuddering and protesting. This was alternated with shouts and commands—it made a steady rhythm: a shout and a shudder, a command and a creak.

We entered the glade and caught our first sight of the looms. They were heavy wooden structures—giant moving frames set at odd angles to each other. They rocked steadily back and forth at each command, and it looked as if the cloth appeared between them. Some of the looms were covered with spiderweb traceries of threads, others with half-pieces of brown undyed cloth stretched across them.

The team leader caught sight of us then, and his command stuck in his throat. The frameworks halted in their busy motion, slowed and came to a stop. Their flashing threads were stilled. The novices and journeymen turned to stare as one.

"No, no," said Purple; "make them continue, make them continue."

Lesta snapped orders at his weavers. They looked at him

questioningly—Weave? With strangers here? He growled menacingly.—I could see why he was head weaver. The apprentices went nervously back to work. The team leader swallowed and issued his command, the looms began grinding again.

The young men sweated as they pushed the heavy wooden frames back and forth, back and forth, while the younger boys played a form of catch with a ball of yarn between the two frames.

I had never seen weaving before, and I was entranced by the process. Lesta explained it: there are two vertical sets of threads, each set in a separate frame and independent of each other, but interlocked in such a way that they alternate. The horizontal threads are laid on one at a time, the frames are moved so as to reverse their positions, and another horizontal thread is strung.

Purple nodded slowly, as if he understood everything. Perhaps he did. He examined a sample of the cloth they were weaving and asked, "Could you not weave it finer than this?"

"I could, in principle—but where would I find loom teeth fine enough to string the threads so close? And where would I get thread fine enough to use on such teeth?"

Purple ran his fingertips along the cloth. "Where does it come from, your thread?"

"This is from the fiberplant. Sometimes we use wool from sheep when we can barter for it, but usually it is too coarse or too scarce."

"There are no finer threads available?"

The other shook his head.

Purple muttered in his own language. "Too primitive even for basic industrial facilities . . ." Though they did not understand what he was saying, the weavers bristled. His tone made it clear enough—he was disparaging their work, perhaps even cursing it.

He looked up, "There is no other way of making cloth that you know of, is there?"

"If there was, I would be making it that way," said Lesta perfunctorily.

"You have never heard of *rubber?*"

"*Rubber?* What is *rubber?*"

Purple turned to me and Shoogar, "Do either of you know

of any kind of tree or plant that leaks a sticky kind of sap?"

We shook our heads.

"There is the sweetbush plant," offered Shoogar. "It has a sticky secretion."

"It does?" Purple was eager.

"Yes, the children love to suck on the sweetdroppings."

"No," sighed the magician. "That will never do. I need a kind of sticky substance that hardens into a gummy lump."

We all looked at each other, each wishing the other to come up with the answer.

"Oh well," sighed Purple again. "I knew it wasn't going to be easy. Look, I need some kind of material that can be heated and molded—liquid that dries in sheets or layers."

We all shook our heads again.

While Purple continued to describe his mystical sticky substance to them, I moved closer to examine the looms. The weavers looked at me with ill-concealed hostility, but I ignored them. The teeth of the looms were carved from hardwood limbs. Each section was about one hand-length and set into a slot at the top of the frame.

"Are these the finest teeth you have?" I asked.

"No, we have one set finer than this," quavered the apprentice I had spoken to. "But we never use them because they are too fragile and break. We have to go very slowly when we use them."

"H'm," I said. "Why don't you carve the teeth out of bone?"

"Bone?"

"Bone-carved teeth would not only be stronger, but you could carve them much finer than this. You could carve two or three times as many teeth to a knuckle-length."

The man shrugged. "I don't know about those things."

I examined the frame again, climbing up on the platform to do so. I wanted to check the slot to see how each piece was fastened. Yes, it would be possible to carve bone to fit into that slot. I pulled out a measuring string and began tying measuring knots into it.

Abruptly Lesta saw what I was doing and broke away from Purple, "Hey, what is that? You're stealing our secrets!"

I protested, "No, I'm not. What would I do with them?

Do you want finer teeth for your looms? I can provide them within a hand of days, maybe sooner."

He looked up at me, Purple and Shoogar moved up behind him. "How?" he asked. "There are the finest and strongest teeth possible."

"I will carve you better ones out of bone."

"Bone!" The old man was horrified. "You would desecrate the cloth with the soul of an animal? Cloth comes from trees and fiberplants. You must use the teeth of the tree, not the teeth of the animal."

"But I can carve teeth four or five times as fine as these!"

At that Purple's head perked up. "You can? Lant, that will be great. That would be almost as fine a weave as we need."

"Hah!" said Lesta. "I can achieve a weave that fine already —if I wanted to."

"How would you do that?" I demanded.

"I would compact the weave, that's all."

"Compact the weave?" asked Purple.

He nodded, "It is a simple process. We use the same number of threads, but we press them inward so they take up less width. You see that loom over there?"

We looked. The framework had a half-finished piece of cloth on it. It was a small piece of cloth, less than one half the width of the loom, but at its edges the threads stretched and spread evenly to every tooth on the frame.

"There," said Lesta, "that cloth is compacted. You want a fine weave? That is how we will get it."

Purple had gone over to examine the cloth.

Lesta followed. I jumped down from the platform and ragtagged over. Lesta was saying, "Of course, if we compact it, you won't have as wide a cloth as—"

"I'm not concerned about its width," Purple said. "If necessary we'll weave more of it. I'm concerned about its tightness."

Lesta shrugged. "As you will."

Purple turned to him. "If Lant were to carve new loom-teeth out of bone, could you compact that weave as well?"

"Of course—you can compact any weave you want," said Lesta. "But you will not use bone on my looms."

"But it's the only way—"

"There will be *no* bone teeth on my looms," repeated the weaver.

Shoogar was standing right behind him. He said, "Do you want to get hit with the termite blight?"

The old man paled. He whirled on Shoogar, "You wouldn't."

Shoogar was rolling up his sleeves, "Want me to try . . .?"

"Uh—" Lesta eyed him warily. Obviously he didn't. He took a step back, then another, a third and he bumped into Purple. He jumped away and looked at us, glanced nervously at his looms, then said, "Well, I suppose I should keep up with the latest developments in the craft, shouldn't I . . .?"

"A wise decision, old man!" Purple boomed. He clapped the weaver on the back. "I am glad that is settled. Lant will begin carving the new teeth immediately."

I was delighted. If nothing else, I would unload most of that runforit skeleton after all. What luck! The carving of the teeth would take care of most of the flat bones and all I'd have to worry about then would be the hundred and twenty-eight ribs.

Now, let's see, I'd probably still have to sand some of the pieces flatter, then carve slits into them—the best way might be to use a cutting thread to slice very narrow lines. H'm, it would be like carving a bone comb, but faster because I would not have to carve so deep. I could use a framework of cutting threads, and cut all the slots in a section at once. If I measured it precisely enough, each section would be the same as every other one.

The *same* as every other one—that was an interesting thought! If one broke, you could replace it immediately; there would be no delay in carving a new piece to fit. You could always keep a couple of extras around. That seemed practical. Hmm . . .

I wondered; I might be able to finish the teeth even sooner if I could find some apprentices—but no, there was not enough free labor in either of the villages. The only thing we had an excess of was women—and most of them were less than useless.

We discussed some of the details for awhile longer, until at last Purple stretched his arms over his head and stared up into the sky. "Ah," he yawned, "let's call it a red day."

"Good idea," I said. "My wives will be preparing the

midnight meal. Tonight I would like to get to it before darkness falls."

We climbed toward the Upper Village. We were far enough past the interpassage that there would be a period of darkness between red sunset and blue dawn. Shoogar might even get a glimpse of the moons.

"I'm sure we would all appreciate a rest," I said.

"I know I would," Shoogar muttered. "I have a housetree cultivation ceremony to perform at blue dawn."

"Why don't you come?" I said impulsively to Purple. "You'll enjoy it."

"I just might do that," he said.

As we entered the Upper Village we could see Damd the Tree Binder preparing the virgin tree for cultivation. A wild housetree is a thick sturdy giant with pliable limbs; it must be bound and strengthened before it can hold a house. The lowest branches must be softened and treated, and then bent into the ground to grow into roots. The upper branches must be twined together to form a cradle for the nest. Within a hand of days the nest weaver can begin his work.

At Wilville and Orbur's insistence, Purple ate with me and my family. Ordinarily, I would never have invited him anywhere near my nest, but the alternative was to publicly refuse—and that might have offended the men of the Lower Village.

As it turned out, I need not have feared. Purple and Wilville and Orbur were so excited about their project that they spoke of nothing else throughout the whole meal—and we were having fresh sea leeches too! The three of them argued back and forth about methods of construction and the principles by which the machine would work. I tried to follow as best as I could, but most of it was beyond me—at last I had to give up and turn my attention instead to calming my nervous wives. All this talk of flying machines and airbags was upsetting them enormously. The two of them twittered nervously in the background and refused to approach except at my sternest command. Finally, I had to threaten to beat them and refuse them our table scraps.

Shoogar had been invited to join us too, but he had declined. Instead, he had spent the whole twenty minutes of darkness up on Idiot's Crag, straining to catch a glimpse of the moons. At blue dawn he was furious. Only one of the three largest moons had shown, and that only for a second as two clouds parted. Shoogar had been unable to tell which moon it was.

It was just as well. I knew what he wanted from the sky, and I would be just as glad if he never found it.

Purple had never seen a cultivation before. He stood and watched as Shoogar offered the seventeen blessings in Quaff borrowed from the Lower Village.

Shoogar was relaxed as I had not seen him relax since his confrontation with Purple. It did him good to get his mind off the complexities and unknowns of a flying spell. A cultivation is mostly a simple rote reciting, so basic and foolproof that even the position of the moons cannot change it.

Purple watched politely while Shoogar chanted in his brightly marked robe and heavy headdress, prayer shawl and beads. When Shoogar sprinkled the quaff at the base of the tree, he muttered something about *comparative somethings* and *fertility rites*. Demon words again.

At last we reached my favorite part of the ceremony. All of the women and children shed their clothes and began dancing around the newly sanctified tree, singing, and painting stripes round and round the trunk in bright colored dyes. Purple's interest immediately perked up. "What spell is this?" he asked.

"What?" I didn't understand his question.

"What is the purpose of this spell? Perhaps you hope to frighten away the red strangling crabvines, or the termite blight, or—??"

"No, Purple. They're doing that for fun."

"For fun—" Purple's naked face turned pink. He watched a bit longer, then gradually lost interest in the ceremony. It did go on for a very long time. He wandered off morosely.

It was only when Shoogar got to the tree-bleeding that

Purple's attention returned. He was sitting dourly off to one side, lost in thought. Now, as Damd the Tree Binder began tapping into the veins of the tree and Shoogar began chanting again, he looked up.

"What are they doing now?"

"Bleeding the tree," shouted one of the children derisively. What kind of a magician was this, who did not even recognize a simple cultivation ceremony?

We watched patiently as Shoogar blessed the blood of the tree and anointed the tied limbs and roots-to-be. Guided by Damd's ropes and Shoogar's chanted instructions, the lowest limbs would become additional sections of trunk. The higher limbs, which had been bent downward and tied together, would grow into a strong circular framework for a nest.

The spell was nearing completion when Purple abruptly stepped into the middle of it. He brushed through the circle of chanting women and ran a finger through the blood of the tree.

The chanting stopped instantly. We stood frozen in shock, wondering why Purple would break a treespell. And Shoogar, furious, reached for a pouch at his waist.

Thoughtfully Purple said, "It may be that we can use this sap." He turned to Shoogar, his sticky fingers outstretched.

Shoogar was taken aback. He hesitated, he forgot the pouch in his hand, and doubtless he remembered his oath. But his voice was thick with fury as he asked, "Is that why you smashed the delicate web of my magic?"

"Shoogar, you don't understand." Purple rubbed the sticky substance between his palms, savoring its feel. "It may be that I can use this substance for the air bags."

"Housetree blood for a flying machine? *Housetree blood?*"

"Certainly," said Purple, "why not?"

The murmur of voices around him should have told Purple why not. It didn't, of course. I stepped quickly through the crowd, took Purple by the arm and led him out. He stumbled along with me almost in a daze, he was murmuring excitedly in his own tongue.

Behind his back I signaled Shoogar to start the ceremony again. I moved off to one side with Purple and tried to get some sense out of him.

"It's like natural rubber, Lant. I'll have to try it, of course, but it may be just what I need to hold the gas in the bags—"

"Forget it, Purple. You can't use housetree blood. Housetrees are sacred."

"Sacred be damned. I must have an airtight container. Will you stop jumping around like that?"

"Then stop using those horrendous curses!"

"What curses—??" He looked puzzled. "Oh, never mind." He went back to examining the sap on his hands.

"Can't you use something else besides housetree blood? Infant blood, for instance—I'm sure we could—"

"No!" he gasped. "No! Definitely not—no human blood—it wouldn't work anyway."

"You said that if your cloth was watertight it would be airtight. What about pottery? Could you hold your light gas in large pottery containers?"

"No, no, they're too heavy—much too heavy—we've got to try the housetree blood. It may be the only way. You see, the cloth we've got just isn't good enough—but if they can weave the finer cloth, and if we can soak it in housetree sap and then dry it, perhaps that might work. We'd have to try different arrangements, of course—"

"But—but—" I sputtered. There had to be a way out of this mess. Purple was desperate to fly; but Shoogar and the villagers would never permit housetree sap to be so defiled. A duel was in the offing, unless——

A weird thought occurred to me. I would have dismissed it instantly, even with my layman's knowledge of magic. But Purple was so oddly unorthodox——

I said, "There is one chance. Now, don't laugh, Purple, but could you possibly use the sap of a *wild* housetree in the same spell—?"

"Yes, of course. Why not?"

"Huh?" I was incredulous. "You mean you could??"

"Of course." There was an odd expression on Purple's face, a delighted expression. "Sap is sap."

"Uh, it isn't, you know—" but he wasn't listening. He was fidgeting impatiently.

"Lant," he said. "I will need to experiment. I will need

a wild housetree and some pots—and some cloth—and—
and—"

"See Wilville and Orbur. They will help you get what you
need. You do know how to recognize a wild housetree, don't
you?"

"Of course. The roots and branches won't be bent." And
off he went.

It was the right answer, of course—but I was still surprised. Purple was *so* unorthodox.

By the time I had finished the first set of loomteeth,
Purple and Shoogar had finished their first set of experiments with wild housetree sap. Purple knew what he wanted
to achieve, and Shoogar knew best how to achieve it.

The heated sap could be treated with certain other
magician's chemicals to make a putrid and foul smelling
soup. Cloth could be dipped into this soup, and it would form
an airtight seal. However, the seal was neither as tight nor
as permanent as Purple had wished and so they continued
to experiment.

On the day I began carving the third set of loomteeth,
Purple announced that he had reached a solution to the
problem of weaving a watertight cloth. Instead of dipping
the whole cloth into the housetree soup, he would dip the
spun threads before they were woven. When the thread dried
it was impregnated with the sap and it had a smooth and
shiny feel.

Cloth woven from these treated threads could then be
treated in a modified housetree-binding solution and dried
again. The threads, already soaked with housetree blood,
would swell and join and become one solid material, im-
permeable to air and water.

Purple was delighted. If thread could be woven fine
enough, and if my bone loomteeth would work as expected,

then surely we could weave a cloth light enough and tight enough for the flying machine.

By the time I had finished the third set of loomteeth, Lesta had already woven several swatches of fine aircloth for Purple. It was smooth and shiny, and the weave was almost invisible to the eye.

"Isn't it beautiful, Lant?" Purple exclaimed.

I had to admit that it was. Old Lesta beamed with pride.

Purple had been running from person to person, stopping them, and demanding that they feel his cloth. "Why, when the rest of the loomteeth are finished, we will be able to make a cloth of such quality———" He was so overcome with emotion, he could not finish the sentence.

Lesta was only slightly more subdued. "Lant," he demanded, "I must have more of those loomteeth. I must have as many as you can carve. We are going to weave nothing but aircloth!"

"That will be great!" cried Purple. "Thank you—I will be able to use all you can weave!"

Lesta stared at him. "Do you think it's for you, you fuzzwort? This cloth will be in demand for miles around—we must prepare for that. When the waters go down again and the trade routes are reopened, we will be prosperous indeed!"

"Aaarggh!" said Purple. His face was red and blue and several other colors at once. "Betrayer!" he cried. "You must first weave enough cloth to satisfy my needs and purposes."

"Nonsense," muttered Lesta, "we have no agreement."

"Snakeroot slime we don't! I was to show you how to weave a finer cloth," he raged, "and in return, you were to weave enough for my flying machine!"

"Blither-blather," snarled Lesta, "it's a magician's duty to continually improve the way of life of his people. You were merely performing your duties, Purple—and for the first time, too!" he added.

"Wait a minute," I cried. "Let me settle this."

They both looked at me.

"It is my duty to aid the magicians whenever and wherever possible. This is precisely the type of situation in which I must arbitrate."

"Lant is right," said Purple. "Go ahead, Lant."

Lesta glared at me. "Let's hear what you have to say first," he grumbled.

"Go on, Lant."

"Well——" I said. "It is quite obvious to me what the situation is here. Purple is the magician, Lesta is the weaver. Purple has shown Lesta how to weave a cloth of a quality so fine that hitherto it has been unknown to men. Purple is now demanding payment for such knowledge, correct?"

They both nodded.

"However, Lesta has charged that he owes Purple nothing. Purple was merely performing his sworn duty as village magician to uplift the way of life of all men. Still correct?"

Again they nodded.

"Well, it is all quite simple," I said. "It is obvious; Lesta is right."

"Huh——?" Purple's jaw fell open with a snap.

Lesta beamed. "You are right, Lant. I will abide by your decision." He threw a mocking glance at Purple.

"Now wait a minute, Lant——" Purple began.

"You heard him," rapped out Lesta. "And you said you were willing to abide by his decision!"

"No, I didn't—I said I'd wait to hear what he had to say——" cried Purple. "Lant, what are you doing——?"

"Wait a minute!" I shouted again, "Wait a minute!"

Again they looked to me.

"I have not finished speaking," I said.

They quieted.

"Lesta is right," I repeated. "He owes Purple nothing. However," I said slowly, "he does owe me——"

"Huh?"

"For the loomteeth," I said. "You are using my loomteeth. I carved them, they belong to me."

"You?" he said. "What would you use them for?"

I pretended to shrug nonchalantly. "Oh, I don't know," I said. "I might rent them out to various weavers; or I might become a weaver myself."

"We would smash your looms!" he snarled.

"And risk the wrath of Shoogar?" I said. "No, you wouldn't. Instead, you will pay me a fair price for the use of the teeth—as any other weaver would."

"I am not any other weaver!" shouted Lesta. "I pay no

price. You should be willing to do this out of sheer graciousness and goodwill for being allowed to settle here in this region."

"It is a poor region," I said. "I do not need it. Come, give me my loomteeth—I must go and talk with Hinc the Weaver."

"Uh—wait a minute," said Lesta. "Maybe we can work something out—"

"I'm sure we can. You will be making profit beyond your wildest dreams. You should not begrudge me a fair price for my labor."

His eyes narrowed. "And what is your so-called 'fair price?'"

Purple was gaping open-mouthed at this exchange. I said, "Enough cloth for Purple to build his flying machine, plus five per cent more for me, for my own uses including trading."

"Gack—" said Lesta. I thought he would choke and die right there.

"I have made it possible for you to weave a cloth better than any you have ever woven before!! Do you want to use these loomteeth or not?"

He eyed the flat bone pieces I held. I could see that he wanted them badly—and he knew that I would not hesitate to deal with some other weaver. Already the word was out about this fine new cloth—there was not a weaver in the land who would not jump at the chance to make it.

"Humph," he said. "I will offer you half that—"

"No. It is either all or nothing."

"You ask too much! I cannot——"

I turned and started to walk away. "I think I saw Hinc over by the river—"

"Wait!" he called. I kept walking. "Wait!" He hurried after me, grabbed at my arm. "All right, Lant, all right. You win, you win. I will weave the cloth for Purple, and five per cent more for you."

I stopped walking. "Fine. I will take a guarantee of it."

"Huh?" He stared. "Is not my word enough?"

"No," I said. "Else we would not have had this argument. I will take a guarantee. Two syllables of your secret name."

"Two—two—syllables——??" His mouth worked sound-lessly. He swallowed hard, "You jest——?"

I started up the hill again.

Again he caught my arm, "All right, Lant. All right." He was subdued now, almost chastened. He looked around warily, then whispered into my ear. Two syllables.

"Thank you," I said. "I hope you will never betray me. If you do, I will see that those secret syllables are no longer secret. The first person I'll tell will be Shoogar."

"Oh no, Lant, you have nothing to fear."

"I'm sure of it. Thank you, Lesta. I am glad that we could come to such a pleasant agreement. I will expect the first consignment of cloth within a hand of days."

"Yes, Lant; certainly, Lant; anything, Lant—ah—"

"Yes—?"

"The loomteeth that you're holding——?"

I looked down. "Oh, yes. You'll need them, won't you?" I handed them over.

Purple came up to me then, "Thank you, Lant."

"For what? I was merely doing my duty."

"Yes. Well, thank you for doing that. I appreciate it."

I shrugged. "It was nothing. I am just as eager to see you leave in that flying machine as you are to do it."

I think he misunderstood. He said, "Oh, it will be a sight to see, all right."

"Yes," I said, "I can hardly wait."

Wilville and Orbur were grumbling.

"We've built four bicycles, Father, since we've arrived here—and now we can't use or trade any of them because of your deal with Gortik."

I sighed, "Gortik will tire of his new toy soon enough. Besides, you have more than enough to keep you busy with the flying machine."

"Hah!" grumbled Wilville testily. "Gortik is such a lunk,

he cannot even ride the machine. Seven times already Orbur and I have tried to teach him."

Orbur shook his head, "He keeps crashing into trees."

"He doesn't steer very well," explained Wilville.

"And besides, the flying machine cannot feed us. The bicycles are to trade for food and cloth and tools. Unless we are allowed to ply our trade, we may starve." Orbur shook his head again and sat down on a rock. "And there will never be any profit in flying."

"Well," I said, "I will see what I can arrange. You build your bicycles—I will figure a way for you to trade them." I added, "Besides, I do not believe that Gortik's injunction prohibited you from trading bicycles in your own village, only in his."

They looked dubious, but at my insistence they returned to their work. They spent their mornings on the flying machine and their afternoons on their bicycles, although lately they were spending more and more time on the flying machine.

Purple had decided that they should line the hull with aircloth inside and out—it would make it more watertight. The boys were delighted with this suggestion. They had been having trouble with the balsite wood anyway. It was the lightest wood they had been able to find, but it was hard to work with. They had been using it on a frame of spirit pine, but it was too weak. When they tested it in water, the balsite became waterlogged and soggy. It came off the frame in shreds. The only way to keep the boatframe in one piece was to keep the balsite wood dry—and that was impractical: the machine had to be able to land on water. Purple's suggestion to use aircloth lining solved that, and the boys went eagerly back to work on the large boatframe. But they needed aircloth —and the production of it was still our biggest problem.

"There is not enough thread," Lesta grumbled. "We have not the men to spin, and not enough to weave!"

"I don't understand—" Purple was saying when I arrived on the scene. "You have enough spinners for all your other types of weaving—why not for aircloth?"

"Because aircloth isn't just woven! The thread has to be spun fine and dipped, then it has to be dried. That requires three times as many men working on spinning. Then after the cloth is woven, it has to be dipped again. That's a whole new step! Where am I to get the men for such work? It takes almost twice as long to weave a patch of aircloth as it does to weave anything else———and that patch is only one fourth the size of what we could be weaving because you want it *compacted!*"

"It would not be aircloth if it weren't compacted," said Purple.

"Fine," said Lesta. "You want aircloth, you'll get aircloth. It'll take only eight hundred years."

"Nonsense," said Purple, "there must be a way to—"

"Not if you want it the way you want it—" Lesta was adamant. "It takes nearly a hand of days to spin enough thread for a single patch of the stuff."

"Well, then bring in more spinners—"

"And where am I to get them? I cannot ask my weavers to accept such a demotion, and there are not enough boys in either of our villages to take on as apprentices."

"Why not hire spinners from the other villages on this island?"

"What?—and let them have the secret of aircloth too?"

"They would not have to know about the final step of the dipping of the cloth," I offered.

"Hm. You are right there—but they will never do it."

"Why not?"

"What would their weavers do for thread?"

"Hire their weavers to help spin."

"And how will we feed them? We are but a poor village."

We thought about it. During the time of ungrowing, most food came from the swollen oceans. If Ang, who had turned to seafarming, had enough nets at his command, he was likely to catch enough sea leeches and crawlers to feed the army of weavers Purple was trying to assemble. Of course, Ang would need some help, but we could bring in some extra seafarmers as well.

We discussed it that evening at a special joint meeting of our two Guilds of Advisors. We met in a clearing in the Lower Village. There were almost *a hand of hands* of tradesmen in evidence, and more were arriving all the time.

Almost everyone who spoke, began with: "We cannot do it—"

Ang, for instance: "We cannot do it—I have not enough nets."

"Weave some more."

"I cannot do it—it will take too long to weave enough nets to feed that many people."

"Perhaps Lesta's weavers can help."

"Nonsense, we cannot—my men do not know how to weave nets."

"It's a form of weaving, isn't it?"

"Of course, but——"

"Then they can learn. Ang, will you teach them?"

"Yes, but—"

"There are no buts about it. If we spend the next hand of days just weaving nets for Ang, by the time the new weavers arrive we should be able to feed them regularly. By that time we will have enough aircloth thread on hand to demonstrate the proper weaving techniques to them."

"We cannot do it—" That was Lesta again.

"Why not?"

"I have been figuring. We have enough fiberplants and fibertrees. We will have more than enough thread. As long as there are wild housetrees, we will have the sap—we do not have to worry about these things. But we still do not have enough spinners *in proportion to the weavers*. Our problem now is that we are not producing enough aircloth thread to keep our own weavers busy—if we bring in new weavers and spinners, we will only be multiplying our own problem by five. We will have five times as many weavers sitting around idle waiting for thread. We cannot do it."

"Nonsense," said Purple. "The problem is that we have not enough people spinning, that's all."

"That's all?" retorted Lesta. "Isn't that enough? If we can't find enough people in our own village to make a significant difference, do you think we will be able to find them in another?"

"I have been doing some figuring too," said Purple. He held up a skin which looked suspiciously like a blue-drawing. However, he did not attempt to explain it, he merely waved it conspicuously about. "Now, using our present number of weavers and looms, at the rate of one patch of aircloth produced per hand of days, it will take almost 12 years to make enough for my needs."

This produced a mutter and mumble of voices among the advisors. "Sure, it's fine stuff, but who needs it if it takes that long to weave——"

Purple ignored the interruption. "Now, if we bring in all the weavers and all the spinners of the other villages on this island, that multiplies the rate of production by five and cuts the waiting time down to two and a half years."

"Oh, fine," muttered Lesta. "I'm not sure I could survive even one more year of Purple, let alone two and a half."

Gortik shushed him. Purple ignored this interruption as well. He said, "Now, let's consider the problem—it's not that it takes such a long time to produce a piece of aircloth that is delaying us, not at all—it's just that we don't produce enough of it. If we had more looms and more men to operate them, we could produce larger amounts."

"Of course," nodded Lesta; "and if I were a bird, I could fly—and I wouldn't need aircloth at all." This produced laughter from all the men—and an angry look from both magicians. Shoogar spat in Lesta's direction—it sizzled when it hit the ground.

Purple waved his skin at Lesta. "I have figured this out very carefully. Counting all the weavers in all five villages—and counting all the journeymen and all the novices—and even all the apprentices, there are more than enough——"

"Pfah! Nonsense!"

"—more than enough," Purple repeated. "If all of them are weaving."

"And who will spin the thread for them if all are weaving? Little creatures will come in at night and do it?"

Again laughter.

Purple was one of the most patient men I have ever seen. He cleared his throat and said slowly, "Not at all. First off, I'm surprised you didn't ask where they will weave this cloth."

"Without the thread it doesn't make any difference."

"Let's take this one thing at a time. If every man who is a member of the weaver's caste could become a full-fledged weaver, and if we had enough looms for all of them and each man worked a full day at his loom, we could make as uch aircloth as I need within four—huh, let's see—huh, well efore Lant's wife delivers her child."

"A little more than two hands of hands of days," I said in xplanation.

Lesta was scratching in the dust. "Purple, you're a fool— hat's 175 looms we'd need. We have but six in this village. Vhere are we supposed to get the rest? You'd change us from weavers to loom builders—and we'd be building for the next ive years."

"Wrong," said Purple. "And you exaggerate besides. First of all, we don't need 175 looms. We only need 60—" He waited till the hoots of laughter had died away. "—we only need 60, but we will *use them continually*, all day and all night!"

There was a murmur of reaction. "Use them continually? Are we to give up sleeping now?"

"No, no—" cried Purple. He was insistent now. "Listen, you only work during blue days, right? When the blue sun sets, you stop. Well why can't you work just as well during red daylight?"

Another murmur of reaction. Purple ignored it.

"Look, the light is just as bright at night as it is during the day. One team of men can work at night, another team of men can work during the day—we'll call them shifts. That way we only need one third as many looms. Each man still works a full shift, but they don't all have to work during blue day. Why should the looms stand empty and unused when there is light? One shift will work in the morning, another in the evening, a third during red morning, a fourth until red sunset. Each shift will work nine hours—"

The noise drowned him out then. "You'd have us violate the weaving spells? Defile the gods?" The weavers were on their feet, waving their fists angrily. "You'd call down the wrath of Elcin on us!"

"Wait a minute! Wait a minute!" Both Gortik and I were calling for order. Purple was saying something, but could not be heard. Finally Shoogar tossed a large fireball calmly into the center of the ring. It sputtered and spat and silenced the weavers.

Muttering, they shrank away. Their protests sank to a whisper. Gortik said firmly, "We have agreed to listen to

Purple's proposal and discuss it logically. He is a magician—
we have all seen a demonstration of his power. Now, if h
feels that there is no danger of offending the gods, then ob
viously he knows what he is talking about."

"And if there is any doubt, we have Shoogar here fo
a second opinion," I added.

Gortik turned to Shoogar, "*Is* there any danger?"

Shoogar shook his head slowly. "Well, I'm not tha
familiar with weaving spells," he said. "But what I do knov
about weaving suggests that the time of day the cloth i
woven is unimportant. However, if there is any seriou
concern, I can construct some modifying spells to alleviate an
danger."

This seemed to pacify most of the weavers. They sank bacl
to their seats.

"But still," said Lesta, "Purple has called for sixty looms—'

"We do not even need to build that many," said Purple
"You have six. Each of the other four villages has at least
that many. Lant tells me that Hinc and some of the weavers
of the Upper Village have already built one of their own
That is thirty-one right there. If all the weavers—*all* the
weavers—were to spend only one hand of days building
looms, we'd have our sixty looms before the fourth day."

Lesta's eyes narrowed. He didn't trust that figuring, but
he wasn't going to challenge it until he had a chance to
check it himself. "And what will we do about loomteeth?" he
said.

They all looked at me.

I was unprepared for the question. I had not known that
it would be asked. I said, "Well, it takes time to carve them
—almost four days per full set."

"Hah! There—you see!" snapped Lesta. "That means more
than 240 days of carving by Lant before there are enough
teeth for all of the looms—and what will we do about break-
age in the meantime?"

"You know something, Lesta?" I said. "You're kind of
stupid."

He stood up at that, glowering.

I stood also. "If we can bring in extra weavers and loom
builders, then we can certainly bring in extra bonecarvers—"

"But there are no other bonecarvers on the island, you fungus-head!"

"Then I will train some! Any apprentice who can learn weaving can certainly learn bonecarving."

"I wouldn't let even my worst apprentice be so degraded!" Lesta snapped. He sat down, smiling grimly, arms folded across his chest.

"Then what will you do for aircloth?" I asked.

His smirk faded.

Purple said quickly, "If you lend Lant ten boys, two from each village, the loomteeth will be finished ten times as fast."

"Er—" I said. Purple looked at me. "What will I use for bone?" Across the clearing, Lesta snorted. "As big as a runforit skeleton is," I said. "I have only enough for twenty or so looms."

"Why do you have to use runforit bone?" asked Purple.

"I don't—but it's the hardest available."

"Do you have to use the hardest?"

"Well, no—but the teeth will wear down or break faster. Wet bone is not as strong as dry."

"But it would work?"

"Yes," I admitted. "It would work. You will just have to replace them more often."

"How often?" asked Lesta.

"I don't know," I shrugged. "I haven't had a chance yet to see how fast they wear."

"Well, give me an idea—how long would a set of wet bone loomteeth last?"

"I can't even give you an idea. It's a totally new situation for me. I'll guess four hands of days, maybe more, maybe less—how's that?"

Lesta curled his upper lip in disgust. Obviously he didn't think it was good enough. But Purple said, "That's fine, Lant, that's fine." He looked at his skin of figuring. "Even three hands of days per set would be fine."

"Good," I said. Already I was eager to start training apprentices.

"Then I guess that settles everything, doesn't it?" asked Gortik.

"No," said a voice. Lesta's.

We all looked at him.

"There's still one question that hasn't been answered—where will the thread come from?"

"Oh, yes," said Purple. "The thread. I should think the answer would be obvious to you by now."

It wasn't. We all shook our heads.

"There is a large untapped source of labor already right here in our midst," said Purple.

We looked around at each other curiously. What was he talking about?

"I'm referring, of course, to the women."

"The women!" It was a shout in unison from more than a hundred horrified throats.

All was uproar. Men were standing, shaking their fists, cursing and spitting. Not even a half dozen fireballs from Shoogar could quiet them. It wasn't until Shoogar threatened to call down Elcin himself that the noise began to subside.

"Let me explain! Let me explain!" Purple was saying. Before anyone else could interrupt, he went on, "Listen, there is nothing sacred about spinning—even old Lesta admits it. The only reason you use boy apprentices to do it is that there is no weaving for them to do. Well, now that there is weaving for them to do, they don't have to spin any more. The success of this whole plan depends on using the women for spinning—and your apprentice weavers can move up to being novices. Your novices can be promoted to journeymen. Your journeymen will all become team leaders."

At this there was a great shout of joy from the assembled tradesmen. At least one part of Purple's plan was going to be popular.

"But women?" declared Lesta. "Women? A woman is so dumb she cannot chew sweetdrops and walk through the forest at the same time."

"Nonsense," said another man, "you are still living in the days of your cubhood, Lesta. We are intelligent men—and intelligent men realize that women are more than dumb beasts of burden. They would have to be—they birthed *us,* did they not?"

This was greeted with a chorus of agreement from some of the other young men around the circle.

"Hah!" snorted Lesta. "Cubs still whining for the nipples."

He was hooted at. The man who had spoken, a man of the Lower Village unknown to me, continued, "These are modern times, Lesta. We know more now than when you were young. We no longer treat our women as poorly as our ancestors did because we are beginning to understand them —and because of it, we are getting better usage out of them. Harder work, Lesta!

"When was the last time you saw a whipherder and his flock of poor women, eh? Women are more than beasts of burden or dumb animals—and they should not be treated as such. Women are domestic creatures capable of many simple tasks. Why, I'll bet that there is not a man here who does not let his wives do his foodgathering for him—and I know some who don't even bother to hobble or chain their wives any more."

"Fools," snapped the old weaver. "Fools and foolishness. You will be sorry."

A few of the other older men cheered, but not many.

"Wait a minute," I said, stepping into the center. They all looked at me. "I would like to suggest something. There is not one of us here who is not eager to see the aircloth woven —am I not right?"

There were nods of assent.

"Purple has shown us that it is possible—that it *may* be possible—for us to weave more cloth in one season than has ever been dreamed of—and all of it *aircloth!* We have accepted most of his other suggestions with a minimum of fuss and debate—he has shown us that his ideas are practical. Unorthodox, but practical. Purple's speedy departure depends upon all of our cooperation."

"What is it you are proposing?" someone called.

"That we give Purple a chance to prove himself. There is only one way to find out if the idea is practical. I have two wives. I will allow one of them to be taught the skill of spinning. If she can handle it, that will teach us that it is a practical thing. If she cannot, then it is a foolish idea."

"Lant speaks sense," cried the man who had refuted Lesta earlier. "I will lend two of my wives to the experiment."

"I will lend one of mine," cried another. And immediately the air was full of pledges of women—each young tradesman was eager to outdo the rest by showing how smart his wife or wives were.

Purple beamed in delight at this development. He was going from man to man, grasping their hands and thanking them.

Old Lesta raised his hand. The noise quieted somewhat. "And what will you impetuous young fools do when you are struck by Elcin's wrath, eh?"

"We have nothing to fear from Elcin," mumbled someone, but not too loudly.

I said, "If we see that the women are desecrating the cloth, we will have them killed. Surely that would satisfy any offended god—but it is *worth* the experiment."

There was a general chorus of agreement.

As it died away, Shoogar stepped into the center of the clearing. "You are arguing about nothing," he said. "It is a simple matter to work up a spell that will allow a woman to work without offending the Gods. Women are so stupid that they cannot help but offend the Gods, so we have an all-purpose spell which excuses them because they are ignorant. They cannot help being what they are, or doing what they do. Thus, once a woman has been sanctified, she can literally do no wrong. We do not need to worry at all about the Gods. The only question is whether or not the women are smart enough to spin—and we will soon find that out.

"There is no point in discussing this matter any further," he said, "until we know one way or the other. I call for the adjournment."

He was right, of course. On both counts. We cheered his speech and broke up the meeting.

The experiment to see if the women could spin was held the following blue dawn.

Seventeen had been pledged. Fourteen showed up, being herded along by their suddenly nervous and uneasy husbands.

In the cold light of morning, suddenly it no longer seemed like such a good idea.

I too was beginning to regret my offer. I could not offer my first wife for the test because she was on the verge of childbirth. That left only my number two wife, the thin hardworking one with the lightcolored fur. I did not like the idea of losing her to Purple's experiment, but I had no choice. I was honor-bound.

I could understand why the other men were grumbling. With only one wife foodgathering, meals would be skimpy and uneven—for me the problem would be even more severe. It is bad luck to beat a woman with child.

Ah, well, if worse came to worse, I could always go down to the bachelor's compound and be served by the unclaimed women. An unappetizing prospect at best, but at least my stomach would be full.

We waited nervously on the hillside, milling about and saying little. The mood of the women ranged from fearful to delighted. All of them were obviously excited or upset at the prospect of a new kind of task. Few of them understood what would be required of them, but any change in their condition, they could only assume, must be for the better.

When Purple arrived, he was flanked by Lesta and several of his weavers. These were the men who would actually teach the spinning. Already several novices were beginning to assemble the spinning devices.

They began by demonstrating what spinning was all about. "You will be making thread—do you understand? Thread—it is very important—we will weave cloth out of it."

The women nodded their heads, dumbly, mutely.

"I will show you how it is done," said Lesta. He sat down on a little stool before the spinning device and began to spin, carefully explaining each step of what he was doing. Lesta was a good teacher. As I watched I felt that even I might learn the craft.

But the women—they missed the point entirely. "Look!" they murmured. "He sits! He sits! He works and *sits* at the same time!"

My wife tugged at my arm, "My husband, my husband, will I be able to sit too?"

"Hush, wife, hush—pay attention."

All the wives were murmuring now, pointing and whispering excitedly among themselves. "He sits! He sits while he works!"

At last, old Lesta could stand it no longer. He stopped spinning and leapt from his stool. "Yes, dammit, I sit! And you stupid creatures will sit too, if you can learn how!"

Immediately they were quiet.

Lesta surveyed the group, "Now, who wants to try it first?"

"Me! Me!" All of them pressed forward eagerly. "Me first, me!" Each wanted to see what it was like to *sit* and *work* at the same time.

Lesta chose one and sat her down on the stool. She giggled hysterically. He put the tools in her hand, and the pieces of combed fiberplant and bade her do as she had seen.

And, Lo! She spun!

She spun the fibers into thread!

The weavers gasped in horror—it was possible! The husbands gasped in shock—could a woman possibly be this smart? I gasped—just because I had never seen such a thing. The women gasped—she sits while she works, she *sits!*

And Purple? Purple was bouncing with delight. "It works," he shouted, "it works—she works, she works!"

And all the while, the woman continued to spin.

Of course, her thread was uneven and unusable—she was inexperienced and did not fully understand what she was doing. But it was obvious, even here, that it was *possible* for a woman to spin.

Purple could build his flying machine.

With experience and training—and careful supervision—all of these women might soon be spinning thread as fine as the best of them.

In fact, as the day progressed, it soon became obvious that a woman was a better spinner than an apprentice boy. An apprentice is smart—he knows that he will soon be a weaver—his heart is not in the spinning. His mind wanders and he pays little attention to it because it is such a mechanical and boring task. Boys will be boys.

On the other hand, to a woman, spinning is an enormously complex task. They must use both hands and one foot simultaneously in three separate and coordinated tasks. It requires all their concentration—it is a challenge. And if they fail, they know they will be beaten. Because a woman must continually pay attention to what she is doing, she is always watching the thread, always careful.

By the end of the day, many of them, including my own wife, were spinning thread fine enough to be used for aircloth.

Already, Purple was organizing. We had almost six hundred unwed women in our two villages. There was little work for them to do except for their own foodgathering and grooming.

But now we could make good use of all that wasted labor: we would put them to work spinning. And if that were still not enough women to produce thread for Purple, we would let our wives work as well.

The experiment was definitely a success.

Purple was not one to waste time. Quickly, he appointed the apprentice and novice weavers to a variety of new tasks.

The boys were eager and willing when they found out what their tasks were to be. Purple was creating a new trade —womenherders. These boys would be supervising the work of the women. They were delighted when they realized that finally they would be giving orders instead of taking them.

The herd of unwed women would be split into three groups; one group to spin, one to gather the raw fiberplants and wisptrees, and the third to comb the fibers smooth for spinning. There were approximately two hundred women in each group, but these were split into smaller herds of thirty to fifty each.

Even old Lesta was impressed. "I have never seen such a work force as this. I would not have believed it possible." And then realizing that he had just complimented Purple, he added, "It'll never work, of course."

But it did. Purple appointed another team of men, this time weavers, to go out into the hills each day and gather housetree blood. They had giant urns which Bellis the Potter had made for us. Once the urns were sealed, the housetree blood would stay fresh until we were ready to use it.

It was no secret that we were going to need it in vast quantities. We would need everything in vast quantities. We had already dispatched runners to the other villages with

samples of aircloth and invitations to their weavers and their
women. If Lesta had thought Purple's army of labor was
impressive with only six hundred women, he had not seen
anything yet.

As the thread was spun, a team of novices would dip it into a vat of seething housetree blood, then slowly, slowly roll
it up on a high suspended spool so it would have a chance
to dry in the air.

It soon developed that Purple was unhappy with this
method. If the thread should happen to touch anything while
it was still wet, it would pick up flecks of dirt just barely
large enough to be seen by the naked eye. Purple would
rave and swear—the gas, he insisted, would leak around the
particles of dirt and his flying machine would fall into the
sea.

Further, the boys were complaining about the heat from
the vats of boiling sap. The season made it all the more
stifling.

The solution was to move the spinning wheels and the
vats up onto Idiot's Crag. The boys enjoyed the change, for
it was cool and quiet up there in the wind; and the women
did not seem to mind the extra half hour's walk up the slope.

More important, the dipping and drying process was im-
proved. As each thread was soaked, a great loop of it was
stretched far down the crag, around a pulley, and back up
again to be wound on spools. The wind held it aloft, and the
boys pulled it from the housetree blood as fast as they could
wind it through the wringers. The thread was clean and dry—
and even shinier than before.

I stood up on the ledge with Purple one day. The work
was progressing smoothly—with a minimum number of ob-
stacles. Along the cliff edge were nearly two hundred women
and spinning devices. There were fifty boys tending the vats
of housetree blood. Loops of newly spun thread stretched out
before them. Another twenty boys were winding it up on
spools.

Wilville and Orbur had built several great spool winding
devices. Each consisted of a rack of spools, a set of pulleys
and two cranks. Each was powered by four boys, two on
each crank, and wound up the thread faster than ten boys
could do working alone.

Below, in the villages, there were almost ten looms now, each producing three patches of aircloth every five days. It was still not enough—but we were getting there.

Already, weavers from other villages were arriving, eager to learn this new secret. Many were shocked when they saw we had women spinning or that we had bone teeth on our looms—but most stayed to learn and to work. New looms were going up every day.

Purple and I stood on the edge and surveyed the scene below us. The waters of the sea were already lapping at the Lower Village, and several of the housetrees had already been abandoned.

"How high will the water rise?" I asked. "Will it menace the looms?"

"I hope not. Look below. You see the tree line? That's where Gortik says the waters rose to last year. Apparently that's as far as the sea carried the new soil. You are lucky to have a fresh water ocean here, Lant. Where I come from, the seas are salty."

"That sounds unpleasant," I said. I looked out over the greasy blue water, remembering how it had been aching desert only a short time ago. "I wonder where all the water comes from."

Purple said absent-mindedly, "When you pass between the suns, the ice caps melt."

I looked at him oddly. After all this time, he still spoke gibberish. Probably he would never lose the habit. Abruptly, I realized just how accustomed to Purple's presence I had become. I no longer thought of his strange ways as being strange—just different. I had stopped thinking of him as something queer and alien—it was only when he said something undecipherable like this that I was reminded that he was not of our people.

Indeed, I had even become used to the sight of his naked and hairless face.

Until, suddenly, I looked again—

"Purple," I exclaimed. "Did you miscast a spell?"

"Huh? What do you mean?"

"Your chin, Purple—you are starting to grow hair all over your chin and on the sides of your face!"

His hand went to his face. He rubbed—then he started laughing, a deep booming laugh.

I didn't think it was funny at all. There were many, like Pilg, for instance, who were still bald from head to toe because of a miscast spell.

Still grinning, Purple took a fist-sized thing from his belt and said, "Do you see this, Lant?"

"Of course."

"It is a—magic razor, moved by a particular kind of magic called *electrissy*." I think that was how he said it. "I will need the power in my razor to help make the lighter-than-air gas. So I have stopped removing the hair from my face."

I peered at him curiously. "You mean you *can* grow hair?"

He nodded.

"But you have been removing it willfully?"

He nodded again.

Strange. Very strange. I peered again. "But, Purple," I asked, "if you are going to stop removing the hair from your face, why do you not stop *completely*?"

"Huh?" he said. Then realising that I was referring to the rest of his naked face, he started laughing again.

I still did not see what was so funny.

The next day, Purple attempted to separate water into gases. Men of both villages came to watch.

The magician had obtained two lengths of copper wire from the coppersmith. These he attached to the rim of a large pot of water, using wooden clips, so that the end of each length of wire trailed in the water.

We watched as he disconnected a spell device from his belt. It was a flat bulging object like the one in the light tube he had given Shoogar many months ago—only bigger. He called it a battery.

He explained that it stored the magic called electrissy.

When it was connected to his impact suit spell-belt, it powered several of the other devices attached there. He indicated, but did not explain. The only devices he had that did not depend on his battery were a lightmaker which had a tiny battery of its own, and a radiation counter, which Purple said needed no battery at all.

The battery was a heavy object—heavier than one would expect for its size. There were two shiny metal nodes at one end of it. Purple twisted the free end of each copper wire around these nodes, one to each one.

"Now," he said, "all I have to do is turn the battery on. This dial tells me how much power I have. This knob controls the rate with which I release it. When I switch the battery on here, I will activate the spell and the gases will separate."

With a knowing look, he did so. We waited.

I heard a—sizzling—and looked into the pot.

Tiny bubbles were forming on the ends of the wires, breaking free and streaming toward the surface.

"Ah," said Purple. He turned the knob. The water began bubbling more vigorously. He smiled proudly. "Hydrogen and oxygen," he explained. "From this wire comes oxygen. From the other comes hydrogen, which is lighter than air. We will want to trap the hydrogen. It will lift the airbags."

"Oh," I said. I nodded as if I understood. I didn't, but I felt that I should at least pretend. Besides, I had expected something more impressive.

I stayed long enough to appear polite, then returned to my bone carving. I had seven apprentices now—and although they were quite capable of doing the work without me, I still felt it my responsibility to check on them as often as I could.

We were using sheepbone now. We had great amounts of it drying in the sun. It would not be the petrified bone that was so hard, of course, but it would still be usable. Such was the difference between wet bone and dry bone.

The apprentices themselves were working busily. Purple had suggested that they work in a new manner. One lad cut the bone into flat segments, another sanded the pieces down to fit into the loom slots, a third cut grooves into the bases so they would lock into the frame, a fourth and fifth cut the slits into the edges, while the sixth polished the finished pieces. The seventh serviced the tools of the first six and kept them sharp. Thus they were able to produce more loomteeth than they could have working alone.

Purple called it a "division of labor"—every job could be reduced to a few simple tasks. If all a person had to do was learn one task only, it would simplify and speed up all methods of production. Nobody had to know everything.

Except Purple, of course, but then—he was the magician.

He had set up his put-it-together lines all over the village. There were put it-together lines to spin the thread, to weave the cloth, to build the looms, to make the spinning machines. Everywhere there were great numbers of things to be made, Purple taught the people his put-it-together magic.

In fact he once explained to me that the whole region had become a put-it-together line for a flying machine. We could build others in the future, he said, if we so wished. All we had to do was keep the put-it-together lines going, and we could build as many as we wanted.

It was a staggering thought!

When he heard it, Shoogar's ears perked up. It was no secret what he wanted. An evil gleam came into his eyes, and he headed off to the mountains, to await the fall of darkness and a chance to glimpse the moons.

Fortunately, the nights stayed cloudy.

Purple had odd ways of speaking—even odder ways of doing things—but if we gave him the chance, his ways worked.

He proved it time and time again.

For instance, he had figured out a way to keep Gortik from crashing his bicycle into trees. He had suggested that Wilville and Orbur add a pair of smaller wheels to it, one on each side of the rear wheel. It kept the machine from falling over.

Gortik was so grateful at finally being able to ride his

bicycle that he allowed Wilville and Orbur to trade their other machines in the Lower Village—but only if they did not have "Gortik wheels" on them. He wanted to be the only one with a "crashproof" bicycle.

Wilville and Orbur were pleased at this turn of events. They had figured out a put-it-together line of their own—with only four apprentices they might be able to build as many as two bicycles per hand of days. They were eager to try it out as soon as they finished the flying machine.

At the moment, however, they had more than they could handle building spell devices for Purple.

For instance, he wanted bagholders—great frameworks to hold the aircloth bags over the bubbling pots of water. Thus he would trap the gas as it rose from his hydrogen wires.

Bellis the Potter had been asked to make great funneled pots for these frameworks, and had already finished the first one. In addition to the opening at the top through which the water would be added, it had two long spouts reaching up from either side. One was narrow and delicate; the gas-making wires were set so that the hydrogen gas would rise up through this spout. The other gas would bubble away harmlessly through the other spout which was wide and stubby.

An airbag—completely empty—would be hung on the framework over the pot and its mouth would be attached to the proper spout. When the wire was attached to the battery, Purple hoped the bag would fill with hydrogen.

But none of the airbags had yet been sewn together, only two of the frameworks for holding them had been built, and only one of the water pots had been finished. Bellis the Potter was being recalcitrant.

Originally he had been delighted at Purple's request for great amounts of pottery—but he was not delighted at Purple's suggestion that he use women to help make the pots. Not for gathering clay, he said, not for turning his wheel; not for polishing the finished pots, and not for cleaning his tools—not for nothing! No women, he insisted. Women were for breeding—and that was all they were for.

Purple said that it had already been proven that women could do such simple labors as spinning and gathering.

Bellis shook his head. "Spinning does not require much thought. Pottery does."

"H'm, that's what Lesta said. Only he said it was pottery that did not require much thought."

"Lesta is an old fuzzwort. There will be no women working on my pots—"

"Is that your final word, Bellis?"

"It is."

"Oh, dear. I had hoped you wouldn't say that. Ah, it's just as well. I have already sent for some potters from the other villages. They have said that they are willing to work with women. I guess I will have to deal with them. I will be seeing you—"

"Wait!" said Bellis. "Maybe it is possible. We will have to try it and see."

In other words, everybody wanted to work with Purple now—even it it meant changing one's way of working.

And something else: just as we were learning from Purple, it had become obvious, just from listening to him bargain, that he had learned something from us as well.

B y now Shoogar had completed the cultivation and consecration of every housetree in the region except for three wild ones he had left for Purple to use for his aircloth.

For a day and a half, then, Shoogar wandered around the village looking for things to do, amusing himself with minor spells here and there to patch up minor problems.

Finally he complained to me. "Everyone has something to do with the flying machine, but me! There are no spells that I have to cast to make it work properly—all of them are Purple's spells."

"Nonsense, Shoogar. There are many spells you can cast."

"Name six!"

"Well, ah—surely you can use your skill on the preparations for the flying machine. The aircloth for instance."

"What is there to do with the aircloth? They weave it, they dip it—it holds air."

"But surely, there should be a blessing over it, Shoogar, shouldn't there? I mean, it is like trapping Musk-Watz the Wind God. There should be some kind of amelioration spell."

Shoogar thought about it, "I believe you are right, Lant. I will have to investigate this—certainly the Gods should be involved in this flying machine."

I followed him down to the weavers' work area, a great pasture just under the crag. There were more than forty of the giant looms thrusting back and forth now. The noise was tremendous—each loom creaked and shuddered and protested mightily. The racous cries of the team leaders tumbled one upon the other until I wondered how the various weavers could tell who was commanding what.

We held our hands over our ears as we strode through the row upon row of machines—each with a tiny patch of aircloth growing in its heavy frame.

I noticed with some dismay that the field here had been ruined by so much traffic—the blackgrass had given way to dirt, and dust hung heavy in the air. That was not good for the cloth. Even though each piece was carefully washed before it was dipped, it still was not a good idea for it to be exposed to so much dirt.

Doubtless we would have to move the looms farther apart.

We found old Lesta down near the end, supervising the construction of three additional looms. Shoogar pulled him away from the work, and away from the noise. "I must talk to you," he said.

"What about? As you can see, I'm very busy—" Even as he spoke, he fidgeted with his robe and growled at the scurrying apprentices.

"Well," said Shoogar. "I have been doing some calculations—"

"Oh, no—not more calculations!"

"It is about the aircloth—we cannot weave it without offending Musk-Watz—that is, we can weave it, but we must offer a spell of appeasement for every piece and over every loom—"

"I cannot afford it," groaned Lesta. "I have enough magic already to make my hair fall out—"

"You would risk being hit with a tornado—?"

"It would be a blessing," snapped the weaver. "I would at least have a bit of peace." He waved his arm, "Look, you see all these looms? Each one is commanded by a different weaver—and each weaver pays homage to a different God. There is Tukker the god of names, Caff the god of dragons, Yake the god of what-if—more Gods than I have ever heard of! And each of those weavers is demanding that his cloth *be woven in a pattern sacred to his God!*"

"But—but—" I said, "Purple would have a fit—"

"Exactly," said Lesta. "The cloth must be woven in a simple over and under, over and under, a steady alternation— we want it as tight as possible—no twill weaves, no satin weaves, no fancy patterns of threads—just a simple aircloth weave! But no—you see those men over there? They are packing to return to their village—they won't weave anything but satins. They are afraid to offend Furman the God of Fasf—whatever that is—every day we lose at least five more weavers."

He turned on us, "You know what it is? They are stealing the secret of aircloth—they come, they weave for a week, then they find some excuse to run back to their own villages. I cannot keep any workers here." He groaned and sank down onto a log. "Aaghh, I wish I'd never heard of aircloth."

"But why?" I asked. "Surely, you have taken precautions—"

"Of course, of course," nodded Lesta. "No weaver is allowed near the looms without surrendering at least two syllables of his secret name as security—but it doesn't work. They claim that an oath to a god is stronger and more important than an oath to a man—and they are right."

"H'm," said Shoogar. "I might be able to do something about that."

Lesta looked up.

"It is simple," he said, "we will just consecrate all the aircloth to Musk-Watz. Anyone else who weaves it without my blessing, or who weaves it in another pattern, will be risking his wrath."

"But what about the men who keep leaving?" asked Lesta.

Shoogar shook his head, "They are not important. We can swear them to more binding oaths—"

"Oaths more binding than those to a god?"

"Certainly—how about the oath of hairlessness?"

"Huh?"

"It is simple—if they defy you, their hair falls out."

"Oh," said Lesta. He thought about it and brightened. "Yes," he said, "let's try it. Surely, it couldn't hurt."

When I left them, they were happily arguing over Shoogar's fee for deconsecrating all the other Gods out of the cloth.

I went to see Purple at his nest. He was well pleased with the way the work was going. A satisfied grin showed through the black bush that surrounded his chin, and he patted his huge stomach in a jovial manner. For some reason, he reminded me of a huge black tusker.

I told him of the problem with the weavers leaving, and he nodded thoughtfully when I told him of Shoogar's solution. "Yes," he said, "that was very clever. And I would not worry about the ones who have left, Lant. Most of them will be back."

"Huh? Why?"

Purple said innocently, "Because we have almost every spinning wheel on the island—where will they get enough thread for their looms?" And he laughed at his own mighty joke. "They will be lucky if they can make even one piece of aircloth."

"Why, you are right—I never realized that."

"And another thing—we have the only bone teeth on the island. They would not be able to weave cloth as fine as ours anyway; they will be back." He clapped me on the shoulder. "Come, I must go up to the Crag and check on the progress of the spinning."

"I will walk with you part way," I said. "There are several other problems we must discuss." I told him of the noise and the dirt created by having so many looms so close together. "It is not good," I said, "not for the cloth and not for the men."

"You are right, Lant—we will have to separate them, perhaps move some of the looms to other pastures. At all costs, we must protect the cloth. I will arrange it myself."

"I have already told Lesta," I said. "He does not object— at least no more than usual."

"Good."

We puffed up the slope toward the Upper Village. I said, "There is another thing. Certain of the men are beginning to wonder about payment for their skills. They fear that you will be unable to cast enough spells to pay them for their labor—they wonder how you will even keep track of them all. I confess, Purple, even I am mystified as to how you will keep your promises."

"Um," said Purple. "I will have to give them some tokens or something."

"Spell tokens?"

He nodded slowly, "Yes, I guess we could call them that."

"But what would they do—?"

"Well, each one would be a promise, Lant—a promise of a future spell. The person could keep it or trade it as he sees fit, or he can redeem it later when I have the time for it."

I considered it. "You will need a great many, won't you?"

"Yes, I will, won't I? I wonder if Bellis the Potter could—"

"No, wait—I have a better idea!" My mind was working furiously. My apprentices were way ahead in their bone carving. They had more than enough loomteeth carved to satisfy the needs of all the present looms, and even the ones still to be built for at least another hand of days. I did not like to see them sitting around idle—and I still had those one hundred and twenty-eight runforit ribs. I said, "Why don't you let me carve them? Bone has a soul—clay doesn't. My apprentices have nothing better to do now."

He nodded slowly, "Yes, yes, a good idea, Lant. We can give one spell token for each day's labor."

"Oh, no," I said. "One for each five days of labor. That is

the way Shoogar works—it makes his spells worth more. 'Work for a hand of days, earn a spell.' "

He shrugged. "All right, Lant. Go carve."

I was delighted. I left him to go on up to the Crag, and I hurried off to the Upper Village to set my idle apprentices to work. We would cut each runforit rib into a thousand narrow slices—maybe more—and stain the resultant chips with the pressed juices of darkberries.

I found, after a little experimentation, that we could use the same cutting threads that we used for loomteeth. The cutting threads were held in a stiff frame. If we opened up one side of the frame and spread the threads out more, we could use it to cut several slices at a time off the end of each rib. Later on we figured that a larger frame holding more threads could cut more slices at a time.

In fact, there was no reason at all that the threads had to be held in a rigid frame—not for this type of cutting. In the space of that afternoon I must have figured at least six new ways to carve bone slices. One of the most effective involved wrapping a single thread in a loop around the piece of bone and pulling it steadily back and forth—in this way, the rib was cut from all sides at once.

We could cut several slices at a time this way—the only limit was the number of threads that we could string around the bone and pull at any one time.

While we were discussing this, Wilville and Orbur stopped by. They were on their way up to the Crag; each was carrying a bundle of hardened bambooze shoots.

I told them of my latest project and they nodded thoughtfully, "Yes, we can build you a device for cutting many slices of bone at a time. We will use cranks and pullies, and it will be operated by two apprentices. I think we may be able to pull fifty threads at a time with it."

"Good, good," I said. "How soon can I have it?"

"As soon as we have a chance to build it—first we must finish the airboat frame. The spirit pine is too heavy—we are going to try again with bambooze."

"And that means building a whole new frame," sighed Orbur.

They shouldered their loads and trudged on up the hill.

It was well past midnight when I finally grew tired. The red sun was already nearing the west.

It had been a relaxing day. It had been too long since I had concentrated on my bonecarving only, and I had missed it.

I was tired and I ached all over—but at the same time I glowed with the satisfaction of a job well done.

As I trudged across the blackgrass-covered slope toward my home I thought of the pleasures that awaited me there: a hot meal, yes—perhaps even a bit of choice meat; a massage, gentle and warm—I might even let the wives rub precious oil into my fur. It had been too long since I had allowed myself that luxury. And perhaps, if I felt in the mood, perhaps we would do the family-making thing. It would have to be the number two wife, of course—number one was growing heavier and more swollen every day.

Perhaps a hot brushing too, I dreamed—yes, definitely. I could feel the combs already. I quickened my step. My nest-tree loomed invitingly——

I found my wives in bitter argument. The first wife, the one with seniority, was in tears—the second wife, the thinner one, was red-eyed and glaring.

"Have you no sense?" I shouted at her. "You do not badger my number one wife—she has borne me two sons! You have borne me none!"

The woman only glared angrily.

"Go get the whip!" I ordered.

She said, "You may whip me, my master—but you cannot change what is. What is *is!*"

She would pay for such insolence. A man with a wife he cannot control has one wife too many. I stepped over to the other woman and put my arms around her swollen form, "What is the matter, my number one woman?"

She pointed and said through her tears, "That—that *woman*—she—"

176

My second wife interrupted haughtily, "I am not *'that woman'* any more. I am *Kate*."

"*Kate?* What is a *Kate?*"

"Kate is my name. I have a name. Purple has given it to me."

"A *what?* You have a *what?* You cannot have! No woman has ever had a name!"

"I do! Purple gave it to me!"

"He has not the right!"

"He does too—he is a magician, isn't he? He came up to the Crag today where we spin—and he talked to us, and he asked us what our names were. When we told him we had none, he proceeded to give us names—and he blessed them too! *We have consecrated names!*"

Why, the fool would bring ruin upon us all! There is nothing so dangerous as a haughty woman—we should never have allowed them to learn how to spin! And now he had given them names! Names, indeed!

Did he think they were equal to men in other respects as well? I would fear to ask him—he might say yes. And this from a magician?!!

Shoogar would have to be told at once. The other men must be warned. Purple must be chastised. If women could have names, then they could be cursed through the power of those names. A man is strong enough to bear such responsibility and avoid such cursing. But a woman? How could a woman even realize the danger? They would be so delighted at having names, they would run to tell everybody.

My first wife turned to me in tears. "Give me a name, my husband. I want to *be* somebody too."

I stormed out.

The village was in an uproar. The sky was smoky and red, and angry men stood about in clumps, shouting foolishness. As if they would dare attack a magician!

Pilg the Crier stood on a tall housetree stump, shouting into the uproar, "Torchlight procession—burn the——blasphemed against—"

A lot of help he was. And Pilg didn't even have a wife any more! What had he to complain about?

This had gone far enough—a voice of reason was needed here. I climbed the stump behind Pilg and pushed him hard in the small of the back. He stumbled forward and off, waving his arms.

I filled my lungs and bellowed, "Listen to me, towns-people—"

But there was too much noise—and suddenly they were all going away.

Torches appeared as if by magic, red flames bright over dark crazed heads. I was off the stump and shoving through the jostling crowd. Where was Shoogar now that we needed him?

There was only me to stop them as they streamed toward the river, toward Purple—

I pushed and fought my way to the front of the crowd so that they could see me. "Listen to me! Listen to your Speaker!"

And then the mob from the Lower Village charged into us, and there was no point. Nothing human or demon could have been heard above the roaring.

We were a raging torrent of men bent on murder. I was still trying to reach the leading edge, trying to turn it aside, somehow deflect it——

And then we spilled out onto the riverbank and there was Purple.

He was kneeling beside one of Bellis's funneled pots, hugging a kind of bag against his chest, an inflated bag as big as a small woman. As the mob rolled toward him he turned in astonishment, letting go of what he was holding.

And it fell up.

It was as if the villagers had run into a stone wall. They stopped joltingly short, and then they moaned as if in agony.

Purple's *thing* tumbled slowly upward into the red-black sky. It was a flimsy-looking bag of wind, made of aircloth, shiny and bright and flickering back the glow of the torches. It danced as it rose . . .

"Lant!" Purple cried. "What's—what's happening? Why are they here?"

I tore my eyes off the bag of wind. "Purple—why did you name the women?"

"Why not?" He seemed doubly confused. "I couldn't just keep calling every one of them 'Hey, you,' could I?" There was a moan from somewhere behind me. I ignored it.

Purple continued, "I had trouble remembering the order, Lant. There were too many of them. I mean, it was easy to remember to call a woman 'Trone's wife,' but she got insulted if I forgot to call her 'Trone's second wife.'"

"Third," I remembered.

"Third. You see? It was slowing things up. So I made up some names—*Kate, Judy, Anne, Ursula, Karen, Andre, Marian, Leigh, Miriam, Sonya, Zenna, Joanna, Quinn*—it made things so much easier."

"Easier?" I looked about me. Perhaps a score of villagers remained. They seemed to huddle together, holding their torches high against the night. The others had not fled, but seeped away into the darkness while Purple and I were talking.

I glanced nervously at the sky—but his *thing* had vanished.

"Easier?" I repeated. "They're here to burn you, Purple. Or they were."

"Um," he said. He looked vaguely about him. "Where's my balloon? It was right here a minute ago—I was holding it—"

"You mean that *thing*—that *thing* that went up into the sky—?"

His face lit up, "It did? You mean it worked?"

I swallowed hard and nodded.

"It actually *worked!*" He peered excitedly upward, squinted at the darkness. Abruptly he looked at me, "Eh, did you say burn me?"

I nodded again.

It didn't seem to bother him much—he still kept glancing at the sky. He was preoccupied with that balloon. "For what?" he asked. "For naming women?"

"Purple, you're a magician—you should have known

better! I suppose you named them right out in public, in the hearing of others, so that every woman who spins now knows the names of every other woman! Well, did you?"

"Certainly. Why not?"

I groaned. "Because they'll use magic on each other! And magic is too powerful to be placed in the hands of fools and women! They'll get above themselves, Purple! First you have given them a profession, now you give them names. They'll think they're as good as men!"

"It bothers you, doesn't it?" he said perceptively. "Very well, Lant, what would you like me to do? Shall I take their names away?"

"Could you?"

"Certainly. I'll do it for you—I'll memorise their numbers and their husbands' names instead—anything to make peace."

I couldn't believe he would give up so easily, so casually. As casually as he had given them . . . Timidly I repeated, "You'll take their names away?"

"Of course," said Purple, "what do you think I am? Some kind of fiend?" He laughed boomingly, showing his teeth. Twenty villagers moaned softly and pushed closer together.

Purple bent back to his water pot again, began fiddling with his battery wires. I watched as he fastened a large piece of cloth to the funnel of the pot. "Another airbag?"

"Huh? Oh, yes—another balloon." He spread the cloth between his hands. "We made the first ones today." Slowly, the bag began puffing up. He held it so it would fill evenly. "Watch!" he said, "Watch—it's filling with hydrogen!"

I took a step forward, curious in spite of myself.

Behind me, the small knot of men who remained also edged forward.

The bag was puffy now, almost its full size. It grew rounder as we watched. I fancied I could hear the bubbles flowing up through the water, through the spout and into the bag. Purple watched it narrowly. At last he lifted the windbag from the pot spout and tied its neck. He let it go.

It wasn't quite as large as the other, nor was it as full— but it lifted into the air *and flew!*

It floated toward the little knot of twenty.

"It works! It works!" Purple was exultant. He did a little dance of delight.

We backed away as the thing drifted nearer. Pilg held his torch before him to ward it off. The bag ignored the warning, floated closer and—

Suddenly was a ball of flame!

A bright orange flash of heat and light!

I don't know what happened after that. Most of us reached home, one way or another; but Ford the Digger ran straight off a cliff, and nobody could find Pilg at all.

But the trouble didn't end that easily.

When Purple told the women that they could no longer have any names, there arose such a weeping and wailing that one would have thought that all the men in the village were beating their wives in unison.

In fact many of them took to beating their wives in order to stop them from wailing—but that only increased their anguish. In a short time it became apparent that we had a spontaneous revolt on our hands.

Quite simply, the wives refused to work, to cook, and even to do the family-making thing unless we granted them the right to bear names.

"No," I told my own wives, "the old ways are best. If I let you have names, the Gods will be angered."

They looked at me adamantly, "But, La-ant, beloved master and faithful husband—"

"There are no buts about it," I insisted. "There will be no names."

"Then there will be no family-making thing either." They said it with a whimper.

I looked at these two women. The number one wife I had purchased while still wearing the fur of youth. She had been with me for many years and had borne me two fine sons and only one daughter. She had been a faithful companion, and I had trained her to my moods well. She was no longer as sleek as she once was, but I would not discard her to the vagaries of the old womens' compound. No, she was too well suited for the duties of running my home.

And the number two wife, sleek and sassy. Young she was, and only a wife of three cycles. She had borne me only daughters. She was spoiled and shrill.

Abruptly, I found myself mourning the loss of the number three wife, the modest and sweet one. She had talked little, and the others had bullied her, but she had been the most gentle. She had borne one son, but both she and he had been lost in the destruction of the old village.

I wondered about the possibility of gaining a new wife. Perhaps I should discard these two if they were going to be so difficult. After all, there were plenty of women around— they would jump at the chance to marry a man such as I.

But then, most of the good women were already married. It was only the flightier and shriller ones who were still single —and even the most comely of those was none too attractive.

Besides, if any other men were thinking in the same manner as I, there would be such a demand for wives that many would go without.

The possibility of trading my wives for the wives of someone else also occurred to me—but who wanted to inherit someone else's bad habits? No, I would just as soon keep these women——

But, no family-making thing.

I could try taking them by force—but they would probably make such grimaces and terrible expressions that there would be no enjoyment in it.

No—I must be the master in my own house. If they would not accept my wishes, then I would discard them and bring in new wives. I could have my pick of the village. After all, was I not the Speaker?

But most of the wailing was in the compound of the unwed women!

These were the women who did most of the spinning— and they were the ones wailing the loudest about names.

But surely, I thought, surely there must be at least one or maybe two of these women who would be willing to forsake her name for the privilege of keeping my house and bearing my children. Surely there would be one who would do the family-making thing with me.

I was mistaken.

Too many other men had had the same idea—too many other men were too eager.

And the women wanted names.

We held another council meeting.

Hinc stood up and said, "I propose that we beat our wives thoroughly. Tell them we will allow them no names and will not permit a strike——"

There was a chorus of cheering. Clearly, it was a popular idea.

But a man of the Lower Village shook his head and said, "It won't work, Hinc. We have *already* beaten our wives—and still they won't work. They want names and no amount of beating will erase that desire."

"But it's unthinkable!"

"The women do not think so!"

"The women are incapable of thinking!"

"But we are not! Think about it! Beating will only increase their resentment!"

We thought about it.

We went home and beat our wives and thought about it some more.

We held another meeting. At last, we decided that a *compromise* might be in order. The word was Purple's—as was the solution.

The women could have names—but names only to be used as identifiers. They would be unconsecrated names with no religious significance at all. Just words, so to speak, that might let us know which woman we were speaking of.

In other words, a woman's name would be outside the influence of the Gods.

Shoogar grumbled at this—something about undermining the foundations of modern magic. He said. "By their very definition names are part of the object which they are the name of. You can't separate the two. A flower is a flower is a flower."

"Nonsense, Shoogar; a flower by any other name is still a flower!"

"Wrong, Lant—it's only a flower because you call it a

flower. If it weren't a flower, it would be something else. It would be whatever you named it!"

"But it would still smell the same!"

"But it wouldn't be a flower!"

We were getting off the track, "I'm sorry, Shoogar, but these names cannot be retracted. The best thing we can do is deconsecrate them and make the best of a bad situation. Make the women spellproof. Let the names be only meaningless words."

"That's just it, Lant. There are *no* meaningless words. All words have meanings, whether we know them or not. There can be no words that are not also specific symbols of the objects they are names of—and a symbol is a way to manipulate the object. When Purple says we must deconsecrate the names, he is talking foolishness. You cannot deconsecrate a name."

"Unh," I said, "but Purple thinks so."

"Purple thinks so!—Who is the magician here? Me or Purple?!!"

"Purple," I said meekly.

That brought him down. He glared at me.

"Well, this is his territory."

Shoogar harrumphed and started picking through his spell devices.

I said, "Shoogar, you are as smart as he—surely there must be some way—"

He frowned. "H'm, yes——" He considered it. "Yes, Lant, there is. I will simply consecrate every woman with *the same name*. Therefore no one will dare cast a spell on anyone else's woman, because he will also be casting a spell on his own. And no woman would dare curse another because she would be cursing herself as well!"

"Shoogar—you are brilliant!"

"Yes," he said modestly. "I am."

The next day he went out and named all the women *Missa*. Gone were the Kates and Ursulas and Annes and Judys. Gone were the Karens and Andres, Marions, Leighs, Miriams, Sonyas, Zennas and Joannas. Gone were the Quinns.

Now there were only *Missas*. Trone's Missas, Gortik's Missas, Lant's Missas.

It was the perfect solution. The men were happy, the women were happy—excuse me, the Missas were happy.

And best of all, they went back to spinning and working and doing the family-making thing.

Purple could call them whatever he wished—it wouldn't make any difference. Their consecrated names were Missa. That was the only name that had any power.

The men of the village breathed a sigh of relief. Now we could get back to normal—the business of making a flying machine.

In order to disturb the production of the aircloth as little as possible the looms were being separated at the rate of only three a day. New looms were being built on other slopes instead of in the same general area as the first ones.

When Lesta had been told that he would have to separate the looms already built and working, he had groaned in dismay—the thought of moving all forty-five looms was frightening. But Purple had quickly pointed out that he need move only twenty-two; if he removed every other loom from the line, he would leave plenty of working space between the rest.

Shaking his head, Lesta went off to issue the orders.

Half of the new cloth was allocated to Purple's construction. The rest was divided on a percentage basis. Each weaver was paid in product, the amount determined by his importance and by the labor he had performed.

Purple paid for his cloth with spell tokens. I had carved them, or my assistants had, to meet his needs. The first set of chips was given to Lesta to be distributed to his workers in the same proportion as the cloth.

At first neither Lesta nor the weavers understood their purpose, but when we explained that each was the promise of a future spell, they nodded and accepted them.

Within a few days they were trading them back and forth

among themselves in exchange for various labors. One group
of men was found rolling the bones for them: a common
game, except that they had thought of exchanging chips ac-
cording to the way the bones fell! Shoogar decided it was an
offense against the Gods to trifle so with magic. They were
severely warned, and their chips confiscated.

Still another man was found trading his wives' family-
making privileges for chips. We confiscated his wives.

Because the put-it-together lines were so efficient, the total
production of aircloth was more than twenty percent greater
than all of the villages' previous cloth production combined.
Of course Purple's share comprised half of that production,
but few of the weavers minded—without Purple, there would
have been no aircloth at all. They knew that they would be
able to trade it for much more than the old cloth.

For a while Purple considered appropriating all of the
cloth for his flying machine, but he let himself be talked out
of it. If the weavers felt they were working only for Purple's
benefit, they would be resentful and careless. If they knew
they were working for themselves as well, they would treat
each piece of cloth as if it were their own—as it might very
well be, after the distribution.

Distributions were held every second hand of days. Most
of the men received enough of the cloth for their own uses,
and enough more for trading. The lesser weavers, the apprentices and novices whose labors did not add up to
enough to make even one piece of cloth, were paid with a
spell token. If they saved up three of them they could trade
them for a piece of cloth.

That the cloth was highly valued was no secret. It soon
became a mark of status to wear an aircloth toga, and trading
for the material was fast and furious. Several men, head
weavers in their own villages, took to clothing their wives
in aircloth to show their own importance. But we put a stop
to that soon enough.

It was not that they had not the right to parade their
wealth, but they should not use their women for the purpose.
The women were proud enough as it was—just with names.
We didn't need our wives complaining that so-and-so's wife
was wearing aircloth and why couldn't they wear aircloth too?

Hurriedly, we stifled that trend.

Chastened, the weavers wore the clothes themselves—as many as they could. For a while it was the fad to wear one's fortune on one's back, but it stopped after a few days. This was still the wading season—the season of sweat.

There was another incident too. We had our first *theft*. They were two of the lesser weavers—boys really—they had coveted Purple's huge store of aircloth. They were from one of the other villages on the island and did not truly comprehend the importance of the flying machine project. They were only here for the weaving—and for the marvelous new aircloth.

But, being only apprentices, they weren't paid in cloth, only in extra spell tokens, and they were bitter about it.

Most of the weavers, not needing airtight cloth, took it as it came from the looms. The threads of the linens were highly polished due to the dipping in housetree blood. The cloth had a luxuriously smooth, starchy feel to it.

Purple's share of the cloth was set aside for its later treatment. It would have to be dipped again, this time in housetree-binding solution. It was this stockpile of waiting cloth that had tempted the boys.

They had been caught, of course. Although it was past midnight and most people were asleep, still the red sun was high in the west. Purple, whose sleeping habits were not like the rest of us, had accosted them—indeed had blundered into them, their arms laden with his stolen cloth.

The boys made the mistake of running for the weaving fields, Purple in hot pursuit, yelling, "Stop, *thief!* Stop!"

The midnight weavers did not know the word. But they saw two boys running and a screaming magician following, and they knew something was up. They headed off the boys, and held them for Purple.

At blue dawn we held a council: the magicians, the head weavers of the villages, and five Speakers including myself and Gortik.

"I don't know how they expected to escape," Purple confided in me. "Is there a standard punishment for—" He seemed to search for a word, "—this crime?"

"How could there be? Such a thing has never happened before. I don't know what we will decide."

Purple looked astonished. He seemed about to speak; but then the proceedings began.

I said little. This was not a matter for me to decide. It was for the Speaker of the boys' village. The boys stood trembling, off to one side. They were much the same age as my Wilville and Orbur.

The Speakers argued for most of the morning. There was no precedent, no basis for a decision.

At last it was Shoogar who decided it. Grumpily he stepped to the center of the ring. "These boys have committed a *theft*," he said. "The word is Purple's. Purple tells us that a *theft* is an offense where he comes from.

"Personally, speaking for myself, I consider it an act of foolishness—taking something from a magician is downright dangerous!"

There was a murmur of agreement.

Shoogar continued, "Obviously, because the property taken was a magician's, this is not a matter for Speakers. It is a matter for magicians."

This time the Speakers agreed heartily. Shoogar was taking them off the hook.

"It was aircloth that these two *thieves* wanted—" said Shoogar, advancing on the boys. They shrank away from him. "Therefore, I propose that the punishment match the offense—I say we give them aircloth!"

And with that he unfurled the huge bolts of cloth the boys had taken from Purple. They were long strips, the first ones sewn together for the airbags. "Wrap them in it!" commanded Shoogar.

"Now, wait a minute—" began Purple.

Shoogar ignored him. The head weavers shoved the boys forward and forced them onto the ground, flat on the strips of cloth. "Roll them up!" said Shoogar. "Tight! Roll them tight!" The weavers did so.

"But—Shoogar," Purple protested, "they'll *suffocate*."

"I do not know the word," said Shoogar, not taking his eyes from the struggling bulks in the cloth.

"It means to—to run out of *oxygen*."

Shoogar threw him a glance. He may have remembered the word, but what of it? Oxygen was the gas Purple threw away when he made hydrogen from water. Throw-away gas.

"Fine," he said. "They will suffocate."

"You mustn't," said Purple. He was quite pale.

Shoogar turned away with a grimace.

Purple made a sound in his throat. I thought he would go after the other magician; but he did not.

The boys were completely bound up now, the weavers were tying the cloth firmly about them. They looked like giant sting thing larvae, long and brown and shapeless.

"We will leave them here until the next rising of the blue sun," said Shoogar. "You will post men to see that no one comes near."

When the boys were unrolled, they were stiff and dead. Even Shoogar was shaken. "I had not expected—"

He shook his head slowly. "So that's what *suffocate* means." He circled the bodies. "A strong spell it must be. Look, not a mark on them."

We looked. Their faces were dark and cold. Their tongues protruded, and their eyes bulged in amazement; but of wounds there were none.

When we told Purple, he made a sound of pain—but as if he had expected it, I thought. He went down to the clearing himself to see. "I shouldn't have let him," he said. "I should have stopped him."

When he saw their stiff forms, he recoiled. He sank down upon a log and buried his head in his hands and sobbed. Even Wilville and Orbur edged away from him.

The fathers of the boys arrived then. They had been summoned from the other side of the island, and it had taken them almost a day to make the journey. When they learned what had happened, they began to wail. They had come to participate in a punishment ceremony, not a funeral.

I myself felt strange, empty, taken with a terrible sense of loss.

Gortik gathered up the *thefted* cloth, handling it with new respect, and presented it to Purple. Purple raised his head, looked at the offering. He shook his head vehemently, shrinking back. "Take it away. Take it away."

In the end, we buried the boys in it.

* * *

Afterward I found Purple alone. He was sitting morosely on the unfinished airboat frame.

He looked at me, "I told Shoogar. They'll *suffocate*. They won't get enough *oxygen*."

"Curse your throw-away gas anyway! They didn't get any air, Purple! Your aircloth holds air out as well as gas in!"

"Yes, of course." He looked puzzled.

"You knew? You knew!" I cried wildly. "You knew they would die! If you'd sat on Shoogar and *made* him listen—or told *me!* The boys had done nothing so very wrong—"

"Stop it!" he moaned.

"You let them die, Purple! For so small a thing?"

"But that's the way it is in many savage societies——" he said. He stopped then and looked at me. Speechless.

"Savage societies?" I asked. "Is that what you think of us—that we are savages?"

"No—no, Lant, I——" He flailed about. "I thought that—I have never seen a punishment here. I did not know what your penalties were. I thought Shoogar knew what he was doing. I—I—I'm sorry, Lant. I didn't know—" He covered his face.

Suddenly, I was calm. Purple was outside all human experience. We had been assuming things about him just as he had been assuming them about us.

I asked, "Do they kill for theft, where you come from?"

He shook his head. "It is not necessary. When one commits a major crime, our—Advisors can tamper with the thief's—soul, so that he can never do it again."

I was impressed. "It is a powerful spell."

"And a powerful threat," said Purple. "A killer who has been so treated cannot even defend himself, or his children or his property. A treated thief could not theft water, though his house was burning . . . But, Lant, I do not understand—how can theft be so rare here? The boys took a thing that did not—pertain to them; they did not build it or earn it or trade for it. How can this be unusual?"

"It is unheard of, Purple. It has never happened before."

"But——" He seemed to search for words. "What do you call it when one takes another's bread?"

"Hunger."

He was flustered. "Well, what would you do if someone took your carved bone?"

"Without payment? I would go and get it back. He could not disguise it. No bonemonger ever carves exactly like any other. I never carve even two pieces alike—except for loom-teeth, of course."

"Uncarved bone, then. You have a good store of uncarved bone. What if someone took it?"

"For what? Who could use it? Only another bonemonger. I would know them all, in any region. I would go and get it back."

"This is nonsense. Lant, surely there must be *something* for thieves to take. Secrets!" Purple cried wildly. "Lesta guards his weaving secrets as a mother her children."

"But if one took his secrets, Lesta would still have them. He could still make his cloth, though others could also. One cannot theft a secret without leaving it behind. One cannot theft more food than one can eat before it spoils. One cannot theft a house, or anything too heavy to lift. One cannot theft tools; tools belong to a trade; one would have to learn the trade also. One cannot theft a profession, or standing in a community, or a reputation."

"But—"

"One cannot theft anything easily recognized, unless one can flee faster than men can follow. In fact, the only things one can theft are things that look exactly like a great many other things." My mind was searching as I talked, and I was beginning to understand Purple's confusion. "Things that look like other things. Cloth, or spell chips, or grain—"

Purple was horrified. "Why, you're right!"

"Cloth and spell chips. Yes. Until your coming, one could not theft enough cloth to be worth the effort. So much cloth did not exist. And how could one theft the services of a magician? The idea was nonsense until you arrived, Purple."

"I've invented a new crime," said Purple dazedly.

"Congratulations," I said, and left him.

The search for fiberplants and wild housetrees had been extended even into the wilderness hills. Four teams left the village each blue dawn to search for materials, and they often did not return till long after Ouells had winked out in the west.

Too often they came back with their gathering baskets and urns only half full.

The fiberplants were not as big a problem as they might have been. They grew fast and the cropmongers had begun experimenting with planting them for the weavers. Already the new shoots were springing up and it looked like we would have fiberplant all year long.

It was the housetree sap, though, that was really slowing us down. We were running out of trees. Shoogar had consecrated all the trees in the region, except three—and those three were nearly tapped dry. Indeed Purple didn't want to bleed them any more for fear of killing them. Already they were losing their leaves.

There were wild housetrees of course, but the effort involved in dragging the filled urns back from the wilderness hills was prohibitive. They were great heavy things, and it took eight men to move them. Bellis had made them out of oaken barrels lined with aircloth, then reinforced them again with extra bindings.

He'd made larger ones as well to be used as vats. These had been made out of heavy bricks of reinforced clay. They were beautiful.

But we did not have enough housetree blood to fill them.

Meanwhile the piles of untreated cloth continued to grow. We had only enough sap for the spinning, not enough for the second dipping.

And the boatframe was rapidly taking shape on the peak.

The first boatframe had become much too heavy and had to be scrapped. The boys had taken it apart and thrown out everything heavier than spirit pine. Then they threw out the spirit pine too, leaving only one length of it for the keel.

Instead, they used bundles of bambooze, bound together and made rigid by judicious hardening. Shoogar had helped them on this, although we rarely saw him otherwise. He was too busy with loomblessings and other spells.

The second boatframe was almost entirely bambooze. But, so far, it was only a framework.

The boys abandoned their idea of aircloth-covered balsite. It turned out that the balsite was unnecessary and that they could use the aircloth alone. The hull could be made of many stiffened layers of it stretched tightly over the bambooze frame. Wherever possible, the aircloth would be used instead of lumber. It would be hardened later by the application of many layers of housetree blood to make it watertight.

Once the boys began thinking about it, they came up with many ways to keep the airboat as light as possible. Instead of wooden planks for seats, they used stretched cloth over simple frames, and Purple would sit on those. Instead of planking on the sides of the two cabins—one a storage compartment, the other a sleeping room—they would use aircloth again.

The boys were ecstatic over their work. It would be watertight; it would be strong. Best of all, it would be so light that Purple could afford to be extravagant with the rest of his weight allowances.

The only part of the boatframe that had to be wood were the deck slats along the floor. The boys had already tied and glued them into the frame; it was a narrow walk running the length of the boat. The rest of the hull was still open to air, but eventually the rigid structure would be covered and firm.

It made me wonder—could aircloth be used in other ways as well?

For instance, could one use it to make a nest? Instead of weaving a home out of fiberplants and stretchvines, one could use aircloth instead. It would be easier and faster and lighter —and it would keep out the rain too.

H'm—perhaps one could stretch large pieces of the cloth across a rigid framework and use it as a rainshelter for the flocks—or to dam a stream. Many thicknesses might be required for the latter, but there was no reason why it shouldn't work. H'm, we might be able to store large amounts of water in aircloth-lined pools as well. It would not drain away. If we put aircloth across the top of the water, not even thirsty Musk-Watz could steal it.

I was willing to bet that there were a great many uses for the cloth that we had not thought of yet. Perhaps I had been too easy with Lesta. No matter, I could renegotiate the terms of our deal after Purple's flying machine was finished.

The finished framework looked like the outline of a boat. It was so light that it had to be tied down against the winds of Idiot's Crag. One man could move it, and two could carry it without difficulty.

The keel was the single length of spirit pine they had saved. To make it even more effective, they had slung it below the boatframe on several spars of rigid bambooze. Then, to hold the boatframe and keep the keel from snapping, they had built a cradle to stand it upright.

Now they were adding rungs to the struts that supported the outriggers. Why rungs? Because, Wilville told me with a happy smile, they would need to be able to crawl from the hull out to the *airpushers*.

Airpushers?

I didn't ask. In time we would know.

The boys continued to work on the outriggers. Soon they would begin stretching the cloth over the frame. Then the only thing holding up the launching of the airship would be the sewing up of the windbags.

And that was being held up by three things.

We needed more aircloth. For that, we needed both fiber-plants and housetree blood.

We needed more housetree blood just to treat the cloth we had already woven.

And thirdly, we needed another way to separate water. Purple's battery had died.

I found out about the battery when I went to tell him about the housetree blood. Purple was sitting on a log outside his house, turning the flat, bulging case over in his hands. From the way he looked, he might have been holding his own death.

I sat down beside him, without speaking, and waited.

"It's dead," he said presently.

I said, "How? Did you starve it?"

He pointed up. Hovering above his housetree were seven man-sized aircloth bags. They hung upward from ropes. "I have been experimenting, Lant—I grew carried away." He waved up at the village. "And I did not want your people to fear the airship—"

A group of young boys came running by, each trailing a shiny aircloth bag behind him on a string. The bags were about the size of a man's head, maybe bigger. "Useless patches of extra cloth," Purple explained. "Not tight enough for the airboat, but I thought if the children could see—that is, if the adults could see that even children could handle the spell——"

I understood. Purple had seen our terror on the night of the riot. He was trying to lessen that by showing this was a simpler spell than we had thought.

Now, he mourned over his battery and stroked it sadly.

"Is there no way you can make a new one?"

"You don't know what you're asking!" he exclaimed. "My whole civilization is based on the kind of power that was in this battery. I am not a—a—magician of that type, I don't have that training. I am only a student of how savage men can live together!"

I ignored the insult, for clearly he was upset. I forced him to sit down and would not let him say another word until he had drunk off a bowl of Quaff. His face twisted into extraordinary shapes.

195

"I've been an idiot," he told me. "For eight months I shaved my face with the *electrissy* I needed to get home!"

"But what about those airbags?" I pointed at his housetree.

"Those wouldn't be enough. Besides, by the time we finish the boatframe, those will be empty again. The gas leaks out, Lant. Very slowly, but it still leaks."

I handed him another bowl of Quaff. "But surely, you can make some kind of power source to separate the water."

"No. That was it. You don't have the tools to make the tools to make the tools."

"Is there nothing else that would activate a flying spell?"

"Hot air. Hot air is lighter than cold air. That's why smoke rises. The cursed trouble is that hot air gets cold. We'd sink into the sea and stay there; we couldn't possibly get far enough north in a hot-air windbag."

I sank down onto the log next to him and poured myself some Quaff. "Surely there must be some way, Purple. It was not so long ago that you thought an airboat was impossible. Is there nothing you can do about your battery? There must have been a first source of electrissy some time. How was it done?"

He looked at me, bleary-eyed. "Oh, no, Lant—" And then his eyes narrowed. "Wait a minute——I did make something in school once! A spinning motor made from paper clips and copper wire and a battery. But—"

"But you don't have paper clips—" Whatever that was.

"Oh, that's no problem. The paper clips were only for structure."

"But your battery is dead—"

"That's no problem either. In that—spell, I was using the battery to make the spinning section go round." He grabbed me excitedly—we tumbled backward off the log; he didn't notice. "It will work just the same the other way! I can reverse the spell and make a spinning section to recharge my battery!"

I grabbed the Quaff bladder before too much spilled. I took a drink. "You mean, you can restore its power?"

"Yes, yes!" He began dancing about, paused, took the bladder from my hands and drank. "I can make as much electrissy as I need. We can even make some for you too, Lant—"

"Uh, no thank you, Purple—"

"But it is great magic! It can help you! You'll see. And I won't need to take it all with me—oh, my goodness—we'll have to turn the spinning section by hand, won't we? Well, we can use a crank and—gears! Migosh, yes—we can gear it up and—"

Abruptly he stopped. "No, it won't work."

"Huh? What's the matter?"

"Lant, it was so long ago. The thing I built was so small. I'm not sure how to do it any more, and I don't know if it would make enough electrissy."

I poured him some more Quaff and sat down on the log again with the bladder. "But you're going to try it, aren't you?"

"Of course," he said. "I have to—but I hardly remember—" He sat down on the log next to me. "Making an airship isn't as easy as I thought."

I nodded. "It's been nine hands of days since we started. I thought this would take only a few at most, but it has gone on and on."

"And on," he added.

I took another swig. "You know," I said, "I've got some more bad news for you."

"Oh? What?"

"There won't be any more aircloth. We've run out of wild housetrees. The weavers can keep weaving, of course, but unless the threads are dipped, it won't do you any good."

"Wonderful," he said. His tone suggested that he thought it was anything but. "Of course, it hardly matters, if we can't make more gas."

I took another drink. So did Purple.

"Of course," he said, "I do have enough aircloth for a small airship—one that would carry me alone——" He trailed off. He hiccuped and said, "If I have to make a hot-air flying spell, I'll do it. Just so that Shoogar can't call me a liar. I promised." He drained his bowl and held it out. I filled it again.

"I'd sell my hope of flying for a quart of good Scotch right now. Well, if we can't bleed the wild housetrees any more, let's bleed the tame housetrees!"

"Blessed housetrees," I corrected him. "Consecrated housetrees. If you try that, they'll burn you for sure. Tampering with a wife is one thing, but a housetree is quite another."

"Can't bleed consecrated housetrees," said Purple. He was having more trouble than usual talking. "Can't bleed consecrated housetrees." His face lit up. "We can deconsecrate them first!"

"Nonsense."

"Why? Shoogar deconsecrated the other villages' weaving patterns. Shoogar deconsecrated the womens' names. Why don't I get to deconsecrate something?"

He was right. "Why not?" I agreed.

"Because I don't know a deconsecration spell," he answered.

"Nobody does," I said. "There are no spells for deconsecrating housetrees."

"Nobody's ever needed one. I'll make one up. Am I not a magician?"

"Certainly," I said.

"Best magician in this whole spiral arm, and two more besides." He was trailing off into gibberish. What he needed was another bowl of Quaff. Me too.

We trudged up to the Upper Village, and climbed into my nest. I dug out a fresh bladder.

Purple took the first swig. Somewhere along the way he'd lost his bowl, so he drank it straight from the bladder.

"How are you going to deconsecrate the trees?" I asked.

Purple lowered the skin from his mouth. He gave me a dignified look of reproach and staggered to his feet, "Let's go look at one and see."

Somewhat unsteadily, he lowered himself from my nest and together we tottered through the village to one of the largest housetrees—that of Hinc the Lesser. Purple took another swill of the Quaff and surveyed it thoughtfully. "To which God is this tree consecrated?" he asked.

"Um, this is the tree of Hinc the Lesser. I believe that it is consecrated to Poup, the God of Fertility. Hinc has fourteen children—all but one of them girls."

"H'm," said Purple, "I would need to deconsecrate it with potions of sterility then, wouldn't I? H'm, Quaff being alcohol is a cleansing medicine. Yes, Quaff can be used to make things sterile. Quaff should be used in the deconsecration spell. And let me see, we should use the petals of the prickly plant which blooms only once in fifty seasons, and . . ." He mumbled on and on like this. I took another drink of the Quaff and followed him back to his nest.

He disappeared up into it, still mumbling. A hail of objects, vials, potions and other magical devices began falling out of the nestdoor. "Junk!" Purple bellowed. "It was all Dorthi's junk. I had to learn the names of each and every—Damn, I'm out of prickly plant petals. Can I substitute?"

"Isn't that dangerous?"

"Do you want to wait fifty family-making years?"

"No."

"I don't either. I'll substitute."

After a bit he dropped out of the nest himself, landing unsteadily on top of the by now large pile of spellcasting items. He started gathering them into a large pack. "It's obvious to me, Lant, that we need to research this a little further. Let's return to the village and look at the trees again."

Again we surveyed Hinc's tree. The sun was red in the west. We had perhaps an hour before blue dawn. "Is this a nighttime or a daytime spell?" I asked.

"I don't know. Let's make it a dawn spell, a five o'clock in the morning spell." He took another drink of Quaff. The bladder was badly deflated by now.

He hiccuped and pulled out a clay mixing bowl. He began mixing a potion, changed his mind abruptly and discarded it. He started another, but poured that one out too—it sizzled on top of the first. Finally he started mixing powders and things in his pottery bowl.

Pottery. I wondered if I should be insulted.

Purple sniffed his mixture and wrinkled his nose. "Ugh! Almost—almost. This should do it, Lant. All it needs is—" Abruptly he straightened and announced, "I have an urge." He lifted his robe and looked around for a bush to step behind. There were none. He looked at the bowl before him, shrugged, "Why not?"

There was a hot spattering into the bowl.

"Purple!" I cried, "That is sheer genius—defiled water will make the spell twice as powerful—*defiled magician's water!* Yes, yes."

He lowered his robe modestly, "It was nothing, Lant. It comes naturally." He reached for the Quaff, explaining, "I may need more later." He drank, then returned the bladder to me.

He hefted his spell-potion bowl carefully. "Now, there is only one thing left to do."

I lowered the skin and said, "What's that?"

"Why, *try* the spell of course——" Immediately he began singing and dancing in a circle around Hinc's tree. On his second round, he almost tripped over his robe, but fortunately he caught himself before he fell into his bowl. Quickly he divested himself of the robe, and picking up the bowl once again began dancing around the tree and singing, "Here we go around the prickly plant, the prickly plant, the prickly plant—here we go around the prickly plant at five o'clock in the morning."

I wondered if I should tell him that it was not a prickly plant he was deconsecrating, but a housetree, when suddenly Hinc shoved his head out of his nest and shouted, "What is that terrible noise?" He wrinkled his nose, "And what is that terrible smell?"

"It's nothing," Purple called as he came around again. "Go back to bed, Hinc. We're only deconsecrating your housetree."

"You're what?" Hinc's neck-fur bristled. He dropped angrily out of the nest.

"Calm down, Hinc," I said. "Have a drink of Quaff while we explain." He did and we did. We told him how we were short of housetree blood, how Purple needed it desperately in order to complete his flying machine and leave this world. We told him how desperately Purple wanted to go home, and how he was doing Purple a great favor. We told him how it would only be for a day or two, and then Shoogar would be glad to reconsecrate the tree.

By the time we finished telling him, Hinc was almost as drunk as we.

He nodded agreeably as Purple gathered up his bowl again and began singing and dancing around the tree, sprinkling it gently with the potion. We watched for a bit and couldn't help laughing.

Purple called out, "Don't stand there laughing. Help me."

We looked at each other and shrugged. Hinc dropped the robe he was holding about himself and easily joined Purple. After pausing for a moment to finish the Quaff I did too.

When we had finished deconsecrating Hinc's tree, we found we had potion left, a lot of it, so we moved on to the tree of Ang the Fish-Farmer and Net-tender. He peered out of his nest at the noise and shouted, "A festival? Wait! I will join you."

Almost immediately he dropped out of his tree, stripping off his clothes, but Purple had stopped singing. "No, it's no good—we're out of Quaff."

"No! No, we're not!" cried Ang. He disappeared back into his nest and reappeared almost immediately with another full bladder. "Here, let the celebration continue!"

After we had danced about his tree five times, Ang suddenly turned to me and asked, "By the way, Lant, what are we celebrating?"

I told him.

"Oh," was all he said. Whatever the magician wanted was fine with him. We kept on dancing.

The noise awakened several other people nearby, and they joined us, with Quaff. We deconsecrated their trees for them too, and were about to start on mine—when abruptly we were out of potion. "It's not fair, Purple. You've deconsecrated everybody else's tree—you've got to deconsecrate mine!"

So we made some more potion.

This time, though, we all provided the defiled water.

By this time the sun was close to rising, we could see the blue-black glare of it behind the horizon. Most of the men in the village were awake now and eagerly joining the line to put defiled water into the potion pots—of which there were several now. We passed around the everpresent Quaff bladders. As soon as one was emptied, another full one seemed to appear from nowhere. The new arrivals kept bringing them. The wives watched nervously from the nests.

And then we were ready to resume the dancing and singing. We danced and sang around every tree we could, until the sun flashed over the horizon. We danced and sang in the harsh blue light until it disappeared behind a cloud bank and abruptly we were in the midst of a raging rainstorm.

"Hurrah! The deconsecration spell has worked!" We skipped down the slope and began to dance around Purple's housetree and the seven giant airbags hanging over it. "The Gods are angry! The Gods are angry!" We sang, "It's raining, it's pouring! All the Gods are roaring!"

Lightning and thunder shattered the sky—the warm drops felt good against our naked fur.

And then—

A crackle of shattering brightness—our hair stood on end —a giant *KKK-R-R-R-ummmmppp!!!* And a ball of orange flame enveloped Purple's airbags, housetree and all.

For a moment I stood petrified—had we gone too far? Was Elcin about to destroy this village too?

And then it was over, and silence reigned. Only the quiet spattering of raindrops.

"Well," said Purple in the stillness. "I guess that's how you deconsecrate a magician's tree."

W hen I awoke, the crimson sun was glaring.

Shoogar was standing above me, also glaring.

"Shoogar," I said and groaned. The sound of my voice hurt my left eye.

"Lant," he replied. His voice hurt my right eye.

"Shoogar," I said.

"Lant," he replied.

"Shoogar," I said.

"I mean to know the meaning of your dancing this morning."

"Not my dancing, not mine." I lifted myself up on one arm. "It was Purple's. He deconsecrated some housetrees so he could use their blood."

"He what??!!"

"Shoogar," I whispered. "Please don't shout. He only did it for a little while. You can reconsecrate them again."

"I can what?!!"

"You can reconsecrate them as soon as we tap their blood."

"When?!!" he screamed. I winced. "I have cloth to bless, airboat frames to bless, threads to bless, nets to bless, weaving to bless. When do I have the time to consecrate house-trees?"

"You'll find time, Shoogar. We didn't deconsecrate that many."

"How many?"

"Um, not that many."

"How many is 'not that many'?"

"Um, let me figure it out. There was Ang's and Hinc's and Kif's and Totty's and Goldin's and . . . um . . . and . . ."

"Come on, clothead. Remember!"

"I will, I will, don't rush me. I think we deconsecrated mine and maybe Purple's—but I don't think we have to worry about Purple's. After we deconsecrated it, there was nothing left. And I think we did Snarg's, but not . . . or maybe . . ."

"Lant, you're such a bloody blithering bowl of bladder-worts—if you don't remember, I'll have to reconsecrate every tree in the whole fang-sucking village!"

"Um, I'm sure I can remember, Shoogar. Just give me time."

Shoogar was preparing to reconsecrate every tree in the village.

But we wouldn't let him. To do that meant that all the other work would have to wait until he could bless it. We would just have to pass out spell tokens to the housetree owners until Shoogar could redeem them. Like Purple's, they would be promises of future spells, and he could catch up later.

"Um," said Shoogar, surveying the village. It was obvious he didn't like the idea. "Well, I still need to know—would you mind telling me just how you and Purple did your spell?"

"It's all every vague. I remember we sang and danced and had a lot of fun. Purple was singing something about 'It's raining, it's pouring, all the Gods are roaring.' "

"I can imagine."

"Oh yes, he also sang, 'Here we go around the prickly plant, the prickly plant, the princkly plant—' "

"He turned the housetrees into prickly plants?"

"Only symbologically, Shoogar—"

"Only symbologically—?" He groaned. "Of course, only symbologically. How else can you turn a housetree into a prickly plant?"

He turned and stared across the hillside, toward the village of prickly plants. "Well," he sighed, "there goes the neighborhood."

The sap-gathering was well under way. I headed down to the Lower Village. Bellis the Potter would have to supply us with everything he had that we could use to hold housetree blood—we weren't going to run out again.

When I told him, he was delighted. It meant a great deal of work, he kept bouncing up and down and shouting, "Oh, goody, goody, goody—spell tokens, spell tokens!"

I shrugged and left him. My head still hurt. I went up the river to look for Purple. I couldn't even find where he had been working. The surf was already crashing in around his blackened housetree stump.

Half the Lower Village was underwater, the Speakers' clearing and the graves of the two boys as well. The river had long since seeped over its banks.

Lower Village families had been trickling up the hill to occupy the housetrees we had prepared for them for some time now, but I had not realized just how high the water had risen. It had been a while since I had been to this part of the village.

I found Purple with Trone the Coppersmith. The two of

them were hard at work with wood and metal. I couldn't fathom what they were doing, but it seemed odd that Trone, a layman, should be working on a magical device.

When I pointed this out, Trone only snarled at me. Purple said, "I need his skills, Lant. He's the only man who can make what I need. We've got the copper wire—now, I need a way to *insulate* it."

"*Insulate?* I wish you'd speak like a man, Purple."

"It means trap the magic in the wire. That way it can't take short cuts. I can make it go round and round in a spiral, but if the wire touches itself—I wonder, maybe if I coated the wires with sap . . ."

"We have more housetree blood, Purple. The gathering crews are busily working in the Upper Village right now. All those trees we deconsecrated—"

"I remember, I remember." Purple clutched at his head. "Ooh. I've got a head you wouldn't believe . . ."

True enough. I hadn't believed Purple's head the first time I saw it. But I had come on weightier matters. I said, "Your housetree was destroyed last night, Purple—"

"No matter. There are others—"

"But your battery—?"

He held it up. "Safe!" he said. "I have kept it with me always."

"Have you worked out a way to restore its power?"

"That's what we're working on now." He indicated the device on Trone's bench. "This one is only a model, but as soon as Trone gets more copper wire, we will be building larger ones. We still have to wind these two iron uprights with copper wire. Then, between them, we will mount a long cylinder of iron so that it can spin between the two uprights. We must wind *that* with wire too, as much as can be fitted on. Then we must run leads for half a mile."

"Half a mile? That's a tradesman's ransom in metal!"

"In your old village it may have been," snorted Trone. "Here metal is more plentiful."

"Besides," said Purple, "we dare not risk bringing the electrissy maker any closer. A stray spark from it might set off all the hydrogen bags."

"Set off?"

"Explode," said Purple. "Catch fire."

"You mean like the ones over your housetree—?"

"Exactly," said Purple. "Only we will be using bigger air-bags for the flying machine—we must be very careful with them."

"Oh, yes," I said. "Oh, yes. By all means. Use a mile of wire if necessary, two miles—a dozen—as much as you need."

Purple laughed at that. "Don't worry, Lant. The danger will be minimal."

"That's what Shoogar said, just before the last conjunction."

He missed the point, began poking at his device again.

"What is it that will make the magic?" I asked.

"The spinner here—" he pointed at the iron bar which would be mounted between the other two uprights. "One must turn this core to make the magic flow. When the wire is wrapped properly, the core will resist turning. We have already mounted the crank here. For the larger ones we will use a set of bicycle pedals and a seat for the pedaller."

"That means more work for my sons," I said. "They will have to build a bicycle frame for your devices, won't they?"

He frowned, "Yes, they will. I hadn't thought of that. I'll go and tell them."

"Don't bother. I'm going up there; I will mention it to them."

"Yes," said Trone to Purple, "you will have to stay here and help me melt this copper into wire. You work the bellows."

Up on Idiot's crag the women were still spinning thread, a pleasant and pastoral scene. Great loops of silvery thread shimmered out over the edge, glistening wetly in the wind.

I climbed past them to where my sons were just finishing the outriggers on the boat. Every day saw them making more and more adjustments with the masts and rigging. All they needed now were the windbags.

The women, of course, did not know about Purple's windbags. All they saw was a great flatbottomed boat with a fin on the bottom and two pontoons mounted far out on the sides.

Naturally, the women gossiped among themselves. Occasionally one of my wives would relate to me the latest rumor —the most recent being that Purple's strange machine was going to fly off the mountain by flapping its wings. Purple was only waiting until Orbur and Wilville could cover the outriggers with fabric and feathers.

We had tried to stop the rumors by showing the loudest of the women the small airbags that Purple had made for the children. *Those* we said would lift the airboat. It did little good. Most of the small airbags had grown flaccid over the few days since they had been filled. They drooped.

I could see what Purple was talking about when he said it was imperative that his battery be recharged—when he took the flying machine on his long journey he would have to be constantly renewing the hydrogen in the balloons.

Wilville was applying another hardening layer of housetree blood to an aircloth-covered side. Orbur was just fastening a bicycle frame to one of the outriggers and stringing pulleys to an odd, bladed construction.

A bicycle on an airboat?

"What in the name of Ouells is that?" I asked.

"It's an airpusher," said one.

"A windmaker," said the other.

"What does it do?"

"It makes wind," said Orbur. "Shall I show you? We have the other one hooked up right—I think." He crawled across the outrigger, into the boat, out the other side and across that outrigger—

"Hey!" cried Wilville. "Be careful!"

"Sorry," said Orbur, still climbing.

"Is it safe to climb on those?" I asked.

"Oh, yes," he called down, "they're designed for it. Whoever is working the airpushers will have to climb out there to sit on the bicycle frames."

"Oh," I said.

He pulled himself onto the bicycle seat, explaining, "If it were in the air, I wouldn't be able to stand on anything but the outrigger. Wilville and I have been practicing, crawling from the boat to the bicycle and back again."

I nodded. "Yes, that makes sense."

"Stand just behind that bladed thing there—not too close." I did so. Wilville paused in his painting to watch.

Orbur began pedaling then—the airpusher started to spin. A wind blew against my face. Harder and harder—it was a pocket hurricane! It was coming from Orbur, coming from that whirling bladed device! I stumbled back with my arm across my eyes.

My sons laughed. Orbur released the bicycle pedals. The spinning slowed and so did the wind.

"You see," said Wilville. "It makes wind. When we get the airboat up in the air, we will lower these slings with the pushers on the end. They hang one manheight below the airframe. We will be sitting on the bikeframes and we will pedal. The pulleys turn the shafts, and the blades make wind. The wind pushes the airboat, and it moves."

"Oh," I said, "but why are there two windmakers?"

"You need two to steer."

"But that means that someone else will have to go with Purple!"

"Two people," corrected Wilville. "One person could not bring the airboat back alone. He would be stranded there."

"But—but—who—who is so foolish as to—?"

"Father," said Orbur. "Haven't you been listening to a thing we've said? *We* are going with Purple."

I felt suddenly stricken. "You're what—?!!"

"Somebody must—who is it that knows the airboat better than us?"

"But—but—"

Orbur climbed down off his bicycle frame, climbed down from the airboat cradle, and came up to me. Gently he put his hands on my shoulders and began to guide me down the hill. "You go home and think about it, Father. You will see that it is the wisest choice. Somebody must see that Purple leaves. Somebody must make sure."

I went. Wilville and Orbur were right.

I trudged back down the hill toward the village. Spread below me was another facet of the airboat's construction. Great swatches of cloth had been spread out across an unused slope and Grimm the Tailor was sewing them together to make the first of Purple's giant airbags.

This was cloth that had already been treated in houseblood and tested for its watertightness. As it was sewn together, the seams would also be treated. The cloth was light and airy, and a gusty wind swept across the hill making ripples in its surface, despite the weights that were holding it down.

I had not realized that we were this far along. I had imagined many more hands of days before we had enough cloth. Apparently, Purple's prophecy had been correct, "It may seem like a long time before we see any results, but when they do happen, they will seem to happen overnight."

Now, all of a sudden, the airboat was almost complete, the first of the bags was being finished and Purple was making a large-scale gasmaker.

As I approached I noticed Shoogar also was working with Grimm. He was holding a copy of—of Purple's blue-drawings! He seemed to be directing something. When I came closer I realized that Shoogar either had figured them out or——

No, it soon became apparent. He was directing the transference of the pattern onto the cloth. Knowing that the bag would form a sphere when inflated, Shoogar wanted the proper spell markings on it. Accordingly, he was using the best flying spell available—Purple's. After all, weren't the blue-drawings the airship itself? Wouldn't it be necessary to have blue-drawings on the balloon in order to make it lift? Shoogar had taken on two apprentices, and they were painting the lines in wide swatches.

I continued on down to the village, where I ran into a disgruntled group of villagers. They were setting up tents beneath their housetrees. "I am not going to live in a prickly plant," Trimmel was saying. "I absolutely refuse."

Others murmured their agreement. I tried to quiet them the best I could. "As your Speaker—" I began.

"Some Speaker—you were part of the dancing!"

"Uh, it is necessary for the Speaker to be on good terms with the magician," I said. "He invited me to dance. I couldn't very well refuse."

"All right," grumbled Snarg. "What are you going to do about it now."

"I'm not going to do anything—Shoogar is. He has promised to reconsecrate all your housetrees as soon as he gets a chance."

"As soon as he gets a chance? That could be days!"

"Don't worry," I said. "He has authorized me to give you blue spell tokens. You will be able to redeem them later."

There was some grumbling at this, but no serious dissent. Spell tokens were accepted in both the villages now.

A voice called, "So where are the tokens?"

"My apprentices are making them," I said. I hurried back to my work area and quickly stained some bone chips blue. I directed my assistants to stain as many blue ones in the future as purple ones. We would need both.

I returned to the villagers and began distributing the tokens. There was a little more grumbling about the house-blood-gathering teams. Some villagers felt that the magicians had no right to take their housetree blood, even if it was a prickly plant now. I paid them a purple token for Purple, and they were satisfied. They disappeared into their nests to sleep.

I wandered downward to the weaving pastures. The weavers were grumbling because Shoogar had not shown up today to offer the morning blessings. I gave them some blue spell tokens in lieu of the blessing. "These are spell tokens too. Shoogar spell tokens. They are just like the Purple ones, only Shoogar will redeem them."

They eyed the blue chips warily. They hadn't liked the purple ones that much, but they had been forced to accept them. Now they were having another chip introduced, and they liked it even less.

I prevailed upon them. "Shoogar will redeem these as soon

as he has time. This is only the promise of a spell. As soon as he catches up with everything else, he'll come by and consecrate the cloth. Go ahead and weave."

Glumly they did so. Now they were getting paid in blue chips and purple chips.

I pocketed the balance of the tokens; I was carrying several of each, and wandered back up to the village. Here and there were a few people I had missed earlier in the day, still moaning about not wanting to live in prickly plants. I gave them some tokens, blue ones for the reconsecration spell, purple ones for the use of their housetree blood.

Having solved those problems, I felt that I had earned my pay as Speaker and went downslope to see Ang the Net Tender. "Ang, have you a fish for my dinner?"

He produced a fine flatfish, already plucked. "I will trade you for it," he said.

"A bone utensil?"

"No," he shook his head, "bone rots here."

"H'm, how about some of the new cloth?"

"No, I already have some new cloth."

I put my hand into my robe fold and found one last blue token. "How about a magic spell?"

"You're not a magician."

"No, but Shoogar is. I will give you this token, which is the promise of a spell."

"H'm," he eyed it warily, "I would rather have one from Purple."

"I can do that." Fortunately, I still had a few Purple tokens with me. I gave one to him for the fish. He handed me the fish and a blue token. "Here is the difference between the value of the fish and the value of the purple token. One Shoogar."

"How did you get a blue token?" I asked. I had just distributed them a few hours earlier. I had not given one to Ang.

"I traded a fish for three blue tokens earlier. Also, I traded for some cloth, but they didn't have enough for me, so they gave me some tokens in exchange, telling me I can trade them back later."

"Oh."

Something about that troubled me. While my wives prepared the flatfish for dinner, I realized what it was. People

212 THE FLYING SORCERERS

were trading those spell tokens as if they were the actual spells themselves. But they weren't. They were only the promises of the spells.

But then again, a promise is a symbol of an act, and a symbol is the same as the act itself.

They were trading magic!

It suddenly occurred to me that it was possible for a magician to make enough "promises" to release an inordinate amount of magic into the village. There would have to be controls of some kind. Oh well, it was Shoogar's problem now, not mine.

Three days later, Grimm finished the first of the giant airbags and began working on the second.

Shoogar and Purple, Wilville and Orbur had already claimed the first one and folded it carefully over the giant filling framework that Wilville and Orbur had built so many hands earlier. Three other filling frameworks waited empty nearby.

"Only four windbags?" I asked.

"No," said Purple. "I hope to use more. But we will probably only need four frameworks. We can only fill one bag at a time, and it will take a while to lay each empty one on a framework. While we're doing that, we can fill the others. We'll do it in rotation."

"Oh," I said. "What is this trench that runs below?"

"That's for the water—instead of using water pots, we are going to use a trench. See these funnel affairs on the side? That's where we will attach the hydrogen-making wires—the airbag mouths will attach here. The oxygen-making wires we will put down at the other end of the trench. We won't need them."

"By using a trench," said Orbur, "we will be able to generate much more electrissy—"

"No," corrected Purple, "we will be able to make better use of it. It will fill the balloons faster."

"We can fill four balloons at once," said Wilville, "or one balloon four times as fast. It all depends where we put the wires and funnels." He held up an odd-looking aircloth bag, a collection of sleeves. "We can attach this to several gas-making funnels, and lead all their hydrogen into one balloon."

"It looks as if you have been doing a lot of work," I said. "All you need now is the electrissy." Purple winced when I said the last word. He always did when I spoke of electrissy. I asked, "Have you and Trone succeeded in making a magic maker?"

Purple sighed. "Yes. Elcin's wrath, but that gave me trouble! Trone did everything right, mind you, but I wound the wire wrong, and then it took me a while to figure out a commutator—"

"A what—?"

"Alternating current, Father," said Wilville. "We can't use it."

"We have to change it to direct current—" said Orbur.

"Never mind. Pretend I didn't ask."

"Okay," said Purple. "Anyway, it's working now. It doesn't make as much electrissy as I'd like, but Trone is building the bigger machines and hopefully, they will be ready before the airbags are. Would you like to see them?"

He didn't give me a chance to refuse, but led me up the slope to where one of the ever-present apprentices was sitting on a bicycle frame and pedaling wildly—but getting nowhere.

"What is he doing?" I asked.

"Look," said Purple. "Isn't it obvious? He is making electrissy."

I looked. All I saw was a complicated arrangement of cranks and belts and pulleys making a spinning thing turn as fast as it could. Two wires led from the spinning thing to Purple's battery.

"He is restoring its power?" I asked.

"Oh yes—he could never restore all of it," said Purple, "but he can make enough electrissy so that it will not run out on the journey."

We trudged farther up the slope. We found Trone and half a dozen other men, working with some giant frameworks of

iron and copper. I had never seen so much metal in my life.
"Where did you get so much?" I asked.

"We practically had to ransack every smith on the island,"
he grunted. Apparently he wasn't too happy about it, but
then Trone was rarely happy about anything.

"When will the bicycle frames be ready?" he asked.

Purple groaned. "Oh, no—I knew I forgot something." He
looked at me. "Your sons have been building bicycles and
bicycles—all without wheels. They have built them to power
the airship, and to make electrissy for my battery—now they
will have to build more, many more. As many as possible to
power these spinning things."

"How many will you need?"

"At least ten or more for each spinning thing. If we have
more, we can turn them faster."

"And how many spinning things are you hoping to build?"

"At least four—but we won't have to wait until they are
all through before we can use them. As each one is finished
we will put it to work storing power in the battery."

I nodded. I was doing some figuring, "But, Purple, you are
asking for forty bicycle frames—without wheels. That's a lot
of bicycles. It takes time to build that many machines."

"I know, I know. We had better go back down and talk
to the boys. We may have to start another put-it-together line.
This time for bicycles."

As we trudged downslope, I noticed that a different apprentice was on the bicycle now. The first was resting. "It is very
tiring work," explained Purple.

"Oh, come now," I said, "I've ridden bicycles—"

"It's not the bicycle," said Purple. "It's the generator. Try
turning that crank on its other side."

"All right." I took the handle in both hands. I waited while
the apprentice dismounted from the bicycle. He was panting
heavily.

The crank did not look that hard to turn. I pushed on it.

The crank turned easily when I moved it slowly, but the
faster I moved it, the more it fought me. An invisible
spirit was pushing back. I felt my fur trying to stand on end.

I let go of the handle and backed away slowly. The crank
whirred to a stop.

"There—now you see why we need a boy on a bicycle."

Legs are stronger than arms. Even so, they still get tired. Can you imagine how hard it will be to make a big machine spin?"

I nodded my head. "I can see, I can see. You will need more than ten bicycles to a machine."

"Right," said Purple.

When we explained the problem to my sons, they nodded understandingly. "We may have to recruit every free man in the village to make a bicycle put-it-together line."

"Do it," said Purple. He turned to me, "You will have to make some more spell tokens, won't you?"

I nodded.

Wilville and Orbur did not seem as depressed as I had thought they would be when Purple told them of the number of bicycles they would have to build. Apparently they had been talking about their bicycle put-it-together line for some time. This would give them a chance to try it out sooner.

Purple began talking over the details with them, "Of course, we will want to fill all the airbags at one time—that means we won't launch the flying boat until all four generators are working. But as each one is finished we'll put it to work storing power. My battery will hold as much electrissy as any of these machines can turn out. The best part about it is that we can use it to supplement the power from the generators when we are ready to launch the boat and fill the airbags that much sooner."

"Won't you run the risk of making it dead again?" I asked.

"Not really. It has a power meter on it. That tells me how much power I have left. I have figured out how much we will need to be sure of making the trip north safely. As long as there is that much in the battery, we are okay. Anything over it we can use for the launching. I can regulate the outflow of the power, Lant, so as to fill the balloons as fast as I can on launch day."

I nodded knowingly. I hadn't understood a word he had said—but I felt he needed the reassurance.

The waters continued to rise. The surf crashed higher on the slope every day. The tides came in—and in and in and in, until most of the people of the Lower Village were forced to move up the slope. Only the tops of the housetrees marked where the major portion of the village had been. Occasionally a nest would break free, and be seen floating away.

The Upper Village was fairly crowded, but we were able to manage with a minimum of doubling up. Wilville and Orbur were able to recruit quite a few men for their bicycle put-it-together line. It gave many of the villagers something to do while waiting for the waters to recede, and there were those who were eager to earn extra spell chips.

By the time the first twelve bicycle frames were finished, Trone had finished the first of the big spinning things— generators he called them. The boys connected up the bicycles that same day.

Shoogar had recruited twelve good men for the first test. They stood nervously to one side and grumbled to themselves. They were unhappy about the prospect of making electrissy. Shoogar kept fumbling with his magic kit, and every time he did, the men twitched in response.

No matter. As long as we could perform the test.

Purple checked over the wires that led across the hill to the water-filled trench. When he was ready he signaled Shoogar with a wave of his hand. Shoogar bade the men mount the bicycles.

At another command they began pedaling. The generator began spinning, slowly at first, then faster and faster—it was making electrissy. Sure enough, down by the trench there was activity—other men were clustering around the wires.

I left the generator crew and approached the water trench. From one end, oxygen bubbled steadily upward. At the other, Purple was just fitting a clay spout over a water-immersed wire. To this he attached a small airbag. Within a few minutes it was full.

He tied it at the neck and released it. It drifted gently upward. This time though, there was no panic—only a cheer. We were becoming more and more used to this spell. Indeed, it was almost commonplace by now.

Purple was delighted. He signaled Shoogar to stop the pedaling. He then trudged halfway up the hill and connected his battery to the leads from the generator.

"All right, Shoogar," he called, "start them up again."

Shoogar growled an order and the twelve men began pumping again. It looked strange to see them pedaling as hard as they could and getting nowhere—but it was only a foretaste of things to come. Purple wanted a whole army of men up on the hill, pedaling wildly.

The smaller generator—the one powered by one apprentice on a bicycle—was dismantled then, and its parts cannibalized for the larger generators. It was one less bike frame to build and that much more wire that could be used.

Wilville and Orbur were pleased at the success. That the twelve bicycle frames had been built so quickly testified to the efficiency of their put-it-together line. "I figure we could have at least fifty bicycles before another hand of days is up," said Orbur.

We started trudging up the slope to where the airboat waited. Wilville replied, "I think only part of it is the put-it-together line, Orbur—remember, we have an awful lot of people working for us too."

"Yes, but we had to teach them."

When we got to the Crag the boys pointed out what still needed to be done on the airboat. Some of the rigging structures to hold the ropes for the balloons had not been secured yet, and Wilville wanted to add at least one more coat of hardener to the sides of the airboat. It felt hard enough to me, but then it was my sons who would be flying in it, and if they felt they wanted it hard, it was their boat.

Orbur explained that he had adjusted the airpushers as well as he could, but he wanted to experiment some more with "higher" gears. He wanted to try putting smaller wheels on the spinning sections and larger wheels on the bicycle frames. The connecting pulleys should then make the airpushers spin

even faster. But he needed new pulley cloths first. He hoped
to have them before this hand of days was over.

Wilville sighed as he began heating his hardening solution.
"I'm glad that most of the other building is over—we could
have had this boatframe finished months ago had it not been
for all the bicycle frames and filling frameworks and cranking
machines we have had to work on."

"Yes," I agreed. "But the boatframe couldn't have gone
anywhere until all the other work was done first. You needed
the aircloth and the generators and the cranking thing for
making loomteeth and—"

"It's just as Purple said. You have to make the tools with
which to make the tools to make the tools," Orbur called
from above. "That's just what we have been doing. You can't
just build an airboat—you have to build the put-it-together
line which can make the pieces which will make the airboat."

"Imagine the size of the put-it-together line for Purple's
black egg," replied Wilville.

I tried to, but I couldn't.

I noticed a figure trudging up the hill then—it was Shoogar.
He had come to inspect the flying machine.

"Oh, not again," groaned Orbur. "He's up here almost
every day now, asking questions and annoying us—"

"He's only trying to understand the spell," I said.

"He will never understand the spell," said Wilville. "He is
a—"

"Watch it," I cautioned, "whatever else he may be, he has
phenomenal hearing."

Shoogar arrived then and *tsk-ed* satisfactorily over the
progress of the work. "But when will you hang the sails?"
he asked.

Orbur said, "Sails? We won't be hanging any sails, Shoogar.
We don't need them."

"Nonsense," said the magician peering up at Orbur who
was hanging in the rigging. "How many times must I
explain to you—you can't be pushed by the wind without
sails."

Orbur began climbing down. I could see that he was sighing to himself. He swung down a rope to the boat's cradle,
then dropped off the edge to the ground. He walked around

to Shoogar, "Purple has explained it to us over and over. We won't need sails. We have the windmakers instead."

Shoogar stamped his foot impatiently. "No, Orbur—if you have windmakers then obviously you are planning to use sails. The windmakers will make wind and push the sails, and the boat will move."

"No, Shoogar—the windmakers push the air backward and the airboat moves forward. *Without sails.*"

"Without sails, what will they have to push against? The boat won't move at all through the air."

"The boat will move."

"It won't."

"Purple says it will."

"And I say it won't."

"I say it will!"

"Are you arguing with a magician?!!"

"Yes! We have tested the windmakers already—and when both Wilville and I are pumping as hard as we can the boat seems to edge forward as if it could hardly wait to leap into the air."

"It may get into the air," said Shoogar, "but it'll never move an inch without sails!"

"But—"

"Don't try to correct me, Orbur. I've already ordered the sails from Lesta. You and Wilville had best plan on masts for them."

"Masts?" asked Orbur. "And where will we put masts?" He pointed at the boatframe. It sat gently on the cradle, its two outriggers stretching wide on either side, its heavy keel hanging below on a spar of bambooze. It had a flimsy looking set of bambooze rigging above, empty and waiting for the air-bags. It looked strangely incomplete. I tried to imagine it finished and in the air, but could not.

Shoogar peered at it. He circled the boat thoughtfully, stepping around Wilville who quietly and calmly continued to paint.

He climbed up on the launching cradle and peered into the boat itself. Orbur and I followed. He climbed in and rapped on the floor. "What's this?"

"It's *sand-ash wood*. We're using three thin planks to add stability to the floor."

"It's too thin. We can't possibly mount masts in it."

"That's what I'm—"

"We'll have to hang them from the outriggers."

"Where? There's no room at all behind the airpushers!"

True enough, there wasn't. There was a bicycle frame at the back of each outrigger. The airpushers hung a good man-height below the bicycle seats and well behind the pedals— so that the pedaller would not be riding in his own wind.

"You'll have to put them in front," said Shoogar. "Plenty of room if you do that. Put the masts and sails in front of the windmakers, then pedal in reverse. The wind will blow forward, into the sails. You'll be facing in the direction you're going."

"But pedaling in reverse is hard work!"

"Then reverse the gear!" Shoogar snapped. "Do I have to do all your thinking for you?"

"We do not need any sails!" Orbur shouted at him.

"All you have is Purple's word for that." Shoogar's voice suddenly turned persuasive. "Set the masts now, put the sails on before you leave. Then you'll be prepared for anything. If the sails don't work, you can take them off!"

"Well—" Orbur hesitated. He looked at Wilville. Wilville studiously ignored him, slapped the paint on extra fast.

"It wouldn't hurt," I suggested.

"There!" said Shoogar. "You see—even your own father thinks so."

"Yes, but—"

"No buts about it. The sails will be ready in seven days."

Pleased that he had won the battle, Shoogar began climbing down from the boat. As he dropped to the ground, he rapped sharply on the sturdy side of hardened aircloth. "Good construction," he noted. He grabbed my arm and started dragging me toward the village, "Now then, Lant, we have to get straight on this matter of the spell tokens. The blue tokens are obviously not being properly appreciated by the villagers."

"What do you mean?"

"They are trading four Shoogars for one Purple—why just this morning Hinc the Lesser told me that it was because I was only one fourth the magician that Purple is. Excuse me, Hinc the Hairless told me."

"Oh," I said.

"Now tell me honestly, Lant—could you agree with a point of view like that?"

"Uh, well—" I began.

"Don't be afraid, Lant. You can tell me the truth."

"Well, Shoogar—it is well known that you do much more work than Purple. You do most of the spellcasting in the village, and Purple hardly does any. That makes Purple's magic much rarer and worth a lot more. The people know that they can always redeem your coins for spells—but Purple's magic is rarer, and hence they seem to think that it is more valuable or else he would use it as freely as you do."

"H'm," said Shoogar.

"Well, you wanted me to be truthful."

"I didn't mean for you to be *that* truthful." He grumbled on down to the village. Certainly he had the right to be miffed.

But there was no help for it. Already the villagers were calling Shoogar's blue tokens "quarters." The custom was now fixed in the language.

Orbur was having some trouble with his gears. He had dismantled the whole assembly and rebuilt them from scratch. When finished, he had increased the speed of the airpushers so that the boat had to be tied down when he tested them.

He had connected three sets of pulleys to each windmaker in descending orders—Purple called it "high gear." There was the large wheel which was turned by the man pedaling. The pulley from this was looped around a very small wheel which was caused to turn very fast. On the same shaft as this small wheel was another large wheel. A pulley from this large wheel was connected to the shaft of the bladed airpusher.

Orbur had also changed the pulley cloths, alternating the loops in order to reverse the spin of the airpushers. Now they threw their wind forward, toward the masts.

Purple came to inspect the progress and nodded in satisfaction. Then his eye caught the masts that protruded below each outrigger, and he asked, "What are these?"

"For the sails," Orbur explained.

"Sails? Are we going to have to start that again?"

"No, but Shoogar—"

"Shoogar. I might have known. Shoogar wants sails, does he?"

"See for yourself. When they're mounted, the wind from the airmakers will blow right into them. We won't have to wait for a breeze—if it works. In fact," said Orbur, "it ought to work for boats too. If—" But he had to stop there, for Purple was leaning against the hull, chortling, while his nude face grew redder and redder.

"You think it won't work," Orbur said sadly.

"Yes, yes, I think that. But try it anyway. What harm can it do? There is only one way Shoogar will ever be convinced that we don't need sails. We'll have to let him try it." He turned to go, but turned back. "Just be sure we can remove the sails after we prove they don't work."

Down the slope Trone had finished two generators, and there were more than twenty men pumping away on each of them. All of their power was going steadily into Purple's little battery.

Purple was growing more and more impatient every day. He hovered around the workers like a bumble-sting, prodding and poking. Grimm, the tailor, had finished sixteen airbags for him. Each, when inflated, would be nearly six manlengths in height.

Purple estimated that ten airbags might lift the boat, but thirteen would be necessary to carry the additional supplies he wanted to take—and sixteen balloons would give him a margin for error in case they leaked faster than he had figured. He was worried about the seams.

Grimm also made three additional airbags to be taken along in case of emergency. If one of the airbags developed a leak too big to be patched, or was otherwise damaged, Purple would have a spare with which to replace it.

In short, we were taking no chances—when Purple left, we wanted to be sure he was gone.

Right now he was directing the anchoring of the filling frames. He had suddenly realized how light they were, and did not want to risk a balloon suddenly lifting up and taking a filling frame with it.

With Grimm's help they had worked out a system of harness and anchor ropes for the balloons, and as each one was filled, six men wearing weighted belts would ferry it up to the Crag where Wilville and Orbur waited. The rigging ropes for the airboat were laid out across the launching cradle in a set pattern, and the harness ropes had to be attached in a specific order. Then—and only then—would the anchoring ropes be released. Purple did not want to risk losing even one of his giant balloons. They had taken too much time and effort to build.

Originally he had planned to use many smaller balloons, each the height of a man—but then he had done some figuring—he could hold the same amount of gas in fewer but larger balloons—and it would not need as much cloth. He would still be able to fly, and it would not take so long to make his windbags.

Purple and Shoogar had created a whole new trade—airmen. These were the various crews who were tending the generators, the filling frames, the water trenches, the anchoring of the airboat—everything that was needed to fly.

More and more villagers came to watch or help. We had little else to do now that the seas had reached their peak—even the lower slope of the Upper Village was under water now. Most people were living close to the working site anyway. That was fortuitous for Purple—he always had need of men to pump on his bicycles, and the demand for his spell tokens was so great that there was never any shortage of volunteers.

Purple grew more and more impatient with each day. The only thing holding him up was the production of electrissy.

Apparently, it took fantastic amounts to make enough hydrogen.

The fourth generator had not even been begun when Purple began filling his airbags. He was experimenting, he said. He wanted to see how long it took to fill each one, and he needed to know how fast they lost their gas. Besides, it would be easier to pump a limp airbag taut than to start from scratch. And in any case, it would take several days to fill all the balloons.

That he was eager to see how well his flying machine worked was no secret. There were almost thirty men on each generator now and he had more than enough power in his battery to fill all the airbags. He would use it if he had to, he said, but he hoped to save it for his journey where it would really be necessary.

We watched as he arranged the wires in the trough. The women began filling that channel with water. Fortunately, they did not have to carry it very far, only half a mile uphill, and the slope was gentle.

There was some hassling then with the filling crews, the boys who had been hired to watch the filling of the bag, but finally Purple straightened out their instructions and they began laying one of the finished airbags across the frame.

Shoogar and Gortik and I exchanged a glance. "You know," said Gortik. "I actually think he's going to do it——"

"I've never doubted it," I said.

Shoogar only snorted.

"All that work, all that work—" Gortik murmured. "Frameworks and looms and bicycles——all that work, just to build a flying machine."

"He said it was a complicated spell," I put in.

Shoogar snorted again.

"It's necessary though," I added. "Otherwise, he can't go home."

"He must want to go home very badly," Gortik said.

"Not as badly as we want him to," Shoogar snapped. "And the sooner the better. I think I'll go help him." And he tottered off down the hill. "There are supplies to gather and sails to pack."

It was a strange scene—four giant frames, three covered with cloth, and the fourth holding a gently puffing mass of rising airbag. A trench of water ran below, and bubbled furiously at its free end. At its other end a nozzle and hose attachment reached up to the giant bag.

Farther up the slope, more than a hundred and twenty men were pumping wildly on their bicycles. Great spinning generators whirred loudly. One could hear their high-pitched whine all over the hill—but we had become used to that sound. It had become a part of our lives.

Nine airbags had already been filled and ferried up the hill. Wilville and Orbur were climbing excitedly about on the airboat frame, making last minute adjustments in the rigging.

All over the slope we could see the imposing frame of the craft—and at last we saw what Purple had visualized all this time. Not all the airbags had yet been attached; yet the nine straining upward from their ropes gave us an idea—a cluster of moons swelling gloriously in the red and blue light.

It had taken nearly five days to fill this many bags. Already the first bags filled were starting to droop, and others were showing ripples in the wind—signs that they were not as taut as they should be.

But Purple had counted on a certain amount of leakage during the time it took to fill the bags. He intended to use his battery to replenish the hydrogen in each of them just before departure.

By now the affair had turned into quite a festival. There was much singing and shouting and drinking of Quaff. The men working on the generators had organized themselves into teams and had begun competing—each team trying to see how long they could go at full speed—each team trying to prove it was stronger than the other.

Purple was delighted. He offered two extra spell tokens for every man on the winning team. As soon as one competition was ended, another promptly began, fresh teams replacing the tired ones on the bicycles. The process of replacement was always fun to watch—one man at a time would hop off his bicycle, leaving the pedals still spinning wildly. Another would then hop on and match the rate of pumping. The next man in line would then hop off his bike and so on.

As soon as all the teams were replaced the signal would be given, and another competition would begin with a roar from the spectators. Purple had even permitted a certain amount of side-wagering with his spell tokens although Shoogar and I had expressed some misgivings about it. "Why not?" Purple said. "It makes them more enthusiastic."

He was right about that. Often the teams would bet large amounts of spell tokens against each other so that it was possible for a generator team to *lose* chips while they worked. But if they didn't mind . . .

Trone and his men were eager to finish the fourth generator—they hoped to form a bicycle team themselves and earn some of those extra chips. His would be a formidable team, I thought. Trone's arms and legs were strong and thick from years of coppersmithing. I might bet on him myself.

Meanwhile, the eleventh balloon was already puffing up. The tenth was just being removed from its filling frame for its transfer up the slope. Purple was directing the transfer, with much swearing and threats of curses.

It was an eerie sight: Six strong men bouncing slowly up the hill under the *absence of weight* of the giant balloon. Once a sudden gust of wind caught them, and they bounced high in the air and floated slowly down. All were laughing—except Purple. He was white beneath his beard as he followed them up.

Then they were on the Crag, and the harnessed bag was attached to the rigging. The rope transfer was made and the men released the balloon—it snapped upward to join the others. They were blue spheres with white lines inscribed upon them, looking tiny from here. The airboat tugged at its mooring, and Purple kept climbing in and out of it, pulling at its rigging and anchoring ropes.

Satisfied, he came bounding down the hill again, shouting, "Two more balloons, Lant. Two more and I can go flying!"

"I thought you wanted to use sixteen—"

"But it works so well, look! See how it tugs at its ropes—and that's with only ten balloons! And see how some of them are limp. Imagine how it will lift when I pump them up again with the battery! Two more balloons should do it. Those will be for the weight of the supplies and the passengers. We will be able to test it today!"

And he bounded on down the hill to supervise the filling of the eleventh balloon. I followed slowly in his wake. Thoughtfully.

I couldn't get used to the idea. Purple was actually leaving!

He had actually built his flying machine, and he was actually going to leave in it. Soon we would be rid of him.

I shook my head as I looked over the fantastic activity below me—things would not be the same with him gone.

A group of boys stood down near the unused end of the trough, cheering the balloons and giggling hysterically.

Some were rolling in the blackgrass, others were peering into the bubbling water. Trone's generator wires led into the water right at that point, and apparently the boys liked to watch it bubble.

They had been gathering at this point for some days now, ever since Purple had begun filling his airbags.

I began to wonder about this. Curious, I approached that end of the trough and observed. The water was bubbling furiously as the gas rose from the wires. The young men would put their faces near it and inhale deeply, then fall back among their fellows and giggle happily.

Their behavior was much like that of one who was drunk

on Quaff—but that was silly. These boys were still unconsecrated and not allowed to drink Quaff.

But then, what was producing this strange effect?

I pushed my way through them and asked, "What's going
on here?"

They shook their heads shamefacedly, but would not say.
I bent over and sniffed at the bubbling waters, but I could
smell nothing. Curious, that. I took another sniff. Still nothing. It was interesting though. I took another sniff, a deep
one—I felt just a wee bit light-headed.

I took another sniff—was it possible that this gas made
people light-headed? I wondered about that. The other gas
made things light——this gas made people light. No, I'd
have to think about that. I took another sniff. The other
gas made things rise above other things. This new gas made
people's view of things rise above other things.

Another sniff—how strange! I knew what I meant. Why
weren't there words for it? I lowered my head again——

Abruptly I was being pulled away by Shoogar, "Lant,
Lant—what is the matter with you?"

"Um—ah, oh—hi, Shoogar—"

He dragged me downwind of the bubbling water. "What
are you doing?"

"Um, I was investigating the bubbles."

"You will turn into a bubblehead—like those wastrels!" He
gestured at the boys once again gathered around the trench.
"They talk about the strange gas that makes them light."

"I didn't know you'd investigated it, Shoogar." I was beginning to feel heavy again. "Is it dangerous?"

"Of course it is—if only because it teaches the young
to enjoy themselves."

"Something should be done," I said.

"Right." Shoogar fumbled in his sleeve. "I'll toss a ball
of fire at them." He reached and pulled and—

Fwoof! It went off in his hand, burning and sizzling faster
than I'd ever seen—

Shoogar yelped and plunged his hand into a water pot.
He shouted, "See? I told you the bubbles were dangerous!"

When it happened, it happened in broad double daylight. Red sunlight and blue lit the sky. The windbags glowed like moons; one side red, the other blue.

There was always a crowd on the Crag now, and Purple had posted men to keep them back. Mongers moved among the people, trading sweetdrops and spicy meats for small tokens.

Wilville and Orbur were just storing the last of Purple's supplies. Each packet had been wrapped in aircloth to protect it from the wet and cold Purple said they would find in the upper sky.

I stood below, leaning on one of the taut ropes that led from the boat to the ground.

Purple was up on the landing cradle with three large pots of water. He had his battery connected to one of them, and a neck of cloth hung down from one of the balloons. It was tied tightly to the water-pot funnel, and as we watched, this last giant sphere swelled and tightened.

Abruptly one of the mooring ropes parted. One end of the boat swung upward.

There was an *"Oooooo!"* from the crowd.

Purple jumped back in surprise, knocking over one of the water pots. Wilville and Orbur had been thrown to the floor of the boat—they stuck their heads up confusedly.

"The other end! The other end!" Purple was shouting and pointing, "Go stand at the other end!" He pointed to the nose of the boat which was aimed eagerly at the sky.

Wilville and Orbur scrambled quickly up the boat. As they did so, that part of it started to settle. Purple began directing men to secure it with new mooring ropes. He bent to disconnect his battery, and hurriedly began tying off the neck of his balloon.

And then Shoogar arrived, leading an excited team of men, bringing with them the twelfth giant windbag. He

229

caught sight of the eager airboat and cried, "Purple, Purple—don't leave without your balloon!"

The murmur of the crowd rose behind him—a gabble of voices and conflicting opinions. "Shut up, Shoogar—if he wants to leave without it, let him!"

Wilville was leaning out over the edge, pointing and waving at the men with the balloon—"No, no! That's the wrong rope—don't attach it there!" They couldn't hear him.

"Wilville! Orbur!" I cried. "Get out of the boat!"

But Purple was crying, "Stay in the boat! Stay in the boat!" He jumped off the landing cradle and ran over to where Shoogar and the others were trying to attach the windbag. "Not here, you slithy tove!" He began pulling them around to the other side—"This is the rope, here!"

For a moment I thought they were going to lose it—the bag was as eager as the rest to leap into the sky. Thank the Gods for the anchor ropes. If we lost a balloon, we would lose many days of work. The anchor ropes prevented that. The balloons could not escape their tethers. If we let go of one, it would only snap upward until we could pull it down again.

Under Purple's direction the men were able to fasten the bag to the proper rope without losing it. It snapped upward, and the rope strained as taut as the others.

This last windbag seemed to do it. The boat hung upward at the end of its mooring ropes. The chatter of excited voices rose.

"Ballast!" Purple was crying. "Get the ballast bags—"

"I'll do it!" cried Orbur and started to climb out of the boat—"

"No!" Purple swarmed up the cradle and pushed him back in—he fell to the deck slats with a thump. "You stay in the boat! We need your weight to help hold it down."

Shoogar was bouncing around the base of the launching cradle, barking at the men struggling to tie more mooring ropes. Heavy wooden stakes were being pounded into the ground.

Other men came running across the slope—each carrying two heavy ballast bags with him. They swung ominously back and forth. Trone the Coppersmith brought four.

The ballast bags were also made of aircloth, and filled

with sand. Purple had realized their need only a hand of days ago, and Grimm had had to hurry to sew them up. Trone had taken the responsibility of seeing that they were filled.

Now the men came jumping up onto the cradle and practically threw the bags at Wilville and Orbur—Orbur slipped under their weight and disappeared again into the bottom of the boat. There was a muffled curse.

The bags had been finished and waiting since this morning. Purple said they were needed to provide extra weight that was expendable as the gas leaked out. A thought occurred to me—why hadn't he put them in the boat as they were finished, instead of waiting till the last moment like this. It certainly would have been easier.

"More bags! More bags!" He was calling. The men took off again, dashing to get another load. Wilville and Orbur staggered to stow them evenly.

Purple then jumped into the boat to help. He grabbed the ballast bags as each one was brought up, and directed their distribution about the craft.

I jumped up on the cradle. "Purple," I screamed over the noise of the crowd and the ballast runners. "It has been a great honor to have you here—we will miss you greatly—your memory will never be forgotten—we wish you the speediest of journeys—"

"Shut up, Lant—you blithering wart! I'm not going anywhere. I'm only going on a test flight! That's why we only need twelve balloons for now. We'll need the other four for the longer journey, but right now we only want to see how well she handles in case we have to make any modifications—"

"Don't forget the sails! The sails!" Shoogar came screaming up. His arms were laden with great folds of cloth, and he was followed by two apprentices, also laden with cloth.

"Yes," said Purple. "We can use them as ballast—Shoogar, what are you doing?!!"

Shoogar paused. He was climbing into the boat. "What does it look like I am doing?"

"It looks like you're getting into the boat—"

"That's right, I am. You cannot take from me the honor of the first flight."

"Honor?!! Shoogar, this might be very dangerous—"

"It will be even more dangerous if you don't take the sails—you will have no way to move through the air." His assistants began handing them over the sides to him.

Purple shrugged. He grabbed one last sandbag from Trone. Did the airboat seem to sag? Had the mooring ropes slackened momentarily? "All right, Shoogar," he said. "You can come. I guess I do owe you a ride in my flying machine."

"*Our* flying machine," corrected Shoogar.

"All right," sighed Purple. He climbed up a rope ladder to get a better view. "Trone!" he called. The coppersmith looked up. "Be sure that you and the rest of the flight crew pump up the other four balloons! We will be needing them. And organize that ground crew that I told you about—we will need them when we return!"

Trone waved and grinned. "Don't worry, Purple."

Purple waved back. He climbed higher up the rope ladder and began checking the rigging of the balloons. "Wilville," I whispered loudly, "be careful! Do not let the magicians kill each other!"

"Father," he called back, wide-eyed, "do not let the magicians kill us!"

"Don't worry—they won't. They need you to pedal the bicycles and turn the airpushers. Just be careful—don't fall off."

"We won't—we are going to tie safety ropes around our necks."

"Try your waists," I suggested. "It'll be even safer. Good luck with the sails."

He groaned. "We'll need it. Shoogar will not be convinced —he is sure we will need sails."

"What do you think?" I asked.

Wilville shook his head. "Purple's first flying machine didn't have sails. I think he knows what he's talking about. So does Orbur—"

We were interrupted by a voice from above. Purple had completed his check of the rigging and he was calling, "All right, *cast loose! Cast loose* the ropes!"

"Huh? What—? Talk like a man, Purple! Not your demon language!"

He screamed, "*Cut the ropes, curse you!*"

I paled and grabbed for a knife.

"Try to cut them all at once!" he shouted.

I started hacking at the first of the mooring ropes. Both Shoogar and Purple were yelling at me from above. As soon as I cut it, that side of the boat leapt upward, throwing it into a violent slant. Purple and Shoogar screamed excitedly, "The other side! Cut the ropes on the other side now!"

I ran around to the other side and cut a rope there, but then that side leapt upward. I ran back to the first side and cut another rope, but now the front of the airship was hanging lower than the back, and so I had to cut another and meanwhile all of them were screaming, Wilville and Orbur, Purple and Shoogar, Trone and the ballast crew, the roiling crowd—even Lesta, upset because the ropes had been bound from his finest cloth.

And then there was only one rope left—the airboat was pointed severely at the sky. I cut it and——

It leapt upward, and there was a great echoing cheer from the crowd. I collapsed on the cradle, rolled over on my back, and watched them shrink into the sky. I was glad that there had not been more ropes. I was panting heavily.

The sky was sparkling blue. The airboat was a slender shape, hanging under a cluster of swollen grapes. The crowd *ooh'd* and *ah'd* as it floated up and away from them.

It was not the first time I had seen a flying machine. But I felt a surge of pride as it rose into the sky—as if I had built it myself. It was so much lovelier than Purple's black egg had been. And after all, hadn't I helped to build it?

A white sail bloomed beneath one of the outriggers.

Then another.

Still the flying boat continued to rise. I thought I could hear voices floating back to me, tiny from the distance, but shrill with emotion: "We don't need your guilty-of-incestuous-rape sails!"

"We do!"

"We don't!"

"We do!"

But perhaps it was only the wind.

The wind pushed the tiny speck of the airship over the mountains and out of sight, and we settled down for a few quiet days of recovery.

Lesta and his weavers continued to make their cloth, the women relaxed into a more leisurely pace of spinning. The airboat was finished now, and there was no longer an urgent need for dipped aircloth. Indeed, Lesta was considering abandoning the dipping steps altogether, except for small amounts of thread and cloth specifically set aside for the weaving of watertight fabrics.

Trone finished the fourth generator and attached the bicycle frames to it. There were forty men on each generator now, but still, those on the bicycle-put-it-together line kept building. No one had told them to stop. Besides, more and more men wanted to join the generator pumping teams, and the only way to do that was to increase the number of bicycles.

The four balloons were filled in just a little more than one full day. They hung tautly in their filling frameworks. With all four generators working it was possible to fill a balloon faster than ever—indeed, they grew and swelled as we watched. The oxygen bubbled furiously from the other end of the trench, and the bubble-heads giggled hysterically.

My assistants were carving nearly three sets of loom-teeth a day, just to replace the ones that had worn out. Every afternoon was spent carving new chips for Purple and Shoogar.

Damd the Tree Binder was busier than ever. Many of those who had emigrated from other villages were tired of their tents, and wanted to move into proper housetrees. Because of the shortage, Damd had begun binding trees to hold two or three nests whenever possible. In a way it was a lost effort. The trees would be under water before they would be ready for nests.

Ang had commissioned three more giant nets from Lesta, and was working out new ways to increase his catch of fish every day. One set of nets was strung across the river. Another set of nets hung from an overhanging ledge of rock which had not been submerged by the rising seas. The third set was used in the most ingenious way yet. Ang had built a boat, much like the hull of the flying machine. Each day he and three of his apprentices would row out a ways, trailing the net behind them. They had to be careful though—once they caught a submerged housetree.

In short, life had settled down to a regular and steady pace. Neither of the magicians were present to consecrate anything, and Shoogar's two apprentices were neither skilled enough nor trusted enough to handle even routine consecrations, so I took it upon myself to distribute tokens as necessary.

Of course I levied a small charge for my carving services upon both Purple and Shoogar—it was the least they could do for me. Hence, as monitor of all the carved chips, for every nine I carved for them, I kept two for myself. It was a fair rate.

Of course I had other sources of wealth as well. Lesta and I had renegotiated our contract for the use of the loomteeth. I would provide him with as many loomteeth as he would need, in return for which I received seven percent of his total output, payable either in spell tokens or cloth.

I was beginning to think about the purchase of a third wife. The gods knew I was entitled to it. I had had three wives before, and had never been happy with the demotion to two-wife status. It was not fitting for a Speaker to have only two.

I decided, however, to wait until the airship returned. If this first airship worked well, we might be able to build others. We could perhaps use such ships of the sky for trading expeditions. Yes, that would enrich us considerably. Large bodies of water would no longer be barriers to travel, and we would not be cut off from the mainland every wading season.

Gortik and I and Lesta and the other advisors discussed the idea eagerly. Lesta, who was now the head of the newly enlarged Clothmakers' Guild (formerly the Weavers' Caste), was one of the strongest adherents of the idea. Of course he had the most to gain—it was his cloth that they would be trading. But still, there was little opposition from any of the rest of us. Aircloth had enriched all of our lives considerably.

We spent those three days resting—and making exciting plans for the future—and speculating about the fate of the airship. We had not been told how long they would be gone. Purple had said only that they would take as long as necessary, until they had determined how best to steer and control the *Cathawk*—for that was what he had decided to call the boat.

It did not look like a *cathawk* to me, but it was Purple's spell, so I did not question it.

Without the magicians the village seemed strangely quiet —and I began to wonder, was this how it would be after Purple was gone? A strange thought that—I had grown so used to Purple's presence, I could not imagine this village existing without him.

I spent one afternoon helping Trone and his ground crew. They were practicing the mooring of the *Cathawk* when it returned. One group of men stood on the launching cradle and threw down ropes, pretending to be the returning airship. The ground crew stood below. When we threw down the ropes, they would chase after them and grab them as fast as they could—then they would pull us off the cradle.

It quickly turned into a competition. We would throw down our ropes and try as hard as we could to keep the ground crew from catching them. The ground crew would try as hard as they could to pull us from our perches. As they were some of the burliest men in two villages, they always won.

Afterward, panting, sweating and covered with dirt, I went up to Trone and asked him if he thought all this effort was truly worth it. After all, the *Cathawk* would only be making this one landing, and then we'd never see it again.

Trone grunted, "Purple is paying me and my men to see that the *Cathawk* is grounded safely. It is to our own benefit to see that it does. If anything should happen to the airboat, Purple will only want to build another—and that might take another three hands of hands of days. You want to see him gone, don't you?"

I couldn't argue with that.

Shortly after that a rumor started that once Purple returned, he would outfit the *Cathawk* immediately for his journey north, and leave without redeeming any of his spell tokens.

I tried to stop such foolish prattle, but the villagers would not be convinced. They felt that if Purple did not cast spells in return for his coins, they were worthless. I said that this was nonsense. The coins were symbols of the magic and, as such, were magic themselves. They were as good as a real consecration. Just keep the spell token near the object to be consecrated.

They didn't believe me.

Instead, they argued about the *Cathawk.* Trone took credit for it by saying that it was his generators that made the gas that put it into the air. The pumping crews said that the generators wouldn't have done any good at all without their effort. Lesta laughed at them both, saying that it was his cloth that had done the job. Nonsense, said the weavers, it was their effort in weaving the cloth. Yes, agreed my apprentices, but they couldn't have done it without my loom-teeth. Grimm claimed it was his work in sewing up the air-bags, the thread-dippers claimed it was their housetree blood, and even the women murmured about the thread they had spun. But the heights of idiocy were reached when the ballast-stuffers claimed it was their sand that allowed the *Cathawk* to fly—it flew when Purple threw it out.

It would have been funny; except that they were all taking it so seriously! Ang was making a small fortune selling dried fish—the same kind, he said, that Purple had taken with him on his historic flight.

The speculation went on about the flight itself. I wondered if they had used Shoogar's sails. Wilville and Orbur believed that Purple's airpushers didn't need sails, but——

I was bathing in the ocean, on a hot still day, when a shout rose up. "The *Cathawk* is returning! The airship is coming back!"

I didn't bother to dry myself, but snatched up my robe and ran for the Crag. Others had the same idea. A great

crowd materialized out of nowhere, and streamed up the
hill, shouting and cheering. As I rounded the crest I could
see it—slender boatframe and great swollen bags bright
against the sky.

I wondered why the *Cathawk* was flying backward.

Then I saw that there were no sails. Purple's method of
airpushing had worked! Wilville and Orbur were right again!

As the boat approached I could see my two sons pedaling
wildly on the windmakers, pushing the boat closer and closer.
Occasionally one of them would stop or pedal backwards
for a few seconds, and the *Cathawk* would shift ever so
slightly in its direction.

Purple was hanging in the rigging again. He was fiddling
with the neck of one of his airbags—apparently he was re-
leasing the gas in calculated amounts to control their descent.

He was shouting too: "Where is my ground crew?!! Where
is my ground crew?!!" The boat sank sideways through the
air.

On the ground, Trone and his men were running around
wildly, the big Coppersmith shouting orders, the others
trying to take up positions around the landing cradle.

"Okay," Trone was shouting. "Bring 'er in—right over
the cradle—and we'll grab the ropes!"

"No! No!" Purple shouted back. "You bloody blind fools!
You have to come out and grab the ropes where they fall and
pull the boat over the landing rack! Then you pull it down!
We can't control it that fine!" He swung around in the rigging,
"Wilville, Orbur, throw down the mooring ropes!"

Trone shouted at his crew, "Move out! Move out! They
can't get it over the landing rack—we'll have to do it for
them." His ragged group of men ran down the slope toward
the *Cathawk's* trailing ropes. They were waving gaily in the
wind. Wilville and Orbur were pedaling as hard as they could
just to keep the boat in place.

"Grab the ropes! Grab them!" Purple exhorted the ground crew. "We've got to come down on the landing cradle or we'll snap the keel." Boys and men were running hither and thither, trying to catch the trailing ends of the ropes, but the constant wind across the Crag kept snatching them away. One boy, very light, grabbed onto a rope only to find himself lifted into the air. He let go, and fell back to the ground.

Other controllers were having troubles too. They would seize a rope only to find themselves dragged across the hill. It was Trone who saved the day, by pouncing on one of these men—four other controllers pounced on top of him, and the *Cathawk* came to a jarring halt in the air.

The other ropes were slowed enough then to allow other men to grab them. It was great sport, with ground crew and villagers alike chasing after every rope still waving free, but at last nearly every rope had a controller or two hanging breathlessly onto the end of it.

Trone released his rope then—there were three other men on it—and shouted to his crew, "All right, pull it up the slope—over the landing rack!"

Shouting and cheering, the men dragged the *Cathawk* along, like a child with one of Purple's tiny airbags. The villagers waved excitedly at the heroes above. Wilville and Orbur had ceased their pedaling and were waving back, big foolish grins across their faces.

The flight controllers were just positioning the airboat above the landing rack when one of them called, "Wait!— If Purple leaves in this boat, our tokens won't be worth anything."

The others looked at him, "So what?"

"We've got to do something about it—"

Meanwhile, Purple was shouting, "The landing cradle! The landing cradle! Pull us to the landing cradle!"

They ignored him while they argued amongst themselves. Trone was insisting that they obey his orders, but the others were too insistent and they ignored him. Finally one of the men shouted skyward, "We're going on strike, Purple!"

"Huh? What's that?"

"The flight controllers are going on strike—"

"The what—?!!"

"We want you to guarantee your tokens!"

"Of course, of course! Anything—"

Suddenly we saw Shoogar's head over the railing. He had a ball of itching balls in his hand, and he was taking careful aim at us below. Three of the flight controllers started to let go of their ropes, but their leader marshaled them back. "If you drop it, Shoogar, we'll let go and you'll never get down."

I backed away. I knew Shoogar.

Sure enough, he dropped it. It struck and burst and tiny flecks of black spotted the air, alighting on the nearest people—the ground crew.

From the air came Shoogar's voice, "If you want to be cured, pull us down!"

Some of the men were trying to rub the back flecks away. Others had let go of their ropes and were rolling on the ground. The *Cathawk* swung out of position.

Shoogar called, "In about an hour you're all going to be screaming for a magician!"

That did it. They swarmed for the ropes and started pulling.

Shoogar apparently wanted to drop more itch balls, but Purple was climbing down from the rigging and motioning frantically. Wilville and Orbur, no longer needed on the airpushers, slung them up into the outriggers exactly as planned, and began climbing back into the boat proper. They too were remonstrating with Shoogar.

"No more itch balls! We're pulling! We're pulling!" called the flight controllers.

Shoogar, Wilville and Orbur vanished below the side of the boat. There were curses and muffled noises. Purple was peering over the side and directing the landing maneuver, "All right, all right—easy now. Watch the keel, the keel! Pull us to the landing cradle—the cradle! Don't snap the keel!"

Grumbling and cursing the men pulled the boat down and into the cradle. They looped their ropes loosely around stakes in the ground. Gradually the boat was hauled down out of the sky. The keel slid into its slot in the landing frame, and I heaved a sigh of relief.

A gust of wind caught the clustered windbags then, just

at the right angle and the wrong moment—there was a
cra-a-ack! of bambooze. The keel had snapped.

Purple leapt out of the boat cursing. It bounced back into
the air, but the men pulled it down again. Others dragged
sandbags over, and quickly tossed them into the boat. It hit
the cradle with a thump.

Wilville and Orbur got off Shoogar then. They had been
holding him down on the floor of the boat. The three
scrambled out.

Even the sandbags were not enough then. A sudden gust
of wind caught the boat and swept it down the slope, bouncing and gliding. It was too heavy to fly with the sandbags in
it, but too light to resist the force of the wind. It swept down
the slope and into the water.

Ang's fisherboys had to recover it.

When he saw it bobbing in the water, its outriggers balanc-
ing it gently against the waves, Purple's only comment was,
"H'm, I guess it didn't need a keel after all."

The next few days were busy ones indeed.

The waters had risen higher than ever, even to the middle
slopes of the Upper Village. The tents which had served us
so well in our journey across the desert were brought out
again, so that affected families could move up to the Crag
itself.

Trone and his crew of ground controllers carried the
airboat back up to the Crag. They had little difficulty because the airbags offset most of the boatframe's weight.

After some additional modifications and repair work
by Wilville and Orbur, the last four balloons were added.
This time there was more than enough ballast in the boat,
and extra mooring ropes to hold it down.

We did not slow down the generator teams though. Purple
attached the lead wires to his battery, and the output of all
four machines was stored in that tiny device. Once I asked

Purple about it, and he explained that as far as we were concerned the battery could hold an almost infinite amount of power.

There were advantages to its use. For one thing, Purple could release power at any rate he chose. It might take two hundred men five days to pump up all sixteen balloons, but if Purple had stored all that pedaled electrissy in his battery, he could fill the airbags almost as fast as we could add water to the pots and change the fittings on the funnels.

So it did not matter that the balloons up on the Crag were starting to droop. Purple would recharge them just before his departure. He planned to leave after two more hands of days had passed. That way, he estimated, he would have enough power to recharge the balloons two and a half times —maybe more.

Also, he said, he did not want to recharge the balloons before then because so much stored hydrogen could be dangerous. And this would give him a chance to measure their rate of leakage even more accurately.

"Danger?" I asked, when he said this. "What kind of danger?"

"Fire," he said, "or *sparks*. That's why we can't even take a bicycle type electrissymaker with us. Besides not being fast enough—even with four people working it—it makes sparks. A spark could set everything off."

A spark, he explained, was a very small dot of lightning. "Remember the way my housetree exploded?"

Lightning? Was that what we were working with? Was it lightning that fought back when we turned the pedals of the generators?

I shuddered—*lightning!*—Purple was definitely not one for half-measures!

He had proven it now. While the teams of men continued their roaring competitions on the generators, while Wilville and Orbur tended to the further provisioning of the *Cathawk*, Purple went about healing every sick person he could find.

"It looks like I can replace my first-aid kit pretty soon," he told me. "I was saving it because I might need it myself, but now——might as well make use of it." He cured Hinc the Hairless and Farg the Weaver; both began to grow new hair. Other men lost the sores they had carried for so many hands of hands of days—Purple blew wet air onto their skins from a tiny cylinder in his medicine kit, and within hours their flesh began to heal.

He didn't stop with the men. He cured the wives of their hairlessness too. He treated Little Gortik, a boy of four conjunctions, whose arm had been small and withered from the day he was born. "Forced regeneration," Purple had chanted over the boy, and had made him swallow two oddly translucent capsules. Now the boy's bones had gone soft, and the arm seemed to be straightening out.

Purple moved daily about the Upper Village and among the tents above the timberline, with his spell kit in his hand and a fierce, eager light in his eyes, as if he suspected sick people were hiding from him.

When Zone the Vender fell out of a tree and broke his back, Purple actually came at a dead run! He reached Zone before the man could finish dying; he sprayed Zone's back with something that went right through the skin, and forbade him to move at all until he could wiggle his toes again. He was there now, beneath the tree that had nearly killed him, while his wife fed him and changed his blankets. He was not dying, but he was getting terribly bored, and Purple had taken all his tokens.

They started trading Purple's tokens for Shoogar's at a ten-for-one ratio.

About this time my first wife finally gave birth to the daughter Shoogar had predicted. She was red and ugly and totally bald—not even a fine layer of glistening down-fur. When Shoogar spanked the child to life, her skin gleamed with womb fluid only.

He took the damp towel I held for him, and began cleaning the child's eyes and nose and mouth. He handled her tenderly, and there was a strange expression on his face.

"Is there something the matter, Shoogar?" I asked.

He never took his eyes off the baby, "As I feared, she is a demon child; but in all my years, Lant, I have never seen a demon child such as this."

"Is she a good witch or a bad witch?"

He shook his head. "I don't know. It's too early to tell." He maneuvered her around in his arms and continued rubbing softly. From her birthing cot, my wife watched wide-eyed. Most women fear to carry a demon child. My woman had born it stoically—I would have to reward her somehow.

Shoogar said, "This much I do know—this child must be protected and cared for. Perhaps even treated as well as a male—"

I stared at him in fear. "Shoogar—" I started, but he cut me off.

"Lant, I do not know. This is something I have never seen or heard of. We can only watch and wait. If this child is a good demon, then for sure we will want to please her—if she is a bad demon, just as surely we will not want to anger her. In any case, it never hurts to take care in an unknown situation."

I nodded gravely. There had been cases of demon daughters before—the children had been treated as sons, named and consecrated, and in some cases even admitted to the Guild of Advisors. But there had also been cases where demon daughters had caused the destruction of whole villages.

Both situations were rare, happening perhaps only once every hundred conjunctions. I had never expected it to happen in my lifetime though, let alone to my wife.

When he heard the news, Purple came running. The villagers parted in awe, as his chubby bulk came pelting across the slope. Excitedly, the villagers trailed in his wake, gabbling eagerly. On top of all that had happened to us previously, this new development was merely one more topic for the gossipmongers.

Purple burst into my nest and stood looking down at my bald red demon daughter. He was grinning all over his partially naked face. "She's beautiful, isn't she?" he said.

Shoogar and I exchanged a glance. Perhaps to Purple she was—but to us she was a thing of fear. What did children look like where Purple came from that such a thing would be considered beautiful?

He approached Shoogar tentatively, "May I hold her?"

Shoogar backed away, shielding the child in his arms. His eyes glared angrily. Purple looked shocked and hurt.

I touched his arm, "Purple, will she grow hair?"

He shook his head. "I don't think so."

"Will you cure her then?"

"I can't."

"My apology—I did not mean to insult you, but you have been doing such curing lately—"

"Anything that will hold still long enough—" Shoogar snapped.

Purple put out his hands, "You misunderstand. She is not sick, Lant. She is merely bald, like me." He advanced toward Shoogar again, "Let me hold her, please." He held out his arms.

Shoogar refused to give up the child. He shook his head firmly.

"But she is mine—" Purple said. "I mean, I sired her—"

"So? Do you think that gives you any special rights? It was Lant's wife who bore her. The child is his."

Purple looked at Shoogar and at me. He had an expression of confusion and hurt. "I do not mean—that is, I only want to hold her—just for a little bit—Lant, please—?"

He looked so pitiful, I wanted to say yes, but Shoogar only shook his head. At last, Purple bowed his head in sad acquiescence. "As you wish. Will you at least let me insure her health with a _____?" He used a word from his demon-tongue.

"What kind of a spell is it?" asked Shoogar.

"It is a spell of—luck," answered Purple. "Luck and protection. It will make her stronger and more healthy. She will have a better chance to gain maturity—"

At first, I thought Shoogar would refuse. He narrowed his eyes suspiciously. I said, "Shoogar, remember, we must please her—"

"All right," said Shoogar. "You may approach." And he let Purple spray essences through her skin with a thing from his medicine kit.

Purple did not ask to hold her again, and when he left, his step was slow and confused. We did not see him for the rest of that day.

In all, the villagers did not redeem a large percentage of Purple's tokens—not even when the sick and crippled began arriving from the other four villages by the boatload. People who were already healthy preferred to keep the tokens, partly because they might be needed for some very strong act of magic later, and partly because they were magic in and of themselves. They would bring good luck.

After they were cured many of the pilgrims decided to stay on. Intrigued by our flying boat and our electrissy generators, they formed an ever-present crowd of curious onlookers. They began trading for spell tokens so they could bet on the various pumping teams.

Others came in hopes of joining our growing Clothmakers' Guild, or of joining a bicycle put-it-together line or a generator team. Still others came to trade, and they were followed by those who prey on those who trade. Others came out of curiosity. They had heard of our flying machine and wanted to see it for themselves.

Our combined Guild of Advisors had grown to a size almost unmanageable, and there were ominous mutterings from various elements who felt they had been slighted in its growth. Clearly we were going to need some reorganization.

And finally came the day that Purple announced his battery was charged. He would depart for the sky before the next dawning of the blue sun.

And this time he meant it; —this was no test flight. This would be Purple's actual departure. Once the airboat lifted from its cradle, he would be gone from our village and our lives forever.

He spent almost all of his time on the Crag now, checking lists and counting supplies. Often he could be seen poking carefully at the boat's rigging or testing an airbag.

"Look how the boat strains at the ropes, Lant—isn't it beautiful? We have food aboard for at least four hands of days; we've got four or five manweights of ballast; we've got a few extra windbags in case we rip any. I say we're ready, Lant. How about you?"

"Huh? I'd say you're ready, too."

"No—I mean, are *you* ready?"

"Huh?"

"Aren't you coming with us?"

"Me?!!" I squeaked. "I wouldn't set foot in that—I mean, I have no intention—that is, I'm needed here. Business requires it! I'm a Speaker! I—"

"But—but—your sons said—"

"My sons?"

"Yes—they led me to believe that you were going to come too. We planned for you."

"This is the first I have heard of it."

"You do not want to come then?"

"Of course not; I can see no reason at all why I should."

"Well, neither did I," said Purple. "But Wilville and Orbur seemed to think it necessary."

I shuddered. "No, thank you, Purple. I will forego the honor." I did not add that I would rather be in a village with no magicians, than in a flying machine with two mad ones.

B ut later that day, in the heat of double daylight, a time when most of the villagers were sleeping, Shoogar took me aside. "Lant, you've seen how he has devalued my magic!" he said bitterly. "You must come with us, Lant. I will need you to help with the spell against him—"

"Spell? Oh, no, Shoogar—"

"I will be free of my oath when we leave this locality. But I will need you for a witness that I have killed him. You are the Speaker. Your word is law."

"Shoogar, can you not leave well enough alone? Purple is leaving. You will be the only magician here—and this is the greatest village of all! There may be as many as 5,000 men living here, maybe more! Never has there been a village of such size! Why must you risk it all by starting another foolish duel?"

But at that Shoogar snarled and left me. He grumbled off down the dark slope, scattering villagers and women alike.

Later, after the blue sun had winked out, Wilville and Orbur came to see me. As soon as I saw them, I said, "What nonsense have you been telling Purple? He says that you want me to come along on this fantastic journey."

They nodded. "Father, you must! You are the only one who can control Shoogar. Surely you must know that he is planning another duel as soon as we are out of this region."

"Yes. He's mentioned it."

"Well then, you must come along to stop it. We will never return if you don't; even if we should be lucky enough to survive this time. He'll insist that we put on the sails again. He's still not convinced! Father, you must come or we'll never get home."

"I'm sure you can manage without me, sons—you did all right on your test flight—"

"Yes, but that was only a test. Shoogar knew no more about the flying machine than anyone else. Now that he has been up in it once, he is convinced that he is an expert. Surely you have heard the tales he has been telling of his exploit."

I nodded. "But you have all been telling tales—and no two of your tales agree. The villagers don't believe any of you. That fact alone should keep Shoogar from dueling. If he has no credible witness along—"

"Father, he is not interested so much in a credible witness as he is in killing Purple." Orbur lowered his voice. "You don't know, do you, what he tried to do on our test flight?"

"Huh?" I shook my head. "I have not heard—"

"That is because Wilville and I have kept it quiet. We do not want to start even the hint of a rumor that there is trouble between our magicians."

Wilville nodded in agreement and said, "Shortly after we took off, they got into an argument about whether or not we needed sails. Shoogar got so mad that he tried to throw a ball of fire at Purple—"

"A ball of fire?!! But—the airboat? The hydrogen?"

"We were lucky," said Orbur. "Purple screamed when he saw it. I thought he would jump out of the boat——; but Wilville was thinking fast, and he threw a bucket of water on Shoogar."

Wilville said, "And then Orbur jumped on Shoogar and held him down. We drenched him all over with another bucket of water and then made him strip. We made him throw away all of his fire-making devices. Purple was as white as a cloud—"

"I can imagine." I was thinking of a blackened stump of a housetree.

"But that's not all," said Orbur. "Later, he tried to push Purple out. Purple was climbing on the rigging—you know, father, for a man like that, he is remarkably brave; he climbed across those ropes as if he had not the slightest fear of falling."

"He did slip once, though," said Wilville. "Fortunately, it was only a few feet, and he fell into the boat."

"Well, we all had to get used to it," Orbur said to him. "Nobody has ever been in an airboat before. There is no one to teach us what to do—"

"Except Shoogar," said Wilville. He looked at me imploringly, "Father, Shoogar is convinced that only he knows the vagaries of Musk-Watz the wind god, but somehow his magic doesn't seem to work right in the upper sky. His sails didn't work, his fireballs almost killed us—"

"My sons, you survived that experience, didn't you?"

They nodded reluctantly.

"Good, then I have faith that you can survive another. From what you have just told me I am all the more sure that I am not getting into that airboat."

I returned to my nest tired and irritated.

It wasn't just the way everyone badgered me. It was the

crowds. By now every family in the five villages was here on the Heights. The nearly bare rock was a maze of tents, practically edge to edge, the meager gaps filled by a swarm of sprats and women and strangers. The sea had swallowed the rest of the island.

The only clear spots were on Idiot's Peak, around the launching cradle, and the wide servicing area that now led all the way down to the water. Keeping those areas clear enough to work in only made the rest of the Heights more crowded.

My tree, like a few others, still reached partway above the waters. We still used the nest and thus avoided some of the crowding; but we had to wade waist deep between nest and Heights.

The sea was tepid and very wet. I was still bristling from the need to push my way between the tents and among the hordes of strangers when I climbed into my nest, my fur dripping. I sank gratefully onto my cot.

"Wives," I called, "I am ready for a hot brushing. I have had such a day as to try even the greatest of men!"

"Oh, our poor Lant," they mourned. "Surely even the greatest of tribulations is only child's play to a man so brave as you—"

"Naturally, but the effort is tiring. Purple wants me to come on the airboat with him; so do Wilville and Orbur—"

"Oh, no, not my brave Lant! Not in the airboat! You might fall!" cried one Missa.

"You mustn't, my husband! You will never return! What would we do if we lost you?" said the other whose nonname was Kate.

"Of course, you told them that you wouldn't!" said the first.

"You have your carving to tend to," said the second. "And there are other things besides. The nestwalls are leaking and must be repaired—"

"Wait a minute," I cuffed them into silence. "What is this noise you make? You dare to tell me what I should do—?"

"Oh, no—" They flung themselves at my feet.

Missa, the second, looked up and said, "It is just that we love you so much, we do not want you to go—"

Missa, the first, said, "It is such a dangerous thing to do—

maybe even too dangerous for such a brave man as our Lant."

I looked down at them, "How dare you even suggest such a thing. I am the Speaker of my village—I have tamed two of the wildest magicians ever known, and, I kept them from killing each other. I have guided the construction of an actual flying machine—"

"Yes my husband, but that does not mean that you should fly in it!"

"Yes—leave that honor for somebody else—"

"And why should I?" I demanded. "I have as much right as anybody to voyage on the *Cathawk*, perhaps even more."

"Oh, but we are so afraid for you—"

"You think I am afraid of the dangers?"

"Oh, no, my brave Lant—but we are—"

"You think too much, wives—it has addled your brains. I am fully aware of the dangers of such a voyage. You think I am not? Let me tell you this though: if I did not think it was a safe journey, I would not be planning to go."

"Oh, my husband, my brave, brave husband, you do not need to prove it to us. We know you are the greatest of all husbands. Just stay with us, and we will not even protest your purchase of a third wife—"

"You will not what—? What makes you think you have even the right to do so? If I want a third wife, I will buy one. If I want to go flying in a flying machine, I will do that too! And I am going to do both! And neither one of you will say another word about it or I will beat you! Now bring me my supper! And be grateful that I am not yet too angry to do the family-making thing tonight!"

Red sunset, still and quiet, a hot mugginess in the air—the memory of the blistering heat of day.

Trone and four other men were holding a line; Wilville and Orbur were up in the rigging rearranging the position of two of the balloons in the cluster. On their signal, Trone and his crew released the rope and the balloons snapped into position.

Purple had spent this day recharging the tired windbags. Even now, he was just filling the last from a water pot balanced on the narrow deck slats.

Shoogar and I stood quietly to one side. I was carrying a narrow pack and wondering how I had gotten myself into this position. I kept replaying the conversations of the day over and over in my head, but somehow the why of it still eluded me.

I had been ready enough to change my mind when I left my nest. But, in their zeal to persuade me not to risk my life, my wives had been busily asking the advice of a great many other women. And those women had been telling their men . . . I soon found out that every man, woman and child on the Heights knew that Lant the Speaker would be aboard the *Cathawk* when it rose into the sky at red sunset.

Wilville and Orbur climbed down from the rigging then. Purple made a mark on his checklist. Orbur turned and burrowed under a cloth-covered pile of supplies. "The blankets are under here, Purple."

"Good," he replied, "I would not want to leave them. Have we plenty of drinking water this time?"

"More than enough," said Wilville; he looked at Shoogar as he said it.

Purple came over to us then. "I am glad you are coming, Lant. It will be a long journey, and I welcome your company." To Shoogar, he said, "You have brought no fire-making devices, this time, have you?"

Shoogar shook his head dourly.

"You remember what I told you about them, don't you?"

He nodded.

"Fine."

He went back to the boys and told them. Wilville and Orbur looked over at us and exchanged a glance. They excused themselves from Purple and climbed out of the boat. "Oh, Shoogar," they said, "could we speak with you a moment; we have a question about one of the finer points of the spell—"

Shoogar toddled off after them. They disappeared behind a clump of blackbushes.

There was a sharp cry and the sound of a struggle. Another cry and then silence. After a moment, there was a sputtering and the sound of water being poured out of a pot. Wilville and Orbur returned then, smiling. A few moments later a soaked Shoogar followed them. He was glaring angrily.

He came up to me, "If they weren't your sons—"

"And if they also weren't necessary to the success of the journey home," I said calmly, "you would do what—?"

"Never mind," he grumbled. "I'm just glad that you decided to come along, after all. I am going to take a revenge on Purple such as no one has ever dreamed of!"

Despite the hour there was a considerable crowd gathered on the slope. Many of them were from the other villages, people who had heard of our wondrous machine, and had come to witness our ascent. Still, there were quite a few people from our own village as well, proudly pointing out what part of the machine they had worked on. Again, there were mongers selling sweetdrops and spicy meats. I had eaten some the last time, and had been sick for hours afterward. This time I had resolved not to eat anything; if I was going to be sick, I didn't want to be so in an airship.

"All right, Lant," said Purple. "You can get in now." He gestured. "Shoogar?"

We went. Purple directed us where to sit, far forward in the boat, one on each side of a cloth-lined bench. Purple took up his position at the rear. He peered about him anxiously, as if he had forgotten something.

I was petrified. My heart was pounding—I could not believe it—I was actually here—in a flying machine! And I was going to rise up into the sky in it!

A voice was calling, "Lant! Lant!" I looked over the side. There was Pilg the Crier.

"Pilg!" I cried. "Where have you been?"

"I have been coming back," he called. "Lant, are you really going flying with Purple the Magician?"

"Yes," I said. "I am."

"You are a brave man," he said. "I shall miss you."

Farther up the slope I could see both my wives with Gortik. They were sobbing copiously. Little Gortik waved happily.

"All right," Purple was saying, "ground crew take your positions."

I looked around me, thousands of faces were looking back—

Wilville and Orbur waved at them. They had climbed onto their bicycles, and were just tying their safety ropes. Underneath, the boat rocked gently. "You know," I said suddenly, "I think I ought to stay behind, after all. I—"

Shoogar pulled me down again. "Shut up, Lant—you want everyone to think you're a coward?"

"I'd just as soon they know it for sure—let go of me, Shoogar!"

Purple was standing at the rear of the boat, one hand on the rigging to balance himself. He was gesturing at the ground crew. I pulled myself away from Shoogar and looked. Trone and his men were stationing themselves around the cradle. Each had a heavy knife and was waiting by a mooring rope.

"All right, now," Purple shouted. "All the ropes have to be cut at once, so wait for my signal. We will do it just as I said. I will count backwards—ready, now? Ten, nine, eight—"

"Shoogar, let go of me!" I said. "I'm not going—"

"Yes, you are!"

"—to do anything foolish!"

"You are too!"

"Seven, six, five—"

"Shoogar!"

"Four, three—"

There were fifty jarring *thunks!* as the knives came down on the ropes. We shot upward! The crowd cheered. I yelped. Shoogar screamed and clutched at me. The boat rocked wildly and I grabbed at something to keep from falling—there was a tearing sound—it was Shoogar's spell belt—

We were in a tumbled heap at the bottom of the boat. I pulled myself into a sitting position, and back up onto the bench. Purple was cursing furiously, "You addle-brained idiots! You can't even count right!! I didn't even get to finish—"

"Finish what?" I said "Three is the spell number, Purple. All spells start with three."

He looked at me stupidly, then he turned away muttering: "Of course, Purple; three is the spell number, Purple; how can you be so stupid, Purple—Oh, what I wouldn't give for a—" His words were whipped away by the wind.

I looked around. Shoogar was peering curiously over the side.

"What is the matter?" I asked.

"My spell belt, you fool! You ripped it."

I joined him at the rail. The boat tipped precariously, but Purple shifted his weight in the rear, and we balanced again. "It must be the lack of a keel," called Orbur from his outrigger.

And now, for the first time since the ascent, I had a chance to look down. Far below us was the Crag, red sunlight slanting severely across it. Blue shadows stretched outward to infinity. Tiny people, getting tinier every moment, moved below. I could see the landing cradle, the housetrees, the foamy edge of the sea, and the rippled surface of it stretching out to the end of the world.

On the other side were the peaks of the mountains. We were even above them.

Shoogar was still looking down. "What are you so upset about?" I asked. "Most of your spells are here at the bottom of the boat."

"I know," he said, "I saw them—but the one you ripped —it spilled out. It's going to hang in the air over the village for days."

"Oh," I said. "What is it?"

"A powder. You remember the dust of yearning?"

"The spell we used on Purple the day we destroyed his black egg?"

"That's the one."

I shuddered. I remembered it well. After just a few sniffs of it, Purple had gone into the village and done the family-making thing with my wife. Repeatedly.

"I wonder," said Shoogar. "I wonder . . ."

"Well, we must go back," I said. "You must show them the proper herbs to chew—there isn't another magician in the region. There will be chaos—"

"Go back?" said Shoogar. "You are jesting. You will not bring this craft down to the ground again until the airgas gets tired of working and sneaks out of the balloons. Besides, we are moving strongly north—"

He was right, of course. I left him at the railing and moved to another part of the boat. It swayed sickeningly under my every step. Wilville called across to Orbur, "I think we should put the keel back on!"

"Me too!" he answered.

"No," said Purple, "all you need do is rearrange the rigging. Spread it out farther at the bottom. It will give the *hoist* a wider *stance*."

"The *who* a *what*?" they called.

He sighed. "Never mind."

The wind was strong this high in the sky. Idiot's Crag had shrunk to a spear of black on the horizon. Below us the sea was many colors. Spots were brown and opaque with mud. In some places reefs showed through. There were groves of submerged trees as well, spines of mountain rock, and even a tall cairn to Musk-Watz. You could see them all sticking out of the water. There were churning whirlpools and vast rippling tides, and the surface of the water was gray and foamy.

Purple was sighting against the sun and marking something on a skin which had been stretched across a framework. Strange lines speared out from the center of the skin to its edges. "It's a direction-telling spell," explained Purple. "We're headed almost directly east."

"I could have told you that," I said.

"Huh?"

I pointed below. "See that spine of land there? That's the way we followed on our migration. It leads directly to the old village."

"It does?" Purple leaned far over the edge and tried to follow it with his eyes. I feared for his balance, but even more I feared for Shoogar who watched us with eyes gleaming.

He straightened then. "Wilville, Orbur! We want to change course. Unsling your airpushers!"

They nodded and began to do so. First one of the bladed wheels swung down to hang a manheight below the precarious outrigger, then the other on the other side. I shuddered as I watched. I would not trade places with either of my sons. You would not get me out there, with nothing between me and the sea but empty air.

"We have to come about," called Purple. "Turn toward the west—left about ninety degrees." I didn't understand that last, but the boys apparently did. Wilville began backpedaling while Orbur pedaled forward. Slowly the *Cathawk* turned in the sky. The red sunlight seeped through the rigging, and the shadows shifted across our faces.

Purple watched carefully on his measuring skin. A small rod stuck up from the center, and he watched the position of its shadow. He called, "All right, stop!" He waited until both airpushers were still, then checked the shadow again. "Not enough," he called, "another ten degrees."

When we were finally pointed in the right direction, he gave another order. "Quarter speed," he called. The two boys began chanting and pedaling. They had removed the extra twist in the pulleys, so that the airpushers blew their wind sternward again and the boys faced in the direction they were going.

The chant was at a set rhythm, and they pedaled in time to it. Purple watched them for a while, then he peered over the side again. After a bit he said, "Ah." He straightened. "We are on the right course. We are traveling parallel to that spine of land you pointed out, Lant. If the wind lets up at all, we will try to get directly over it."

He went to the back of the boat then and stretched out on a cot of aircloth over a wide frame. "You know, Lant," he called, "if I didn't have my responsibilities elsewhere, I might almost be willing to settle down here. This is a very relaxing way of life."

"Oh, no, Purple," I reassured him. "You would not be happy living with us. You had best return—"

"Fear not, Lant. That's what I intend to do. But I tell you, I have truly enjoyed myself here." He pounded himself on his stomach. "Look, I think I may have even lost a few pounds."

"Have you looked behind you?" muttered Shoogar.

"Sh," I hissed. "We are all going to be together for a very long time. At least try to get along."

"With him?!!"

"You didn't have to come, Shoogar!"

"I did too! How else can I ever—"

"Never mind! If you can't say anything nice, don't say anything at all. At least so long as we're in the air!"

Shoogar snarled at me and went forward to the front of the boat. I sank down tiredly on a pile of supplies and blankets.

For a while I watched my sons as they pedaled. It was a funny sight, a bicycle so high in the air——with no wheels at all, yet they were pedaling so steadily, I had to laugh. They glared at me, but kept chanting and pumping.

Above us the clustered windbags were like a distant roof. Large enough to be covering, but high enough so that they were not oppressive. It was a feeling like being sheltered, but also one of being strangely free.

Occasionally the boys rested—and then all was silent. That was the most peculiar thing about the airship. Once in the sky, it neither creaked nor shuddered. There were no sounds at all, except perhaps that of our own heartbeats.

We had stopped rising now. And a good thing too. The air was cold—almost biting. Purple pulled out some blankets and passed them around. Wilville and Orbur were wearing extra layers of clothing. It had been tied to their outriggers so they could pull it on as they wished. They also had water bottles and packs of hardbread. There was no need for them to come into the boat itself at all, if they did not wish to.

The last of the red sun finally seeped below the horizon.

"Are they going to pedal through the dark?" I asked Purple.

"Uh huh. As long as the wind keeps up, someone has to keep pedaling. You see, Lant, the wind is blowing us northeast. If we pedal west, then we cancel out the east and go only north. But the wind doesn't stop at night, so neither can we. The only other choice is to land—and that means letting air out of the bags."

"And you don't want to do that, do you?"

"Right. We know the boat will float in water, but I'd rather not have to depend on it, Besides, even if we did come down on the sea, the wind might still push us. So we might as well stay in the air and keep pedaling all night. The boys know how to pace themselves. As long as we stay near that spine of land under the water, I won't worry."

In the dark the steady chanting and pumping was an eerie thing—coming, as it did, from outside the boat. Fortunately, the time till blue dawn was little more than an hour away—we would have naught but a brief flash of darkness at this time of year. Followed by seventeen hours of pure blue sunlight, an hour of double sunlight, and another seventeen hours of red sunlight. Then darkness again. Later in the year the darknesses would stretch, as would the times of double sunlight. The single-sun hours would shrink as the suns moved closer and closer in the sky—toward the inevitable red conjunction.

We pedaled on through the darkened sky.

F̲ar to the east the horizon's edge was limned by a faint blue glow. Blue Ouells was sneaking up behind it, soon to shout and leap and flash brightly over the edge.

Below, the sea was a dark platter, greasy and wrinkled. A cold wind whipped around us. I pulled my blanket tighter against it. The boat rocked gently. The swollen balloons seemed motionless above; the sea motionless and flat so far below.

My sons pedaled steadily. I fancied I could see the churned air stretching out in a line behind us, but that way was as dark as the way ahead. Their pumping was a steady sound, sensed rather than heard—a constant vibration filled the boat.

And then it was morning, sharp and blue—bright Ouells was a pinpoint at the edge of the world, sleeting light sideways across our eyes.

Wilville and Orbur rested then, while Purple sighted for the spine of land under the water. It was a barren range of hills, barely higher than the land around it. Beneath the risen ocean it would appear with a lighter color.

At first he thought we had lost it, then he sighted it off to our right. Apparently, during the dark, the wind had slackened somewhat. The boys, having no way of knowing this, had kept pedaling, and so had carried us farther west than Purple had wanted us to go.

Fortunately the wind was still blowing northeast, so Purple told Wilville and Orbur that they could rest until such time as we were again over our guide. The boys climbed into the boat, but did not remove their waist ropes until they were safely inside.

They sucked eagerly at a skin of Quaff, passing it back and forth between them, then each stretched out on a cloth-lined framework, the *Cathawk*'s equivalent of a cot. Within moments they were asleep.

I picked my way forward, past bundles of supplies. Shoogar was just stretching and yawning. He greeted me with a surly grunt.

"Haven't you slept?" I asked.

"Of course not, Lant. We only had an hour of darkness. I was watching for the moons. The moons," he yawned grumpily, "I need the moons."

"Shoogar," I said, "you do not need the moons—"

"Yes, I do—do you want me to lose my duel?"

I could see that he was unapproachable. "Go aft," I said. "Go aft and get some sleep."

He was fumbling in his sleeve, but all he found was a damp husk-ball. "Curse it," he said, "they ruined it, your sons ruined it. I had hoped it would dry out, but—" he shrugged and tossed the sodden mass over the side. "I'm going to sleep, Lant," he mumbled and tottered off.

I moved to the front of the boat and peered out. Here was a view, unobstructed by either balloons or rigging. I was suspended above a silvery-blue sea, miles above it. I seemed to be floating in silence. The stillness was overpowering. Deafening.

The air was crisp and, at the same time, hot. Blue Ouells was already heating up the day.

"Beautiful, isn't it?"

I looked around. Purple had come up beside me. He placed his hands on the rail and looked out at the ocean blueness on all sides. "I love the way it changes," he said. "The changing light of the suns keeps changing the look of the water."

I nodded. I did not particularly feel like talking yet. My bones still ached from the cold of the night, and the sun had not yet begun to bake that out.

"Lant," he said, "tell me about your journey again. I am trying to figure out how far you traveled, and how long it will take us to cover that distance in the flying machine."

I sighed. We had been over this many times already. It was on the basis of our migration that Purple had calculated the number of balloons and amount of supplies he would need. "We journeyed for a hundred and fifty days, Purple. We followed that range of hills because the seas were rising so fast. We needed every advantage we could get."

He nodded, "Good, good," then fell silent and became lost in thought, as if he were making figures in his head. After a while he brought out his measuring skin again and began sighting the sun. "We will be drifting over our course line again," he said. "I had better go wake up the boys."

Afterward, when we were again vibrating to the tune of the whirring bicycles, I tottered aft and joined Purple for a bite of breakfast, my first meal since coming aboard the aircraft. Shoogar was snoring loudly on a cot.

Purple bit into a sour melon. He said, "For some time I have wondered, Lant. Why do you call me Purple?"

"Huh? That is your name."

He cocked his head at me, "What do you mean? I knew you had a word for me in your language, but it wasn't until my speakerspell was destroyed that I found out it was your word for purple."

"But you told us that was your name, long ago."

"I couldn't have. It isn't."

"It isn't? But—" I thought hard. "But your speakerspell said it was—"

"Oh," he said, "the speakerspell." As if that explained it. "Yes, Lant, sometimes we do have troubles with speakerspells."

"I thought so," I said, "I sometimes wondered if it was working correctly. It said some very silly things."

"Just what did it say?"

"It spoke wildly of dust clouds and other suns—"

"I mean, about my name."

"Oh. It said that your name was *As A Color, Shade of Purple-Gray*. We thought it distinctly odd."

Purple looked distinctly confused. He wiped a bit of melon dribble off his chin. "As a color, shade of purple-gray? I don't see how—" And then his eyes lit up behind his black bone frames. A delighted expression came across his face, "Ah, it's a *pun!* A *pun!*" He began chortling hysterically. "Of course, of course—how right that I should have a translator that makes *two-language puns!* As a color, shade of purple-gray! As a *mauve!* Oh, how delightful."

I looked at him oddly.

He explained. "It must have tried to translate the syllables individually, Lant, from my language to yours."

"Then Purple isn't your real name?"

"Oh, no, of course not—that's just a poor translation. My real name is—" and he spoke in the demon-tongue.

At that I felt a cold chill—no wonder Shoogar's first curse hadn't worked—he had used the wrong name!

Behind us Shoogar's snoring had stopped—he was lying on his back. His eyes were narrow slits—had he heard too?

The wind had died completely.

Purple signaled Wilville and Orbur to take a rest while he measured the suns again. "It's very difficult," he said. "There's no *north star* in this world, and even a magnetic compass isn't that much help. I have to rely mostly on the suns to tell me which direction is which."

The boys had climbed into the boat again and were thirstily swigging Quaff and chewing hardbread. "Relax," Purple told them, "because we are becalmed, you can take all the time you need. We do not have to worry about being blown off course."

The boys stretched out for a short nap then. Shoogar was up at the front of the boat, offering a chant to Musk-

Watz, trying to restore the wind, and Purple decided to climb up into the rigging to check his balloons.

I climbed forward. So far, this journey had been very boring. There had been nothing to do but sit.

Shoogar finished with his *cantele* and sat down on a bench. He began packing away his spell-chanting equipment. "Bung-smelling apprentices!" he cursed. "Forgot to pack my filk-singer flute."

"You should be grateful you even have apprentices," I said. "They have been most hard to come by recently. Most of the young boys in the village want to become weavers or electrissy makers. There are few who want to follow the old ways."

"Hah!" snorted Shoogar. He looked at me. "And what will those others do now that the airboat is finished? Eh? There will be no more demand for aircloth, no more need to pump on the generators. All of a sudden there is no more work for them."

"Oh, I don't know," I said. "Last hand I heard Gortik and Lesta discussing the possibility of building another flying machine, a bigger one, to carry trade goods back and forth between the village and the mainland."

Shoogar grunted. "It's possible—but I still have yngvi-infested apprentices. They left out my locusts, my trumpets, my appas—"

"Then you have not trained them properly," I said. "I've had no trouble with mine."

"Hah, it is not so easy as you think, Lant, to train a magician. I remember my own training——" He trailed off suddenly.

"What's the matter?" I asked.

"You are right, Lant. I have not been beating them enough."

"I don't understand."

"Of course not; training a magician's apprentice is not like training a bonecarver or a weaver. First off, you must beat them three times a day so they do not become presumptuous. Then you must beat them three more times so they will pay attention. Then you must beat them three more times so as to instill in them a healthy fear of you—else they will carry a grudge all their lives, may even one day turn against you."

"That's a lot of beating," I said.

He nodded, "It's necessary. The greatness of a magician is directly proportional to the amount of beating he has taken."

"Your training must have been frightful—"

"It was. I was lucky to live through it. Old Alger would not rest until he had beaten all resentment out of Dorthi and me. We set over five hundred different spell traps for him. Not one of them worked—he saw through them all."

"You mean an apprentice magician keeps trying to kill his teacher?"

Shoogar nodded. "Of course, that's how you get to be recognized as being better than he. It's not necessary, but it is always tried by the apprentices because it is a short cut to greatness. It is easier than waiting for a formal consecration."

"But Shoogar," I said, "your apprentices—they will try to kill you."

"Of course. I expect it. But I am greater and smarter than either of them can ever hope to be—I'm greater and smarter than both of them put together. I have no worries about them. They have not yet learned even how to curse a stream. Besides, every time they fail, I beat them for it, severely. Thus they are inspired to do better next time— it will force them to plan more carefully. They will fail, of course. They always do—but a contest of wits like this is always great fun for a magician."

I shook my head. I did not understand many things in this life—and this was one of them.

I wobbled aft to get some sleep. The boat rocked gently under the swollen balloons, and within moments the cares of magicians had slipped away.

W e spent a miserable hour of darkness drifting, all five of us huddled together at the bottom of the boat. Keeping watch would have done little good. There was little to see but black water.

After a while Purple gathered his blanket around him and stumbled off. We could hear him pacing back and forth at the stern of the boat, we could feel the pad-padding of his feet through the deck slats.

"He's restless and impatient," murmured Orbur.

"Let's hope a wind doesn't come up for a while," said Wilville. "It's cold enough without having to go out and pedal."

I peeked out from under my blanket. Purple was peering upward at the balloons. They were illuminated by the eerie glow of his flashlight. They shone brightly in the dark, ominous and impassive. He was muttering something about hydrogen leakage.

Wilville and Orbur exchanged a glance. "He doesn't want to land," said one.

"We'll have to," replied the other. "If we have to recharge the balloons, we'll have to."

I shivered. Below, we could hear the water lap-lapping, and the occasional splash and groan of a cavernmouth fish. Best we do not land at all, I thought—although, if the hydrogen was leaking, we would have no choice at all in the matter.

I longed for a fire, blessed warmth, but Purple would allow us none—no flame, no fire, no spark-making device of any kind. Nothing that might endanger the violently explosive hydrogen.

Had it not been for the ample supply of Quaff, we would have been twice as unhappy and twice as cold. But Shoogar and I passed the flask back and forth between us, and after a while the sun came out and we didn't care any more.

Purple sighted our course then, and Wilville and Orbur climbed out onto the outriggers. They turned us in the proper direction and began pedaling across the sky. Purple retired to his sleeping cot in the back of the boat. He snored like an awakening mountain.

Shoogar was grumpy again. The few times he had poked his head out from under his blanket during the darkness, there had still been no moons. The first time of dark, there had been mist. The second time had been clear, but there were still no moons! It was annoying and frustrating: the sign of Gafia, when all the gods have stopped listening.

Shoogar was unapproachable. He climbed up into the rigging, onto a little platform Purple called a *bird's nest*, and sat there moodily.

Later, when Purple awoke, he asked why Shoogar was so angry. I told him that it was the moons. Shoogar needed them and he could not see them—I didn't tell him why he needed them though.

Purple called up to him, "Shoogar, come down—I will explain to you about the moons."

"You?" he snorted. "You explain about the moons?"

"But I can tell you about them," Purple insisted.

"It wouldn't hurt to listen," I called.

"Humph," said Shoogar to me, "what do you know?" But he began climbing down.

Purple pulled out an animal skin and began marking lines on it. "Before I brought my flying egg down, I studied the paths of your moons, Shoogar. Apparently they are all fragments of one larger moon and they stay close together in its *orbit*. At least they are all together now. I suppose there are other times when they are all far apart."

Shoogar nodded. This much at least was correct. "They change their configurations often," he said. "But they go in cycles of close configurations alternating with loose ones."

"Ah," said Purple. "Of course, they interfere with each other too, and some get lost, and others get picked up from the stream of rocks that follows in your sign-of-eight orbit; but for a while, at least, the moons should behave like this. Especially this one, which is very important to me—"

I stopped listening and wandered to another part of the airship. I am no magician and shop talk generally bores me.

Later though I noticed that Shoogar had kept the spell chart that Purple had made, and was poring over it interestedly. He had a fierce look in his eyes, and was muttering grumpily and happily to himself.

Blue dawn of the third day revealed us to be only a few manheights above the water. Great swells swept before us, the water rising and falling in constant uneasy motion. As Wilville and Orbur climbed out onto their bicycles they muttered about our lack of height. "The wind is more effective at pushing us higher up." Orbur said.

Purple nodded thoughtfully. He was peering up at his balloons.

I was peering uneasily down. The surface of the water was greasy and black, and crinkled with flecks of light. I could see the foam on the waves, and smell the wetness in the air.

We had been moving erratically north for two days now, sometimes pushed by the wind, and sometimes by the airpushers. Whenever the flying machine had dropped too low, Purple poured sand out of the ballast bags until we rose again. But we only had one sandbag left, and Purple was beginning to worry.

He had been measuring the balloons regularly since the first night. Periodically, he would climb up into the rigging and poke one experimentally, then climb down, tsk-tsk'ing and shaking his head. The windbags were drooping sadly now; we could see that without climbing the ropes.

He spent all morning leaning over the rail trying to estimate the distance to the water below.

I spent long hours leaning over the rail myself, but little of it was in contemplation of the water. The continual height had begun to unnerve me—and the motion, the constant sway of the boat, the uneasy rocking whenever someone shifted his position——

It was Purple's observance of me that gave him the idea of how to measure our height. He would drop an object and time how long it took to fall. He could do that even in the dark if he listened carefully for the splash.

After his latest calculation—made by dropping a sour

267

melon over the side—Purple announced that we were losing
gas very rapidly and would have to pump up the balloons
as soon as possible.

He climbed up into the rigging then, while Wilville and
Orbur manned the bicycle frames. Hopefully, he said, after
we came down in the water, the *propellors* would keep us
balanced and headed in the right direction. He began untying
the neck of one of his windbags.

He hung from the ropes above us, a puffy figure against
a background of limp and bloated cloth, and he called instructions to the rest of us. "Lant, Shoogar, pull hard on that
rope—I must push this balloon aside. Loosen your pace,
Wilville! Orbur, backpedal now! Hard right! Keep on course."
Carefully, he manipulated the long hose-like neck of the
windbag, and let some gas seep out. We sank toward the
water.

He let more gas out, then tied the neck of the bag again.
He readjusted himself in the rigging and grabbed another
bag. We continued sinking. "How high are we?" he called.

I looked over the edge. We were less than one manheight
above the water. Already the *propellors* were slashing across
the tops of the swells, dipping in and out of them, churning
them to froth. A foamy wake appeared behind us.

"Check to see that the boat rudder is straight, Lant!" Purple called. I wobbled to the back of the boat to where the
rudder was mounted. It too was an aircloth-hardened frame.
I straightened it out, and looped a rope around it to hold
it so.

"How high are we?"

I looked again. We were still one manheight over the
water. We had stopped sinking.

Purple loosed a little more gas from the bag and we sank,
sank—*oof!*—smacked into the water, slid sickeningly downward, then up again, across the tops of the swells, up and
down, up and down. Wilville and Orbur kept pedaling. Amazing! The airpushers kept churning the water behind us, and
we moved steadily forward—the airpushers worked in water
too! What a marvelous device they were!

Purple then unslung the hoses from the windbags, so that
they hung down into the boat frame. Sixteen long nozzles—
I looked up and thought of a milkbeast's belly.

Purple brought out a wooden frame which Pran the Carpenter had made for him. There was a slot in it to hold the battery. Two copper wires led out across separate arms. One of them ended in a clay funnel. To this Purple attached the first balloon nozzle. He hooked the whole affair over the boat rail and let the wires and funnel arm dip into the water. He made an adjustment on his battery. From the oxygen wire came the familiar furious bubbling. We could not see the bubbling on the other wire, it was inside the funnel. But we did see the gentle puffing of the balloon neck, and we knew that the gas was leaping upward through it.

Suddenly there was a yelp from Orbur, "Hey! We're rising again!"

Sure enough, we were. The annoying up-and-down motion of the boat across the swells had stopped. We had swung back into the air. I could see our shadow slipping across the water beneath us. Only the propellors still skimmed through the surface, and then they too were free.

"Curse it," said Purple. "I never thought of that."

There was a wind pushing us along. We watched glumly as our wake disappeared behind, lost in the swells.

"What do we do now?" I asked.

He switched off his battery. "We wait."

"But there's hardly enough gas in the balloons to lift us, Purple. We'll be hitting the water again in five minutes."

"I know that, Lant. That's what I'm hoping for."

He began looking around him. He laid aside the recharging framework and started rearranging the supplies in the bottom of the boat; checking and tying the aircloth covers to see that they were secure. "Find me a pail," he called.

There was one in the bow of the boat. We had been using it to hold wash water, but it was empty now. Shoogar brought it back to where we waited.

As soon as we were skimming through the tops of the swells again, Purple leaned far over the rail, the bucket trailing in his hands. He pulled it up, half full, and emptied it into the boat. Again he leaned over the edge.

When he had poured ten bucketsful into the boat we were again splashing through the waves. Another ten bucketsful and we were dipping into the troughs. Ten more and we were firmly in the water. Up and down. Up and down.

"We need ballast," he explained. "And there's nothing else to use." He peered over the side and measured how low the boat was riding in the waves. He poured fifteen more bucketsful into the boat before he was satisfied. It was up to our knees at its deepest point.

He picked up his battery and funnel device again and started to lean over the side— "Eh? What am I doing? I can just as easily use this water—" He sat down on a cloth-covered seat and placed the device in the water before him. It began bubbling and he beamed delightedly.

We were all delighted. On all sides splashed the restless ocean. If Purple's gas-making magic were to suddenly stop working, we would be trapped here, a tiny craft bobbing across an uncaring sea.

Whether Purple worried about this or not, I did not know. Apparently he had full confidence in the power of his battery and he worked steadily. Within seven hours, he had recharged all sixteen balloons. They hung taut and full-bellied overhead. Several times we had added more water to the boat to offset their increased lifting power. There were more than a hundred bucketsful in the boat now.

At last though, Purple tied off the last windbag, and began disconnecting his battery wires. He tsked thoughtfully as he did so, "H'm, we have used more power than I thought we would. We will have to be careful."

He put the device aside and began gathering up the empty ballast bags. "Fill these with water," he instructed. "We will use that as ballast instead of sand."

While Shoogar and I did as he instructed, he began bailing the water out of the boat. After fifteen bucketsful had been poured out, the boat began rocking harder in response to the waves. A few more bucketsful and we were splashing through them, the swells smacking the bottom of the boat. A few more and we were level again while the water skimmed harmlessly below.

"Are we off the water?" Purple called to Wilville.

Wilville nodded, "By half a manlength easily." He and Orbur were still on their bicycles, still hanging down onto the sea—they were pumping steadily, and keeping the air-pushers spinning to maintain our heading in the proper direction.

Purple bailed one last bucket and straightened up. "Do you want me to bail for a while?" I asked.

He shook his head. "Uh, uh. There's no need for any more bailing, Lant." He put the pail aside.

While I scratched my head in confusion, he splashed forward to the *Cathawk*'s toolbox. He came back carrying a drill, and proceeded to make a small hole in the narrow deck slats.

It took only a few moments, and then he stood up proudly and wetly. Almost immediately Orbur called, "We're on our way up again!"

Indeed we were. The ocean dropped away at an ever increasing pace. The water spilled out of the hole at a steady rate, and gradually there was less and less water in the boat. Like Purple's first windbag so many hands ago, we fell upward.

I leaned over the railing in excitement. "Why, it works just like the sand ballast," I said. "When you throw it away, the boat rises."

"Of course, you nit!" said Shoogar. "That's part of the ballast spell."

"It's the weight, Lant—it doesn't make any difference what your ballast is. It's the throwing away of weight that makes the boat rise."

"Nice thinking," commented Shoogar. "The ballast goes automatically. No jerks, no bumps."

"Thank you," Purple beamed. It was the first compliment he had ever gotten from Shoogar.

He checked our course heading then—the wind was blowing almost directly north—so the boys could either rest or pedal in the same direction, as they chose. They chose to rest and stretched out on their outriggers. There had to be one son on each outrigger at all times, or no son on either— otherwise the airboat slanted all askew.

Purple dried himself off as well as he could, then climbed into the rigging to tie up the airbag nozzles. They were still hanging down. By the time he had finished, all the water had drained out of the boat. He toddled back to where we waited and pounded a heavy bone plug into the hole.

Once more the sea glistened far below us. Indeed, it seemed we were higher than ever. When we dropped a sour melon over the side, it dwindled to a distant speck and vanished without a splash.

We were aloft for the rest of that day and most of the next, before we again had to dump ballast. Purple always waited until we had sunk below a certain level before he would throw any away. Otherwise, he said, we were just wasting it. "The idea is to stay aloft as long as possible," he explained.

We were standing in the front of the boat looking down at the glass-colored water. All was blue and red with the fairy-tale quality of double daylight. Above, massive cloudbanks covered half the sky, the multi-colored sunlights painting them in gaudy hues and stark relief. Purple eyed them with a worried frown. "I hope the weather holds up," he said.

The blue sun hesitated on the horizon, then winked out, leaving everything rose-colored. The silence of the upper air was perfect, but for the *sssssss* of the bicycles and the low chanting at the rear of the boat where Shoogar was trying to change the direction of the wind. It was northeast again, and the boys were pedaling west.

"How much longer do you think the voyage will take?" I asked.

Purple shrugged, "I estimate that we are covering fifteen miles an hour, maybe twenty—that is, in the direction we want to go. If we had a steady wind we could cover the whole fifteen hundred miles in three full days. Unfortunately, Lant, the winds over the ocean are most erratic. We have been journeying for three and a half days and still no land is in sight."

"We were becalmed for a full day," I pointed out. "That did not help any either."

"True," he admitted, "but I had hoped—" He sighed and sank down onto a bench.

I sat down across from him. "I don't see why you should be so impatient. Your test flight took at least this long."

"Yes, but we didn't go that far. Then the wind was blowing west, and we were swept over the mountains. We spent the whole three days just coming back."

"You were fighting the wind?"

"Oh no. It had died away by that time, but we needed to figure out how best to handle the boat in the air—and then we had to prove to Shoogar that his sails wouldn't work. It took a full day just to rig them, and then Shoogar would still not be convinced. He made us try over and over and over again. He kept insisting that the airpushers needed something to push against.

"All the time we had those damned sails up," said Purple, "we were powerless to fight the wind, so we were blown even farther away. Shoogar didn't want to let us bring them in, but we would have never gotten home otherwise. Once we got organized though, we made good time, and later on the wind gave us a push too."

"You weren't over the island the whole time, were you?"

"Oh no. Just before we started pedaling for home we were getting very close to the mainland. There was a very excited crowd there on the beach, but we didn't try to approach."

"It was well that you didn't—they might have stoned you or worse—" I started to tell him what Gortik had said about the mainlanders, but a distant cough of Elcin interrupted.

Purple started at the sound. His eyes went wide and he leapt to his feet. "Thunder!" he yelped.

"What? What about it?"

"Thunder means lightning, Lant!" He was leaning forward, shading his eyes with one heavy hand. Frantically he searched the sky and the blood-colored clouds. He didn't see what he was looking for and moved nervously backward to peer out across the side. He began climbing up into the rigging for a better view.

Abruptly there was another *KKK-R-R-u-umpp*, this time noticeably closer.

Purple yelped again. He didn't wait for a third cough, but swarmed up to the top of the rigging and began untying the windbag nozzles.

"What is it?" both Shoogar and I cried.

"Thunderstorm!" he screamed. "Get up here and help me! Wilville, Orbur! You too!" My sons abandoned their posts immediately and began climbing inward.

"I don't understand," I said confusedly, "what is the danger?"

"Lightning!" shouted Orbur. He was already into the rigging.

"You mean lightning strikes airboats too?"

"*Especially* airboats—remember what happened to Purple's housetree? We have to land and drain all the hydrogen out of the airbags. The slightest spark and we'll all blow up!"

He didn't have to repeat himself. I followed Wilville up the ropes. Shoogar was right behind me. Purple had already untied three of the bags and was working on a fourth. The airboat lurched sickeningly. I could not tell if the sinking sensation I felt was me or it.

There was a flash of light and another crashing slam. It was directly above us. We were headed right into the storm. Purple was muttering wildly to himself, "Damn the bloody— I should have thought about emergency deflations! Orbur, this is too slow and we will never get all the gas out of the balloons through the nozzles. Somebody is going to have to climb up to the top with a knife and cut holes to let the gas out! We'll patch them up later—"

"Not now," I yelped. "If you cut holes now, we'll fall!"

"No, not now—after we hit the water," shouted Purple. "We can't risk doing it in the air or the balloons might rip!" He untied another nozzle. Seven of them were waving free now, spewing their precious hydrogen unseen to the reddened thunder.

Another crash of light and sound limned us in stark relief —and sparked us all to move still faster. The black water below rushed up at sickening speed—

"Tie off the balloons," shouted Purple. "Slow our descent!"

Orbur swung precariously from a rear mast section, Wilville only a few yards away. A frantic Shoogar clung to the *bird's nest* platform. Purple and I were in the forward section of the rigging. All of us were grabbing furiously for the free swinging hoses——

The wind whistled and shrieked. I pulled at the aircloth

hose and wrapped it around itself. I swung out on the rigging grabbing for another—

"Hold on!" screamed Purple. "Wait—"

A precious moment of stillness while we fell through the angry sky. Still too fast, too fast—were we slowing at all?

Another crash of thunder—this one closest of them all. A second flash of whiteness——

Purple was a stark silhouette. He was grim-faced, but suddenly stern. He stared at the uprushing water with no sign of emotion. Had he miscalculated? Would we hit the water too hard?

The image of a splintering airboat filled my mind—why had I ever come on this god-cursed journey——?

"Ballast—" he shouted and disappeared from his post. For a moment I thought he had fallen, but with the next crash of thunder I saw him below, tugging at the ballast bags. Wilville was already there, just emptying one over the side—

"I'll help!" I hollered, but he yelled back, "Stay where you are, Lant—it'll be safer—tie off the airbags! Don't release any more gas until I tell you to!"

He cast about frantically then, looking for things to throw overboard. His eye lit on a pile of cloth—"What the—?"

Shoogar yelped from the rigging, "Those are my sails!"

"Good!" And with that, he snatched them up and heaved them over the side. Shoogar began screaming curses, but they were lost in the loudest crash of all.

The spare windbags followed the sails, as did half our food and water. Wilville had emptied all the ballast bags by now and was helping Purple.

We were still falling. A sickening sensation in the pit of my stomach told me we were about to die.

Purple called for me to unreel a windbag nozzle, but not to untie it. What was he planning? He grabbed it as it fell, and hooked it to his funnel. He had a ballast bag between his legs; he plunged the nozzle and battery device into the bag of water. I saw him turn the battery up to its maximum release of electrissy. Great gulps of gas roared up the hose— the windbag expanded terrifically.

Purple waved to Wilville. "Get up in the rigging!" he bellowed. "It'll be safer!"

I could see long streamers of foam below us. We were
falling at little more than a fast gallop—the sea was a
wall of blackness—I could see the individual waves—

Cra-a-ack—the boat smacked down with a great splash
that sent water in all directions. For a sickening moment all
the ropes were slack—then they snapped taut again as the
balloons leapt back. There was a yelp from behind me—Shoogar—I turned in time to see Orbur lose his grip and fall into
the water, but he surfaced again almost immediately and began paddling for an outrigger.

Wilville was climbing down from the rigging then to see if
Purple was all right, but the magician was screaming: "The
balloons! The balloons! We've got to finish deflating the
balloons!"

"Then you'd better disconnect *that!*" pointed Wilville.

Purple looked, saw his battery and funnel device lying
in a puddle of water at the bottom of the boat. The puddle
boiled. Purple yelped and leapt for it.

The boat rocked as Orbur climbed into it, his fur plastered
wetly to his body. He started up the rigging to join us, then
stopped. He cocked his head oddly— "Wait a minute!" he
called. "Don't deflate the balloons yet."

"Huh?" Purple cried. "What are you—" Then he stopped
too. There was a distant cough of thunder. Behind us. Far
behind us.

"The storm is over," said Orbur. "We're past it."

"We fell through it," muttered Shoogar. He began climbing
down. The *bird's nest*, where he had been holding onto it,
was bent out of shape.

The rolling sea lifted us up and dropped us down. Lifted
us up and dropped us down.

The boat lay askew in the water. One of the outriggers

had snapped halfway off and had to be retied before we dared to ascend again. Wilville and Orbur were working on it now.

The balloons—nearly empty now—drooped flaccidly above us. They had barely enough gas to hold themselves aloft. We had been sitting in the sea for half a day now. The red sun was seeping into the west, and the day was ever darkening. Purple sat glumly in the rear of the boat with his battery and his filling framework. Shoogar was half-heartedly bailing water. Apparently we had sprung a small leak somewhere.

I staggered aft, stumbling once. "How bad is our situation, Purple?" I asked.

He shook his head. "It's not good, I can tell you that. I used an awful lot of power in my attempt to pump up the balloons."

"But you had to—you had no choice."

"I shouldn't have panicked though. I was so afraid we were going to be struck by lightning that I let the gas out of the bags too fast, then I used up too much power trying to replace it. And I don't think I did that much good. All I did was make steam. I'm sure some oxygen got mixed up with the hydrogen." He peered upward at the limp airbags. "I'm afraid this may be the end of our journey, Lant."

I looked around me. Fortunately, Shoogar and the sons had not heard. Or, if they had, they showed no sign. "Are you out of power completely?"

"No, but I'm not sure there's enough to refill the balloons, Lant—"

"There's only one way to find out."

Purple nodded, "Yes, of course—we will have to try it. The only thing is, I have to save some power with which to call down my flying egg. I'm not sure I have enough to do both." He scratched thoughtfully at his chin hair.

I thought hard. "Why don't we use another ballast spell? Throw away some more weight?"

He started to shake his head to that, then— "Wait! You're right, Lant. We can lighten this boat considerably. We can't be that far from land—" He stood up, began looking around for things to throw overboard.

He tugged at a bundle. "What's this?"

"The spare windbags. Orbur found them floating in the water."

"Oh," He started throwing them over again. "I'm sorry, Lant," he said to my shocked expression, "But it's the same situation as when we were falling. It's either us or them. Now, what else—what's in here?"

"Quaff skins, water skins, sour melons, sweet melons, smoked meats—Purple, what are you doing?"

"Throwing it overboard, Lant. We packed enough food for three or four weeks. We don't need that much. I'm keeping only enough for two more days." He began dropping armloads of it over the side.

"Not that!" I protested, but he ignored me—the Quaff went too.

We stumbled forward, looking for other things to throw out. The sea rolled around us, rocking the boat and carrying away our hard-won treasures. Our Quaff.

The blankets followed the food, all but three—which Purple agreed might be necessary. He picked up a twisting tool, "Orbur, are you through with this?" Orbur nodded.

"Good," said Purple. It splashed over the side. He moved forward again. "What's this junk—"

"Not that!" yelped Shoogar. "That's my spellcasting equipment!"

"For God's sake, Shoogar—what's more important, your life or your spells?"

"Without my spells I wouldn't have a life," snapped Shoogar.

For a moment I wondered if maybe Purple wasn't considering throwing Shoogar over too. But instead he thrust his spell kit back at him. "Here, this must be as important to you as my battery is to me. If something this light is enough to make a difference—well, if we're that far gone it won't matter one way or another. Keep it." Shoogar took his kit and examined it carefully.

Purple stumbled forward and began to empty out the small cabin framework there.

Wilville climbed back into the boat then. "The outrigger is fixed," he announced.

"Good," said Purple, dumping an armload of things. He wobbled back to us and began throwing the tools overboard.

That done, he straightened and said, "I guess we're ready to ascend now. Orbur, will you pull down the first of the windbag nozzles while I ready the gasmaker?"

Orbur nodded and started to climb the rigging—that is, he tried to—what happened was that he pulled the balloon down to where the rest of us could reach it. "Umph," said Purple, "that is limp, isn't it?"

He attached the hose to the funnel and battery and lowered it into the water. "I am going to fill these very carefully," he said to no one in particular and switched on his battery.

While he worked the rest of us began to fill the ballast bags. "You won't need those," said Purple when he saw what we were doing. "We're going to have to make it without ballast."

"Yes, but we're going to need some in the boat while you fill the balloons," I said.

"Yes, of course—you're right, I forgot." He turned back to his gas making.

After two balloons had been filled, Wilville and Orbur climbed out onto the outriggers and began pedaling. The boat rode up and down the ocean swells. Five balloons later, it stopped riding the waves. Instead, the water just slapped at the bottom.

Shoogar and I exchanged a glance. "We need more water in the boat," he said and reached for the bucket. I helped him for a bit, then something occurred to me.

"Why are we doing it the hard way?" I asked. "Just pull the plug and let the water flow in." As I spoke I was already tugging.

There was a yelp from the stern. "No!" shouted Purple, but it was too late. Water spurted up and struck me in the face.

"Stop it, stop it!" Purple cried. "Stop it!"

"Why?"

"Just do it! Don't ask why! Just do it!" He dropped his gasmaker and came splashing back, slipped in the water and fell. "Stop it, Lant!"

"But—but—" The water was rapidly filling the boat and I began to understand. "I can't! I let go of the plug when the water hit me!" And then we were all down on our hands and knees feeling around for it under the rising water. It was cold and it surged into the boat eagerly—a spouting fountain marked the spot where the hole was.

We scrambled around frantically in that cold wetness and then suddenly I had it—something small and round and hard. The plug! I tried to jam it back into the hole, but the water was up to my thighs already—I went down on my knees, but then I had to stretch my neck to hold my head above water, and after a few seconds even that didn't work. Shivering, I took a deep breath and went under. I pressed hard on the plug, but I couldn't get the leverage, and the water continued to pour in too fast.

There was another pair of hands on top of mine—Shoogar's—he was trying to help. But it wasn't working—— Even the two of us couldn't press hard enough. I surfaced for air. Wilville and Orbur were shouting at me from their outriggers. They were up to their necks in water already—and still pedaling furiously. Purple was bailing frantically with the bucket.

And then the water stopped rising.

It was up to our chests, and waves were sloshing over the sides of the boat. We had stopped sinking. The windbags held the boat just a few hand's-breadths from total immersion. We stood there up to our chests in cold sea water and glared at each other. I said, "Well, don't just stand there treading water, Purple! Do something!"

He glared at me. Shoogar glared at me. Wilville and Orbur glared at me.

The bags of wind hung over us, the restless sea tossed around us. The red sun began to seep behind the horizon. We had perhaps an hour and a half of daylight left——

Well, since nobody else was going to do anything——

I trod water to the center of the boat and ducked under. I came up with a ballast bag, pulled it to the rim—I could not have lifted it without going under—opened the mouth and poured the ballast over the side. I ducked, found another bag and emptied it.

Purple began to laugh.

Shoogar had gotten the idea and was helping me empty the bags of water overboard. It wasn't enough. The windbags tugged upward on the boat frame, but they couldn't lift it.

They could only keep it from sinking into the uneasy swells. Shoogar searched around for some more ballast bags, ducking under and feeling around with his hands. The dumping of ballast did not help noticeably. The rim of the boat frame continued to show only as an outline in the water.

Purple had been clinging to the rigging and chortling helplessly while we worked. It seemed a singularly rude act. Now he found his voice and said, "Stop. Please stop. You're only emptying water out of water."

"But it's ballast," said Shoogar.

"But it's water too—it just replaces itself as fast as you bail it." He swam over to us. "Put the plug in first, then bail."

I looked at the plug in my hand and shrugged. Why not? —I ducked into the water and felt around for the hole. There was no pressure to fight this time, and the plug slipped in easily. I surfaced with a gasp.

"Is it in?" asked Purple. I nodded. He dove under to check it himself. He came up beside me. "All right, it's firm enough." He gave Shoogar and me a look. "You two start bailing while I finish refilling the balloons. Wilville, Orbur, keep pedaling."

"We have to," they called back, "otherwise we'll sink."

Grumbling, Purple splashed aft. Shoogar and I grabbed buckets and set to work. We bailed fast and furiously. By the time Purple had two more balloons refilled, we had the water level down to our thighs. "You know," I mused, "this might be a good way to keep boats from sinking—hang them from windbags."

Purple only glared at me.

I went back to my bailing.

The red sun seeped down behind the horizon, leaving only a festering glow across the western edge of the world. We worked in shivering darkness. The water splashed coldly about our knees.

After a while I became aware that we were rocking more noticeably. "Purple," I called, "we're riding higher in the water."

He looked up from his battery device, peered over the edge. "So we are." He tied off the neck of the balloon—the tenth to be filled and slogged forward to where we stood.

"One more balloon and we should be out of the water altogether."

"How is your battery holding up?"

"Better than I had hoped—" He tugged at the rigging, pulled down another nozzle. "—it's getting awfully cold, isn't it, Lant? Why don't you break out the blankets?"

"You threw them overboard," I said. "All except for three —and those are soaking wet."

"*Everything* is soaking wet," grumbled Shoogar.

"Oh," said Purple. He sloshed aft for his battery. There was nothing more to say.

Shoogar and I paused in our bailing to hang the sodden blankets across the rigging, hoping to dry them out. I imagined that tiny icicles were forming on the ends of my body fur.

"Our food supplies are a mess too," said Shoogar, sniffing at a package. "The hardbread *isn't*." He tossed it soggily over the side.

"You should have said a ballast blessing over it," I said, but it was a cheerless joke.

He didn't appreciate it anyway—this was no time for joking. Purple was just filling the twelfth balloon, and we were miserable and cold.

"Shoogar," I said.

He looked at me from where he was huddling in his damp robe. "What?"

"Feel! We're not rocking any more! We're out of the water!"

"Huh?" He turned to the railing and looked. I joined him. In the last fading glow of red sunset, we could just make out the black water skimming effortlessly below.

There was no doubting it—and every moment we rose higher and higher. The twelfth balloon was bulging taut overhead. "Purple," I called, "we're in the air!"

"I know," he called back. "Wilville! Orbur!" he shouted to the outriggers. "How high are we?"

"At least a manheight. The airpushers are just out of the waves——"

Purple unclipped his flashlight from his belt and aimed it at the balloons above. Only four still hung limp, the rest were swollen with the familiar and friendly bulge of hydrogen gas. He stepped to the side of the boat and aimed the

light over the side. The water gleamed five manheights below.

"I will pull the plug," I said. "It must be safe to drain the
rest of this water now." I splashed toward it; the water was
still knee-high in the boat.

"No!" shouted Purple and Shoogar together. Wilville and
Orbur too. "Don't touch that plug."

"Huh?" I stopped, my hand on the bone cylinder.

"Don't do it, Lant! Don't touch the plug unless I tell you
to!"

"But we're so high above the water. Surely there's no danger now."

"I still have four balloons to refill. Where will I get the
water I need if you will pull the plug?"

"Oh," I said. I let go of it quickly.

"Wait a minute," Shoogar said suddenly, "you can't use
that water for your hydrogen gas. That's ballast water. It
makes us go down, not up."

"Shoogar, it's water. Just water," Purple said patiently.

"But it's symbological nonsense to think that the same
water can make us go in two directions!" And then Shoogar
could only make gulping sounds. For Purple had casually
dipped up a double handful of water from the bottom of
the boat, and was drinking it. Drinking the *ballast!*

Shoogar choked in impotent rage; he tottered off.

"Why don't you go sit down too?" Purple suggested to
me. "Let me worry about the boat."

"All right," I shrugged and sat down on a bench. It was
cold and wet like everything else on the *Cathawk.* From the
stern came sounds of damp rigging being pulled and
stretched. Purple was just starting to fill another windbag.

We sailed on through the dark, shivering and miserable.
Wilville and Orbur pumped and chanted. Purple filled the
balloons. Shoogar and I froze.

A wind came up then and started pushing us north. Any
other time we might have appreciated it. In this sodden darkness though, it only set our teeth to chattering. Wilville and
Orbur gave up on their pedaling then—it was too cold to
continue. They huddled at the wet bottom of the boat with
the rest of us. After a while even Purple joined us. Being

wrapped with cold soaking blankets was still better than being exposed to the biting upper air.

Or should have been. My fingers were so numb, I could not even pull the icy cloth tighter about myself.

Sleep was impossible. I muttered constantly. "There's no such thing as warm, Lant. It's all your imagination. You'll never be warm again. You'd better get used to freezing, Lant—"

When Ouells—bright blue and tiny—snapped up over the eastern horizon an hour later, we were still damp with chill, and there was a thin layer of frost on everything in the boat.

The morning was crisp, but rapidly warming.

The sea was a plate of restless blue far below. We seemed higher than we'd ever been in the airship. The edge of the world was almost curved.

Purple said that was an optical illusion. We were much too low to see any real curvature. Gibberish again.

We stretched the blankets across the rigging to dry them in the sun. Our togas as well. Even Purple shed his impact suit and stretched out against the bright morning.

The wind continued to blow steadily north, and Wilville and Orbur were resting on their outrigger cots.

I splashed around in the front of the boat, looking for any foodstuffs that either Purple or the water had missed. I found a half of a sour melon and glumly split it with Shoogar. None of the rest wanted any.

We still had water in the airboat, up to our knees, but Purple refused to let us dump it. "Look how high we are already," he said. "There's no point to throwing this water away. Later, when the windbags leak a little more, then we'll need it. Besides, I may want to make some more hydrogen first."

"Do you have enough electrissy?"

He smiled sheepishly. "I—uh, I sort of miscalculated when I filled the windbags. I didn't realize they still had as much hydrogen in them as they did. I have enough power left to fill three airbags. Or to fill four if I don't want to call my flying egg down." He looked about him. "That should be enough. We should have at least four days of flying time left before the balloons are too weak again and I'm out of power. If we can't make it by then, we'll never make it."

We sailed on hungrily; and steadily, steadily north.

We fought crosswinds for a while, but always the general direction of our motion was north.

We had lost our course line of hills under the water sometime during the thunderstorm. That we had been unable to find it again didn't worry Purple as much as it might have. He still had his measuring devices, and he charted our course by them.

When I asked him about it, he shrugged it off, "Well, it seemed like a good idea, Lant—but I think those hills of yours are too deeply submerged now to be seen. Maybe we'll be lucky though, and see them again when we get over shallower water."

The next day, he recharged the windbags, leaving himself only enough power to fill two bags completely until full, or one windbag and a call to his flying egg.

Toward evening we finally pulled the plug and drained away the knee-high water which had been our companion for the last two days. "I had thought this trip was going to be over water," Shoogar grumbled, "not through it."

Purple grinned as he watched the water spill away. We were too high to see if we were rising, but the feel of the craft told us that we were. He said, "But it was obvious, Shoogar, we should have thought of it sooner—always keep a quantity of water in the boat. It helps us to balance the craft so that it doesn't rock so much when we move. It's there for recharging the airbags—we never have to go down to the water any more. And we can use it as ballast too."

"I tell you that that's nonsense!" Shoogar exploded. "Ballast, drinking water, gas-making water, wash water—— What kind of a spell is it when you arbitrarily change the name of the object to suit your needs?"

And he stamped off to the bow to sulk, his sandals making wet squishy sounds as he went.

He was still there when darkness came, peering forward at the sky and chanting a moon-bringer spell.

It was Orbur who spotted our course line again. Far off to the left, a lighter-colored patch of sea could be seen.

We were lower now, despite the dumping of six bags of water. Purple said it was due to the airbags leaking faster than before. They were stretching, he said, and the seams weren't as strong as he had hoped. He ordered the boys to come about and head the boat in a course that would eventually bring us over the spine of hills again.

I chewed thoughtfully on a lump of moldy hardbread. That the hills were visible under the water again meant that we were nearing shallower seas. Soon we might be over land, and our journey would be over——

The windbags above were taut, but rippling slightly in the wind. Soon the ripplings would increase some more, folds of cloth would hang loose, the bags would droop heavily—and all the while we would descend lower and lower.

Purple began emptying the last of the ballast bags—all except two which we would save for drinking water. Shoogar moaned, when he said that. The boat rose some as he dumped the ballast, but not by any significant amount. "Well, that's it," he said. "We make it on the gas we've got left, or not at all."

Wilville and Orbur pumped silently and steadily. They no longer chanted happily while they worked. Rather, they seemed almost in a trance, trying to endure from one moment to the next. They had both developed sores and blisters on their hands and buttocks. Purple had sprayed them each with a salve, but then they had gone back out onto the outriggers, and I suspected that the salve would not do much good.

We took up our position over the spine of hills and pumped steadily north. I wobbled to the front of the boat and joined Shoogar. Although the red sun was still bright in the west, he wanted to miss not a moment of the impending darkness. "The moons," he chortled happily, "the moons should be visible soon."

I ignored him. I was not so much concerned with what was above as with what was ahead. Was that a line of narrow darkness on the forward horizon? It was too dark to tell.

I called it to Purple's attention. He shouldered roughly past Shoogar and peered eagerly forward. "Umph," he said, "I can't see."

"Use your flashlight," I suggested.

"No, Lant, it hasn't enough power to reach that far."

"Attach it to your big battery. That still has some power left in it."

He smiled. "I could do that, but it hasn't got enough power left in it to turn the flashlight up that bright. Besides, blue dawn will be here in slightly more than an hour. If it is land, we'll see it then."

The red sun faded away then, and we throbbed impatiently through the darkness, only the steady *sssssss* of the bicycles reminding us that we were moving. Purple paced restlessly in the back of the boat, while Shoogar chanted steadily in the bow.

I tried to sleep, but couldn't.

Morning snapped up over the east and as one, Purple and I rushed forward. Wilville was already crying, "Land! I can see it! Land! We've made it! We've made it!"

"Keep pedaling," Purple shouted. "Keep pedaling!"

We were lower now—much lower—the airbags were not holding their hydrogen as long as they used to, and we were only a few manheights above the water.

It mattered not. Far ahead of us we could see the craggy shore of the North, and behind it, jagged hills rising toward a familiar mountain range—The Teeth Of Despair.

"Oh, pump, Wilville, pump!" cried Purple. "Pump, Orbur, pump!" He peered so far forward out of the boat, I thought he was ready to leap out and swim for land. "Just a little bit farther!"

The sea below us was mottled and ugly. We could see

jagged reefs below us—and here and there a whirlpool. All slid past, but we were sinking lower and lower.

Purple noticed it too. "What the—" He moved back inside the boat and began tugging experimentally at the rigging.

"One of the bags must have a leak—" He started climbing upward. "Is it this one?" He pulled at a rope. "No. Maybe it's that one. Yes, the seam there—see it?"

I looked. Just above him, one of the airbags had a narrow slit of darkness in its belly. Purple took a step higher in the rigging—

And then it happened.

The seam ripped wide open—a great stretching and tearing sound. The bag folded open, and the boat gave a sudden lurch as it collapsed. Huge lengths of aircloth began falling across the rigging. Wilville and Orbur screamed.

"Throw some ballast! Throw some ballast!" cried Shoogar. He ran frantically about the boat, but we only had two ballast bags. He pulled at them furiously.

"No!" shouted Purple. "That won't do any good. There's not enough!" He half climbed, half fell from the rigging. "Lant, get my airmaker!"

"Where is it?"

"In the back of the boat, I think! Hurry!"

We were losing altitude fast. And I could see why he wanted me to hurry. A swirling whirlpool lay below us, hungry and sucking. It was huge—

Purple already had a windbag nozzle untied and waiting above an open sack of water. He grabbed the airmaker and shoved its funnel into the airhose and into the water, both in one motion. He snapped his battery on. The windbag swelled frantically, strove to rise. The airboat gave a lurch.

Purple flung away the empty water bag. "Give me the other." Shoogar shoved it into position before the words were out of his mouth, and again Purple plunged his wires and funnel into it. Again the windbag puffed with a mixture that was half hydrogen, half throw-away gas.

We could hear the roar of the whirlpool now—and little else. We were less than two manheights above the water. Wilville and Orbur were frantically pulling their airpushers up so they would not get caught in the maelstrom below.

But we had stopped our descent!

The great whirling walls of water slipped thunderously past us—crashing and black. We could feel the wet mist across our faces. Foam sprayed the boat.

"The Mouth of Teev," whispered Shoogar. "It appears at the end of every summer. As the seas recede, it sucks up everything within its reach, men, boats, trees, rocks——"

"But summer isn't over yet," said Purple. His face was white, and the bones of his knuckles showed where he gripped the railing.

"No," said Shoogar, "but it's starting to wane. By summer's end the Mouth will be much bigger than this. Its roar will be audible for miles."

Purple peered nervously backward. The dark thundering water was slipping steadily behind us. Wilville and Orbur lay clenched across their outriggers.

"I never thought I'd live to see it that close," Shoogar said weakly.

Purple grunted thoughtfully. He was looking at his air-maker.

"What's the matter?" I asked.

"My battery. I think it's dead."

"What? No! Again?"

"I think so." He disconnected the battery and shook it experimentally. "Look, the dial doesn't even light up. We used up all the power we had."

"We needed it. We'd be in the Mouth of Teev if we hadn't made more gas."

"We could have swum for it. Or cut the boat loose and hung onto the ropes! Or—anything——" He put his face in his hands and made sounds of pain. Then suddenly he stood up, picked up the battery and—for an endless moment I thought he was going to fling it overboard and perhaps follow it.

Instead he called briskly, "Wilville! Orbur! Back on the bicycles. We're so close to land, you don't want to quit now!"

I could see that he was only acting. He didn't want the others to see how deeply he felt his loss. He pretended to busy himself checking the rigging, but several times I caught him staring off into the sky with a faraway look.

The boys unslung the windmakers again and Shoogar

began to chant with them—the *I Think Icon,* a fast chant, strong and purposeful.

The shore line loomed ever nearer—the surf was white and foaming; Shoogar steadily increased the pace of the chant. Even so, we kept sinking lower and lower toward the water—not as fast as before, but it was apparent that the airbags were no longer as tight as they had been.

The water slipped past us, the windmakers dipping through the higher waves; then cutting through the swells themselves, becoming visible only in the troughs between the waves; and at last, no longer visible at all. The outriggers hung low along the sides of the boat, and pushed us through the surf. The balloons hung in silent stillness overhead, and the sea splashed below. An occasional spray of wet foam came through the rigging.

Shoogar interrupted his chanting to call, "Lant, look! Do you recognize where we are heading? Come look!"

I climbed forward. Ahead lay a bleak and forbidding land-scape of jagged black and brown. It was streaked with gray and purple, and ominously stained whites. All was pitted and scarred. Here and there a flash of red testified to a scorch-blossom's attempt to take root, but little more was visible. Except—was that the fire-blackened shell of a wild house-tree? It looked like a gaunt hand frozen in an anguished skyward grasp.

"Lant! It is the Cove of Mysteries—or what's left of it. We are not far from the old village, just a few miles south of it."

Purple came up behind me, a clicking device in his hands. I had noticed it on his belt before, but he had never ex-plained its use. Now he tapped it experimentally and frowned. At last he smiled, "The level of—" He used a demon word here, "is not as high as I thought it would be, not much higher than the normal background level. Certainly not dan-gerous, anyway. It will be safe to walk in this area."

The boat was splashing through the waves now, and Purple directed the boys to head for a place where the ground sloped gently into the water. We could see one not too far ahead, and the boys shifted direction to make for it.

Purple peered ahead. "Lant, how far are we from Critic's Tooth?"

"Well, it used to be over there, Purple," I pointed. A few cracked, half-melted slabs of rock marked a conspicuous gap in the mountains to the north.

He misunderstood. "That peak is Critic's Tooth?"

"No, that's Viper's Bite—one of the lesser foothills before Critic's Tooth. Critic's Tooth is gone."

"Oh."

"The whole range of jagged mountains is called the Teeth of Despair. Critic's Tooth was one of the sharpest peaks. The region is ruled by the mad demon, Peers, who gnashes and gnarls mightily. He attacks natives and strangers alike. We should approach no closer, lest he blame us for the damage to his Teeth."

Purple was looking at his ticking thing again, waving it and pointing it. "A good idea."

We bounced through the surf. There was a gentle bump as the nose of the boat slid up onto the sand. We had reached the northern shore.

"The *Cathawk* has landed!" shouted Wilville. "The *Cathawk* has landed!"

As one person we jumped for shore, Shoogar and Purple and I scrambling over each other.

At last we stood on solid ground again. The land was desolate, mostly naked rock, blood-colored in the westering light of Ouells and the overhead glow of Virn, but it was solid. No more standing in air, no more standing in water. No more standing in both at the same time.

If ever I returned safely home, I swore, I would never again risk my life in so foolhardy a venture. The skies were *not* friendly

Wilville and Orbur had slung up the airpushers and pulled the *Cathawk* high on the shore, out of reach of the lapping waves. Immediately they began filling the ballast bags, and the interior of the boat as well, with a low level of water.

They began checking the rigging, the bicycle frames, and even the watertightness of the boatframe and the balloons. They acted as if they expected the *Cathawk* to fly again. How, I could not imagine. The gasbags were all limp from leakage, and I did not trust the seams on several of them. They still extended upward from their ropes, but none were very determined about it.

How they hoped to refill the windbags, I did not know.

Shoogar was walking around and chuckling to himself. "I won't have to acquaint myself with the local spells or the local gods at all. I can start as soon as I check the moons . . ." and he wandered off toward a distant blackened hill, carrying his spell kit.

A strange black crust covered everything. It shattered when one stepped on it and left miniscule shards, or stinging dust which went up in wisps before the surly wind. Curious, I crunched across the ground toward the hill where Purple stood. He was attaching his big battery to another of his endless spell devices.

He looked both sheepish and defiant as I came up. "Well, I have to try it, don't I?"

"But you said it was dead."

"Perhaps I've come to believe in magic," said Purple. "Nothing else seems to work." And he finished attaching the wires to the disc-shaped thing from his belt.

He twisted a knob, but nothing happened.

"This yellow eye should light up to show it's working," Purple explained, smiling foolishly. He twisted the knob again, harder this time, but the yellow light still did not appear.

"Magic doesn't work either," he said. He sighed.

I knew just how he felt then. I longed to be going home myself.

How strange!—that I should consider an area that I had lived in for only a short time as my home; while this bleak map, the blasted remains of the village where I had spent most of my life, was no longer *home* but a strange and alien land. "Home" was a new land and a different life across the sea.

For that one terrible moment Purple and I were alike.

Two strangers, marooned on a bleak and blackened shore, each longing for his home, his wives, and his Quaff.

"All I needed was one surge of power," said Purple. "Shoogar was right. You can't mix symbols."

He picked up his useless devices and trudged slowly down the hill. The ground crunched beneath his feet.

There was nothing to eat. I lay there in the darkness and listened to the roar of the surf and the rumble of my stomach. Man was not meant to live without bread alone. I was dizzy with hunger. My thoughts didn't even make sense any more.

Purple had spent the red day wandering dully up and down this landscape of despair. I and my sons waited. There was little else we could do. Shoogar was the only one with a sense of purpose. He had positioned himself patiently at the top of a nearby slope to wait for the moons. He chanted a song of triumph.

Purple muttered incessantly. "When the seas recede, we could walk back. Lant's people did it before. We can do it again. Yes, we could walk back. The generators are still there, the looms are still there. I could recharge my battery. We could make another flying machine. Yes, of course. And this time, we would know better. I would have my battery fully charged. *Fully* charged. We wouldn't have to make the same mistakes again. That's it, we left before we were fully ready. We weren't tested or experienced enough. But we came so close, so close. Next time, we'll do it better and we'll succeed. Next time, next time. Next time—"

He crunched through the dark, mumbling insanely. He would pick up rocks and examine them, then throw them down again and stumble on.

I stared up into the dark at the twinkling moons. There would be no next time. I was sure of that. Shoogar wasn't going to let there be a *next time*. From his hill there was only silence now.

I turned over on my blanket and raised up on my elbows. "Purple," I called, "you should try to rest."

"I can't, Lant," he called back. There was a skidding sound and a thump. "Ow—"

"What's the matter?" I leapt to my feet, thinking Shoogar had struck in the dark.

But no—Purple's flashlight went on revealing that he had tripped over a boulder. He lay there in his impact suit, grinning foolishly.

I walked over and helped him up. The night was stale and still; the surf was a distant rumble. We stood in the dark, Purple's light the only thing in existence, casting an eery white aura into the chaotic blackness.

Purple switched it off. "I guess I'd better save my power," he said—and stopped.

There was deathly silence. Not even insects still lived in this accursed land. "Save my power," Purple repeated quietly. His hands clamped on my shoulders and he screamed, "Power! In my flashlight! In my flashlight, Lant!"

"Let go, curse it!" He was as strong as an old ram.

"Power, Lant! Power!"

"Don't get your hopes up, Purple. Wait until you get a response from your mother nest."

He sobered instantly. "Yes, you're right, Lant." There was a scraping sound in the dark as he removed the flashlight's small battery, another sound as he pulled the calling device from his belt, an incomprehensible curse as he tried to attach the wires in the dark. He worked eagerly, impatiently—I could not blame him.

At last he said, "I'm ready." There was a click as he switched on the device. A dial on its face gave off a soft glow. Before he even pressed the call button, he peered at this dial. "There is power enough, Lant. More than enough. I can call my mother nest ten times, maybe more, with the power in this battery."

"Is it enough to recharge the windbags too?" I asked hopefully.

His face was a dark blur. "No, not that much. That requires vast amounts of power, Lant. It needs a heavy-duty battery like my other one—but don't worry. When my mother egg gets here, I'll see that you and your sons get safely home.

"Home," he repeated. "I'm going home. No more double shadows. No more furry women. No more black plants—"

"Green, Purple. Plants are green."

"Green is a bright color where I come from. No more odd food and foul drink. No more scratchy clothing. No more *medicine* shows for *yokels*." He chanted this litany in man's tongue and demon's tongue. It was a homegoing spell and he spoke it intensely. "I'll have *books*, music, normal weight—"

"You intend to diet?"

He laughed at that and kept laughing from sheer joy. "I'm going home!" he bellowed into the night.

"Why not try your calling device?" I was getting impatient.

He said, "I'm afraid to."

"Oh."

He turned the knob. A yellow eye opened brilliantly.

"Hah!" Purple shouted. "And the red eye means that the mother nest has answered."

"What red eye?"

Purple twiddled the knob impatiently. "Come on," he whispered. "Come on."

Nothing happened.

He shook the device. "Come on, damn you! I want to go home!"

The yellow eye burned steadily. There was no red response light.

"We're far enough north," said Purple. "Close enough to the *equator*. The seeing should be good; the curve of the *planet* isn't in the way. What could be wrong? It *can't* be sending the wrong *frequency*," he mumbled. If he was making magic, it wasn't working.

"Perhaps it's your battery," I suggested.

"It's *not* my battery. Why doesn't it answer? Why doesn't it answer?" He jumped to his feet and went raging off into the dark. After a moment, I followed him.

I found him sitting in ashes and despair. He had his device on the ground in front of him and was banging on it with a rock.

He hadn't damaged it though—only pounded it deeper into the soft dead earth.

"Purple, stop," I said softly. "Stop."

"Why should I?" he said bitterly. "We've come all this way for nothing. All of your devices have worked, Lant. None of mine have. Your aircloth got us here, your generators got us here, your airpushers got us here—but my calling device doesn't work. So why did we bother to come at all. The only one who's going to get any benefit out of this will be Shoogar."

"Huh?" Did he know about the duel? Had he realized?

"Yes, Shoogar," he answered my questioning look. "He needed to know about the moons. He had to come north. The rest of us might as well have stayed home." He started pounding again.

"Perhaps we have not come far enough north," I suggested.

He made a sound that suggested he thought me a fool.

I was grabbing for ideas now, anything to restore his spirit. "Or perhaps there is still a *planet* in the way." Whatever that meant. He had used the word before.

For a moment, there was silence. "What did you say?—"

I opened my mouth to repeat it.

"Never mind. I heard it the first time." There was a sound of digging in the dirt. A scraping and a crunching. "Damn me. I'm so stupid sometimes—"

"What are you talking about?"

He stood up, a blur in the darkness. He held his device in his hands. "Lant, you are a genius sometimes. And all this time I thought you didn't understand a thing I was talking about but were only being polite and pretending that you did. *Of course* there's a planet in the way," he stamped his foot. "This one."

"H'm," I said, pretending to understand. Who was I to shatter his illusion?

"Don't you see? My egg hasn't risen yet. Like the suns, it's probably on the other side of the world. I will have to wait until it is in sight, before I try calling it again. That's probably why it didn't work before."

When magic doesn't work, a good magician usually has an explanation ready. Purple was one of the best. I wondered if he understood his own explanation. I asked, "How long will it take before you can call it down?"

"A couple of hours should be all I need. I'll try calling it every fifteen minutes. Its *orbit* is only two and a half hours. I couldn't possibly miss it, no matter how low on the horizon it is."

I left him mumbling happily to himself, explaining things to no one in particular.

B lue dawn snapped up over the eastern rim, revealing a world even bleaker and drearier than before—if such was possible.

Aching with hunger I stumbled up a black hill to find Shoogar tracing a gigantic pattern in the greasy dust. He was using a brilliant white powder and mixing it with various colored potions as he trickled it into graceful curves. Every so often he stopped to consult a parchment in his hand.

I recognized the skin, with its circles and ellipses looping around a central dot—then I recognized the larger pattern. "Shoogar! What are you doing?"

"What does it look like I'm doing? I'm casting a spell!"

"And your oath of fealty?"

"You know perfectly well that I swore by the local gods. Different territories imply different gods and different oaths. Now we're on my home territory. Here, I painted the runes of the duel against Purple. Here, that duel is still in progress!"

"But so much has changed—" I stopped, for he was right. "And you stole his map of the moonpaths."

"No. He gave it to me, the fool. I'll use his own magic against him. And his own name—his real name! Of course, he wasn't worried before. He knew I couldn't hurt him because his speakerspell hadn't told his true name. But this time—"

"Maybe he was lying," I said quickly.

Shoogar gave me a contemptuous look. "Lant," he explained patiently, "the act of saying 'my real name is,' is a consecration spell. Even if he was lying when he said it, the act of saying it made it as good as his real name. And it can be used against him! If this were not so, a magician would have no power at all. People would change names at will to avoid local spells."

"But why the moonpaths?" I said. Then it dawned on me. "No—you can't!"

"I can—and I will. I'm going to drop a moon on his head."

I felt a strong urge to laugh. It was insane. Wildly, incredibly insane.

And he meant every word of it.

"Shoogar," I said. "A moon did fall once. Do you know what the results were?"

"I have seen the *Circle Sea*."

"*Circle Sea* was once a rich farming area. Now the sea rolls in a circular depression of blasted stone, where nothing grows at all."

Shoogar shrugged unconcernedly. "This place is already accursed, Lant. What harm can a falling moon do here?"

"It can kill *us!*" I almost shouted.

"I'll pick one of the little ones—"

"Even a *little* one can kill us—they say that the Circle Sea was a ring of molten rock for many years, before the sea stopped boiling and moved in to cover it."

"Probably, they exaggerate."

"But—"

"Lant," he said, "I can do no less. Consider: Purple has insulted the Gods themselves. He has claimed repeatedly that they do not exist at all—and he has had the incredible effrontery to build a flying machine that proves it! In his violations of reason, such as his games with the ballast concept, he mocks the laws that even the gods obey."

Shoogar paced furiously as he spoke, red-eyed and wild. "He has insulted custom, Lant. He has given names to women and taught them the trades of men! He has interrupted housetree consecrations, and turned housetrees into prickly plants. He has reduced our village life to chaos. Some of our traditional trades no longer exist, while others, like coppersmithery, have swollen monstrously in importance."

He stopped pacing and looked at me. "He has introduced new concepts to us, Lant. He has taught us evil things that lessen the value of life and increase the importance of *things!*

"But most of all," he said. "He has insulted *me*. He would

not teach me to fly, until he needed to fly himself; and he still has not taught me the spells that make electrissy. We depend on his charity for his lightning boxes and airmakers! He has undermined my authority with his spurious cures, so that they trade my spells for his at ten to one!

"I was bound to him by an oath of servitude, but he never asked for my help in anything. Never, not once. He even threw my sails overboard!

"No little death spell would retrieve my honor," Shoogar screamed. "I will bring a moon down upon his head! This one last time I must show my might, before he escapes me forever!"

"I won't help you," I said feebly.

"You don't have to, Lant. I'm sure it was your help last time that *yngvied* me up."

"How long will this take?"

"Not long. I will finish this soon and then I will chant. I will chant until the red sun is high in the west. Then we will move off and wait."

"I would rather you do something about finding us some food," I grumbled.

"Forget your stomach for once, Lant. Before the blue sun rises again, Purple will be destroyed."

P urple tried his calling thing three more times. On the third try the red light flashed. It began winking steadily.

Purple screamed with delight and threw the device joyously into the air. He capered about wildly, singing and dancing. "I'm going home, I'm going home—I'm going home."

He flung himself on the ground and rolled and kicked. He jumped up with a holler and ran furiously in all directions. Back and forth, in a great circle about me, he pranced and yelled.

At last—it seemed like days—he tired and came gasping up to me. "Lant, I can hardly believe it. It has been so long," he panted. "But it's true. It's happening. My mother egg has heard."

I glanced nervously at the hill where Shoogar still worked. He was sitting and chanting now. "Uh, how long will it take before your egg gets here, Purple?"

He frowned. "Who cares? It's coming—that's all."

"I care!" I almost screamed.

He gave me a peculiar look. "I hadn't realized this meant so much to you."

"Well, it does," I said, in a slightly quieter tone. "How long will it take?"

"Maybe a day," he said. "Maybe a little longer. The egg was on *standby*. It will have to activate itself, come to full power, take bearings, check its systems, plot a course, make an approach—it will take time, Lant. The egg could not possibly be here before blue sunset."

I groaned.

"I know how it must pain you, my friend. But fear not. I have waited this long. I can wait a little longer."

I groaned and trudged away, clutching at the ache in my stomach.

I went down to the shore. The sea surged restlessly at the slope where Wilville and Orbur worked.

"Father, you look ill," said one.

"I am," I said. "I am tired and hungry and I hurt all over. I long for a decent bed and a decent meal—"

"Wilville has found some cavernmouth eggs," said Orbur. "Do you want one?"

I groaned. But it was better than nothing. I took the heavy sphere and bit at its rind. A salty-sweet taste flowed into my mouth. "Oh, that's awful," I said. I took a drink of water from a ballast sack.

"Don't let Shoogar see you doing that."

"Curse Shoogar—" I said. "Do you know what he's doing? He's trying to call down a moon!"

Orbur snorted. Wilville didn't say anything.

"Didn't you hear what I said?"

"We heard you," said Wilville. "Shoogar is trying to call down a moon. At least it will keep him out of our way."

"Oh," I said. Apparently they were so intent on what they were doing, they were oblivious to what was going on around them. "What are you working on?" I asked. I squatted down on my haunches to look.

They explained. One of the pulleys had worked loose from a bicycle frame. But they had almost no tools at all to work with. Purple had thrown them all overboard. They were working now with rocks and sticks and shreds of aircloth. "If we can get this working again, we can use the boat to get away from here, whether we have windbags or not."

I nodded and offered my help, but Orbur said I would only be in the way. I gathered up the cavernmouth eggs and took them off a ways. I found some driftwood and made a small fire to roast them. They were still awful, but they were food.

I took one up to Purple, but he had spread out a piece of aircloth from the ripped balloon and was snoring blissfully and peacefully; it was the first time that I had seen him completely relaxed since I had known him.

I let him sleep and trudged across the slope to Shoogar. He shook his head at the sight of the egg, "I will have it later, when I finish my chant."

I looked at his gigantic spell pattern. "Why don't you draw it around Purple?" I asked.

"Why bother? If a moon falls on him, it won't matter if it hits him directly or not—it's going to make another Circle Sea."

"Oh," I said. I went back to my sons and watched them work.

They worked for most of the day, stopping only to chew on a piece of roast cavernmouth egg or to swill down some water. By the time night had fallen and the red sun was seeping into the west, the bicycle pulley was working again as well as it would ever be.

The day was rapidly nearing its end. Purple's egg had still not arrived, and Shoogar was still on the hill chanting.

My sons stretched out tiredly on their blankets and chewed gratefully on the rubbery eggmeat. Had they had their tools, they might have finished the job in less than an hour, but encumbered as they were, it took nearly all day. They were exhausted from the frustrations involved.

I lay on my back and stared into the sky. Already one of the moons had emerged in the darkening east, and others would join it shortly. I watched with a helpless feeling. I had been unable to dissuade Shoogar in his spellmaking. Warning Purple would do no good; I knew what he thought of Shoogar's magic.

I tried to guess what pattern the moons had assumed. Two of the three big ones made a diagonal across a line of four small ones, so tiny they barely showed their colors.

The sign of the Bent Cross?

No matter. Whatever sign it was, Shoogar would think of a way to use it——

He came running over the hill then. He pulled me roughly to my feet, "Come on, Lant. It's time to retreat."

"Huh?" I said sleepily. "What—?"

"I've finished my spell. All we have to do now is wait." He pulled at my arm.

I followed him down to the boat. He was grabbing things at random and throwing them into the craft where they splashed into the water. "Come on, Lant, come on—we haven't got any time."

I woke my sons. They were just as confused and upset as I—and twice as grumpy. "If Shoogar's spell really does work," I insisted, "this is no place we want to be." They allowed themselves to be pushed down the slope. Wilville pulled the plug to drain the water from the boat—it was no longer needed—the airbags were so limp they could no longer hold up even the rigging.

Orbur gathered the last of the aircloth shreds we had been using as blankets, and the remaining cavernmouth eggs. We pounded the plug back into the hole, and shoved the boat roughly into the water.

"Hurry, hurry," snapped Shoogar. "The moon will be falling soon!"

"Does Purple know?" asked Orbur.

"Of course not. Why should I tell Purple?"

"Oh, no reason," Orbur said as he pulled himself out of the water and onto his outrigger. "Except that he might have died of fright, and then you wouldn't have needed to go through with the spell."

Shoogar snorted and climbed into the boat. I followed. Our robes were wet from our thighs down. We had had to push the boat out past the breakers before we could climb in.

Wilville was the last to mount. He swung the boat around so that its stern was toward the sea—it would have taken too long to try to turn it the other way.

He swung himself up on the bike frame, and the two boys unslung their airpushers and began backpedaling furiously. Within moments we were moving away from the shore. Purple, up there in the dark with his many-eyed calling device, did not notice at first. But by and by he came strolling across the sand to call, "What are you doing?"

"Testing the boat!" Shoogar called across the black water.

"Good idea," Purple called back. He went back up the hill. There was sufficient light from the moons and the still westering sun to see him as a puffy form on the crest of the slope.

Wilville kept backpedaling then, while Orbur began pedaling forward. The boat swung around to head away from the Teeth of Despair. Bow forward, we moved across the water.

We made little progress though. The wind was headed shoreward and hampered our efforts.

"Pedal faster," Shoogar urged them, "lest the falling moon destroy us!"

"This is nonsense," Orbur complained. "Shoogar can't bring down a moon!"

"Don't you believe in magic?" I demanded.

"Well—"

"You've flown, you fool! How can you not believe in magic?"

"Of course, I believe in magic!" Orbur whispered to me. "It's Shoogar I don't believe in!"

"I notice," I said, "that despite your skepticism you still thought enough to whisper."

"I don't care. He's not the magician Purple is. Even Purple never claimed the power to bring down a moon."

I didn't answer. The boys continued to pedal, but without conviction. Sssss——the bicycles droned, and the water churned.

The boat was a fragile frame with limp bags hanging above it. The sea was restless, like an endless vat of ink; the water was a greasy black oil, flecked with foam. The shore was dark, and Purple was a motionless silhouette on a blackened hill.

I looked at the moons—two were disks, pink on one side, blue-white on the other. Four were too small to show as disks—and there was something wrong up there, something dreadfully wrong.

The boys felt it too. The *sssss* of the bicycles rose frantically. The boat bounced across the water.

I continued to stare, frozen.

One of the little moons, the tail of the crooked cross, was drifting out of alignment.

I looked toward the shore. Did Purple suspect?

He was a doll-sized silhouette capering wildly on a darkened mound. Yes, he must be trying to force it back into the sky. Even now as we watched, he was jumping and crying— but this was Shoogar's home ground.

I glanced over at him as he leaned out the back of the boat. His teeth gleamed as he watched. My sons pedaled furiously, frantically. Our wake was a churning froth.

The moon grew larger.

At first it was a bright dot against the black sky like the other moons—but moving, always moving—faster than any moon had a right to move! Then it was a clear disk like the major moons, red on one side and blue on the other. It was the largest moon in the sky now.

And still it grew!

It should have been sinking toward Purple—*should have been*. Instead, it seemed to hover overhead growing steadily. The blue-white side suddenly darkened, now dimmed to almost black. The moon grew faster, and the red side commenced to dim also.

In the middle of the nearly black globe a yellow eye stared down at us.

And the moon grew huge, huge, and huger still!

"Pedal! Curse you! Faster! Faster!" Shoogar and I were both screaming.

He had miscalculated, the blithering toad—a moon is too big a thing for one man's revenge! Its weight would destroy a world for one man's pride!

And then it was drifting down, down like a monstrous

soap bubble—Shoogar *hadn't* miscalculated—down to where Purple capered on the black-scarred hill.

It stopped over Purple's head—and directly over Shoogar's design.

"Well, don't stop now!" Shoogar shrieked. He practically leapt out of the boat. "Crush him! Crush him! Another two manheights, is that too much to manage? *Arrrgh!*" For the moon would fall no further. Instead, Purple was rising, rising toward the yellow eye. He disappeared into it.

"It ate him!" Shoogar was flabbergasted. "Why did it do that? It wasn't in any of the runes."

"Maybe it was in Purple's runes," said Wilville.

"Yes! He's right," I said. "I see it now! Your moon and Purple's mother egg are one and the same."

"What do you mean?"

"He's going home in it," I said. "Home. I'm glad."

"Purple? *In my moon?* He can't! I won't let him! Boys, turn around!"

"Do it," I told them. As the boat swung slowly around, Shoogar stamped toward the bow. I followed to reason with him.

"He's probably going to wait for us," I said quietly. "He told me he'd make sure we could get home before he left. What are you going to tell him?"

"Tell him? I'll tell him to get his hairless rump out of my moon! What else would I tell him?"

"And what do you think he will answer?"

"What do you mean?"

"There's only one thing Purple can say if he wants to keep the moon. He'll have to say that this is *his* vehicle; that he brought it down; that you had nothing at all to do with it."

"But that's a black lie!"

"Of course it is, Shoogar. But he needs the moon to get home. He'll have to say it. And as your only witness," I explained softly, "I'll have to tell the villagers that Purple denied your claim that you brought down a moon."

"But it's a lie, a black outrageous lie!" Shoogar was flabbergasted at the mad magician's perfidy. "I did too bring it down! And they'll know it, too! Who will the villagers believe, me or that insane bald magician?!!"

"They will believe their Speaker," I said.

For a moment Shoogar glared at me. Then he stamped back to the stern to sulk. We were twenty minutes pedaling back to shore.

The great black moon waited for us, shedding yellow light on the sand.

"I never thought he could do it," Orbur kept repeating as he pulled the boat onto the shore. "Imagine Shoogar bringing down a moon! And he couldn't even cure baldness."

"Perhaps he had help," I said, jumping out of the boat, splashing into ankle-deep water. "Orbur," I complained. "Couldn't you have beached it a little higher? Look at my robe."

"Sorry, Father," said Orbur. He gave another tug at his outrigger. "You think Purple brought the moon down?"

"Not by himself. Obviously he had to wait for Shoogar's spells. But they both wanted the same thing: a falling moon and Purple's departure. Two such powerful magicians working in concert, is it surprising that they succeeded?"

Wilville came up on the other side of me. There was a splash from behind as Shoogar stamped grumpily from the boat. We turned to look at him.

He returned our stare, pulled himself up to his full height of half a manlength, and stamped forward. He brushed imperiously past us—

"Shoogar!" I called.

He stopped, folded his arms and surveyed the giant glowing sphere at the top of the hill. As I came up beside him, he said, "Let him keep my moon, then, if it will take him home! My oath binds me to drive him from my territory, and that I have certainly done!"

"Well said," I bellowed, "you're a generous magician, Shoogar!"

With not another word the four of us trudged up the hill to where Purple waited. His mood was one of frantic impatience—but the lines of worry seemed to have vanished from his face and he beamed with a smile as wide as the world.

We approached cautiously. That great dark mass hung over us like the Doom of the Gods, and we could see nothing holding it up. It was no windbag, that was for certain—it neither behaved nor looked like one.

"Don't be afraid," said Purple. "It's safe."

We advanced into the cone of the peculiar yellow light that poured from Purple's moon. It was that same color that turned green into something eye-hurtingly bright, and I wondered how anyone could stand it for long. The moon towered brightly above us, seeming as high as Idiot's Crag, perhaps higher.

Shoogar leaned back, back as far as he could, to peer up at its height. Absent-mindedly, he brought out a cavernmouth egg and began scratching a rune into it.

Purple reached behind him then—I noticed a huge stack of items lying there—and handed Orbur a new battery. It was identical with the one Purple had used to charge our windbags, but this one, Purple said, was *fully* powered. There was no danger at all of our running it down. It would fill more windbags than we could make before it would even begin to weaken. "It has enough power to make a dozen journeys like this, Lant. This dial, Orbur, shows you how much power you have left in it. This knob controls the rate at which you use it."

He handed the device to Wilville to examine, and reached behind him for another. This was a large box with a hinged opening on its top. "This is a chest of emergency rations. I have given you five of them. There is enough food here for a one-month journey." He shoved the box forward and reached again. We crowded forward, interestedly. "These are blankets, of course," said Purple. "You will need new ones for the upper atmosphere and—let's see, what else?"

He rummaged happily through his pile, presenting things to Wilville and Orbur. One by one he would hand them to the boys, who would pass them on to me. After examining each one, I put them in a stack behind me. His pile shrank while ours grew.

Shoogar was not at all interested. He kept wandering

around and around the base of the giant egg, scratching runes
on the cavernmouth rind.

"Here are flashlights, and this is a simple medkit. I have
labeled the sprays in here that you will want to use for hairlessness and things. You should be careful with this, even
though there's nothing here that can kill you." Purple picked
up one or two last items, meaningless things. One was a flat
folder of odd pictures—Purple called it a *book*—we would
have to examine it later. But Shoogar gasped when he saw it,
"Spell images!"

Purple tried to convince him that they were not, but
Shoogar wouldn't listen. No matter. Few of the images made
sense anyway. After a while, Shoogar tossed the *book* in
with the other stuff and went back to his egg marking.

At last there was only one item left, a shapeless mass of
glimmering white. Purple didn't even try to pick it up, it
seemed too big for that. He merely pointed at it. "I think
you will find this the most useful of all."

"What is it?" I asked.

"A new windbag," he said. He smiled. "I am afraid that
the ones we made weren't as good as I thought. They hardly
lasted the journey. One is already ripped, and I fear the rest
will rip too. My friends—and I know you are my friends—"

Behind me Shoogar snorted.

"I want your journey home to be as pleasant as mine. This
windbag is used for weather testing on strange worlds. It will
be big enough to hold your weights. Use it with your other
windbags, and you should be able to make it home."

Orbur was already examining it eagerly. The material was
light and transparent and thinner than anything we had ever
seen. "There's no weave!" he exclaimed. "Wilville, come look
at this!"

But Wilville had disappeared. A moment later, he came
panting up the hill. "This is a terrible place to park a moon,"
he gasped. "Why couldn't you have guided it lower."

"Where were you?"

He indicated his laden arms. "I have brought Purple a gift
too." He held out his hands. "An aircloth blanket, Purple,
and—and a sack of ballast. Just in case. You might need it."

Purple was visibly moved. He took the bulging sack and
held it tenderly, like a child. His eyes were moist, but there

was a smile on his face. He allowed Wilville to drape the blanket over his arm. "Thank you," he said, "these are fine gifts." His voice choked as he said it.

He turned to me. "Lant, thank you for everything. Thank you for your help, for being such a fine Speaker. I—wait, I have something for you." He disappeared up into his moon.

Almost immediately, he reappeared; he had stowed our gifts and carried something else. A sphere, with strange knobs and protrusions on it. "Lant, this is for you—"

"What is it?" I took it curiously. It was heavy—as heavy as a small child.

"It is your Speaker's token. I know Shoogar never had time to make one for you. I hope he will not mind if I present you with this. See there—that is my name in the markings of my own language. *You are the Speaker of the Purple magician.*"

I was confused, shocked, delighted, horrified—a tumble of emotions poured across my mind. "I—I—"

"Don't say anything, Lant. Just take it. It is a special token. It will be recognized and honored by any of my people who should ever again come to this world. And should I ever return it makes you my official Speaker. Keep it, Lant."

I nodded dumbly and staggered back with it.

Finally, Purple turned to Shoogar who had stood patiently throughout this all.

"Shoogar," he said, extending his empty hands. "I have nothing to give you. You are too great a magician for me to insult you. I cannot offer you anything at all that you do not already have, and for me to presume that I can would be an affront to your skill and greatness."

Shoogar's jaw dropped. He almost dropped his egg—then his eyes narrowed suspiciously. "No gift—?" He asked. I didn't know whether to feel hurt or pleased for him.

"Only this," said Purple, "and it is one that you cannot carry with you, it is already there. I leave you the two villages. You are now the official magician there."

Shoogar stared at him wide-eyed. Purple stood there, tall and impressive. In that peculiar-colored light, he looked almost a God himself. No longer the pudgy, almost comical figure who had terrorized us for so many months. Suddenly he seemed a kind of nobility itself: generous, loving, all-knowing.

Shoogar managed to say, "You admit it—you admit that I am a greater magician—?"

"Shoogar, I admit it. You know more about the magic and the Gods of this world than anyone—including me. You are the greatest—and you have your flying machine now." He looked at all of us then, a great friendly figure. "I will miss you," he whispered. "All of you. Even you, Shoogar. And your duels."

And with that he rose up into his moon and vanished.

The yellow light glowed brighter for a second, then winked out.

The moon vanished as silently as it had come, rising, rising, ever upward, dwindling, shrinking; snapping brilliant for a second, and then vanishing altogether.

Shoogar was so startled he almost forgot his cavernmouth egg spell. Hurriedly, he bit into it with a noisy chomp.

He started choking then, and we had to pound him hard on the back before he would stop.

The sea tumbled and broke on the blackened shore.

Except for that, all was silent. Above hung the pinpoint brightness of Ouells, blue and glaring. The *Cathawk* lay beached on the shore, her balloons full but flaccid. A larger white one blossomed above them; only one tenth full, it was a narrow cylinder with a gentle bulge at its top. A full load of water kept the boat from rising.

Our supplies lay scattered on the sand to protect them from the water in the boat. The four of us sat there and stared glumly at it.

"I knew we had forgotten something," repeated Wilville. It was the eleventh time he had said it.

"North," said Orbur, "we forgot about north."

"We forgot that the wind *blows* north," I said.

"No matter," shrugged Orbur. He tossed a pebble toward the sea. We're still not going anywhere. Wilville and I just can't pump hard enough to fight our way south." He tossed another pebble. "Curse it, anyway."

"Don't swear," mumbled Shoogar. "Greatest magician in the world, and I can't even change the wind. Curse it all."

"*You're* swearing," said Orbur petulantly.

"That's my job. I'm a magician."

We had tried to lift the boat four times already. Each time the best we had done was to maintain our position over the shore—and each time, as the boys had slackened, the wind had threatened to push us inland. Each time, we had brought the airboat down again.

"I don't care how much power that battery has got in it," Wilville said. "If we're not getting anywhere, we might as well not have it at all. We're only wasting its power this way."

"It doesn't show on the dial yet," I said.

"That doesn't mean we haven't wasted the power we've used," said Wilville. "And if we keep this up, we'll keep going until there's no more left."

We were miles east of where we had first touched shore. It was a spot that had once been below our old village. It was as desolate as the other. I chewed thoughtfully on one of Purple's food sticks—it was soft and brown and had an odd taste. "There must be a way," I said. "There must be."

"Not through the air," grumbled Wilville.

Orbur tossed a rock, "Then let's go through the water."

"Why not? The boat will float, won't it?"

"Yes, but—the whirlpools, the reefs—" I said.

"We lift above them!" Wilville was shouting now. "Yes, I've got it. We put just enough gas in the windbags to hold the boat out of water—but not the outriggers! The airpushers will move water too, and we can pedal our way home. Whenever the wind dies, we can lift into the air."

"But," I said, "if the wind works on balloons like it does on sails—it pushes—won't it push against us in the water too?"

"Yes, but the water will be pushing back. That is, the water will give us the leverage we need to move forward. Besides, we won't pump the balloons as full as they are now—they

won't present as much area to the wind and we won't be
fighting it as much."

Wilville and Orbur were right, of course. They usually
were in matters concerning the flying machine. It was almost
as if they knew as much about it as Purple—certainly more
so than Shoogar. Shoogar had protested their whole discussion
equating the action of the wind on the balloons with the
action of wind on sails. But, said Orbur, wind is wind. And
Wilville and Orbur were right.

The water splashed slowly under us, the airmakers churned
it into froth behind us. The boys had to pedal nearly twice
as hard as they would have in the air.

The sea was sinking again, and rapids and whirlpools were
frequent. Often, we had to take to the air. When we did
this, we would usually slip backwards, but then the boys
would begin driving either east or west, and in this manner
we managed to avoid most of the dangers of our first journey.

Whenever the boys tired of pedaling, we either took on
ballast or released some gas. In the water, our backward
slippage was slight.

We trailed fishing lines behind us. They had been a gift from
Purple and not understood at first, but once they had been
explained we were eager to put them to use. Once we caught
something big and it pulled us eastward for half a day before
we could cut through the line. We had to use a special tool
to do that.

It was not that the food Purple had given us was inade-
quate. It was just that it tasted bad. We ate it only when
there was nothing else available.

On the fifth day we were lucky enough to slip into a
section of water that was receding rapidly southward. We
stayed with it as long as we could until it became too savage.
Then we lifted into the air. The boys were delighted to find
that the wind was behind us now.

The darknesses were longer now—nearly two hours—and
the seasons were changing. The oceans were slipping away
again. They would continue to slip for months, but the
process had begun.

The sea below churned over razor-sharp reefs that were
becoming mountain peaks. There was a period when we saw
nothing but fog: blue fog, white fog, red fog, black fog, blue

fog, and so on, endlessly repeated with the cycle of the suns.

We had lost three of our aircloth windbags by now. Their seams had given way abruptly, one right after the other, smacking the boat solidly into the water. We made up the difference by inflating Purple's weather windbag even more. It was only half full, but more than offset the loss of the others.

We lost two more bags in as many days. Apparently there was something seriously wrong with the glue Grimm had used to seal the seams—and perhaps his stitching wasn't as strong as it should have been. The bags that we still had held their air for little more than a day. Shoogar and I were constantly recharging them. The aircloth had been tight when we had woven it, but it was certainly no longer so. Something tended to weaken it with continual use.

We still trailed our fishing lines below us, they hung like slender threads of shimmering gossamer. I wondered how they were made, and if we could duplicate them.

We sailed into another wall of fog. Blue fog, white fog, red fog——

In black fog we hooked something big, too big to draw in. We dared not cut the line. It was too precious to lose. The wind whistled past us—how fast were we moving?

And then the fog cleared as the blue sun burnt it off, and we saw that we had hooked land.

The desert we had crossed so many months ago—which had been sea bottom for the last few seasons—was a swamp now; a marsh of riotous colors, blooming briefly and frenetically during the few short hands of days it would take it to dry. There were roots to chew down there—and possibly meat.

We reeled in the line and pulled ourselves down.

We were within walking distance of home.

We returned to the peaceful life of the twin villages.

Indeed, life turned out to be even more peaceful than we

remembered it. And Shoogar and I were responsible. On the *Cathawk*'s departure we had dropped the dust of yearning across the cheering crowd. The resultant orgy lasted for three weeks.

Most improper, of course, but it left a feeling of fellowship between the Upper and Lower Village.

Another bond between us is Shoogar himself. He is now resident magician of both tribes.

Before Gortik would let him assume that post though, he secured from Shoogar an oath to redeem and honor all spell chips in the village at their full value. Shoogar had needed some persuading before he would redeem Purple's chips, but Purple's parting words left him in what could only be called a *good* humor. Once, he was even seen *smiling*.

There were one or two who were upset about the arrangement, of course. Hinc, who had invested heavily in Purple chips, felt that they should be redeemed at their old value of ten for one. Hinc has been scratching for the past three hands of days.

But life is peaceful here. In the evenings I sit and listen to the wives quarreling and the children crying and think how good it is to be home. Life has returned to its gentle pace. I carve the bone into chips, and regulate the flow of commerce as I have always done. Others work out the new processes and make the goods and I distribute the chips, blue ones only since Purple has gone.

Weaving is still our major industry here. Traders come not only from the other villages on the island, but from the mainland as well—even from as far south as the Land of Frozen Water. Every five days a new party arrives, always from further and further away. We are a powerful trading village now, gaining power as the fame of our cloth is spreading.

Wilville and Orbur are at work on a new *Cathawk*. The old one sits in a place of honor in a special clearing owned by the son of Trone the Smith. It is Smith's Son's Clearing, and no trader ever comes without stopping to peer curiously at the boat out of water.

The new *Cathawk* will be huge—nearly fifteen manlengths —it will require over one hundred windbags and ten men on bicycles to propel it; but the next wading season will not interrupt our trade with the mainland. The boatmaking and weaving apprentices have never worked so hard in their lives.

At first, when Wilville and Orbur announced their plans, there was some dissent—"What do we need another flying machine for? We've already built one. We've proved we can do it, why do we have to do it again? What a waste of effort and aircloth! Better to use the aircloth for trading!"

"But how will you get it there to trade?" was the answer. "And if we do not build another *Cathawk,* there will be no need for the generators, or for the generator teams—or for the *betmongers.* You will have nothing on which to spend the chips you earn from your weaving, and no place to trade your cloth."

Those who could not see the value of it were soon shouted down. Gortik and I gave my sons the go-ahead, and up on the crag the new cradle rises impressively.

It seems likely that the women will have names forever. Shoogar had thought that after the airboat was finished we could deconsecrate even the Missa names—but as long as we need them for spinning, we dare not do that.

And the plague spreads. The new wife, whom I bought on the mainland, had not been in my home but two days before she too asked for a name. My other wives support her. Somehow they have gotten the idea that all women must have names—even if they are only Missas.

The only exception is my hairless daughter. Shoogar is planning to consecrate her soon. She will have a secret name of her own.

Shoogar is frantically busy these days. He can deconsecrate, bleed and reconsecrate a housetree in almost no time at all. And it costs the nest owner only a spell token. It was lucky that Shoogar discovered that housetree bleeding is a good way to ward off the demons. He resells the housetree blood to the clothmakers for less than one chip per tree load—which is eminently fair of him.

Because of Shoogar's increased status I have had to take on extra apprentices. I have more than ten now, and they carve more chips in a day than can possibly be redeemed by any one magician. Many of the villagers no longer seem to regard the redemption of the spells as necessary. They trade the chips like lightweight, valuable, indestructible goods.

But others still value the chips well enough to keep Shoogar constantly busy. There is cloth to be blessed, looms to be consecrated, housetrees to be unblessed, bled and blessed again, fertility spells and name givings—and always he must watch out for his apprentices who are getting better and better in their attempts to kill him.

"Run and chant, run and chant!" he complains. "Never a time to rest! And do you know, Lant, they are still trading Purple's chips at four for one! Why? Purple is gone!"

"But his magic lingers on. It clings to the chips and makes them lucky."

Shoogar snorted angrily.

"Besides you do a better, more impressive job for a Purple chip. Or so I have been told," I added.

"It's true. It's because I *want* Purple's chips. When I have destroyed the last of them, there will be no sign of him anywhere! And all will be as it was before the mad magician came to us. I will expunge his memory, Lant!"

"I think it is hopeless, Shoogar. The purple-stained chips have spread as far as our new cloth. You will never be able to redeem them all."

"I can try, Lant. I can try. I drove him out—you saw it yourself—I can drive out his chips." And he bustled off to his next appointment.

I returned to my carving and staining. It is a lost cause, of course, for Shoogar. Every time he destroys a purple chip, the rest just go up in value because he has made them that much rarer. The people become less willing to part with them every day. But I will have to see what I can do for him.